ZARA WRIGHT

BLACK AND WHITE TANGLED THREADS

KENNETH

AFRICAN-AMERICAN WOMEN WRITERS, 1910–1940

HENRY LOUIS GATES, JR. *General Editor*

Jennifer Burton *Associate Editor*

ZARA WRIGHT

BLACK AND WHITE TANGLED THREADS

KENNETH

Introduction by
MAGGIE SALE

G.K. HALL & CO.
An Imprint of Simon & Schuster Macmillan
New York

Prentice Hall International
London   Mexico City   New Delhi   Singapore   Sydney   Toronto

G.K. Hall & Co.
An Imprint of Simon & Schuster Macmillan
866 Third Avenue
New York, NY 10022

Library of Congress Catalog Card Number: 94-21459

Printed in the United States of America

Printing Number
1 2 3 4 5 6 7 8 9 10

Library of Congress Cataloging-in-Publication Data

Wright, Zara.
[Black and white tangled threads]
Black and white tangled threads ; and, Kenneth / Zara Wright ; introduction by Maggie Sale.
p. cm.
Includes bibliographical references. (p.).
ISBN 0-8161-1626-1 (alk. paper)
1. Women civil rights workers—Kentucky—Louisville—Fiction. 2. Racially mixed people—Kentucky—Louisville—Fiction. 3. Louisville (Ky.)—Race relations—Fiction. 4. Family—Kentucky—Louisville—Fiction. 5. Domestic fiction, American. I. Wright, Zara. Kenneth. II. Title. III. Title: Kenneth.
PS3545.R848B57 1994
813'.52—dc20
94-21459
CIP

This paper meets the requirements of ANSI/NISO Z39.48-1992 (Permanence of Paper).

C O N T E N T S

GENERAL EDITORS' PREFACE

The past decade of our literary history might be thought of as the era of African-American women writers. Culminating in the awarding of the Pulitzer Prize to Toni Morrison and Rita Dove and the Nobel Prize for Literature to Toni Morrison in 1993, and characterized by the presence of several writers—Toni Morrison, Alice Walker, Maya Angelou, and the Delany Sisters, among others—on the *New York Times* Best Seller List, the shape of the most recent period in our literary history has been determined in large part by the writings of black women.

This, of course, has not always been the case. African-American women authors have been publishing their thoughts and feelings at least since 1773, when Phillis Wheatley published her book of poems in London, thereby bringing poetry directly to bear upon the philosophical discourse over the African's "place in nature" and his or her place in the great chain of being. The scores of words published by black women in America in the nineteenth century—most of which were published in extremely limited editions and never reprinted—have been republished in new critical editions in the forty-volume *Schomburg Library of Nineteenth-Century Black Women Writers*. The critical response to that series has led to requests from scholars and students alike for a similar series, one geared to the work by black women published between 1910 and the beginning of World War Two.

African-American Women Writers, 1910–1940 is designed to bring back into print many writers who otherwise would be unknown to contemporary readers, and to increase the availability of lesser-known texts by established writers who originally published during this critical period in African-American letters. This series implicitly acts as a chronological sequel to the Schomburg series, which focused on the origins of the black female literary tradition in America.

In less than a decade, the study of African-American women's writings has grown from its promising beginnings into a firmly established field in departments of English, American Studies, and African-American Studies. A comparison of the form and function of the original series and this sequel illustrates this dramatic shift. The *Schomburg Library* was published at the cusp of focused academic investigation into the interplay between race and gender. It covered the extensive period from the publication of Phillis Wheatley's *Poems on Various Subjects, Religious and Moral* in 1773 through the "Black Women's Era" of 1890–1910, and was designed to be an inclusive series of the major early texts by black women writers. The Schomburg Library provided a historical backdrop for black women's writings of the 1970s and 1980s, including the works of writers such as Toni Morrison, Alice Walker, Maya Angelou, and Rita Dove.

African-American Women Writers, 1910–1940 continues our effort to provide a new generation of readers access to texts—historical, sociological, and literary—that have been largely "unread" for most of this century. The series bypasses works that are important both to the period and the tradition, but that are readily available, such as Zora Neale Hurston's *Their Eyes Were Watching God*, Jessie Fauset's *Plum Bun* and *There is Confusion*, and Nella Larsen's *Quicksand* and *Passing*. Our goal is to provide access to a wide variety of rare texts. The series includes Fauset's two other novels, *The Chinaberry Tree: A Novel of American Life* and *Comedy: American Style*, and Hurston's short play, *Color Struck*, since these are not yet widely available. It also features works by virtually unknown writers, such as *A Tiny Spark*, Christina Moody's slim volume of poetry self-published in 1910, and *Reminiscences of School Life, and Hints on Teaching*, written by Fanny Jackson Coppin in the last year of her life (1913), a multi-genre work combining an autobiographical sketch and reflections on trips to England and South Africa, complete with pedagogical advice.

Cultural studies' investment in diverse resources allows the historic scope of the *African-American Women Writers* series to be more focused than the *Schomburg Library* series, which covered works written over a 137-year period. With few exceptions, the authors included in the *African-American Women Writers* series wrote their major works between 1910 and 1940. The texts reprinted include all of the works by each particular author that are not otherwise readily obtainable. As a result, two volumes contain works originally published after 1940. The Charlotte Hawkins Brown volume includes her book of etiquette published in 1941, *The Correct Thing To Do—To Say—To Wear*. One of the poetry volumes contains Maggie Pogue Johnson's *Fallen Blossoms*, published in 1951, a compilation of all her previously published and unpublished poems.

Excavational work by scholars during the past decade has been crucial to the development of *African-American Women Writers, 1910–1940*. Germinal bibliographic sources such as Anne Allen Shockley's *Afro-American Women Writers 1746–1933* and Maryemma Graham's *Database of African-American Women Writers* made the initial identification of texts possible. Other works were brought to our attention by scholars who wrote letters sharing their research. Additional texts by selected authors were then added, so that many volumes contain the complete oeuvres of particular writers. Pieces by authors without enough published work to fill an entire volume were grouped with other pieces by genre.

The two types of collections, those organized by author and those organized by genre, bring out different characteristics of black women's writings of the period. The collected works of the literary writers illustrate that many of them were experimenting with a variety of forms. Mercedes Gilbert's volume, for example, contains her 1931 collection, *Selected Gems of Poetry, Comedy, and Drama, Etc.*, as well as her 1938 novel, *Aunt Sara's Wooden God*. Georgia Douglas Johnson's volume contains her plays and short stories in addition to her poetry. Sarah Lee Brown Fleming's volume combines her 1918 novel *Hope's Highway* with her 1920 collection of poetry, *Clouds and Sunshine*.

The generic volumes both bring out the formal and thematic similarities among many of the writings and highlight the striking individuality of particular writers. Most of the plays in the volume of one-acts are social dramas whose tragic endings can be clearly attributed to miscegenation and racism. Within the context of these other plays, Marita Bonner's surrealistic theatrical vision becomes all the more striking.

The volumes of *African-American Women Writers, 1910–1940* contain reproductions of more than one hundred previously published texts, including twenty-nine plays, seventeen poetry collections, twelve novels, six autobiographies, five collections of short biographical sketches, three biographies, three histories of organizations, three black histories, two anthologies, two sociological studies, a diary, and a book of etiquette. Each volume features an introduction written by a contemporary scholar that provides crucial biographical data on each author and the historical and critical context of her work. In some cases, little information on the authors was available outside of the fragments of biographical data contained in the original introduction or in the text itself. In these instances, editors have documented the libraries and research centers where they tried to find information, in the hope that subsequent scholars will continue the necessary search to find the "lost" clues to the women's stories in the rich stores of papers, letters, photographs, and other primary materials scattered throughout the country that have yet to be fully catalogued.

Many of the thrilling moments that occurred during the development of this series were the result of previously fragmented pieces of these women's histories suddenly coming together, such as Adele Alexander's uncovering of an old family photograph, picturing her own aunt with Addie Hunton, the author Alexander was researching. Claudia Tate's examination of Georgia Douglas Johnson's papers in the Moorland-Spingarn Research Center of Howard University resulted in the discovery of a wealth of previously unpublished work.

The slippery quality of race itself emerged during the construction of the series. One of the short novels originally intended for inclusion in the series had to be cut when the family of the author protested that the writer was not of African descent. Another case involved Louise Kennedy's sociological study *The Negro Peasant Turns Inward*. The fact that none of the available biographical material on Kennedy specifically mentioned race, combined with some coded criticism in a review in the *Crisis*, convinced editor Sheila Smith McCoy that Kennedy was probably white.

These women, taken together, begin to chart the true vitality, and complexity, of the literary tradition that African-American women have generated, using a wide variety of forms. They testify to the fact that the monumental works of Hurston, Larsen, and Fauset, for example, emerged out of a larger cultural context; they were not exceptions or aberrations. Indeed, their contributions to American literature and culture, as this series makes clear, were fundamental not only to the shaping of the African-American tradition but to the American tradition as well.

Henry Louis Gates, Jr.
Jennifer Burton

PUBLISHER'S NOTE

In the *African-American Women Writers, 1910-1940* series, G.K. Hall not only is making available previously neglected works that, in many cases, have been long out of print; we are also, whenever possible, publishing these works in facsimiles reprinted from their original editions including, when available, reproductions of original title pages, copyright pages, and photographs.

When it was not possible for us to reproduce a complete facsimile edition of a particular work (for example, if the original exists only as a handwritten draft or is too fragile to be reproduced), we have attempted to preserve the essence of the original by resetting the work exactly as it originally appeared. Therefore, any typographical errors, strikeouts, or other anomalies reflect our efforts to give the reader a true sense of the original work.

We trust that these facsimile and reprint editions, together with the new introductory essays, will be both useful and historically enlightening to scholars and students alike.

INTRODUCTION

BY MAGGIE SALE

Very little is known about Zara Wright.[1] What little is known comes from two sources, a mention of her in John Taitt's *Souvenir of Negro Progress*, published by the De Saible Association of Chicago in 1925, and from the front matter of her novels. Taitt's *Souvenir* includes the same portrait of her that faces the title page of *Black and White Tangled Threads*. Under it are her name, "Mrs. Zara Wright," the titles "Novelist and Dramatist," the characterization "Author 'Tangled Threads,'" and her address, 9 West 21st Street. Her portrait shares the page (one of three pages of such portraits) with ten other important members of Chicago's black community: nine men entrepreneurs, politicians, and professionals, and one other woman, Dr. Fannie Emanuel, physician and surgeon. Taitt's title of "Dramatist" suggests that Wright wrote plays as well as prose, although none of them have been discovered. Taitt's additional characterization of Wright as the "Author [of] 'Tangled Threads'" suggests that not only were her novels known among this community, but that they were well-enough received to qualify her for inclusion in the *Souvenir*. The fact that Wright is the only writer included in the *Souvenir* further testifies both to her stature in the community and to the reputation of her work. In addition, on Christmas Day 1920, the *Chicago Defender*, that city's leading black newspaper, reviewed *Black and White Tangled Threads* and its sequel, *Kenneth*, calling them "remarkable," and asserting that "to read this story will be convincing proof that as a writer, Mrs. Wright is unexcelled."[2]

Despite this auspicious beginning, Zara Wright and her two published works fell (or were pushed) into obscurity. Originally published privately and together in Chicago in 1920, *Black and White Tangled Threads* and *Kenneth* immediately went out of print until they were reissued by AMS Press in 1975. Residing and writing far to the west of New York City's Harlem Renaissance, typically considered the center of African-American culture during this period, Wright has not been within the purview of literary critics.

Although Wright lived and published in Chicago, she shared a number of characteristics with women writers of the Harlem Renaissance, characteristics that have contributed to her obscurity. Wright was among those who, like Angelina Weld Grimké, Jesse Fauset, Alice Dunbar-Nelson, and Georgia Douglas Johnson, wrote as if "reared as proper middle-class, almost Victorian black women, who were trained to be proofs of black female morals and modesty."[3] These women wrote more about mixed-blood, urban, bourgeois characters than about the black folk. In the cases of Grimké, Dunbar-Nelson, and Johnson, foregoing the "hateful" topics of prejudice and injustice, Gloria Hull has argued, "placed them out of the fashionable mainstream to the detriment of their contemporary and posthumous reputations" (Hull, 19). Much of Wright's subject matter, influenced by her race and gender, situates her in the company of other black women writers and largely outside of the male-dominated and -defined Harlem Renaissance.

In her introduction, Wright comments that she hopes her books are "food for sane and serious thought, eliminating much sordidness that often mars a story, leaving the reader with neither desire nor inclination to either remember or discuss its contents afterward."[4] Here she asserts not only the importance of her endeavor, but its possibility for success in influencing others because, in her view, its exclusion of topics of degradation makes it more fit not only for reading, but for rereading and study. It is easy to imagine those critics who called Jesse Fauset prim characterizing Wright as prudish. Her juxtaposition of "sane and serious" with "sordid" challenges not only the appropriateness but the intellectual quality of narratives of racially-motivated violence, critical though they may be. Notably absent from Wright's novels are references to rape, forced concubinage, lynchings, and other forms of torture common to novels and narratives thematizing slavery and post-Reconstruction. Also absent are the immediate context of increasing racial violence in which she personally lived,[5] and any explorations of sexuality more common in male-authored writing of the Harlem Renaissance.[6] One might interpret these absences as an attempt to ignore, obscure, or escape from unpleasant realities on the one hand, and to repress sexual desire on the other. But it is also possible to read these absences as Wright's way of challenging the all-too-common association of black women with sex, illicit or otherwise, and violence.

Male-authored slave narratives of the nineteenth century graphically depict the sexual abuse of enslaved women by white men. These portrayals were part of the literary formula designed by abolitionists and ex-slave narrators to garner support for the abolition of slavery among Northern—and Southern—sympathizers. Two effects of this strategy, however, were the monolithic representation of enslaved women as passive and hapless victims and the association of black women with illicit sex. As Frances Smith Foster has pointed out, when women wrote of their experiences under slavery, sexual exploitation and violence are never presented as the most significant or most profound portion of their story: "Though they document the trauma and grief of sexual exploitation and physical abuse beyond the comprehension of most nineteenth-century (and twentieth-century) white women, the slave women's works do not center around these tragedies. From their narratives it is repeatedly clear that slave women saw themselves as far more than victims of rape and seduction."[7]

Later black women writers similarly recorded such facts of slavery, but they also developed female characters who understood these facts as part of the larger social, cultural, and political environment in which they lived. Pauline Hopkins's Mrs. Willis of *Contending Forces* (1900), for example, argues that "'we shall not be held responsible for wrongs which we have unconsciously committed, or which we have committed under *compulsion*. We are virtuous or non-virtuous only when we have a *choice* under temptation.'"[8] And in the early twentieth century, black women writers, such as those from the Harlem Renaissance, increasingly became interested in creating characters who had not been subjected to and who did not discuss sexual exploitation.

It would be misleading to say Zara Wright eschewed the topics of racial prejudice and injustice. Her strategies for addressing these topics can best be understood, however, as growing out of the literary culture established by works of earlier writers, such as Harriet Jacobs's *Incidents in the Life of a Slave Girl* (1861), Frances E. W. Harper's *Iola Leroy* (1892), and Hopkins's *Contending Forces*, rather than in relation to her male—or female—contemporaries. Wright makes her connection to this culture explicit by taking her title from *Contending Forces*. Mrs. Smith, the central mullata matriarch of the novel, makes the following statement to a British politician just before they discover their familial relation: "There are strangely tangled threads in the lives of many colored families—I use the word 'colored' because these stories occur mostly among those of mixed blood" (*Forces*, 374–75). Jacobs's slave narrative and the novels of Harper and Hopkins deal with the impact on families of the legal, social, political, and economic systems, Northern and Southern, before and after Emancipation, that produced and supported pervasive notions of innate and immutable racial difference, used to justify slavery and segregation. By asserting an absolute and fundamental difference between African and Anglo races, these systems obscured the existence of mixed-race people, and implicitly argued for the degradation of anyone with African blood. The texts of Jacobs, Harper, Hopkins, and Wright, among many others, explore the ways in which these systems twisted relations among family and community members, and in many cases rent them asunder, and the ways in which some individuals nevertheless developed healthy and supportive relations in defiance of those dictates.

Wright also wrote to inspire her readers to live morally upright and productive lives. Like Harriet Jacobs, who exposed the inadequacy of "true womanhood" and developed an alternative standard for ethical behavior under slavery, Wright interrogated the efficacy of cultural dictates for mixed-raced characters. And like Frances Harper, whose "poetics dictated that the writer must first of all feel and say what is 'right,'"[9] Wright wrote with the hope that "the unselfishness and noble qualities of the heroine [may] be productive of good results and an inspiration to those who are too weak to do their duty as they see it and too cowardly to do that which is just and right for fear of criticism" (*Threads*, 3). Thus Wright names generosity, nobility, strength of character, and bravery as the guiding principles of her ethical standard, the principles by which she will judge the actions of her characters as they face the moral dilemmas she sets before them.

In order to reach as wide an audience as possible, these and other black women writers made use of the conventions of popular literary genres, such as melodrama, the sentimental romance, the gothic novel, the novel of seduction, and the slave narrative, as well as of elements of sermonic and other oral traditions. Modifying well-known figures and tropes enabled them to connect quickly with their readers, and to draw them into exploring otherwise difficult themes. These appropriations and transformations were part of a broader movement by African Americans, begun with oral poetry, the slave narratives, and early novels, to invent new narrative forms appropriate to unique and often dangerous subject matter, and to create textual spaces in which to debate with their white contemporaries and amongst themselves.

In the twentieth century, Euro-American criticism, written largely by white men, devalued the literary and cultural innovations of nineteenth-century and early-twentieth-century African-American writers and nineteenth-century Euro-American women writers by labeling them sentimental or propagandistic. The standards and values underlying this devaluing assume and assert that evoking emotional responses and being involved politically are inappropriate endeavors for both writers and scholars. Rather than being objective or transcendental, these standards, as many feminist scholars have shown, were developed in accordance with these critics' own sensibilities and desires. Their privileging of irony, syntactical difficulty, and psychological complexity, for example, degraded the vast majority of nineteenth-century writing, including that of the popular "Fireside" poets, such as Henry Wadsworth Longfellow and John Greenleaf Whittier, and elevated the cultural productions of a handful of white male writers.

Early women writers were devalued within twentieth-century African-American criticism as well. Harper, probably the most popular African-American writer of the nineteenth century, is the most notable example, but other women writers also were devalued first by critics more interested in primitivism, the black folk, and what they considered formal innovation, aesthetic values established during the Harlem Renaissance. This trend was then continued by critics who valued more highly later male writers of the urban experience, such as Richard Wright and Ralph Ellison. This critical privileging of urban life and its cultural productions, especially the male-authored versions of it, held sway until the 1970s and 1980s, when black feminist critics began republishing and writing more extensively about earlier women writers. Although Zara Wright published in 1920, her treatment of racial injustice is often more in keeping with her nineteenth-century female predecessors than with her twentieth-century male contemporaries. Thus twentieth-century shifts in literary, cultural, and political values until recently have relegated Wright's work, along with that of many of her predecessors, to undeserved obscurity.

Black and White Tangled Threads and *Kenneth* follow two families from the generation after Emancipation, with brief flashbacks to the previous generation, until after World War I. The novels are set mostly in Louisville, Kentucky, yet contain a few scenes in England and Italy.[10] The heroine of the first novel, Zoleeta Andrews, is the child of Harold Andrews and Mildred Yates, son of a slaveholder and daughter of a slave. Her parents secretly left the plantation on which they were both reared and fell in love for a life in India. Both die when Zoleeta is quite young. She is adopted by Harold's older brother, Paul, and is brought back to the plantation of her parents' youth, where she is reared as a member of the formerly slaveholding family. Claretta, who is Paul and Harold's sister, hates Zoleeta's beauty and resents being forced to live with someone "tainted" with the blood of the slaves, and she teaches her daughter, Catherine, to feel the same way. Much of the plot of the first novel turns on Claretta's plans to ruin Zoleeta's marriage prospects. Zoleeta is eventually united with the man of her dreams, Lord Blankleigh, who knows and accepts her racial heritage, and she spends three years in England as Lady Blankleigh. She then returns to the United States, without her husband and son but pregnant with her daughter, in order to speak and work on behalf of the newly freed women and men of the South.

In a subplot of *Black and White Tangled Threads*, Zoleeta's cousin Catherine marries a young painter, Guy Randolf, who discovers after his marriage and the birth of their son, Kenneth, that he is the illegitimate son of a wealthy but deceased slaveholder named Guy Slayton and his slave Hebe, a woman who had escaped slavery and, disguised as his nurse, reared Randolf. This revelation of his paternity brings Randolf a large fortune, but also the loss of his wife, who accuses him of being duplicitous regarding his heritage and whose racism makes him and their son repulsive to her. The second novel, *Kenneth*, follows Guy and Catherine's son as a rising young lawyer in Louisville, and also examines the troubled life of Kenneth's dark-skinned friend, Dr. Philip Grayson.

Within the conventional plot twists of these melodramas, Wright explores the complexities of interracial heritage and marriage, race consciousness, and passing, revealing the "strangely tangled threads" of many family trees. Wright's novels differ from earlier novels by African-American women in that her principal focus is not on clearly mixed-race families, as in *Iola Leroy* or *Contending Forces*, but on families who, in most respects, identify and publicly represent themselves as white. Wright explores the decisions and behavior of a different population, not those who chose to live and identify with African Americans in separate or segregated communities, but those very light-skinned persons, reared in white families and communities, who both pass as white and serve the black community. In this respect, Wright's novels may be seen as transitional, coming as they do between those nineteenth-century novels that call for identification with and service to the race and the twentieth-century novels of passing.

While Wright does not explore the lives of dark-skinned people, the most obvious targets of racial discrimination and intimidation, her focus asserts that "white" families everywhere have members who are descended from Africans. When considered in the context of Jim Crow, in which five generations are legally defined as black by one African ancestor, and in which eugenicist notions of innate and immutable racial characteristics and difference were common parley, the implications of this assertion are profound: Anglos and Africans in the United States share a common heritage. Wright implies biologically what cannot be denied metaphorically: that those of us who are white also share the blood of the enslaved. Directed primarily at "white" families, this position disrupts contemporaneous attempts to represent and indeed produce a nation of purely European descent, free from the guilt, as well as the "taint" of slavery.

The behavior and attitudes of Wright's principal characters both challenged the racist underpinnings of stereotypical notions developed by white writers and exemplified standards for ethical behavior in mixed-race relations. For example, mulatto fiction often details the revelation of the African and enslaved heritage of individuals reared as white and their subsequent identity crises. Typically the crises arise, according to Judith Bertzon, when the black heritage of the mulatto characters are revealed and they realize that their physical appearance and cultural and educational attainments have conditioned them to feel more comfortable with the upper class.[11] This realization requires that the mixed-blood characters confront "new" identities in which they become conscious of their own racial and social marginality, thereby necessitating a shift in the habits and attitudes learned over a lifetime.

Wright's depiction of Zoleeta's learning that her mother is of African descent challenges such representations of the "crisis." Zoleeta's moment comes when her cousin Catherine implies to their schoolmates that Zoleeta's fine singing voice is a result of her "negro blood" (*Threads*, 25). Although the heroine's complexion pales, she shows no other sign of distress. She does, however, telegram her Uncle Paul, who comes to her immediately. But upon their meeting, the question she puts to him is not about her heritage but about her parents' relationship: "'Tell me, uncle, oh, tell me. Did my father place a wedding ring on my mother's hand and have I a legitimate right to the name I bear?'" (*Threads*, 32). After assuring Zoleeta that "her father's marriage had been honorable," Paul relates to her the story of her "parents' love and devotion to each other," all the while "fearing to look at that young face so full of anguish and misery" (*Threads*, 32–33). Defying both the expectations of her Uncle Paul and the conventional assumptions of Wright's readers, Zoleeta responds to this news with delight: "I am so happy to think that my father was a prince among men and that I am his daughter . . . If my dear mother had lived, I would have owned her before the whole world . . . I am proud of my parentage." Given the sanction of legal marriage and true love, Zoleeta finds "nothing to be ashamed of" (*Threads*, 33) in her African and enslaved heritage.

The attitude and behavior of Zoleeta's parents, especially Harold Andrews's decision to give up his wealth and position to marry Mildred, is thrown into relief by Wright's depiction of another couple in similar circumstances. Like Andrews, Guy Randolph's father fell in love with an enslaved woman and they had a child together; but unlike Andrews, he did not marry and protect her. In a note to his lost son, Slayton explains why he did not consider his behavior inappropriate: "I had no thought [of marrying her] . . . I did not feel that I was doing a great wrong as the same conditions between master and slave existed all around me" (*Threads*, 135). When read in relation to Slayton's more typical story, Andrews's decision to forego family and status in favor of marriage appears unusually honorable. In this way, Wright reminds her readers that although Andrews does only that which is his duty, according to the ethical standard of her novels, his performance nevertheless stands out from his peers.

Hebe, Guy Randolph's mother, apparently recognized Slayton's legal claim to her as property, but her wistful and pleading looks betrayed her discomfort with their situation. Although Slayton says that she "never asked me to marry her," Hebe does assert herself on her son's behalf, asking Slayton whether he intended "that the fetters that bind the mother shall also shackle the son? And do you intend to give your son a name or shall he remain nameless?" (*Threads*, 135). Slayton agrees that the child should be named after him and is impressed deeply by Hebe's "new dignity" upon "entering the realms of motherhood." (*Threads*, 136) Her outrage at what he considers a generous monetary settlement spurs him to new heights of feeling, and he resolves to marry her, come what may. But his weakness of character, earlier evidenced in his assumptions about the appropriateness of their relationship, asserts itself again, and he marries a "charming young lady visitor" (*Threads*, 136) whom he happens to meet and who favors him. Wright further develops her criteria for good character by having Hebe leave with her son the night Guy Slayton brings home his bride, denying the father the ability to "provide handsomely," as he thinks is his only obligation to Hebe and their son (*Threads*, 136). Given the historical circumstance of concubinage under slavery, Hebe's decision, like that of Harold and Mildred, asserts that monetary compensation is not an adequate substitute for the legal sanctioning of heterosexual love.

Thus Wright's emphasis on true love is more than mere convention. As the example of Guy Randolf's parents illustrates, relations between master and slave, even affectionate ones, typically were not valued by the more powerful partner. In addition, both nineteenth- and early-twentieth-century notions of racial difference, which represented different racial groups as equivalent to different species, implicitly asserted the impossibility of "true love" between the races. Wright appropriates a convention of sentimental romance, the possibility of true love, and transports it into an interracial context in which its meaning changes to an indictment of both sexual exploitation under slavery and notions of innate and immutable racial difference.

Wright's emphasis on legal marriage carries similar indictments. But more than this, as Claudia Tate has argued convincingly, the right to marry legally, long denied enslaved people in the United States, should be read as an assertion of civil rights, one as important as the right to vote. Both are civil contracts that recognize the actors' rights and responsibilities.[12] In the case of Zoleeta's parents, the legality of their marriage figures Mildred Yates as an independent agent capable of entering into a civil contract that at once grants her rights and requires of her certain responsibilities; it makes her a legal subject. This is no small achievement; the *Dred Scott* decision by the U.S. Supreme Court in 1857 had asserted that "negroes" have "no rights that a white man is bound to respect." Harold Andrews's decision to marry Mildred Yates shows that he acknowledges his responsibility to her and their children, and recognizes her as a legal subject, though legally he is not required and socially he is not supposed to do so.[13] Thus he earns from his daughter the title of "prince among men." The love and marriage of Zoleeta's parents prevent any crisis of identity because they argue against the conventional basis of such a crisis: notions of racial hierarchy and white supremacy.

Another common cultural assumption that Wright challenges is the notion that African Americans want to intermarry with whites in order to raise their status, and that they see this action as positive and unproblematic. Mildred's (Zoleeta's mother's) dark-skinned brother, Ralph, who had returned to the plantation in order to foil Claretta's (Zoleeta's aunt's) plot to ruin Zoleeta, decides to leave town to prevent her from being ostracized by her friends. Zoleeta's Uncle Paul, after close scrutiny, has come to recognize Ralph's "intellectual ability" and has become convinced that "he was a man to be trusted, yet there were times when a shadow would flit across Paul Andrews' face when he thought of his lovely niece's kinship to the ex-slave. At those times he wished that his brother had chosen one from his own race to be the mother of his child. . . ." (*Threads*, 142–43). Paul Andrews admires the man but is repelled by the ex-slave embodied in Ralph. But "little did he think that Zoleeta's ex-slave uncle suffered as keenly as he did and . . . wished that his sister had chosen one of her race for her life's companion" (*Threads*, 143). Wright reveals to the reader what Paul does not know, that Ralph also considers Harold and Mildred's marriage to be problematic for their daughter, despite the fact that it has brought her wealth and a place in upper-class society. This revelation makes visible Paul's sense of his own racial superiority and challenges his assumption that Ralph, and by implication other ex-slaves, desires whiteness and the status it brings. The painfulness of Ralph's decision to leave the area in order to protect Zoleeta and her place with her white family testifies to his desire to be with his only kin and yet his willingness to put her welfare first. This complex situation implies that however difficult it may be for Zoleeta's white family to accept her darker kin, Ralph's unselfish attitude is both more difficult for him and more worthy of respect.

Wright addresses this same cultural assumption, that African Americans want to intermarry, with a different set of characters in *Kenneth*, and with different implications. The sequel opens with the handsome, dark-skinned Dr. Philip Grayson treating the victims of a railroad disaster, among whom is Alice Blair, the white daughter of a wealthy banker. Alice Blair not only falls desperately in love with Philip Grayson, who has saved her life, but she pursues him, and eventually becomes deathly ill after he rejects her. Grayson, in love with a younger black woman with whom he grew up, politely explains to Alice Blair that her unlooked-for attentions are dangerous to him and that he may be run out of Louisville, if not killed, if she continues her unsolicited visits to his office. Here Wright points to the common Southern practice of lynching black men for their supposed attentions or insults to white women. But in Wright's scenario, the white woman is the aggressor, concerned only with her own desire and careless of the danger she brings to the man she loves. This scenario challenges the stereotypical notions that black men always desire white women, that relations between black men and white women are always created by black men pursuing white women, and that black men are aggressors and white women are passive victims. Although lynching is not the fate of Dr. Grayson, this situation implies that black men are often lynched not for their own aggressions, but for those of white women.

In addition to disputing common cultural assumptions, Wright enters into a long-standing debate about the development and goals of racial consciousness and the efficacy of passing. Like earlier mulatta characters, Zoleeta's new knowledge of her African and enslaved heritage marks the beginning of her development of racial consciousness. After learning of her heritage, Zoleeta leaves school and returns to her uncle's plantation, where she becomes reclusive and secretly decides never to marry, feeling that she is "'an impostor sailing under false colors'" (*Threads*, 39). Wright presents her readers with a twist on the conventional crisis moment when Zoleeta, faced with a man presenting himself as her mother's brother Ralph, "felt greatly depressed for she could feel no responsive feeling for the man who stood there with outstretched hands appealing to her for recognition of his claim. . . .

She felt that after all her protestations of loyalty to her mother's people and kindred that she was a traitor. . . . The girl realiz[ed] that she was facing the crisis of her young life for now and all future time to come" (*Threads*, 72). Because Zoleeta feels no connection with this man, readers, like Zoleeta herself, might conclude that her feelings are born of racist alienation from her mother's people. But when this man is unmasked as an impostor who has spirited her away in the hopes of making her his own, Zoleeta's instinctive mistrust of him proves well-founded. When she finally meets her true Uncle Ralph, "a sigh of relief escaped her when she beheld that manly man standing there. She felt a responsive chord . . . [t]here was forged a link which bound them together that already joined them by ties of blood and never until the day of their death was there a shadow of regret in their trust in each other" (*Threads*, 121–22). Thus Zoleeta survives her crisis by claiming her real uncle as her own, giving up her betrothal to Lord Blankleigh, bearing the scorn of her friends, and "'doing what [she is] sure [her] parents would approve of, if they were living'" (*Threads*, 141).

But even more important than her sense of duty to and love for her uncle, Zoleeta develops an analysis of race relations that is the basis of her later career as an advocate for freed women and men of the South. She argues,

"Is it not inhuman and cruelly unjust to mistreat anyone on account of his color? . . . I have seen a black horse and a white horse harnessed together, each doing his part without friction, and [yet I also know] the negro [whom] we are trying to impress from the pulpit and platform that God, the creator, made us all equal and tell him it is a sin to oppress the weak, when it is an evident fact that [the] Caucasian race is not only the oppressors but they never stop until the weaker races are crucified on the altar of their greed and ambition. I ask, Uncle, who is responsible for this deplorable state of affairs, that, to me, seems a little less than barbarism?" (*Threads*, 144–45)

Zoleeta's indictment of prejudice based on color is typical of novels of racial protest, as is the way she blames the "Caucasian race" for "this deplorable state of affairs." In 1920, no less so than in 1890 (or in 1990), black writers thought it was important to remind readers of all races that the conditions of radical inequality —economic, social, political, educational, and so on—among the races were the result of hundreds of years of legally sanctioned and institutionalized discrimination. This was perhaps especially the case in Wright's day, the era of segregation in which the white population was developing new strategies for denying its historical responsibility for racial inequities.

Speaking about the responsibility of the white population proves to be Zoleeta's calling. After hearing some missionaries speak about the ignorance and degradation of Southern "negroes," she decides to join the cause of the freed women and men, but in a different manner. She asserts to her husband, Lord Blankleigh, with whom she is living in England, "Do you not see those missionaries are all wrong? . . . I will admit there is much to be done for the uplift of the colored people, but we must first educate the hearts of the Southern whites before we can ever hope to successfully educate the negro's brain. To uplift that race of people, despised and mistreated because their skin is black, we must first change the attitude of the Southern whites and the calm indifference of the prejudiced Northerner" (*Threads*, 164–65). Zoleeta follows her calling and returns to the United States, where she becomes a speaker against racial prejudice and seeks "companionship among the wealthy and influential whites and the middle class" (*Threads*, 168).

Zoleeta's career comes at a high price. Having been forbidden to leave by her husband, Wright notes that "[y]ear after year she sacrificed home, husband and child. She crucified herself on the altar of duty for the betterment of her mother's people" (*Threads*, 170). Lord Blankleigh's attitude requires Zoleeta to be different from earlier models of "race women," such as Frances Harper's Iola Leroy. Zoleeta is more independent than Iola needs to be because she has chosen both a white husband and a life of passing. For Harper, writing thirty years earlier, passing was neither permissible nor desirable. Once Iola learns of her heritage, she learns to claim it openly, spurning her white suitor and the luxurious life of passing he offers. For Iola, the components are connected: heritage, husband, and vocation require and reinforce each other. In Zoleeta's case, acknowledgment moves more slowly and is never fully completed. Although she recognizes her true Uncle Ralph and willingly foregoes her betrothal in order to maintain her relationship with him, as soon as he's dead she marries Lord Blankleigh. Consistent with Wright's criteria, Zoleeta requires that Lord Blankleigh's family know and accept her heritage. Yet this acknowledgment does not move out of the familial sphere into a larger, more public one. Even when she decides to defy her husband in order to work for the cause, she distances herself from "that race of people" whose "skin is black" and maintains her identity as white.

This choice is dictated in part by the way she defines her work. Zoleeta argues that the first step is to open the minds of white people. In order to encourage open communication, she runs separate meetings for whites, and sometimes for blacks, the former of which she would not be able to do if she identified herself as of African descent. Thus Wright suggests that Zoleeta's passing may be judged differently from that of others in that it is attached to a progressive racial agenda. Wright, however, acknowledges the danger of this strategy. Reared in ignorance of her mother's heritage, Zoleeta's daughter grows up a racist, "declaring that if she had a drop of Negro blood in her, she would cut herself and let it flow out. . . . I do not care," she ironically continues, "how fair one is[,] I could tell if they were contaminated with Negro blood" (*Threads*, 310). Thus while Zoleeta may have been a successful lecturer and educator, Wright illustrates that passing perpetuates racism.

At the beginning of *Kenneth*, Wright includes an uncharacteristic segment, perhaps the most striking and disturbing one of the two novels, in which two innocent boys confront the paradox of race. Herbert, the white son of a wealthy banker, is told by his father that he cannot take his dark-skinned friend, James, to a family picnic "until James gets white" (*Threads*, 207). Interpreting literally his father's facetious remark, Herbert rubs onto James's face a strong cleaning solution that he has seen used on dirty floors. But rather than lightening James's skin, Herbert terribly burns his friend, blinding him, probably for life. For the two young boys, "in their baby minds" (*Threads*, 207), whiteness lies solely on the surface, in a person's skin color, not in essentialized notions of racial being or character.

The trope of passing depends upon a notion of race as different from skin color, a notion based on heritage and history, but also one biologically determined by "one drop of black blood," despite the absence of superficial markers of race characteristics. Herbert and James do not recognize this difference. All they see is that James's skin is dark, and they try to "rectify" that situation by attacking the color of his surface. They think that if they can make his skin lighter, then he will be white. But in this novel, as well as in legal definitions, social mores, and many other fictional representations, even those characters with light skins are not all white. On the one hand, this difference makes all the difference because of the social ostracism of and legal limitations on anyone with "one drop" of black blood. On the other, this difference is no difference because the majority of "black" characters in these novels successfully pass as white, and they all (with few exceptions) have exemplary characters. This paradox, made visible by the children's innocence, in turn exposes the internal contradictions of essentialized notions of race.

Careful reading of *Black and White Tangled Threads* and *Kenneth* reveals a deft and informed exploration of racial prejudice and injustice. As Ann Allen Shockley asserts, "the uniqueness of [*Black and White Tangled Threads* was] its mulatto story with a different twist; it showed the effects of miscegenation upon a white antebellum southern family who acknowledges a mulatto as a legitimate family member" (Shockley, 280). Moreover, Wright's novels argue that miscegenation is far less important than appropriate moral behavior, than, as Wright puts it, being "too weak to do their duty as they see it and too cowardly to do that which is just and right for fear of criticism" (*Threads*, 3).

Wright followed her own dictates. Despite its obvious popularity, she argued against including "sordid" material. She pursued instead the purpose she deemed "just and right," and she chose to use the literary forms that she deemed most appropriate to that purpose, despite contrary opinions. Wright's novels challenge us to interrogate the critical standards and assumptions that privilege what we imagine to be new, different, and original, and to thereby discover the significance and originality in the older and familiar.

Published in Chicago in 1920, Wright's novels have not received the attention they would have had they been published in New York. While Harlem certainly was a hotbed of cultural activity, the narrow geographical focus of most African-American criticism on the Harlem Renaissance has obscured the cultural and literary developments of other urban black communities. Recently, Wilson J. Moses has pointed to Washington D. C.'s vibrant and prolific literary community in the same era, a community that included such notable writers as Mary Church Terrell, Paul Lawrence Dunbar, and Alexander Crummell, and that was the home of such publications as the nationally known *African Methodist Episcopal Church Review*. He argues that "much of the Harlem Renaissance did in fact take place there," and that "a Washington Renaissance had predated the one in Harlem by at least twenty years."[14]

No such study of black culture in Chicago exists, despite the fact that it was the site of the largest migration of African Americans in the wake of World War I, its black population doubling from approximately 50,000 to 100,000 between 1916 and 1919. The rise of Jim Crow, the development of a "city within a city"[15] in Chicago's southside black belt, and the conditions leading to the race riots of 1919 have typically been the focus of studies of this time and place. The republication of *Black and White Tangled Threads* and *Kenneth* in this series is an important first step in broadening our critical attention of African-American culture beyond the borders of New York City. Our understandings not only of Zara Wright's work, but of African-American and United States literature and culture more generally no doubt will be enhanced by placing Chicago on a cultural map.

NOTES

[1]Wright is not included in any of the standard reference books on African-American women, Anglo-American women, or African

Americans. Ann Allen Shockley's brief introduction to Wright's "The Little Orphan" in Shockley's *Afro-American Women Writers, 1746–1933* (1988) is the only published commentary on Wright's work and it contains no biographical information. The *Chicago Defender's* combined review of *Black and White Tangled Threads* and *Kenneth* is the only review of the novels from either 1920 or 1975, the year the texts were reissued. J. Edward Wright, Zara's husband, is not listed in *Deaths in the Chicago Defender, 1910–1920* (Park Forest, Ill.: Lori Husband, 1990), even though she refers to him as "dearly departed" in the introduction to *Black and White Tangled Threads*.

²Review of *Black and White Tangled Threads* and *Kenneth*, by Zara Wright, *Chicago Defender* (25 December 1920): 8.

³Gloria T. Hull, *Color, Sex, and Poetry* (Bloomington: University of Indiana Press, 1987), 29; hereafter cited in text.

⁴Zara Wright, *Black and White Tangled Threads* (Chicago: Barnard and Miller, 1920; New York: AMS Press, 1975), p. 7; hereafter cited in text as *Threads. Kenneth* was also included in these volumes, although its title does not appear on the title page, so *Kenneth* also will be cited here as *Threads.* Page number citations in the present essay refer to the 1975 edition, which is reproduced in the present volume.

⁵Wright's 1925 address, 9 West 21st Street, places her in the Armour Square neighborhood of Chicago, between State Street and Heywood Avenue, a blockwide corridor between the largest concentration of black Chicagoans to the southeast and a smaller section to the northwest. This narrow north-south corridor was up to 95 percent black in 1920 and remained so in 1930, although the blocks between 20th and 27th streets on either side had lost some of their black residents, perhaps to the growing community to the southeast. Wright's address was only a few blocks from where the August 1919 stoning and drowning of a young black boy set off a five-day race riot, one of the worst in a period of increasing racial violence in northern urban centers.

⁶Zora Neale Hurston is one of the few black women writers of this period to address sexuality in her writing.

⁷See Frances Smith Foster, "'In Respect to Females . . . ': Differences in the Portrayals of Women by Male and Female Slave Narrators," *Black American Literature Forum* (Summer 1981): 66–70.

⁸Pauline E. Hopkins, *Contending Forces: A Romance Illustrative of Negro Life North and South* (New York: Oxford University Press, 1988), 149; emphasis is in the original. Hereafter cited in text as *Forces.*

⁹Frances Smith Foster, ed., Introduction to *A Brighter Coming Day: A Frances Ellen Watkins Harper Reader* (New York: Feminist Press, 1990), 26.

[10]Although it is not known if Wright was from Louisville, many black Chicagoans had recently migrated from the Southern states. Thus this setting may not be so much a displacement of contemporary life as an imagining of a geographical if not economic and social background similar to that of many of Wright's peers.

[11]See Judith R. Bertzon, *Neither Black nor White: The Mulatto Character in American Fiction* (New York: New York University Press, 1978), 120.

[12]Tate has argued that modernist and postmodernist logics have figured marriage and freedom as antithetical, making narratives that thematize marriage, such as Wright's, appear not only old-fashioned, but restrictive and reactionary. But Tate believes that with a more historicist critical eye, the right to marry legally may be accorded the same significance as the right to vote. See Tate, "Allegories of Black Female Desire; or, Rereading Nineteenth-Century Sentimental Narratives of Black Female Authority," in *Changing Our Own Words: Essays on Criticism, Theory, and Writing by Black Women*, ed. Cheryl A. Wall (New Brunswick, N.J.: Rutgers University Press), esp. pp. 99–104.

[13]Social restrictions against intermarriage were still very strong during the period in which Wright was writing. Consider the following excerpt from closing arguments in the famous Rhinelander antimiscegenation case in 1924: "There isn't a father among you . . . who would rather not see his own son in his casket than to see him wedded to a mulatto woman. . . . There is not a mother among your wives who would not rather see her daughter with her white hands crossed in her shroud than see her locked in the embrace of a mulatto husband." Quoted in the editorial "The Rhinelander Suit," *Opportunity: A Journal of Negro Life* (January 1926): 4.

[14]Wilson J. Moses, "The Lost World of the New Negro, 1895–1919," *Black American Literature Forum* 21 (Spring–Summer 1987): 65.

[15]Allan H. Spear, *Black Chicago: The Making of a Negro Ghetto, 1890–1920* (Chicago: University of Chicago Press, 1967), 91.

BIBLIOGRAPHY

Bertzon, Judith R. *Neither Black nor White: The Mulatto Character in American Fiction*. New York: New York University Press, 1978.

Foster, Frances Smith. Introduction. *A Brighter Coming Day: A Frances Ellen Watkins Harper Reader*. New York: Feminist Press, 1990.

———. "'In Respect to Females. . .': Differences in the Portrayals of Women by Male and Female Slave Narrators" in *Black American Literature Forum* (Summer 1981): 66–70.

Harper, Frances E. W. *Iola Leroy; or, Shadows Uplifted.* 1892. Reprint. Boston: Beacon Press, 1987.

Hopkins, Pauline E. *Contending Forces: A Romance Illustrative of Negro Life North and South.* 1900. Reprint. New York: Oxford University Press, 1988.

Hull, Gloria T. *Color, Sex, and Poetry.* Bloomington: Indiana University Press, 1987.

Husband, Lori, ed. *Deaths in the Chicago Defender, 1910–1920.* Park Forest, Ill.: Lori Husband, 1990.

Jacobs, Harriet A. *Incidents in the Life of a Slave Girl.* Edited by Jean Fagan Yellin. 1863. Reprint. Cambridge, Mass.: Harvard University Press, 1987.

Moses, Wilson J. "The Lost World of The New Negro, 1895–1919." *Black American Literature Forum* 21 (Spring–Summer 1987): 61–84.

Review of *Black and White Tangled Threads* and *Kenneth. Chicago Defender,* 25 December 1920, 8.

"The Rhinelander Suit." Editorial. *Opportunity: A Journal of Negro Life* (January 1926): 4.

Shockley, Ann Allen. Introduction to "The Little Orphan," by Zara Wright. *Afro-American Women Writers, 1746–1933: An Anthology and Critical Guide.* New York: New American Library, 1988, 380–82.

Tate, Claudia. "Allegories of Black Female Desire; or, Rereading Nineteenth-Century Sentimental Narratives of Black Female Authority," in *Changing Our Own Words: Essays on Criticism, Theory, and Writing by Black Women,* ed. Cheryl A. Wall. New Brunswick, N.J.: Rutgers University Press, 1991, 98–126.

ZARA WRIGHT

BLACK AND WHITE TANGLED THREADS

KENNETH

ZARA WRIGHT

BLACK AND WHITE
TANGLED THREADS

BY

ZARA WRIGHT

I found a little rosebud that had been left alone,
   Tenderly I gathered it, watered it with dews of love;
Now I find as its leaves unfold,
   A flower most rare with a heart of gold.

DEDICATED

TO THE

MEMORY

OF MY DEAR DEPARTED HUSBAND,

J. EDWARD WRIGHT,

who inspired me to write this book, hoping to interest and possibly benefit someone. May the unselfishness and noble qualities of the heroine be productive of good results and an inspiration to those who are too weak to do their duty as they see it and too cowardly to do that which is just and right for fear of criticism.

ZARA WRIGHT.

CONTENTS

PREFACE

TO

BLACK AND WHITE TANGLED THREADS

In writing this book I wish to impress its many readers, that this great and beautiful world in which we live, is sufficient in its greatness for all to live in peace and harmony. That in future years there may be no necessity for conflicts and wars to make any country safe to live in. We are commanded to love our neighbor as ourselves. If we followed this commandment, the conditions in which we live would be made more tolerable. We would find fewer obstacles in the path that leads to success and eventually the Heights. I feel that if one person has been benefited by reading the story written in these pages, that my efforts, altho feeble, will not have been in vain.

Every life must have its shadows, and the tempestuous storm
Only makes brighter the beautiful unfolding dawn.

THE AUTHOR.

INTRODUCTION

TO

BLACK AND WHITE TANGLED THREADS.

The lives of each character portrayed in this book remind one of tangled skeins of threads. The heroine of this story portrays a type of womanhood so often sought for, so rarely found. Circumstances having placed her in a false position, she sacrifices her principles of right and wrong to save those near and dear to her from imaginary shame and humiliation. Paul Andrews, a southern planter, vies with the heroine in sharing honors. One cannot help admiring him. He plays an important part in this story. There are other characters that play such distinctive parts that we must leave it to the imagination of the reader to decide which is the most appealing.

In this story you will find food for sane and serious thought, eliminating much sordidness that often mars a story, leaving the reader with neither desire nor inclination to either remember or discuss its contents afterward. I sincerely hope that the many readers of Black and White Tangled Threads and the sequel, which we find under the same cover, may leave a sweet memory and that there will be a genuine sigh of regret when we read the last word, FINIS.

THE AUTHOR.

BLACK AND WHITE TANGLED THREADS.

CHAPTER I.

THE THREE COUSINS.

It was late in the month of September and it had been raining hard since early morning. Now, at the close of day it seemed as if the clouds felt ashamed and disappeared from view, the sun shedding its last rays over the distant hilltops and the valley beneath, the mellow light causing the raindrops that linger on tree and bush to look like pearls. This beauteous aspect of nature makes one loath to leave the scene and enter where art alone is responsible for the beauty of the interior of a grand old mansion, situated on one of the largest plantations of the Sunny South.

Thus felt a beautiful young girl as she stood enchanted while the soft breeze gently blew her long black hair in confusion around her exquisite face.

After repeated calls from her cousins, she turned and entered the house, where they were soon discussing an important event. They were to start North in a few days to enter a select boarding school for young ladies.

Catherine Marceaux was the eldest, just sixteen, the daughter of a haughty, impoverished widow, who was a sister to Paul Andrews, the owner of the mansion.

Paul Andrews, tall and handsome, had married and lost his wife in just one year, leaving a little daughter whom he called Aline after her mother. She was a sweet child, possessed of a sunny disposition that won her the name of "Little Sunbeam," and was beloved by everyone.

The father idolized his child and she in turn fairly worshipped her father and would often leave her play and be found in the library, sitting contentedly at his feet for hours, sometimes falling asleep while waiting for him to put aside his books and papers. Then she would feel rewarded by the welcome he gave her. He often wished that his dead wife could see their lovely daughter.

The third cousin, the heroine of this story, is the most beautiful of the three. Her face is oval and her features are perfect, yet some thought that the nose was inclined to tilt upward. But if you would observe more closely you would find that it was the upward poise of the head that was misleading. Her complexion was fair although of a richer hue than her cousins, and her wonderful jet black hair hanging in long natural curls reached far below her waist and made her look most fair indeed, and no one would suspect that there flowed in her veins blood of a despised race,—the black slaves of the South. But such was the case. Zoleeta Andrews was a full cousin to Catherine Marceaux and Aline Andrews.

The children of two brothers and one sister. Mrs.
Marceaux bitterly resented it when her brother Paul
brought home their orphan niece, making her one of
the family, and as she expressed it, compelling them
to come in contact with that negro child. She declared that Catherine should not recognize her as a
relative.

To make matters worse, her brother was determined that Harold's child should have the same accomplishments and advantages as their children. It
was in vain that his sister cried and pleaded to have
Harold's child sent elsewhere, for Paul was inex-
orable, and she was compelled to abide by his decision.

Eighteen years preceding the events recorded,
Paul Andrews and his sister Claretta, and a younger
brother named Harold, lived with their parents,
General and Mrs. Andrews, in the present homestead.
At the age of eighteen Claretta married a man by
the name of Leroy Marceaux, who was of French descent, as his name would imply.

It was some years later that their brother Harold
ran away with and married Mildred Yates, a slave
girl belonging on the plantation. His mother never
recovered from the shock, shame and humiliation,
but in the end forgave him and begged his father to
forgive him also. Two years later, when General
Andrews was laid beside his wife, Harold was still
unforgiven.

Paul and his sister inherited all of the vast wealth.
The homestead, a fine old mansion, fell to Paul. A
few years later he had it remodeled and refurnished

and no one was much surprised when he brought
home a lovely bride. She was dearly beloved by all,
but died a year later at the birth of their daughter
Aline.

When Claretta married, her father gave her a liberal fortune, which she placed in the hands of her
husband, subsequently she placed in his hands the
entire fortune that she inherited through the death
of her father. A few years later when her husband
passed away, it was found that there was nothing
left of the large fortune that had once been hers. It
was then that her brother Paul went after her and
brought her and her little daughter to take charge of
his handsome home, to rear his child and manage
the servants. She gladly accompanied her brother
and was once more installed in her girlhood home.

Mrs. Marceaux was very domineering to those
whom she considered her inferior and often took her
brother to task for being too lenient with the servants. She was horrified to see his little daughter
Aline walking hand in hand with the little colored
children, but her brother only laughed and said there
was no harm and that the children had but few
pleasures and some of those consisted of being with
his daughter and he had not the heart to separate
them.

In a few years Aline would enter boarding school
and all would be changed. But his sister could not
forget how their brother Harold had disgraced them,
and not having her brother's optimistic views, remained unconvinced of the wisdom of the association.

Mildred Yates, the slave girl whom Harold married, had more education than the average slave girl. Her mother, a trusted servant of old Mrs. Andrews, had taught her to read and write and she had in turn taught her daughter Mildred all that she had learned, and with her limited opportunities and doubtful possibilities, succeeded in inspiring in her child a desire for knowledge. Her thirst for knowledge was so great that when her mother could teach her no more, she still tried to learn, but finding it difficult to proceed without help, went back to the beginning and went over all that she had previously learned.

Thus it was that her young master, Harold, found her one day when he was on a tour of inspection for his father. He was amazed at the sight of a beautiful slave girl, who had a piece of broken slate and a pencil trying to trace letters as her mother had taught her to do.

She arose at the approach of her young master, but not from fear, as she had never been punished or scolded. She was afraid, however, that he would laugh at her; but he spoke so kindly, asking to let him see what she was doing, that she let him take the piece of slate. After looking at it for a moment, he returned it, complimenting her on her successful efforts. He asked her if she would like to learn and she answered very brightly that she would. He promised to teach her if she would not tell anyone. Needless to say, she gave the required promise.

Day after day they met in an obscure place, remote from all danger of discovery. She proved to be a very diligent pupil and learned quite rapidly.

It was not long before she could do her sums in arithmetic. In fact, she made such rapid progress in all of her studies, and was thinking of taking up more difficult work, that when Harold's father decided to send him North to spend two years in college and another in travel, he at first rebelled, and declared that he would not go. He loved his mother dearly, however, and when she placed her arms around his neck and begged him to go for her sake, he consented.

He did not realize how dear Mildred had become to him until the hour of his departure. Besides being beautiful, her superior intellect gave promise of a glorious possibility in the future. He could no longer conceal from himself the fact that he was madly in love with his charming protege. Realizing that his heart was forever in the keeping of this beautiful slave girl, he resolved to have a talk with her before leaving for the North. Mildred had learned to love her young master as ardently as he loved her and unhesitatingly promised to follow his instructions in all things. Leaving her plenty of good books and admonishing her to be a good girl, he promised to return in three years and marry her.

Three years later when Harold returned to his home, he felt more than repaid for the love he had lavished on this slave girl. She had studied diligently and not only did she show mental improvement, but she had grown wondrously beautiful. Dressed in the garb worn by the southern slave, with no other adornment save those with which nature had provided, a beautiful face, a graceful, willowy form that even her coarse garments failed to hide, she looked like some princess in disguise. In Mr. Harold, who treated her with that courtesy and consideration that he would, had she been his equal in birth and social standing, she had utmost faith, and he was never guilty of doing aught to betray the confidence of this poor, innocent, trusting girl.

Ere many weeks had gone by, he had severed the fetters that bound her and they were safely landed in England. They were married without delay. Although he knew his father would disinherit him, that was of small consequence. Having a comfortable fortune of his own—a legacy from his godmother, and being young and energetic, he felt that he would succeed—and he did.

He wrote to his parents after his marriage, assuring them that he and his wife would remain abroad, thus relieving them of any embarrassment that they might feel. He begged their forgiveness and in a manly way, without exaggeration, dwelt on his wife's many admirable qualities. Without defiance, but with that firmness of purpose which a deep and sincere love lends, he closed his letter by saying that he was very proud of his wife and had no regret for the step he had taken.

His father was furious. "Harold has acted in a senseless, idiotic way," said he. "What need to pluck one rose from the stem, when he could have inhaled the fragrance of many?" (Thus unconsciously paying a beautiful compliment to Harold's Afro-American wife.)

Paul felt the absence of his brother keenly, and

greatly deplored the step he had taken. He often longed for his little brother, unmindful of the fact this his little brother had grown to be a handsome, broad-shouldered man.

CHAPTER II.

THE LITTLE ORPHAN.

Some years later Paul received a letter from his brother, telling him that Harold's wife had died two years previous, leaving him a sweet little daughter. The letter also assured Paul that Harold's days were numbered, according to the doctor's statement which said that he might possibly live six or eight weeks. He begged Paul to come and take his little daughter home, assuring him that she was well provided for.

"I came to India soon after my marriage," continued the letter, "and by careful investments and close application to business, have become a successful merchant, more than doubling my wealth."

When Paul received this letter, he was filled with consternation. He felt that he could not do the thing that his brother had not only asked him, but expected him to do.

"No. It is impossible to take that child into my home with a taint of slavery clinging to her ancestors," said he. "I could not let my daughter associate with her. It is not to be thought of."

His sister agreed with him and declared it was an outrageous imposition for Harold to shift his negro child on them. However, it was decided that Paul should hasten to his brother's bedside, take the child and place her in some institution until she became of age, making no other plans for her future, but trusting to time, circumstances and existing conditions to adjust matters satisfactorily to all concerned.

Paul left without delay and it was only by traveling night and day that he succeeded in reaching his brother's side before death claimed him. As he listened to his brother he was convinced that his marriage had been a supremely happy one. Although he seemed loath to leave his little daughter, he appeared anxious to meet his wife, who had preceded to realms above. (Paul had not yet seen his brother's child, and therefore was much disturbed because he felt that he could not heed his brother's last request and asked himself how he could refuse to make his brother's last hours happy.) He was visibly agitated, knowing that his brother's eyes were scanning his face, perhaps reading perplexity and indecision there.

Presently there was a gentle, hesitating rap on the half open door. A sweet, childish voice said "Papa, may I come in?" Feeling sure of her welcome and scarcely waiting for a reply, she softly entered the room. Upon beholding the beautiful child, Paul Andrews was speechless with surprise. She showed no trace of the blood of her mother's people, and was by far the prettiest child he had ever seen. He marveled at the beauty and grace of this little girl scarcely six years old.

The father, propped up in bed, looked on and felt
that he could die in peace when he saw his brother
open his arms and say: "Darling, come to your
uncle." She, unhesitatingly went to him, clasped
her little arms around his neck and with her head
pillowed on his breast, rested contentedly there. Ah!
who knows by what instinct this little girl felt so
content in the clasp of her uncle's arms, though she
had never seen him before. Was it some unseen
power that made it plain to this little innocent child
that in her uncle's arms she would find a haven of
rest, a shelter and protection from life's tempestuous
storms in the trying days to come? Who knows?

Paul Andrews registered a vow as he stroked the
long glossy curls of his niece, to stand by her through
life. Little did he think at that time that he would
be called upon to defend and protect her from the
treachery of those who should have felt near and
dear to her through ties of blood. When the time
came he did not hesitate to do his duty by his dead
brother's child.

Unclasping the little arms from around his neck,
he glanced at his brother and realized that the Messenger had come—that Zoleeta was an orphan. Before she could realize that her father had gone to
join her mother, her uncle had led her from the room.
He told her that her father was now with her mother.
At first, she was inconsolable, but after the first par-
oxysm of grief was over, she allowed her uncle to
caress her while he explained that she would have
two cousins to play with and they would love her
dearly, for he had resolved to take Harold's child
home and rear her in a befitting manner.

In looking over Harold's papers, he found two letters, one addressed to himself and one to Zoleeta to be given her when she became of age. Paul read his at once. His attention was called to a curiously carved ebony box that had been given his brother by an exiled prince, who lost most of his possessions and was forced into exile by existing conditions in his country. The death of the prince soon followed. This box was in an iron safe filled with precious stones, worth a king's ransom. Paul opened the casket containing the jewels and never had he in his life beheld such jewels representing a vast fortune. He hastily closed the box, resolving to say nothing of its contents until Zoleeta was old enough to understand and appreciate their value.

Paul worked hard to settle up his brother's affairs, but it was some weeks before he was ready to sail for home. He wrote his sister informing her of the death of their brother Harold. He also informed her that he would bring their orphaned niece home with him. When she read the letter she became very indignant because he had not placed the child in some institution as they had agreed to do.

Paul and Zoleeta finally arrived. Zoleeta's aunt was dismayed at the sight of the most beautiful child that she had ever seen. She was amazed at this lovely graceful child, who had no badge to proclaim to the world that she had descended from the degraded race of negroes of the South. She could not understand it, and hated her dead brother's child for her rare loveliness. She had no love in her heart for her little orphaned niece; no compassion for this helpless child, thrown on her care.

Paul took Zoletta by the hand and led her to his sister, saying: "Claretta, this is Harold's child." His sister made no attempt to welcome the little stranger to either her heart or her home, and, for an instant, seemed inclined to repulse the child, but a look from her brother changed her mind. She spoke a few cold words to her niece and it was plain to be seen that the little girl would have had a hard time in her new home had it not been for her uncle and Cousin Aline. As it was, there were many times that her little heart ached so badly that she wished she was up in the bright blue sky with her own dear father and mother.

Turning to his sister's daughter, he said: "Catherine, I have brought you a little new cousin. I hope you will help to make her happy." That little miss scarcely spoke to Zoleeta. She knew not why, but she saw that her mother was not pleased and felt that she must show her displeasure, also. Before Paul could speak to his daughter Aline, she had thrown her arms around her little cousin's neck telling her how glad she was to see her.

"I am so glad that you are going to stay with us always," said Aline as she led Zoleeta to see her little pet birds. Catherine followed, but said nothing.

When the cousins had left the room, Paul turned to his sister and said: "Claretta, that is our dead brother's child. Will you not help me to care for her and make her happy in her new home? Women know just what to do for little girls and Zoleeta is a sweet, lovable child. I was in hopes that you would love her for Harold's sake."

"You will find out that you have made a mistake by bringing the child here," replied Claretta, becoming more indignant as she continued, "and if after years, she develops traits and habits of her mother's people to the exclusion of the better blood flowing in her veins, causing us shame and humiliation, you must remember that I warned you and you will have no one to blame but yourself. In a few years, our daughters will make their bows to the world and a girl as beautiful as Zoleeta promises to be will prove detrimental to their prospects. Of course," continued she, "Catherine has enough beauty of her own and will not be disturbed by the beauty of Harold's child, but Aline is such a meek little creature that the chances are that she will be outshown by Zoleeta."

Paul was not disconcerted by this outburst of temper from his sister and was firm in his decision that each one should have an equal chance when they entered the social world.

Neither Zoleeta nor her cousins were aware of the secret of her parentage, and Paul impressed upon his sister that under no circumstances were they to be enlightened. There were old servants about the place who remembered their young master Harold, and that he had gone abroad and married, and who were not surprised when Mr. Andrews brought home the little orphan, telling them that his brother and wife had died abroad, leaving a little daughter who would henceforth remain in his home. No one, of course, had attached any importance to the disappearance of Mildred Yates, as it was not infrequent in those days for slaves to take advantage of every opportunity to escape. Paul felt that as no one except himself and sister knew the secret of Zoleeta's parentage, it was perfectly safe.

CHAPTER III.

CATHERINE'S JEALOUSY.

The years went by, the cousins growing more beautiful each day. Finally, it was decided that they should go North to a select finishing school for young ladies. It was with many misgivings and after repeated talks with her brother, that Mrs. Marceaux was convinced he remained unchanged in his decision that Zoleeta was to enter the same school with her cousins.

If Paul could have seen and read his sister's heart, how she was planning to humiliate and crush her niece, he would have been appalled. The night before the cousins started North, Mrs. Marceaux told Catherine the secret of Zoleeta's parentage, thus betraying the confidence of her noble brother, who was endeavoring to shield Harold's child from the consequence of her father's act in his youth. It was Paul's most sacred wish that no shadow of the past should rest upon her, marring her future and causing her shame and humiliation. It was his fondest hope that she might still cherish in the days to come, the same sweet memories of her father as in the days that were past and gone.

Mrs. Marceaux cautioned her daughter not to let her uncle know that she knew the secret of Zoleeta's parentage as he would be very angry. Thus it was that when Catherine Marceaux departed for the North with her cousins, her mother had placed a weapon in her hand to wound her orphan cousin, and there came a time when she used it most cruelly.

Mr. Andrews accompanied the girls North and left them comfortably settled. He was pleased with their surroundings and before he left had a long talk with Zoleeta, telling her not to hesitate to call upon him at any time, that henceforth she must consider him a father as well as an uncle. She burst into tears and for a long time cried unrestrainedly. Those tears forged a link that already bound them by ties of blood and to the day of his death, Paul Andrews had two daughters instead of one.

On his return home, his sister greeted him affectionately, for, in spite of her cold selfish disposition, she dearly loved her handsome brother. Often when she looked at him she felt very much disturbed for fear he might bring another mistress to preside over his palatial home.

It was decided that the girls should spend their vacations at home, but they prevailed upon Mrs. Marceaux to allow them to accept an invitation to spend the time with a schoolmate. She reluctantly consented.

The following year Mrs. Marceaux was laid up with a sprained ankle and Mr. Andrews had business of importance that detained him at home, making it impossible for either of them to visit the girls.

They were very much disappointed as they had not seen the girls since they entered the school, two years previous. They planned, however, to be present at their graduation the following year and accompany them home.

One day about six months before they had finished their course, the principal informed the school that they would have a musicale and reception. There would be visitors and refreshments would be served. She desired each one to do her best. For days, nothing else was talked about. Finally, the much talked of event arrived. Each one acquitted herself with credit. Catherine gave an instrumental solo, which was well received and generously applauded. Zoleeta was the last on the program. As she arose and moved gracefully forward, there was more than one admiring glance that followed her. Her rich, mellow voice rang out sweetly and held the audience entranced. She captivated the house. This closed the exercise and our heroine was the center of an admiring crowd, all eager to greet this queenly girl who carried off the honors of the day.

The pupils were highly complimented. Zoleeta's schoolmates vied with each other in singing her praises. Her cousin Aline fairly smothered her with kisses and was standing with her arms around her, demonstrating to all how proud she was of her beautiful, talented cousin.

Not far away stood Catherine with a party of young people, some of them being schoolmates and others visitors. It was evident that Zoleeta was the theme of their conversation. Just as the first group named, of which Aline and Zoleeta were the center, had ceased speaking for a moment they heard Catherine distinctly say: "Anyone having negro blood in their veins always has a good voice for singing. That is a characteristic of the race. On my uncle's plantation there are still many negroes who remained and they often sing such amusing songs. Zoleeta is only my uncle's protege."

One of the young ladies said it was outrageous imposition to allow that class of people to mingle with them. One gentleman was incredulous, and said: "If Miss Andrews is contaminated with African blood, it breaks down all tradition concerning the Southern negro and his ancestors."

He immediately sought an introduction to this imperial Southern beauty.

Zoleeta and Aline had heard every word as it was intended they should, but beyond getting a little pale, our heroine showed no signs of having heard or felt the cruel blow. Aline stood horrified and looked as if she would burst into tears, but Zoleeta pressed her hand and led her out of hearing and was soon mingling with the crowd of visitors, all vieing with each other in paying homage to this queenly girl.

At last the guests had departed. Madam had nothing but smiles and compliments for her pupils who had done themselves and her school so much credit and congratulated herself that everything had gone off so pleasantly, nothing to mar the occasion. Her glances rested fondly on Zoleeta, for Mrs. Payne cherished a deep affection for Paul Andrews' orphan niece. She felt as if Zoleeta had been instrumental in making the musicale a success, but had no sooner retired to her room than word was brought to her that she was wanted below.

She found two or three excited and indignant girls, who lost no time in charging her with imposing on them by having a negro girl for their schoolmate. That, furthermore, they intended leaving her school at once. Mrs. Payne was not only mystified, but horrified. She was very indignant at such a charge being brought against her, and at first, could not understand what it all meant, until one of the girls, who had been present when the statement was made told her just as it was told to them and by whom.

Mrs. Payne immediately sent for Miss Marceaux, who unblushingly repeated the story. Mrs. Payne asked the girls not to repeat the story to anyone until she had had time to adjust the matter satisfactorily. She begged them not to leave as it would ruin the reputation of the institution, and she would be obliged to close her school. She assured them that she was perfectly innocent and that it was the first time that she had heard the story and was averse to believe it even now.

Zoleeta went to her room at once but not to bed, nor did she retire until she had sent a telegram to her uncle to come to her without delay, and if impossible, to let her know and she would come to him immediately. She assured him that both cousins were well, thus relieving him of any suspense he might have concerning them.

Aline came to her room and would like to have spoken cheering words but Zoleeta told her that she was too sleepy to talk. As she kissed her cousin a fond good-night she noticed that Aline's lips trembled as if she could scarcely keep the tears back. After carefully locking the door, she fell upon her knees, calling on her dead parents to be near and help her to endure the heavy burden that she was called upon to bear. She knelt there a long time wondering why her uncle never told her that there was a stigma on her birth or a mystery of any kind. She had never heard of her mother's kindred beyond the fact that her mother had a brother who ran away from home when quite a youth.

After the death of her mother she came across an old picture and asked her father whose it was and had been told that it was her mother's brother, and that when she was older he would tell her all about her mother and her mother's people. She had not thought anything about the matter at that time as she was too young to understand. However, she remembered her mother, and now, since her cousin had said that she had negro blood she remembered that her mother was much darker skinned than her uncle, aunt or cousins. Her father had died before revealing anything of the early life of her mother.

It was almost morning when she fell asleep. She arose quite early the next morning as she was anxious to hear from her uncle. About noon she received a telegram telling her that he would leave for the North immediately. She had not told anyone what she had done, but as it was not her nature to conceal her actions, she at once took the telegram to Aline, who was overjoyed at the prospect of seeing her father so soon. Zoleeta knocked on the door of Catherine's room and was admitted. Her cousin was expecting this visit, hence was not surprised but ill at ease, when she noted the calm look on Zoleeta's face. She offered her cousin a chair. At first, Zoleeta thought to refuse to be seated, but realizing that she had much to say, took a seat.

"Catherine, I have a telegram from Uncle Paul in reply to one that I sent him. He will be here on the 17th. This is now the 15th. Only two days more," said she.

Catherine was prepared for an unpleasant interview with her cousin but was not prepared for the announcement of her uncle's expected arrival. For a moment, she was incapable of speech, although her cousin paused for a reply. Finally she said: "I do not see the necessity for your sending for uncle. You have disgraced the whole school and several of the girls are going to leave if you remain."

"I shall return home with my uncle," replied Zoleeta.

"If you had intended to leave school, I think it very selfish and inconsiderate of you to have uncle make the trip," said Catherine. "You could have gone home alone."

"I should not have sent for uncle," replied she "if I could have vindicated myself before the prin cipal and the school that I am no imposter. I was not aware of my mixed blood and felt that an explanation which I am unable to give, was due them.

I came here this morning to ask you how and from whom you received the information concerning my parentage. Our parents were brother and sister."

Catherine, blinded by jealousy and anger, forgetting the fact that her orphaned cousin had always shown her the utmost kindness, drove the shaft farther into the heart she had so cruelly wounded the day before.

"It is true, as you say," retorted Catherine, "that your father and my mother were brother and sister, but your mother was a 'nigger.' "

At these words Zoleeta arose to her feet, the blood rushing to her face for a moment, then a deadly pallor overspread that sweet face so full of anguish. Never did Zoleeta look more beautiful than when she turned to Catherine with flashing eyes, and said:

"My mother may have descended from the negroes of the South, but let me ask you if that was a crime. It is evident that she was a lady or my father would not have chosen her for his wife. My mother was his equal if not by birth, by breeding."

At this unlooked for outburst from her cousin, Catherine fell back affrighted. Zooleeta, looking as imperial as a queen, towered in just indignation over her cousin, who was scarcely the average height, while Zoleeta was much taller.

"I do not know why you cherish such ill feelings toward me," continued Zoleeta. "If we were not united by the ties of blood, the fact that we are schoomates should make it impossible for us to feel otherwise than cordial and happy together, and sincere in our cordiality, but I see that it is not to be, and in the future I hope you will refrain from letting your antagonism lead you to speak ill of my dead mother. Although I have been subjected to many indignities, I have never complained to my uncle, but if it continues, I shall do so at once. I am his ward until I become of age, consequently, I am under his protection until then, and shall demand it. Afterward, if the same conditions exist, I shall be free to go where I will.''

Catherine was older than her cousin, yet she lacked that broad minded intellect—the higher ideas that Zoleeta possessed. In fact, she showed intellectual inferiority, which was clearly demonstrated when she rallied from the momentary surprise occasioned by her cousin's noble defense of her mother.

''Of course, Zoleeta, I feel sorry for you in your inferior position, but I think with your good looks you might find someone who would be willing to marry you.''

At those words, the hot blood rose to Zoleeta's face. She was amazed at her cousin for this unlooked for insult. With withering scorn, she replied: ''I prefer your unconcealed hatred to your secret enmity and pretended interest in my future welfare.''

Without waiting for a reply, she turned and left the room. Not as a warrior, who had been beaten in battle, but as a queen ascending her throne. Nor did she again give way to despair as she did the night before when she had wished she had died in her mother's arms. She was restless but did not in-

trude on the other inmates of the school. She and
Aline spent much of the time together until the arrival of Mr. Andrews.

He arrived at the specified time and was overjoyed to meet his daughter. Aline clung to her
father's neck, kissing him again and again. Catherine greeted her uncle cordially, but there was an
observable restraint. Her uncle kissed her affectionately and complimented her on her improved
looks.

Presently the door opened and Mr. Andrews looked
around. He immediately arose to his feet. Never
before did he behold such a face or form. Surely
that tall, graceful girl could not be his brother's
daughter, yet she had called him uncle. He had not
seen the girl since she entered the school, therefore,
while he was prepared to see some improvement, he
was not prepared to see such rare loveliness as Zoleeta possessed. He noticed, however, that she was
very pale, but attributed that to the gala week at
the school and the loss of sleep. He embraced her
with genuine affection. They all chatted pleasantly
for awhile, then Zoleeta told her uncle that after he
had rested she wanted to have a talk with him.

As the pupils had been severely tasked that week,
they were not permitted to resume their studies until the following week. Zoleeta could therefore talk
freely to her uncle without infringing on the rules of
the school. Sometime later when she returned to the
reception room she found her uncle anxiously await-
ing her. He arose at once and offered her a chair,
but she refused to be seated. Mr. Andrews noticed

that while she was apparently calm she was deeply agitated. She longed and yet dreaded to hear the history of her parents' lives and the mystery of her birth, if there was one.

Her uncle appeared to be as deeply agitated as she. He could not understand why he had been sent for, but felt sure that while Zoleeta was still quite young, she would not have sent such an urgent request for his presence if there had not been grave cause.

She did not keep him in suspense long. Seeing her deep agitation, he held out his arm, and said: "Lay your head on uncle's shoulder and tell him all."

But she exclaimed, "Oh, no! let me stand or I could not breathe. Tell me, uncle, oh, tell me. Did my father place a wedding ring on my mother's hand and have I a legitimate right to the name I bear?"

Paul Andrews' face was awful to see. The tightening of his lips and the clinching of his hands showed only too plainly that the one who had so cruelly stigmatized her birth was not present, but he unhesitatingly assured her that everything connected with her father's marriage had been honorable and that she was the legitimate child by lawful marriage.

Zoleeta, raising her eyes heavenward, exclaimed: "Oh, Father in Heaven, I thank Thee, I thank Thee."

"Now, uncle, there is one more question, and do not fear to speak. Have I negro blood in my veins with a taint of slavery clinging to my ancestors? Who was my mother?"

But Paul Andrews hesitated to tell this beautiful girl that she was descended from the race of black slaves of the South. He hesitated to tell her this and would not tell her that his father had sold her grandmother, in a fit of rage, after he had cruelly punished her for her daughter's act of running away and marrying his son and that she died in chains. She never drew the free breath of liberty. No, he could not tell her this, but seeing the tense, drawn look on her beautiful face, he gently told her that her mother had been a beautiful girl despite the fact that she had mixed blood.

She listened to the story of her mother's marriage to the young master, never once interrupting her uncle, as in a broken voice, he related the story of her parents' love and devotion to each other. When he had finished speaking he bowed his head upon his hands, fearing to look at that young face so full of anguish and misery. He did not lift his head until he heard her speak. Then he was puzzled at the cheerful tone of her voice. Her face was radiant. She threw her head proudly back, causing her hair to fall in beautiful disorder around her exquisite face and making a picture that would have made an artist famous.

She embraced her uncle, exclaiming: "Oh, Uncle Paul! let us congratulate each other. I am so happy to think that my father was a prince among men and that I am his daughter. How proud you must have been of your noble brother. If my dear mother had lived, I would have owned her before the whole world. I have nothing to feel ashamed of. I am proud of my parentage."

By this time tears that did not shame his manhood rolled down Paul Andrews' cheeks. Clasping Zoleeta to his breast, he thanked the God above for this glorious good girl, who was a fit companion for his lovely daughter. When they had grown more calm, he asked when and where she had learned the secret of her birth. She told him that her cousin had told her and that her aunt had given her cousin the information.

Paul was very angry with his sister and determined to have a very plain talk with her when he returned to his home, but Zoleeta would not tell her uncle where and when those cruel words had been spoken, but later on, his daughter told him all.

Both were very much depressed. Aline shed bitter tears while telling of the severe ordeal through which her cousin had passed. Father and daughter both felt that this was only the beginning. Before Mr. Andrews and his niece separated she told him that Mrs. Payne, the principal of the school, had sent for her but that she had failed to go before she had talked with him.

Mr. Andrews told Zoleeta that he had sad news for her, but that she would not be affected by it.

Said he: "I have met with reverses, through the dishonesty of my agents and the failure of the bank that contained most of my funds, leaving me bankrupt. It is my intention to take the girls home with me. I know they have only a few more months before finishing; yet, I feel that I cannot afford to let them remain. I was on the point of sending for them when I received your telegram. Of course, Zoleeta," he continued, "you know there was ample provision made for your education and you can remain until you have finished."

"I cannot remain under any consideration," replied Zoleeta, "but it is my wish to have my cousins remain. You know, uncle, you have made me such a generous allowance that it has not been possible for me to use it all and I have quite a sum on hand at this present time, and the next allowance is most due."

Whereupon Zoleeta's uncle produced a package containing her allowance. She would not touch it, however, but begged him to add to it that which she had on hand for her cousins, Aline and Catherine, that they might remain until they had finished.

At first, Mr. Andrews was reluctant to accept his niece's generous offer and tears dimmed his eyes when he remembered how she had been insulted and humiliated by his sister's daughter, who was to share in the generosity of her lovely cousin. After much persuasion, he gave his consent with the understanding that it would simply be a loan. It was also agreed that the girls should not be told of his reverses as it would mar the last of their school days.

Zoleeta arose, saying that she would go and see Mrs. Payne and in all probability she would want to see him. After she went out Paul Andrews arose and paced the floor in deep agitation until sent for.

Zoleeta found the principal looking pale and nervous. Mrs. Payne felt that she would rather do almost anything than to say to this beautiful imperious girl that which she knew must be said and said at once, and the knowledge that Zoleeta's uncle was under the same roof did not help matters. She felt that she must choose her words carefully for she really loved this noble girl for the many admirable qualities that she had discovered in her soon after her arrival at the school. She was very proud of her as a pupil, and was filled with pleasure to introduce her to her many friends, telling them afterwards that Zoleeta was a great heiress as well as the most beautiful girl in her school. Therefore, when Zoleeta entered her presence she was warmly greeted. Mrs. Payne would have taken her by the hand and led her to a seat, but Zoleeta declined, telling her she would rather stand.

The principal gently told her of the rumors that were rife concerning her birth and parentage, at the same time adding that she was reluctant to believe it, but in justice to the girl herself, she felt it was her duty, although painful, to ascertain the facts, if possible from Zoleeta. Gaining permission from Mrs. Payne, Zoleeta, who, up to this time, had not interrupted the speaker, sent for her uncle. When Mr. Andrews entered the room with all the dignity and bearing of a king, Mrs. Payne completely lost her composure.

Not so with our heroine. Her extreme pallor was the only indication she was passing through the greatest tragedy of her young life, but if she had known what the future held for her, she would have been filled with horror.

In spite of her nervousness, Mrs. Payne greeted Mr. Andrews most cordially; Zoleeta informed her uncle that the principal was desirous of learning something of her birth and its legitimacy. Mrs. Payne would have apologized but Mr. Andrews stopped her, assuring her that it was perfectly right and natural that she should investigate those rumors. He informed her that there was no mystery concerning his niece's birth, that his brother was lawfully married to Zoleeta's mother, and had he known there was any controversy over her birth and parentage, he would have brought the proofs.

Mrs. Payne was much relieved and her face beamed with smiles. "I knew that this lovely girl did not have negro blood in her veins," said she, and was again ready to apologize for the humiliation that Miss Andrews had been subjected to, adding, "I would not have given the matter any credence if Miss Marceaux had not informed me of its truthfulness, and that Miss Zoleeta was only a protege of yours."

Mrs. Payne would have embraced her favorite pupil, but Mr. Andrews told her that she was still laboring under a mistake. "Neither myself or niece have any intention of deceiving you. Her mother was descended from the race of colored people of the South. She was a beautiful woman yet she showed in the color of the skin unmistakable evidence of her dark-skinned ancestors."

Zoleeta who had stood calmly by without uttering a word, stepped proudly forward, and said: "Although my mother was a mulatto, I am not ashamed of my parentage."

Before Mrs. Payne could utter a word, Zoleeta in-

formed her that she was leaving the school and
would return home with her uncle. Thanking her
for the kindness shown her while she was in the institution, she begged for the continued courtesy of
Miss Andrews and Miss Marceaux, who would remain until the closing of the term.

Mrs. Payne was truly sorry to lose Zoleeta, but
was thankful to think the matter had been taken
out of her hands and satisfactorily adjusted.

Aline shed many tears when she found out her
cousin was going to leave school and return home.
Feeling very resentful towards Catherine for being
the cause, she indignantly told that lady so. She
was not deceived when her cousin, Zoleeta, told
her that there were reasons of a business nature
that made it necessary for her to leave, but as she
was of a very cheerful disposition, Aline was soon
smiling and helped her to pack.

Zoleeta bade Catherine a gentle good-bye. Paul
had not notified his sister that Zoleeta was returning home with him, therefore, it came as a great sur-
price when she beheld that beautiful, imperial girl
who called her auntie. She could scarcely believe it
to be her dead brother's child and hated her for her
great beauty and was so busy planning how she
might drive her orphan niece from home in disgrace that Zoleeta had to speak the second time,
saying, "Auntie, have you no welcome for me?"

For the second time on entering her uncle's home,
she was coldly received by her father's sister. However, they spent a very enjoyable evening together,
Zoleeta, careful always to relate to her aunt all of

the most admirable qualities of Catherine, knowing full well that her aunt was very proud of her daughter.

As Paul sat and listened he could not help but notice how little love his sister had in her heart for their orphan niece and again resolved to shield and protect Harold's child while life should last.

Six months had rolled around and the cousins had returned home from school. It was indeed a pleasant homecoming. Aline clung to her father and declared that she would never leave him again. Between her love for her father and her beautiful cousin, she was very happy. Catherine was not very cordial to Zoleeta, who, if she noticed any slight, gave no sign.

One morning Mr. Andrews informed Zoleeta that in a few days she would be mistress of her entire fortune thus making her one of the wealthiest heiresses in the whole country. Zoleeta accepted her new responsibilities with quiet dignity and with her uncle Paul's assistance soon developed into quite a business woman for one so young. She and her cousins were invited everywhere. But her uncle found it difficult to get her to accept invitations. She always said, "Uncle, I feel that I am an imposter sailing under false colors." Although she knew that it was no fault of hers if she occupied a false position, and had it not been for her father's people, she would not have cared as far as she was concerned. She often smiled when she thought of the beautiful romance of her parents' courtship and marriage and wished the whole world might know of it.

One day her uncle and aunt told her that some guests were expected to spend a few weeks. That Catherine and Aline had expressed a desire to have a couple of their school friends included and her uncle thought that she would like to avail herself of the opportunity to invite whoever she wanted, but she declined to invite anyone.

Among the guests in the house was a young widow named Mrs. Marshelda, who was quite wealthy and very fascinating. From the very first she was drawn towards Paul Andrews' beautiful orphan niece.

Ruth Marshelda had married quite young, scarcely eighteen years of age. She had married an old man at the bidding of her father, as she was not in love with anyone else. She made a very good, considerate wife and five years later she was left a widow at twenty-three. She truly mourned her deceased husband, who had been very good and kind to her. She was very wealthy and quite sensible. Her father had died shortly after her marriage, thus we find her without a relative.

Mrs. Marceaux was the mistress of her brother's palatial home, yet Ruth Marshelda noticed that everyone seemed to seek and value the orphan girl's opinion more than anyone else. She had not been a guest in the house many days before she discovered that Zoleeta's aunt and cousin Catherine hated her most bitterly, yet this lovely, imperious girl never gave a sign of being otherwise than happy. This young widow often noticed a shadow on that beautiful young face, however. She also discovered that Zoleeta's uncle and Cousin Aline loved her dearly, but as she always appeared so bright and cheerful, they never gave a thought of her being otherwise than happy.

There were a great many visitors in the neighborhood and it was small wonder that the Andrew' home with three beautiful cousins and a lovely fascinating young widow should be the magnet that drew all the men from miles around.

One of the wealthiest residents of the vicinity was a Mrs. Slayton, the widow of old Colonel Slayton, who had died many years ago, leaving her an only son, Will Slayton. Having finished his college course, he spent two years travelling abroad, and had just returned bringing with him two friends, Phillip Seville, the son of a Boston banker, and Lord Blankleigh.

Seville was a fine looking young man with a frank, open countenance.

Lord Blankleigh, who appeared to be about five years the senior of the other two men, was tall, broad shouldered and of athletic build. He had wavy brown hair that he kept well combed back from his broad, intellectual forehead, but strange to say, his hair was sprinkled with gray. It was learned afterwards that those silver threads were the result of a tragedy at sea that had deprived him of his father and only brother. Lord Blankleigh was the soul of honor and a man to be trusted to the death.

Needless to say the trio spent much time at the home of Paul Andrews and were pleasantly received by the host and the ladies.

It soon became evident that Lord Blankleigh was

smitten with the charms of Paul Andrews' orphan
niece, much to the discomfiture of her aunt and Cousin Catherine, who straightway began to plot how
they might turn his attention to Catherine.

Zoleeta never gave Lord Blankleigh any encouragement, yet she was pleased when day after day
lovely bouquets of flowers found their way to her
room with his name attached.

Catherine also noticed the flowers and had learned
who sent them. One day she was on the lookout,
received the flowers telling the servant that she was
going to her cousin's room and would take them and
save him the trouble of going up the stairs. He
gave them to her to deliver to Miss Zoleeta and took
himself to task for misjudging Catherine whom he
had always thought selfish and indifferent to the
servant's comfort.

It happened that day Lord Blankleigh had placed
a note in the bouquet telling Zoleeta that he would
call that day at four o'clock and had something very
special to say to her and hoped that she would accord
him an interview.

Mrs. Marceaux had seen her daughter intercept
the note and was pleased with her alertness and was
delighted when her daughter brought her the note
to read. She embraced her and told her that she
had done well. That afternoon when Zoleeta was on
the veranda with some of the guests her aunt came
up the walk with a tired expression on her face.

Her daughter asked her where she had been, she
replied that one of the old servants was quite sick,
that she had been to see her, adding, that poor old

Mrs. Brown wanted her to read, but her head ached so badly that she had to refuse but promised to see her on the morrow.

Zoleeta got up at once, as her aunt knew that she would, and said, "I will go and read to her and I am very sorry that I have neglected to go as usual, but Aline had not been well and I remained with her instead."

It was now nearly four o'clock. Her aunt was quite anxious to have her start, which she did as soon as a servant brought a basket containing some wine and other delicacies she wanted to take to the old woman. Soon after her departure Lord Blankleigh arrived, he looked so handsome that even the men could not help but admire him, he was cordially received by Mrs. Marceaux and her guests.

Not seeing Zoleeta, he gladly accepted an invitation into the house, and sent up his card to Zoleeta. The servant soon returned with the information that Miss Andrews was out and she could not tell at what time she would get back.

Just then Catherine came in, looking for her handkerchief. She was very clever and pretended to be very much surprised to see Lord Blankleigh there. After greeting her pleasantly he turned to depart, but Catherine had no intention of losing an opportunity like the present one and detained him for quite a while.

She was a good conversationalist and had the visitor been an ordinary caller he would have found her very interesting. Nor was she blind to the fact that he only remained out of courtesy, but it suited her purpose.

Before leaving he inquired if Miss Andrews was well and being assured that she was enjoying the best of health, he seemed puzzled at her absence and was at a loss to understand her haste to leave the house before four o'clock.

Lord Blankleigh felt that Zoleeta was not indifferent to him although she had not given him any encouragement, yet he felt this was the first time that she had purposely avoided him. The thought of not winning this lovely girl for his wife filled him with despair. He felt that if he could win her he would ask no greater happiness.

Meanwhile Zoleeta had returned from her mission of mercy while Lord Blankleigh was still in the parlor with Catherine. Her aunt, who had been watching for Zoleeta, saw her coming, and going to her told her that she looked very tired and for her to lie down until dinner was ready. She really did feel tired but took her aunt's advice, and passed on upstairs to her room.

She wondered why she did not receive the customary flowers that morning. She took the hairpins out of her hair which fell around her beautiful face and was standing by the window where the soft breeze was blowing through it, cooling her head. She heard someone come out of the parlor, and recognized Lord Blankleigh's voice as he was bidding Catherine a pleasant afternoon. He walked slowly down the path. Zoleeta wondered why she had not been called. Again she thought that it was possible the visit was not intended for her and would not allow her mind to dwell on the matter. Somehow, she felt disappointed and resolutely turned from the window and was soon dressed.

As she passed down the hall, Catherine, who had been watching called to her, saying that she wanted her opinion about a dress. Zoleeta ever ready to assist anyone in every way possible, turned and went into her cousin's room, almost the first thing that met her eye on entering, was a bouquet of flowers, the exact kind that Lord Blankleigh had always sent her. He knew her preference for the American Beauty rose and they were there in profusion, seemingly more beautiful than ever.

Catherine had asked her cousin in for no other reason than for her to see the flowers. She told her that her mother wanted her to wear white, but she preferred pink. Zoleeta told her to be guided by her mother and she felt sure that she would look quite charming in the white.

As Zoleeta was turning to leave the room, Catherine remarked quite carelessly that she would have to hurry or she would be late for dinner, that Lord Blankleigh had detained her so long, but if she had expected to see her cousin start or change color, she was disappointed. Zoleeta only pointed to the little clock on the mantel telling her that she had still three-quarters of an hour.

Dinner passed off pleasantly. There was a merry party at dinner that night and Zoleeta was as usual the cynosure of all eyes. Although her aunt and cousin Catherine watched her closely, they could see no change in that proud face. More than one noticed the absence of Lord Blankleigh as it was a rec-

ognized fact that his heart was in the keeping of
Paul Andrews' niece and was most happy in her
presence.

The next morning some of the guests departed for
their homes, but Zoleeta prevailed upon Ruth Marshelda, the young widow, to remain sometime longer.
She gladly accepted the invitation as she had become very fond of this lovely girl. The next morning, when the customary bouquet of flowers arrived,
Catherine was watching and hastily taking the card
off bearing Zoleeta's name and a note and substitut-
ing one with her own name instead. She had copied
Lord Blankleigh's writing and no one could tell the
difference. Then she carelessly laid the bouquet on
the table in the hall telling the servant she would
carry them upstairs.

Thus it happened that as Zoleeta and her guest,
Ruth Marshelda were passing through the hall they
saw the flowers. Zoleeta, thinking that they were
for her, stepped to the table wondering why they had
not been given to her at once or sent to her room.
Just then Catherine, who had been standing at the
other end of the hall, watching her cousin and Mrs.
Marshelda, came forward and said, "What beautiful flowers you have." Just then Zoleeta's eyes
caught the name on the card and without a tremor
in her voice or any evidence of embarrassment said,
"They are for you, cousin, they are very beautiful.
If I were you, I would have them placed in water at
once."

Catherine did as her cousin advised her to do.
She took the flowers and ran up to her mother's

room, telling her mother the incident of the flowers
as they lay on the table in the hall, then she produced the note that she abstracted from them. It
was a passionate appeal for a few moments talk. He
told Zoleeta that he expected to leave the South with
Mr. Seville on the morrow, but he had decided to
remain until he could see her alone. After reading
the note, Mrs. Marceaux complimented her daughter
on her cleverness and told her to destroy the note at
once, but just at that moment there was a rap on the
door. Catherine hastily picked up the flowers and
was holding them in her hand when Ruth Marshelda
entered to tell Catherine that they were all going for
a stroll in the woods and were going to have lunch in
the maple grove, that Zoleeta had sent her to ask her
to come, as they wanted to start at once.

As Mrs. Marshelda entered the room, she noticed
that both mother and daughter started guiltily, but
attached no importance to the incident at the time.
She also noticed that Catherine slipped something
in her pocket, however. She felt no concern about
the matter and soon after left the room, being assured that Catherine would soon follow.

When Lord Blankleigh came that afternoon, he
seemed very much disappointed at not seeing Zoleeta
Catherine was standing alone on the porch and informed him that the rest of the folks were in the
maple grove where she was preparing to follow.

He gladly accepted her invitation to accompany
her, determined to have an interview with Miss Andrews at any cost, consequently when Catherine
dressed in her most becoming toilet, with Lord

Blankleigh by her side, came upon the party in the
woods she felt that it was the last straw, that Zoleeta would never listen to him now, for she was well
aware of how proud her cousin was.

Perhaps her surmises would have been correct if
Mrs. Marshelda had not had her suspicions aroused,
and if her maid had not found a crumpled note addressed to Miss Zoleeta Andrews which she promptly gave to her mistress who felt that it was well that
it fell in her hands. Somehow she connected the
note with the incident that transpired in Mrs. Marceaux's room that morning when she had gonè there
to deliver Zoleeta's message.

She intended to give the note to Zoleeta, but she
seemed in such earnest conversation with Phillip Seville that she had no opportunity to do so, but when
she saw Catherine in company with Lord Blankleigh
and Zoleeta's determination to ignore that gentleman, Mrs. Marshelda made up her mind to give her
the note without further delay and as soon as they
were through greeting the newcomers she gave Zoleeta the note telling her how she came by it, at the
same time looking straight at Catherine, saying that
servants were so careless. Her eyes did not leave
Catherine's face, which had turned first red, then
pale. Of course, no one else noticed it and the widow
once having made up her mind that those two were
the victims of some treachery, determined to help
those who loved each other so dearly to a satisfactory understanding and turning to Lord Blankleigh,
said, "Miss Andrews' note may be important and as
she reads it, I want to show you an old mansion on

the hill over there. They tell me it is haunted.'' It was too far to go at that time so the party viewed it from a distance, saying that some day they would explore it and drive out the ghosts.

Presently, one of the gentlemen, a Mr. Harding, who was very much smitten with the fascinating young widow announced that lunch was ready and he was very hungry.

Everyone appeared to be in the best spirits. The lunch passed off nicely, but Catherine was very uneasy for she had missed the note and was filled with dismay when it was given her cousin. She felt sure that Mrs. Marshelda suspected that she had been in some way responsible for the note not being in the possession of the rightful owner. Zoleeta seemed as proud as ever yet she had a bright light in her eyes that was hard to subdue. Although she tried to avoid Lord Blankleigh, yet he managed to sit by her at lunch. Afterward he drew her aside and asked permission to call on her that evening. She was very gracious to him and made him supremely happy by granting his request and allowing him to monopolize her the rest of the afternoon.

Mr. Andrews and his sister were seated on the porch when the party arrived home. Zoleeta never looked more beautiful as she walked by the side of Lord Blankleigh, who could not conceal his love for the girl by his side. Aline looked very happy with Phillip Seville, who looked as if he could devour that dainty piece of humanity. Mrs. Marceaux was ill at ease when she saw Lord Blankleigh walking beside Zoleeta. Catherine rushed upstairs to her room, fol-

lowed by her mother, whereupon she told her mother
that all was lost and burst into tears. Finally she
grew composed enough to tell her mother about the
servant finding the note and Mrs. Marshelda giving
it to her cousin, but her mother told her to cheer up
and leave it to her and she would yet be Lady Blankleigh.

Catherine dried her eyes and made a very becoming toilet. Most of the guests had departed except
Mrs. Marshelda and an old gentleman once captain
of a steamboat and a friend of Mr. Andrews. Captain Wade was very genial and very entertaining
and could tell many interesting stories of the South
before the war, he was in sympathy with the North,
but by his tact and high standing and seemingly
upright dealing with the Southern trader, was uni-
versally liked. No slave had ever appealed to him
in vain to escape in those dark days of slavery with
the baying bloodhounds at their heels.

Lord Blankleigh arrived early in the evening and
was at once ushered into the presence of Zoleeta.
She greeted him cordially. He had hard work to
convince her that he had sent her flowers every day,
yet he seemed so truthful that she felt that she was
doing him an injustice to doubt him. She knew that
he had sent flowers, but she had seen with her own
eyes the card with her cousin's name attached.
Again, she had seen him leave the house without
sending for her and her cousin had led her to believe that all would be settled between them. Could
there be treachery and what was she to believe?
Lord Blankleigh had expressed such genuine sur-

price upon learning that Zoleeta had received no flowers for a week, that she had not received the first note and the one of today. By the merest accident, she could not doubt him any longer, but who was her enemy. She knew that her aunt and cousin Catherine did not like her, but she could not believe that they would stoop to anything so dishonorable.

She felt very happy to think that Lord Blankleigh found her pleasing but she sighed when she thought of her birth that would be a barrier to her future happiness, while she always cherished the memory of her dead parents and had always maintained that she was not ashamed of her parentage, yet she felt that no matter how she felt regarding the matter that the world would sit in judgment and characterize it as a stigma. Zoleeta knew, however, that there was only one thing to do, no matter how she felt, she would be truthful.

When Lord Blankleigh asked her to be his wife, she expressed her regret and told him that she was pleased at the honor, but it was impossible, she never intended to marry. She also told him that her uncle was aware of the facts that had caused her to remain unwed, that if he wished, her uncle would explain all to him.

Her lover was not much downcast, but hoped that an interview with Mr. Andrews would remove all obstacles which he thought to be only imaginary. He immediately sought her uncle and for the second time that day Paul Andrews listened to two of the most passionate tales of love that he had ever heard.

First to the man who wanted to rob him of his only

child and now the saddest of all was for him to listen to the passionate pleadings for his intervention in behalf of a suit that seemed almost hopeless, to marry his dead brother's child. All the comfort that he could give this despairing lover was a promise to talk the matter over with Zoleeta and let him know the result.

He promised to communicate with him at the earliest possible moment. He also told Lord Blankleigh that while he deeply sympathized with him, that he would not try to influence his niece in the matter.

The second day after his interview with Mr. Andrews, Lord Blankleigh was walking dejectedly along when he came across two little children who were looking for some pennies they had lost. They were going to buy some oranges for their sick brother. They told him that the pretty lady gave them the pennies and that she had gone into the little cottage. He gave the children more pennies than they had lost. He retraced his footsteps feeling sure that it was Zoleeta. Although disappointed he was pleased to meet Aline. He again retraced his steps to accompany her home, but had not proceeded far before he met his servant with a note for him from Mr. Andrews. He took the note but continued his walk with Aline to the gate declining an invitation to enter.

The note was short but courteous, was more in the form of a request for him to call, that he had much to say, stating that he would be pleased to see him there at three o'clock.

At the specified time Lord Blankleigh was ushered

in. He found Mr. Andrews waiting, he greeted him most cordially and for more than two hours they were closeted together. At Zoleeta's request Mr. Anrews informed him of her mixed blood, the result of his brother's marrying one of the slaves on his father's plantation and as soon as his niece was old enough to discuss her future, they had both agreed there should be no concealment as to her birth and parentage and showed him the letter left her by her father that was also his wish.

Dear Daughter:

Some day there may be someone who may seek your hand in marriage and if you feel that person is necessary to your happiness, let there be no concealment. If he is a man of honor and principle, he will cling to you in defiance of the whole world, if he turns his back on you, then congratulate yourself on so fortunate an escape. He will be unworthy of you.

Your father,

Harold Andrews.

Lord Blankleigh admired the noble sentiments expressed in the letter and wished he could have known that grand man that had shown such nobility of character that he gave up home, kindred and position to marry this slave girl and on dying had expressed true happiness at the prospect of being reunited. Returning the letter to Mr. Andrews, grasping his hands, he said:

"Such a brother, a brother to be proud of." He also handed Zoleeta's uncle a letter to read that he had received anonymously several days before. The letter in question informed him that Zoleeta's moth-

er had been a Negro slave. The only consideration
that he had given it was, that if he knew the writer,
he would drag him to Miss Andrews' feet and force
him to beg her pardon. Paul Andrews echoed his
sentiments. It was well that the writer of that letter
was unknown to those two men.

It was now Mr. Andrews who grasped the hand of
Lord Blankleigh, exclaiming, "And you have known
it all the time! Oh, what a lover, a lover to be proud
of." Almost the same words that Lord Blankleigh
had used to him concerning his brother, adding,
"Go to Zoleeta and may heaven bless you both, I
wish you success," and his voice was tremulous with
emotion.

Lord Blankleigh immediately sought Zoleeta.
Needless to say that he overcame all scruples regarding her parentage and proudly led her to the presence of her uncle. He was delighted and felt that
when he laid down to die, he could do so in peace,
knowing that Harold's child would be sheltered from
the tempestuous storms of a cruel uncharitable
world.

Their engagement was announced without delay,
much to the chagrin of Zoleeta's aunt and cousin
Catherine. Mrs. Marceaux had been expecting this
and had not been idle. Our heroine was agreeably
surprised at the perfect friendliness of the two who
had always shown her so much antagonism. Both
warmly congratulated her and kissed her affectionately. Everyone seemed very happy. Aline received such affectionate letters from her future husband that she was truly a "Little Sunbeam,"

although her father would not hear of her marriage for a year, but now she was in hopes that both weddings could be celebrated at the same time, but subsequent events decreed it otherwise.

The happy lovers would have been surprised a few hours later to see Mrs. Marceaux fresh from congratulating her dead brother's child on her engagement, cautiously descending the back stairs that led into the garden. Presently she emerged from the inside enveloped in a long black cloak. After listening for a moment she went swiftly through the garden until she reached a gate that led into the lane, nor did she slacken her speed until she reached a poor, dilapidated log cabin. She looked around carefully before knocking. There was no answer to the first knock, then she rapped again.

Presently she heard shuffling foot-steps inside and a voice asking, "Who is there?" She replied, "It is I, Uncle Nathan," a title often given to the old colored people of the South). "Open the door." He did as directed.

At first he could not remember who she was until she told him, then he was profuse in apologies for keeping her waiting.

When the war broke out and the slaves were set free, many of the old ones refused to leave, realizing they had no visible means of support and as Paul was both kind and indulgent they did not fare badly. Old Nathan was one of those who refused to leave and with his little grandchild, Lucy, was permitted to remain in the cabin that had long been their home. Lucy was asleep in one corner when Mrs. Marceaux

entered. She knew Nathan's weakness for liquor
so she had brought him a bottle of whiskey and some
tobacco. She also gave him a nice silk handkerchief
and inquired after his rheumatism. While she was
talking she was busily drawing the cork out of the
bottle, she poured him out a liberal drink and patted
him on the arm and said, "Uncle Nathan, this seems
like old times. Do you remember how you used to carry me on your shoulders when I was a little girl and
how you saved my brother's life when he had fallen
into the river?"

Old Nathan replied, with an idiotic leer on his face
that he remembered it quite well. But Mrs. Marceaux did not go there to discuss her childhood days,
but she knew as soon as the liquor began to take
effect that he would become very communicative.
Finally she asked him if he remembered a slave
woman on her father's plantation by the name of
Barbara Yates, he told her that he did and that she
had a very pretty little girl and a boy. The boy he
told her ran away when quite a youngster and some
years later his sister also disappeared. No one knew
where. She was never heard of again.

Mrs. Marceaux saw that he did not know any of
the circumstances of her brother Harold's marriage
and was glad that it was so. Old Nathan told her
that the preacher who preached in the little church
in the hollow had received a letter from Barbara
Yates' son. The preacher had sent him the letter
thinking perhaps that he would remember him as he
had belonged on the same plantation, but as he could
not tell him anything, he had told Lucy to return the

letter. He began calling her to wake up and before Mrs. Marceaux could stop him the child was awake. Her grandfather asked her if she had taken the letter to the preacher. At first the child was too sleepy to understand. He struck at her with his cane that caused her to jump and open her eyes wide. She told him that she had forgotten it.

Mrs. Marceaux was delighted and her heart gave a bound for everything was working more smoothly than she anticipated. Lucy got the letter and gave it to her grandfather and was very careful to keep out of reach of his cane. As his former master's daughter was giving him liquor frequently, telling him that it was good for his rheumatism, she hastily copied the address and handed the letter back to the old man. She told him not to tell anyone that she had been there or say anything about the letter, and as it was no good he had just as well destroy it, which in his semi-conscious condition, he at once threw into the fire. She placed a five dollar bill in his hand and promised to bring him more liquor and tobacco.

By this time the old man had taken so many drinks and his speech was so thick that it was impossible to understand him, so Mrs. Marceaux gathered her cloak closely around her and without another word passed out pulling the door shut behind her and glided out into the darkness. She sped swiftly along and never stopped until she reached her room, which she did in safety.

Nobody knew of the midnight visits to Uncle Nathan's cabin or the amount of whiskey consumed for his rheumatism furnished by his old master's daughter. Consequently some weeks later when he was found dead no one was surprised for he was old and rheumatic. His old master's daughter was overjoyed when she heard of his death for she was becoming uneasy as he was beginning to talk too much and might reveal some things that she might not be able to satisfactorily explain.

She had begun to formulate a plan to remove him out of the neighborhood as she had no further use for him. She did not take in consideration that children have ears. Although Lucy was young she was much older than she looked. She had very little schooling, yet she was a bright comprehensive child and when Mrs. Marceaux made those visits she was supposed to be asleep in the other room as there were only two rooms to this cabin, but there were cracks between the logs and often Lucy was awake and listening and light began to struggle through her brain. She became aware of the fact that something was wrong.

She fairly worshipped Zoleeta ever since one day as she was passing and heard loud screams issuing from the cabin, had pushed open the door and found her grandfather beating her with a cane, which she had promptly taken from him and told him if he ever beat her again that she would take Lucy away and send him to the poor house. Lucy told Zoleeta that she was trying to cook on some logs in the fireplace and had upset the food and in trying to save it had broken a bottle of whiskey that was on the chair close by and that was why her grandfather was beating her.

When Zoleeta's aunt first visited Lucy's grandfather, Lucy did not pay much attention to their talk until she heard Zoleeta's name mentioned, then she pricked up her ears and never lost a word afterwards.

One day she was sent on an errand for her grandfather and as it was so warm she laid down for a few moments under a hedge and before she knew it she was soon fast asleep. She was awakened hearing voices. She peeked through the thick leaves and saw Mrs. Marceaux and her daughter.

She heard the mother say that Zoleeta should not marry some Lord or God, she didn't know which, and the daughter had replied that "she would kill her first."

Lucy got so scared she was afraid to move and stayed so long that she was afraid that she would get a scolding, but she dared not move for fear she would be discovered, for she remembered how Mrs. Marceaux slapped her on one occasion when she thought she had heard too much. Finally they walked away and Lucy ran home as fast as possible. She was glad to find her grandfather asleep, but she could not forget what she had heard and was always glad to see Zoleeta and to know that she had not been killed by that "white trash," for that was all that they were even if they did have beautiful clothes. They did not buy them for she had heard the servants say that they were kept up by Mr. Andrews as they had no money.

Her grandfather had died and she was taken farther away and saw no more of Miss Zoleeta.

Lord Blankleigh had written to his mother a sisters announcing his engagement to this gr Southern beauty, who was also an heiress, but tl fact did not matter to him, but he knew his mothei notion of wealth. She was not only displeased, b wrote and told him so, adding that she had oth plans for him and declared that she would nev give her consent for him to marry an ignoranv Yankee girl, whose reputed wealth doubtless would not pay their servants a year's salary.

She would not have spoken thus about Zoleeta if she could have seen her that morning with her open caskets of jewels that dazzled the eye. She had on becoming of age been generous in her gifts from that casket to her aunt and two cousins, yet, on this day she was puzzled to know what to do with so many rare and beautiful gems, yet, she was glad that she would be able to rank with her husband's people as far as wealth was concerned. She had not rested on her laurels since leaving school, but never stopped until she felt that when she became Lady Blankleigh that her husband would not be ashamed of her. She would have smiled even as her fiance did at his mother's allusion to an ignorant Yankee girl. He was quite anxious to take home his bride and felt sure that his mother and sister would welcome her as she deserved to be, but a man of superior intellect, such as Lord Blankleigh, had even yet to learn a woman's way, that there were times and circumstances that neither wealth or beauty could compensate for the marring of some cherished plan.

CHAPTER IV.

THE NEW TENANT.

On the outskirts of the village, about two miles from the Andrews' homestead is situated a little vine-covered cottage. It had been unoccupied for about a year until the day previous when a middle aged man was seen to enter. He had his satchel in his hand and a wagon was standing before the door. The driver took off a trunk which he deposited on the little porch and drove away. The man meanwhile had unlocked the door and after depositing the satchel inside, came out and carried in the trunk. The house was set back a long way from the roadside.

The neighborhood was sparsely settled yet those who got a glimpse of the newcomer thought him a foreigner. His rich black hair was sprinkled with gray. Although his clothes were good, he did not seem to be of the prosperous type. The sun was setting as he entered the house, throwing a soft red glow that made the interior of the cottage both pleasing and inviting to the new tenant. It was plainly but comfortably furnished, and showed there had been a long period of unoccupancy. He came out on the porch again and seated himself on the one seat and was soon lost in deep reverie, nor did he stir until the shadows began to fall and the click of the gate warned him that someone was approaching.

He was not surprised to see a woman coming up the walk for he had instinctively thought that it

was no man with whom he was dealing. She wore a
long cloak completely covering her dress. He remained seated until she reached the porch, then he
arose and held open the door for her to enter, which
she did at once, he following. On entering she did
not lift her veil, yet it was apparent to the stranger
that he was in the presence of a lady of culture and
wealth. After closing the door he pulled down the
blinds. All this time there had been no words spok-
en beyond the most formal courtesy. Then in a quiet,
gentlemanly manner he asked her if she would lay
aside her hat and veil.

She refused to do so, but straightway proceeded
to business by first asking his name. He promptly
replied it was Ralph Yates. She complimented him in
being so prompt in following her instructions. She
said, ''I have business of importance with you, but I
must first have your promise that all transactions
must be strictly confidential between us.'' Continuing, she said, ''It rests with you whether you will
be a rich man for life or die a pauper.''

Ralph Yates gave her the desired promise that
she would have nothing to fear from him. She took
some bills from her pocket and gave them to him for
present expenses. The amount surprised him very
much. It was more than he had ever possessed at
one time in his life and to further show him that she
would trust him, she lifted her veil. She also told
him that she was the daughter of his old master and
that she was quite a child when he ran away, ''I
could not write you all the particulars, but I hope
that you brought the letters with you as requested.

I wish to refer to some parts of them.'' He went at once to the trunk, and unlocked it and took out a package containing three letters. He handed them to her, remarking, that he had followed her instructions and would continue to do so.

He did not tell her that he had copied them, nor did he tell her that he had done a little detective work on his own accord and had found out something that was important that would help him in his undertaking, but he had to admit to himself that he had not the faintest idea of her motive for bringing him here and defraying all expenses and taking the cottage for him for six months, without any cost to himself, was something that he could not explain, but he was destined to learn that and much more before she left the cottage.

She explained to Ralph that his sister Mildred had run away some years later and married her brother Harold. They went to India and both had died out there, leaving a little girl to the guardianship of her uncle Paul. The child of course was also Ralph's niece. Her father had left a large fortune for his child and she was the wealthiest heiress of the whole country as well as the most beautiful in spite of her mixed blood. She also told him that he was Zoleeta's only relative on her mother's side, and as such it was his piece's place to provide for him. She explained that Zoleeta was very proud and self-willed, but thought if he approached her right that she would rather part with half her fortune than to claim him as a relative, as Zoleeta loved her Uncle Paul very dearly and would agree to almost any terms rather than bring shame upon him. Mrs. Marceaux talked for more than an hour before she arose to leave. While talking to Ralph she had, as she thought, slipped the letters in her pocketbook unobserved, thinking that they would involve her, but he had seen it all and felt that it was a wise thing that he had copied them.

Mrs. Marceaux knew that her brother Paul would be away from home all of the next day as he had to go to a little village some twenty miles distant. She arranged for Ralph to call at the house the next day and she would see him. Arriving at home she passed around the house to the side entrance and unlocked the door and reached the room unobserved.

Catherine rapped on her door but her mother did not open it, saying that she had gone to bed and that her headache was better. Catherine went to her room and was soon sound asleep. In spite of her disappointment at not winning Lord Blankleigh from her cousin, but she had implicit faith in her mother's ability and felt there was still hope. Her mother had not gone to sleep, but was planning one of the worst acts of treachery that one woman could plan against another and that other her dead brother's child. Mrs. Marceaux knew that her brother Paul had lost all of his wealth and that every mouthful that she ate was paid for by her orphan niece, even her clothes and her daughter's wardrobe of fine apparel was provided by the generosity of the daughter of Mildred Yates, once her father's slave.

When Zoleeta came into possession of her wealth she gave her aunt a large sum of money and told her

that when Catherine married that she would settle
a like sum on her so that she would not go to her
husband dowerless. Her aunt scarcely thanked her,
knowing that her income alone was great, she felt
that she could have done far better. It was nearly
morning before she went to sleep.

The next morning as Mr. Andrews was starting to
drive away, his daughter and her cousin Catherine
asked if they might go as they wanted to do some
shopping and Aline wanted to see her dressmaker.
He sent his horse back to the stable and ordered the
carriage. Zoleeta did not go as she had promised
her betrothed to go with him for a ride.

Soon after her uncle and cousins had departed,
Lord Blankleigh rode up on a large limbed spirited
chestnut horse. Zoleeta rode a jet black horse that
her uncle had purchased for her paying a fabulous
price for him.

Luncheon had not been served when they reached
home. Lord Blankleigh reluctantly declined an invitation to remain as he had a pressing engagement
with his host. As he rode away, he turned in his
saddle and looked at Zoleeta as she stood on the
porch in her dark green riding habit and felt that
he was indeed fortunate to win her for his wife. He
pictured the surprise of his mother and sisters when
he should present his wife to them.

Zoleeta watched her lover until he disappeared
from view, then turned and walked into the house
singing softly as she went up the stairs, thus giving
evidence of her happiness. She was never vain, but
on entering the room, she went to the long mirror

and her gaze rested on her reflected image for an instant and felt pleased at the reflection for her lover's sake. Yes, she was very happy. Her aunt treated her with the utmost consideration and Catherine was very kind to her. She began to think that some of her wrongs were only imaginary. She did not see the cloud arising in the sky that seemed so small but was destined to become larger and it was a long time before she ever smiled a happy smile, it was a long time before she knew what it was to be happy again.

After changing her riding habit, she went down the stairs and met her aunt in the hall, who seemed somewhat disturbed. She told Zoleeta that she had something to say to her and led the way to a cozy little room off from the dining room that was called the morning room. It was so called because the ladies spent much time there after the breakfast hour arranging and planning for the day. After they were seated, she told her niece that after she went riding a man came to see their brother and as he was not at home, the man was just leaving as she came in. She saw that he was of mixed blood and a stranger or had no recollection of having ever seen him before.

"As he seemed very genteel, I questioned him telling him that I was Mr. Andrews' sister and that I could probably attend to the business or at least he could leave the message with me. On learning that I was Paul's sister he seemed relieved, but showed some embarrassment. I soon put him at his ease when I told him that he could fully trust me as my

brother's interest was mine. He asked me if I remembered him but I did not and told him so.''

Mrs. Marceaux continued: ''He said that his
name was Ralph Yates and at one time was the property of my father, but ran away when quite a lad. I
told him that although quite small, I remembered
that slaves often ran away, but I did not remember
their names. He told me he had been trying to save
money to buy his mother and sister Mildred, but they
had been liberated by the war between the North and
South. He said he had been unfortunate in many
things and now after many years had returned, to
find that his mother was dead and his sister had run
away and died. He also learned that his sister's
daughter was living in the house, but he would not
tell me the source of his information or in what capacity his niece was residing here. He also stated
that he learned my brother was her guardian. I told
him that I would speak to my brother Paul but if he
had any proofs that I would like to see them. He
showed me a picture of himself and another boy that
had been taken here on this plantation and told me
many things that I know to be true as I have heard
them spoken of,'' Mrs. Marceaux concluded.

Zoleeta had grown very pale but did not interrupt
her aunt while she was speaking. In fact, she could
not. She seemed like some withered flower and felt
a spasm of pain when she realized that her dream of
happiness was over, that she could never wed Lord
Blankleigh and subject him to humiliation. Finally
she spoke, saying, ''Oh, Auntie, that must be my
mother's brother! Go on and tell me all.''

Her auntie described him to be a nice looking mulatto, could easily be taken for a Spaniard. "He is very anxious to see you. He told me he did not want to thrust his relationship on you, but had heard so much of your beauty that he was anxious to see you." She also said, "Zoleeta, I do not think that your Uncle Ralph would do anything to disgrace you, if you will treat him considerately as is due him as your mother's brother, and for that reason I promised to let you talk with him yourself this evening in the summer house at eight o'clock," adding, "I know nothing of his disposition, yet it is best to treat him with kindness and avoid making an enemy of him and you on the eve of a great marriage. No telling what effect it will have on your future and you have not only Lord Blankleigh to think about, but your uncle has not been well lately and it will be best not to worry him. The other day he was saying that he was glad that you had no relatives on your mother's side to come forward and mar your future prospects. He thought probably your mother's' brother might be dead. He also remarked that he believed it would kill him if anything like that should happen, that it would disgrace Lord Blankleigh, who belonged to one of the proudest families in England. I think it will be best for you to see this new uncle, and when he finds how you are situated, he may go away again, if he wants money, give it to him, you have plenty of it."

When she had finished speaking, Zoleeta spoke, and said. "Auntie, I do not value the money and if I should offer him any, it might be construed as the price of his silence, and again, if he should ask me for some, I should not refuse his request. I would feel that he had taken advantage of my kinship, consequently it would lessen my respect for him, even if I could not cherish a warmer feeling for this stranger, who claims to be my uncle." Continuing she said, "If this relationship between he and I be fully established, I will not disown him, though it cost me my lover," but the very thought of losing one that was so dear caused a wave of sadness to steal over her.

She wondered, if she could sacrifice Lord Blankleigh's and her happiness for this unknown uncle. How she would have liked to have gone to her uncle Paul for advice, but her aunt had warned her of the probable fatal consequence of such a course.

Following her aunt's counsel, Zoleeta carefully kept the knowledge of the advent of her mother's brother in the neighborhood from her uncle Paul, thereby, causing untold misery in the days to come. Her aunt also advised her to see Ralph and she decided that it would be best to see this man and discover his object in coming there, and his attitude toward her before she could come to any decision and be guided by the coming interview.

She was very restless all the evening and was truly glad that Lord Blankleigh would not be there. She felt that she could arrange matters so she could explain everything to him. She watched the clock and when she arose to leave the room her uncle would have detained her had not her aunt came to her rescue, and Zoleeta was soon making her way rapidly toward the summer house.

The occupant had heard her coming and came out to meet her, feeling sure of a cordial welcome, he held out his hand at once and in well modulated tone said, "My dear niece, my dead sister's daughter! How glad I am to meet you," and would have embraced her had not Zoleeta stepped back holding up her hands, waving him aside. He stopped looking both surprised and hurt.

Before he could make up his mind how to proceed, she spoke and said, "Sir, you are a stranger to me, and I have no proof that you are my mother's brother, and I will not consider any claims that you may bring forth unless you can produce indisputable facts that your claim is good. You cannot expect me to give credence to the unsupported word of a perfect stranger, one I have never seen before, matters not what claim he presents. I would not only ask the same of anyone else regardless of how exalted his position might be, but I would demand unquestionable proofs of the same."

She paused for a reply, but the stranger gazed at her with admiring eyes, he was unable to utter a word. He was speechless with surprise, at her marvelous beauty, which was discernible by the light of the young moon, which was disappearing behind the trees. To his inexperienced eye, she was of the exact type that a queen should be. He almost wished himself back in his frugal home in London.

Seeing that the stranger did not reply to her, she said, "It is true my mother had a brother, but you have given me no proof substantiating your claim, therefore, I am forced to believe you an imposter," and turned to retrace her steps.

It was then he found his voice, saying, "I have the proofs and it is natural that you should want to see them."

"But first, let me assure you that I have no wish to thrust myself on you or your father's people. I came here hoping that I could learn something of my sister, if alive, but was informed that she and her husband both died abroad, leaving a little girl to the guardianship of Mr. Andrews. I then felt I had a duty to perform that was to care for my dead sister's child, but I am denied that privilege for I learn that you have been abundantly provided for. However, I could not leave this part of the country without seeing you, my only relative. I have been trying to see you, but without success until today. I made so bold as to ascend the steps and ring the bell and was fortunate to meet Mr. Andrews' sister. I did not know her at first, as she was quite small when I ran away. She was very kind to me. She worships her brother, and was very glad that I did not see him as he has heart trouble, and my unexpected appearance might be harmful in his present state of health." Ralph had handed a picture of himself to Zoleeta and as she gazed upon it she felt dispairing and hopeless.

The picture that she held in her hand was the exact counterpart of the one in her desk upstairs. Her father had told her that it was her mother's brother. She could not tell why, but she did wish there was some mistake. She could not make herself feel that this man was her uncle although the proof was there. He related instances that had transpired when he

was a boy and her uncle Paul had told her how Ralph
had saved her father's life when he fell into the
river.　The man standing there related this instance,
thus step by step she saw each link in the chain riv-
eted, and felt that fate was unkind to her.　In spite
of the proof laid before her, she felt greatly depressed for she could feel no responsive feeling for
the man who stood there with outstretched hands
appealing to her for recognition of his claim.　She
thought perhaps when she saw more of him that she
would feel different, but she asked herself the question, did she want to see him any more?

She felt that after all her protestations of loyalty
to her mother's people and kindred that she was a
traitor.　Oh, how very wicked she felt.　Silence had
fallen on them.　The girl realizing that she was facing the crisis of her young life for now and all future
time to come.

Presently she aroused herself, and asked him if
he expected to remain in the neighborhood.　He replied that he had taken a cottage for a short while.
He assured her that he was not seeking aid and had
no wish to embarrass her, but his heart hungered for
one kind word or look from someone who would sympathize with him in his loneliness.　Zoleeta could
not help but recognize his kind consideration of her,
and felt very much ashamed of herself to still cherish
such unkind feelings toward him.　She allowed him
to take her hand on bidding her goodnight, promising to see him on the next evening.

Between her aunt and her mother's brother, always reminding her of her uncle's failing health,

Zoleeta was made very unhappy and secretive against her will.

Had she followed her own desire and inclination, she would have gone direct to her uncle Paul and told him all, but was restrained from so doing by her great love for him.

In so saving her uncle she believed she was doing right. She unconsciously deprived herself of his protection when she needed it most. Never did a girl need a mother's care and a mother's love more than this dear girl did, and the one that should have filled a mother's place was her most bitter enemy and was weaving a web around her dead brother's child that caused untold pain and suffering to more than one innocent person.

Lord Blankleigh came unexpectedly while Zoleeta was in the summer house talking to Ralph. It had been his intention to go with some friend to a distant town for a few days, but for some reason the visit was postponed, so he decided to give his betrothed a pleasant surprise by spending the evening with her instead. Nothing could have suited Mrs. Marceaux better than the presence of Lord Blankleigh at that time.

Zoleeta had spoken of a slight headache earlier in the evening but nothing to keep her in her room. Her aunt informed him of her indisposition, but assured him there was nothing alarming. She sent for Zoleeta, but learned that she was not in. Mrs. Marceaux told Lord Blankleigh that it was quite likely that she was visiting some of the poor people and no doubt would soon return as she seldom ever

stayed out late until quite recently. As her niece
was aversed to having her charitable deeds known,
they seldom ever knew where she was. She told him
that Catherine and Aline had gone to spend the night
with some friends. She was just starting for a stroll
through the grounds and invited him to accompany
her and enjoy the beauty of the evening. He courteously accepted the invitation hoping that he would
yet get a glimpse of Zoleeta before leaving. Mrs.
Marceaux took the path that led past the summer
house. They heard voices issuing from within. It
was a man that was speaking saying, "I feel paid for
coming here already. I feel that you are learning to
love me at last."

Lord Blankleigh turned at once to retrace his footsteps. Mrs. Marceaux was therefore compelled to
do the same. Her companion laughingly, said, "We
came near being a witness to a little love affair, presumably between some of your servants."

She replied that the speaker seemed to be a stranger by the accent of his voice. That reminded her
that she had noticed a good looking mulatto man in
the vicinity for some time and as they had in their
employ some neat looking servants, no doubt, he was
smitten with one of them.

Zoleeta and Ralph had been very much startled
when they heard voices and approaching footsteps
and as soon as the footsteps had died away in the
distance she lost no time in hastening from the spot,
but her aunt was too shrewd a woman to let her
escape without suspicion. Knowing that her niece
would be compelled to pass a certain point before

turning off into the walk that led direct to the house, she determined to keep Zoleeta's lover close by so he could see her, hoping that he would connect her with the incident in the summer house. She dropped into a seat near where he could see her, at the same time remarking, that she must be getting old, and if he had no objections, she would rést there a moment.

They had hardly seated themselves when Zoleeta came swiftly down the path. Lord Blankleigh was overjoyed to see her, but had no thought of connecting her with the moonlight lovers. Her aunt was not satisfied and wished to draw his attention to the matter, laughingly said, "Zoleeta, I believe you also heard a little of those lovers' confidences," and hastened to explain the matter.

Zoleeta replied, that she had neither seen nor heard the lovers. They all entered the house.

He noticed that Zoleeta was very pale and gently reproached her for being out alone. He did not remain late. Mrs. Marceaux saw that her niece was somewhat perplexed and disturbed and as soon as the visitor had departed she sought her at once and explained how she and Lord Blankleigh had happened to be in that part of the grounds, for Zoleeta knew that her aunt was aware that she and Ralph were there. Her aunt told her that she and the visitor were seated on the balcony waiting for her return when a messenger brought her a telegram from the girls announcing they would remain until the next day, she excused herself and went inside to read the message. When she returned Lord Blankleigh had gone into the garden, "so of course, dear Zoleeta

before I could locate him he was near the end of the
walk close to the summer house. I got him away at
once, telling him I thought you had returned. Had
he not dropped his cigar case and stopped to look
for it, we would have been out of the way, but that
detained us a few minutes, then you came along so
quickly.'' As her aunt explained everything so satisfactorily Zoleeta's face cleared, especially when
her aunt assured her that Lord Blankleigh thought
it some of the servants, which he did.

CHAPTER V.

THE ABDUCTION.

As Lord Blankleigh passed out of the gate he saw
a man a few steps in advance of himself and the man
with old fashion courtesy, whether real or assumed,
raised his hat to Lord Blankleigh as that gentleman
with long strides soon overtook him, saying ''Good
evening, Mister.''

And as this Englishman of royal birth never allowed anyone to have more manners than himself, returned the greeting in style and would have passed
on had not Ralph said, ''Excuse me, sir, do you think
I did wrong to walk in the garden with my sweetheart at the house up there,'' pointing to the Andrews' home, ''without permission I would not have
been so bold to ask, sir, only I recognized you as the
gentleman that was with the lady in the garden I
saw through the bushes. I am a stranger here and

would not like to get into trouble.'' When he first commenced to speak Lord Blankleigh drew himself up haughtily for he was not accustomed to discuss the love affairs of his inferiors, but he began to see the humorous side of the affair, so he laughed good-naturedly, saying, ''Oh, you are the chap that was making such violent love in the garden? Well, young man, I do not think you have done any wrong but you must be careful and you will not have any trouble.''

''Thank you, sir,'' replied Ralph. ''I will behave myself. I do not want to stay here long, but my sweetheart does not want to go just yet, but she said she was beginning to love me,'' and with a ''Good-night, sir,'' he turned and went on his way.

Lord Blankleigh was so happy himself that he listened with more patience to this love romance in lowly life than he otherwise would have done and resolved to find out which one of the maids was this fellow's sweetheart and assure her if the young man was worthy, that he would assist them to a start so they could marry soon. He was in that happy mood and wanted to see everyone else happy.

Zoleeta went to her room but it was a long time before she fell asleep. She longed to tell her uncle all, but she remembered that any worry might prove fatal, so she tried to do as she thought best and her aunt told her. It only proved the deep affection she felt for him by not bothering him, besides Ralph had told her he expected to leave soon, and as he did not know of her approaching marriage or her future husband's name it was not likely they would ever meet again.

Zoleeta could not help but reproach herself for her lack of affection for Ralph. She could not even address him as "Uncle," just simply, Ralph. How selfish she was! But try as she would, she felt no responsive chord to his appeal to her. She would have liked to have given him enough money to help him, but the mere suggestion seemed to hurt him and she did not want him to feel that she was trying to buy his silence. She did not know what to do. Here lately it seemed that at every turn she met him.

Once Catherine had seen them together and had asked her who he was. She simply said that at one time he had belonged on the plantation and was there hunting his relatives whom he had not seen in years. She did not see the scorn or triumphant look on her cousin's face, for Catherine knew who he was and was often close when Zoleeta met Ralph, although Zoleeta was not aware of it.

Aline had also seen her cousin talking to the man, but had attached no importance to it, for nothing could change her faith in her lovely cousin. She had often seen Zoleeta cancel engagements to a party or ball to sit by the bedside of some poor sick person, administering to their comfort, but there came a time that Aline's faith in her cousin was severely shaken, yet she was loyal and defended her nobly, only to lock herself in her room and cry her eyes out.

Ralph Yates continued to remain in the neighborhood. Mrs. Marceaux saw him often secretly and had many long talks with him, so their plans were working like a charm. In fact, she gave him no chance to make a mistake. They played on Zoleeta's affection for her uncle Paul, so there was no fear of her confiding in him and her aunt saw that she had no one else except herself to confide in, consequently, when Zoleeta told her aunt that she could not longer bear the burden of the secret and felt as the time for her marriage drew near that it was her duty to tell Lord Blankleigh all. Her aunt was dismayed at the thought of her doing so and counseled her to wait a few days and she would think what would be best.

That night her aunt visited the vine-covered cottage and when she left there Ralph held in his hands a roll of bills, with a promise of more if he succeeded in his undertaking. That night Zoleeta was sent for. Poor Mrs. Brown was taken worse, would she come and read to her a little while. She told one of the servants where she was going, but she would not stay long that she need not tell her aunt or uncle where she was unless they asked for her. She was walking quite swiftly and noticed a closed carriage a little in advance of her, driving very slowly, where a long lane branched off that led many miles into a forest. She would have passed on but the driver had stopped, and as she came near he jumped off the seat. Zoleeta thought she heard some one groan inside the carriage and was about to stop to see if she could be of any service, when the driver hastened to her and asked if she could tell him where No. 10 Cottage Lane was.

He said, "I have a gentleman who has broken his ankle, I fear. The gentleman wants to be taken to that number. I do not know his name, he simply said that it was Ralph."

Zoleeta's heart stood still for that was where her mother's brother lived. She told the driver that she knew the gentleman and would go home with him and see that he had the proper treatment. "Let me speak to him."

She stepped to the carriage door and asked, "Is that you, Ralph? This is Zoleeta." Whereupon he said, "Yes, but I am in great pain." She told him not to worry, that she would see that he had the best of care and would pay the bill. "I will go with you."

After directing the driver where to go, she stepped into the carriage she was very careful not to hurt the wounded limb. She asked him how it happened. He talked slowly as if in great pain. Finally it occurred to her that they were a long time arriving at their destination. She called to the driver and asked him if he had lost the way. He admitted that he had, but was on the right road now and would soon be there.

Presently Zoleeta became very sleepy. Try as she would she could not keep her eyes open, and was soon sleeping soundly. When she awoke she found herself lying on a bed that was spotless, white and clean. She noticed that the bed was one of those tall four-posted kind. She also noticed that the sun was shining through the one window.

At first she thought that she was dreaming. She closed her eyes for a moment trying to recall what had happened, when all at once her memory returned like a flash. She sat up in bed and would have sprung to the floor, if she had not been restrained by a firm hand. At the same time a woman's voice, that was neither harsh or kind spoke to her and offered a drink from a cup that she held in her hand.

Zoleeta was about to refuse, but she was very weak, so she drank from the cup and soon felt refreshed. She wanted to know where she was and why she had been brought there. She noticed the woman was white, although her complexion was very sallow, and appeared as one who is paid to perform a certain task, matters not what it is she will be sure to do it regardless of consequences. She refused to answer any questions, but insisted on Zoleeta eating the nicely prepared breakfast that she had brought her, for old Mrs. Crane had been given to understand that she was to take special care of her charge, and Zoleeta was not to want for anything.

It was most distasteful, however, to the girl to be compelled to do the bidding of this strange woman, and she would have refused altogether to touch a morsel of food, but did not know what was in store for her, and wished to retain her strength. She felt that she had not much to expect from this hard visaged woman, but did not want to antagonize her and lose the chance of making her a friend if possible, at least. She ate a fairly good breakfast. The woman then took the tray of dishes and left the room, carefully locking the door behind her. Zoleeta arose at once and began a tour of inspection.

She found that the one window was very high, seemingly in a tower and heavily barred, as if it had been used as a jail. She wondered much at this, she also noticed that the house seemed to be situated in the midst of a large forest. She looked down into the yard, it appeared to be deserted. Presently she saw a man or boy, but from that distance she could not tell which; but even from afar, she could tell that he was a hunchback. As he walked his arms seemed unusually long. He seated himself on an old tree stump. Presently she saw the old woman go to him and say something and both entered the house. Zoleeta was about to turn from the window when she saw two large dogs walking around. She turned as she heard someone place the key in the lock. The door swung open admitting her uncle Ralph.

She faced him with flashing eyes and said, ''I want to know why I have been subjected to such an outrage. It is almost beyond belief to think that my mother's brother would commit such a crime.''

She could not say that she had been brought there by force as no force had been used. She had simply walked into a well laid trap. Continuing, she said, ''I want to be returned to my home at once. And in spite of the evidence that you have produced substantiating claim as my mother's brother, I believe you to be an imposter. And you shall be made to suffer for this terrible outrage.''

All this time the man stood still, not having uttered a word as Zoleeta had spoken very rapidly. He advanced into the room and said, ''Be seated, I have much to say.'' She scornfully refused to do so and continued standing, and as she looked at him for a moment, a great fear seemed to take possession of her, yet she gave no sign. He had gotten himself up in a gentlemanly manner. His clothes were not only good, but costly. A diamond ring shown on his finger, his curly hair had been carefully oiled and combed, his mustache was nicely brushed and perfumed. And no one would deny that he was a very handsome man and looked every inch a gentleman. Zoleeta stood with one hand resting on the back of a chair. And without another glance at his handsome face, she requested him to proceed.

He hesitated for a moment and if he had been a man of intellect or had he any idea of the girl he had to deal with, or could have seen the terrible results, possibly he would have drawn back from his purpose, and returned the orphan girl to her people. But the man was ignorant and had unlimited confidence in his handsome face and knowing of Zoleeta's mixed blood felt that he had nothing to fear. He again asked her to be seated, she again scornfully refused.

"Miss Andrews," he said, "what I have done and what I am about to say no doubt will surprise you. Up to the present time you have believed me to be your uncle. Such is not the case. My name is Julian Marlow. I was born in Spain. At an early age I came to the United States, finally drifting to New York, where I found employment. I lived here for several years. Then I made up my mind to go to England. On board the vessel I became acquainted with a man who at first, I thought, was of my own nationality, but later on learned that he was a mulatto also bound for the same port. Soon a warm friendship sprung up between us. As neither had any family ties, we decided to cast our lots together. We settled in London and were fortunate to find employment, Ralph Yates was my companion's name. We would often sit around the fire at night and he would tell me of one desire to save up money enough to return to the United States and bring away his mother and sister if alive. He told me that at an early age, he ran away from his master, but had been captured by another slave trader and again sold into slavery, but had found no opportunity to get away until the time that we met on board the ship, so when slavery was no more, he ventured to write to find out what had become of his relatives. He wrote to a church in the vicinity of his plantation home, but it was some months before he received a reply, as no one could be found who knew anything about his people.''

"Finally he received a mysterious letter telling him that if he would consent to come back, he would find out something to his advantage and his passage money would be sent. But he was not to tell anyone and to bring the letters back with him. There were three in all. Ralph was overjoyed and after consulting a lawyer and being assured that it was safe for him to return, he wrote at once and received the passage money as well as identification papers. He took sick just before he started and sent me to represent him. He also gave me the letters that he had received from the parties that had sent for him. I will let you read them presently. Ralph and I were very much alike and as it had been so many years since he ran away, he was not afraid for me to take his place. He had told me so much of his early life on the plantation that it did not take me long to find out everything that would help me in my undertaking, and when I left to come here, I not only had the letters, but also the picture that he had taken when a boy. You remember I showed it to you, in fact, nothing was overlooked or forgotten."

"Well, to make a long story short, everything prospered as I had planned. Of course, there was much to mystify me, but I was soon in possession of the motive that induced the parties to send for Ralph. You were hated by a rival and when I learned that this niece was of mixed blood, I expected to see a fairly good-looking mulatto girl, so felt no uneasiness as to the results. At first, it was intended that I should play the part of an ignorant uncle, one who would disgust the gentleman that you were betrothed to. I was given to understand that under no circumstances was I to reveal myself to your uncle Paul, as he idolized you almost as much as he did his own daughter."

"You must remember Miss Andrews, I had not yet seen you, therefore, I agreed to all plans and also, please remember, that the plans were not of my making, but must say in justice to my employer that they were not aware that I was any other than Ralph Yates, the ex-slave. I met you as arranged and believe me when I tell you, that I was never more surprised in my life. Your loveliness surpassed any that I had ever seen. I was like one who had been groping in the dark and had suddenly come into the dazzling light, and for once in my life I was conscience-stricken. I felt that I could not do this thing that I was paid to do and resolved that when I met my employer that evening, to refuse to go any further, and made up my mind to disclose my identity.''

Ralph continued, ''I thought of your great beauty and how dearly all the poor people loved you, that it would be a shame to spoil your life. Pray do not despise me when I tell you that I presumed to worship you from afar at first, then I became madly in love with you. I thought if I could only win you and take you away from your enemies, that I would be willing to work for you day and night, for I had lost sight of your wealth. I thought only of my love for you, when I saw my employer, I told her that I would not carry out her plan to disgrace you. You understand that it was a woman who was employing me. She seemed frantic with fear and declared that I must go ahead and could name my price, then I told her of myself thinking that she would give up the scheme against you, but the knowledge seemed to give her exceeding joy and said it was better so. Well, I felt that I could not give you up and we were seen together numbers of times that you were not aware of and it had been whispered around that you had a Negro lover as some thought by my complexion that I too descended from the black slaves of the South. I loved you dearly and let matters drift as they would. I know the method I have taken to win you is against me, my only excuse is my great love for you.''

Up to this time Zoleeta had spoken no word, but listened with a very white face, but his acknowledgment of his presumption to love her and daring to confess it, was more than she could stand. She forgot that she was in his power, imprisoned in a turret chamber with vicious dogs guarding the place; she only knew that she had been grossly insulted by a self-confessed villain, who was unfit to mingle with the servants.

She drew herself up to full height, with flushed face and flashing eyes, replied that, "Before I would even touch your hand or submit to your touch, I would cut off my hand, and before I would marry you, I'd beat out my life against the wall." Furthermore, she said, "There is not a negro on my uncle's plantation but what is your superior, and unless you leave me at once, I will find a way to kill myself."

While our heroine was denouncing the Spaniard, she did not notice two red spots that burned on his cheeks until his whole face turned a dark red flame; there was a glitter in his eyes that was hard to conceal, but he calmly said: "I will go now, but I will return again." With those words, he turned and left the room, locking the door behind him, and Zoleeta had made another enemy, for he went away vowing vengeance on Paul Andrews' orphan niece.

When the door closed behind her tormentor, Zoleeta neither fainted nor gave way to tears, but seemed turned to stone, so mute and statuesque she stood. She regretted that she had not demanded those letters that he referred to. Now she doubted if he would ever let her see them. She had ceased to wonder who was her relentless enemy and her remorseless foe. She reluctantly confessed to herself that it must be her aunt, yet her aunt and cousin Catherine had shown her so much affection lately that she could hardly believe that they would subject her to such a contemptible outrage.

Marlo had told her that it was a woman who was pursuing her so relentlessly. She then burst into tears and cried unrestrainedly for some time, not from fear, but her heart was heavy to think that she was the victim of such a cruel plot, and presumably by her aunt. She wondered what her lover and uncle would think, and if they were searching for her. Poor girl, she did not know that those two men who loved her so dearly were led to believe that she was lost to all principles of honor and had fled with a colored lover. She did not know the forged letters placed in her desk purporting to have been written by herself had stricken the life almost out of the good man who had been a father to her. She did not know that the blow that had stricken her uncle so terribly had shattered the hopes and embittered the life of the truest man that ever wooed and won a girl's love.

Marlo did not return to the turret chamber that day. Old Mrs. Crane came and tidied up the room, bringing fresh water and clean linen. Zoleeta tried to talk to her, but the old woman said she had no time to talk. Zoleeta also noted that the old woman eyed her suspiciously whenever she came into the room. Sometimes she seemed afraid of her. Our heroine realized that she had been represented by the Spaniard as being mentally deficient. Marlo had only been to the room twice since their stormy interview, on each occasion had renewed his offer of marriage and each time had been rejected with scorn, until at last he began to threaten; however, she still defied him. She was expecting him that day, although she had no intention of yielding to this man; yet this morning she felt so weary, so utterly crushed, that she felt she must find some means of escape, or some way to communicate with her relatives, for Marlo had given her to understand that unless she consented to marry him that he would find a way to make her suffer untold misery.

Finally she heard the key turn in the lock. She did not turn her head, yet she knew that he stood before her. Not even when he spoke did she turn her gaze upon him. He asked her if she decided to do as he wished. She simply replied: "I have no decision under consideration. My mind was made up from the first and I will never change."

Before he could reply, there was a knock on the door. He hurriedly opened it and stepped into the hall. She saw old Mrs. Crane standing there; then the door was closed. Presently she heard their footsteps as they descended the stairs. She saw him no more that day.

That evening Mrs. Crane did not bring up her dinner. When the door opened she was never more startled in her life. There stood a man or a boy, she knew not which; his arms were long, terribly long, that reached far below his knees. He had a way of grinning that was perfectly hideous. His head was long and flat and covered with red hair that stood up like bristles and the stubby hair on his face gave him the appearance of some animal. He set the tray down and stood there grinning until Zoleeta told him that he could go. He started, then turned back, and before she could prevent him he threw himself on his knees and kissed her hands, then sped away, forgetting to lock the door. Our heroine was waiting for this opportunity, and after waiting a few moments she carefully opened the door and stepped outside. The hall was large and spacious and showed signs of past grandeur.

As Zoleeta stood there uncertain what to do, she heard voices that seemed to come from a room at the end of the hall. She could distinguish Mrs. Crane's voice. She heard her say that she did not intend to wait upon white women and black ones, too, and if the colored one did not get up she could lay there and die. Zoleeta wondered much at this. Could it be one of the servants? Yet she felt that those people could not afford servants. She was sure that they were very poor themselves.

She had just time to step in the room again and old Mrs. Crane came in to clear away the things. She found Zoleeta standing before the window, but she did not turn around when the woman left the room and the door securely locked.

CHAPTER VI.

ZOLEETA IN HER PRISON HOME.

The next day when she brought her breakfast, she was in an ugly mood, but Zoleeta had made up her mind to make her talk. She asked her if she would send her the papers to read. She was anxious to learn if her absence had been made public.

The old woman spoke crossly, telling her that she never had the paper, that she had no time to read, but she seemed glad to speak her mind to someone; so, continuing, she said some days ago Silas was driving home from town when he heard someone groan. At the same time he saw what he thought to be a sack of grain. He was partly correct, but there was more than one sack; there were several that looked as if they had fallen off a wagon. Possibly they were being taken to a mill. He knew that sacks could not talk, so he listened again—this time he heard someone call. He looked around and saw what he thought at first a bundle of clothes, but on going closer discovered that it was a colored woman.

She seemed to be in great pain. She told him if he could take her somewhere, that she would pay him, as she had some money. He had brought her home, but she was tired of bothering with her and was going to put her out. Mr. Marlo had told her to keep her and as soon as she was able to put her to work. This morning she put her to work in the kitchen, but she did not know how to cook, and "I

do not know what I shall do, colored people are so
trifling.'' The old woman continued grumbling until
she had finished tidying up the room. As she was
preparing to go, Zoleeta asked her not to forget the
papers. While Mrs. Crane was speaking, Zoleeta
was thinking rapidly and wondering if it were not
Providence that brought the colored woman to that
house.

Speaking in a careless manner, although her heart
was beating, she said: ''Since the woman is useless
downstairs, she might save you the climbing of the
steps by sending her up to clean the room and bring
my meals.''

Mrs. Crane ungraciously murmured that she knew
her business and left the room. However, she must
have thought the matter over, for the next day when
the door opened there stood the colored woman with
the paper. But she was not alone. The hunchback
was with her and only his presence prevented the
woman from crying out aloud that—it is dear Miss
Andrews.

Zoleeta also had turned pale. She remembered the
girl to be the one that she had saved from her grandfather's cruel beating, but she remained perfectly
calm. She reached and took the papers and in doing
so gave the girl's hands a quick squeeze as a warning to keep still and not to let on that she knew her.
She asked for some fresh water, hoping that Silas
would go. He made no effort to move, and Lucy was
compelled to go for the water. Zoleeta seated herself in the chair and indifferently opened the papers,
but she had become so nervous and excited that she

felt like crying. She could not read a line, but felt happier than she had at any time since she had been spirited away. She was anxious to see the girl alone, but would she be permitted to do so?

She felt if she could only see her before Marlo returned to the room, but such was not to be, as he came while she was thinking about it. She saw at a glance that she had a determined man to deal with. He sent Silas, the hunchback, from the room. Before she could speak a word in response to his greeting he handed her the copy of two letters that had been found on her writing desk the morning after her disappearance, but did not give her the ones that he had referred to on a previous visit to her, the ones that he had brought from England. The first one that she read was the one addressed to her uncle. It read as follows:

"My Darling Uncle:

Pray forgive me for what I am about to do; the one thing that grieves me most is to leave you and Aline and to lose your love and respect, but I suppose it is in the blood, for I love one of my mother's people. I realize that not even a title that I would have married for, is sufficient to make me give up that love. I do not know where we will settle, but will let you know.

In the meantime, uncle, please continue to look after my business interests, and remember, uncle, that I want you and Aline to share with me as long as I have a dollar, and be as generous with aunt and Catherine as you see fit. Hoping that you will not grieve about me, for I love you too well to bring disgrace on you and your household, and that is why I leave. I will be married in a few days, so with love and kisses to yourself and Aline, I sign myself for the last time,

Zoleeta Andrews.

P. S.—Please tell Aline to open my desk and return to Lord Blankleigh all of the presents that he has given me.

Zoleeta.''

The letter to Lord Blankleigh read as follows:
''Lord Blankleigh,

Dear Sir: When you read this I will be on my way North to be married to a man of mixed blood like myself. I find I love him too dearly to perjure myself at the altar with another. Forgive me if you can. I feel that it is better so. Hoping that you may find someone more worthy than I to fill the high position that you can give them, with best wishes, I remain,

Zoleeta Andrews.''

Not until Zoleeta read those letters did she realize how fully she was in the man's power and no hope for help from those who loved her so well. Those letters had sealed her doom. When she finished reading those letters they fluttered to the floor and Zoleeta Andrews lay unconscious at the feet of the man who had brought upon her the bitterness of death, and before night the doctor stood at her bedside giving no hope to those around her.

However, before Marlo left the room to summon aid for the stricken girl, he picked up the letters and replaced them in his pocket, then lifted the limp form of Zoleeta Andrews and laid her on the couch; then with his sallow face turned to a sickly white, he hastened to summon Mrs. Crane, telling her that her charge had fallen in a faint and wanted her to go to her at once, which she did, he following.

But with all their efforts they could not revive the stricken girl. He hesitated to send for a doctor, but at last that had to be done to save the girl's life. Marlo flung himself into the saddle, riding like mad, bringing the doctor back with him.

Dr. Martin told the old woman that she had a very sick girl and it would require the greatest care to pull her through, and he was not sure that she would leave her bed alive. If so, he was afraid that she would never regain her full senses. He asked if she had received a shock, but was told that she did not know. The doctor had seen much in his professional capacity that seemed mysterious and both experience and wisdom always made it a point to closely observe everything of a suspicious character, but he was not prepared to see a lady so young and beautiful, and thought it strange that she should be carried up so high to a turret chamber when there were numerous rooms on the lower floors.

The old woman, watching him closely, seemed to read his thoughts, for she said: "I had the lady brought up here away from the noise." Whereupon the doctor told her that was quite right, but he could not imagine any noise in the forest home. He left after giving instructions for the care of the patient. Day after day the doctor called and administered to the sick girl, whose case at times seemed hopeless.

Marlo felt anything but comfortable on being told that her life hung by a mere thread. He stood watching the pale, sweet face of the sufferer, feeling no remorse for his part in bringing her to the brink of the grave, only as it would detain him longer than he cared to remain, as it was getting dangerous for him. He had been informed that Zoleeta's uncle had begun a rigid search for the girl. As he stood gazing down on that beautiful face, he was resolved more than ever that when he left the South Zoleeta should accompany him, regardless of consequences.

He told Mrs. Crane to take the best care of her and she should receive double pay. The old woman loved money and needless to say she tended her charge as faithfully as her own mother would have done, were she alive; but the old woman must have rest, so Lucy was pressed into service and everything that could be done for the sick girl was done. She began slowly to improve, and finally was pronounced out of danger.

Marlo was overjoyed when he heard the good news. He was anxious to get away, as he had heard that Ralph had left England for the United States. Leaving Zoleeta in the hands of her almost incompetent but faithful nurses, we will return to what was transpiring in the Andrews home.

The evening that Zoleeta left on her errand of mercy to old Mrs. Brown and her failure to return was carefully kept from her uncle. Mrs. Marceaux told the servants that her brother was not well and he would only worry, her niece was possibly detained by someone who was very ill and would come home later. Mrs. Marceaux had no intention of any search being made for Zoleeta that night, knowing that if Ralph, or Marlo, as we now know him, could have a few hours start that he could safely reach his destination and all would be well.

As Zoleeta's wedding was to take place within ten days, there were several guests in the house, including Mrs. Marshelda, who was a visitor there some months before, and who cherished such warm affection for Zoleeta.

Philip Seville was there and Aline was supremely happy. She knew that in a few months she would be wedded to the man of her choice, the year of waiting was almost over. She felt very happy that evening as she sat with her lover, unconscious of the fact that her beautiful cousin was being borne away from her loved ones. Once her father came out on the balcony and asked if her cousin had returned, for he had been told of her visit to the sick woman. Aline replied that she did not know, but would find out. The guests had missed her at first, but it was quite a gay company and when each went to his room, there was no comment on her absence.

Mrs. Marshelda went to Zoleeta's door and tapped lightly, but receiving no response, thought she had retired early, as she had been in such constant demand and had looked a little fatigued at luncheon.

Aline met the servant and told her to tell her cousin that she would not disturb her tonight, but would see her early in the morning. Early in the evening Lord Blankleigh had sent a message of regret to Zoleeta that he would not be able to come over, consequently Mrs. Marceaux was well satisfied that he could not put in his appearance at that time and those who loved our heroine so dearly went to bed and slept soundly until the sunlight was peeping through the window.

Aline went to sleep with a happy smile on her face, yet when she arose in the morning she felt depressed; she could not tell why. She made a hasty toilet and then went downstairs. The other guests had not yet put in an appearance, so she walked out into the garden and was soon joined by her fiance. They strolled around in the early morning sunshine until summoned to breakfast.

The guests were all there, but Zoleeta had not come down. Aline wondered at that, as her cousin was an early riser and was often cantering over the hills on Black Prince, as her horse was called, long before the others were out of bed. Aline's father asked her if she had seen her cousin this morning.

She replied that she had not and thought it possible that she had overslept and would be with them presently.

Mr. Andrews said to his sister: "Had you better not send to Zoleeta's room and tell her that we are waiting breakfast?"

His sister replied, saying: "Zoleeta stayed up quite late and probably is very tired and I think a good rest would do her good."

They all sat down to breakfast, little dreaming that before the shadows of night would fall, the very bitterness of death would settle on that household.

Shortly after breakfast, as Aline was passing

through the hall on her way to her cousin's room, she met her aunt and told her where she was going. Her aunt told her that she had just come from there, but could not get in as no one answered her knock.

Aline looked startled, but her aunt assured her there was no cause far alarm, no doubt Zoleeta was out in the garden. The depression that Aline had felt that morning on first arising came on her again stronger than ever. On leaving her aunt she fairly flew upstairs and met one of the servants with a scared face coming out of Zoleeta's room. She told Aline that Zoleeta was not in the room and her bed had not been slept in.

Aline, with a white face, dropped into a chair and began to cry and called her dear beloved cousin.

The servant hurriedly called Mrs. Marceaux and told her just what she had told Aline. Mrs. Marceaux at once sought her brother, whom she had seen in the library. She told him that Zoleeta was still absent and that her bed had not been slept in.

Her brother partly arose from the chair, then fell back again, just as Aline came rushing into the room and threw herself into her father's arms, sobbing wildly. Paul Andrews for a moment was stunned. He put his daughter from him and arose to his feet declaring that he would find his niece and dedicate the remainder of his life to avenge any wrong that she might suffer, and anyone who saw him then would have doubted that he had heart trouble, as his sister was continually warning Zoleeta. There was such a dangerous look in his eyes that Mrs. Marceaux shrank from him shudderingly. Well she might, for if her brother found out how she had persecuted their dead brother's child he would forget that the same mother bore them both and would show her no mercy.

Mr. Andrews sent for Lord Blankleigh and was expecting him at any moment; while waiting for him he said to his sister: "I will go to Zoleeta's room and possibly discover something concerning her mysterious disappearance."

His sister replied: "I have the key, for I thought it best that no one should enter."

Together they went to Zoleeta's room. Everything was in perfect order. The flowers in the vase were fresh and their fragrance filled the room. They looked around but saw nothing unusual until his sister opened the writing desk and discovered the two letters. One was addressed to himself, the other to Lord Blankleigh.

Paul took both letters and went at once to the library, giving orders that as soon as Lord Blankleigh arrived to show him in. With trembling hands he tore open the letter addressed to himself, and when he read what was written there he was stricken almost to death.

An hour later when Lord Blankleigh was shown into the room, he found the master of the house in a dazed condition. He seemed to have grown ten years older. The happy lover expected to find Zoleeta with her uncle, but on looking around and not seeing her and noting the troubled expression on Mr. Andrews' face, he became alarmed and asked for her.

Zoleeta's uncle only pointed to a chair and it was

some moments before he could speak. In the meantime Lord Blankleigh's suspense was terrible. Finally, Mr. Andrews told him of the discovery of his niece's disappearance.

He sprang to his feet, exclaiming, "Has nothing been done?" and picking up his hat started for the door, when Mr. Andrews stopped him.

He gave Lord Blankleigh the letter addressed to him. He read it a second time before he realized what it meant to him. It meant that he was never to be happy again, that his trust in woman was gone forever.

He exclaimed again and again: "Oh, why did she do so!" And laying his head on the table, he sobbed like a child.

Then without uttering a word, Paul gave him the letter to read that his niece had written to him. When he read that letter he made a vow that never while life lasted would he ever willingly call her name or look upon her face again.

Each felt that it would have been easier to have laid her in her grave. They agreed there was nothing to be done. She had taken her future in her hands to make or to mar, although feeling that she had made a mistake. Lord Blankleigh silently clasped Mr. Andrews' hand, promising to see him on the morrow. As he reached the gate he met Catherine, who looked quite pretty in a dainty white dress with blue ribbons. She was startled at his extreme pallor; however, she was too wise to attempt to console him in words.

She gently laid one hand on his arm, saying: "My lord, the carriage is at your disposal."

Not until then did he remember that he had ridden over on his big chestnut horse. It was brought at once from the stable where it had been taken on his arrival. Bidding Catherine a courteous good-bye, he mounted his horse and rode away, feeling that henceforth life was not worth living.

The next day when Lord Blankleigh called to see Mr. Andrews, he was surprised to see the change in him. The day before he had left him a crushed and heartbroken man, who looked nearer sixty than forty-five. Today he looked younger than ever, with a plainly written resolve on his face. He grasped Lord Blankleigh's hand vigorously. He told him that he had reconsidered his decision concerning Zoleeta's disappearance and was determined to leave no stone unturned to find his niece. He said he had been hasty in accepting the statement in those two letters and was convinced that she was above reproach and intended to vindicate her before the whole world and believed her innocent until with her own lips she said that she was guilty.

Lord Blankleigh replied, saying: "My dear friend and almost uncle, your resolve is a noble one, but we have her written confession and that tells the whole story. Oh, how I wish I could believe otherwise! I still love your niece—God only knows how much. Never while I live will another take her place in my heart; but were she to appear before me now, I could not forgive her. I only pray that we may never meet again."

Little did he think then that he would ever have cause to reproach himself as bitterly as he did, but there came a time that he realized that he had cruelly misjudged this poor girl almost beyond pardon.

Nothing could change Paul Andrews' resolution to find his niece, who was encouraged by his lovely daughter and her fiance, who offered his assistance in every possible way. Mrs. Marceaux and her daughter once spoke very slightingly of the absent girl, and her uncle's foolish undertaking. They never spoke so again, as Mr. Andrews had silenced them in no gentle manner. Aline always defended her cousin so loyally that even her lover was surprised at the wealth of love and affection cherished in her heart for her absent cousin.

The guests had all departed for their homes after first being assured that there was nothing they could do after they had proffered their aid. Mrs. Marshelda at the earnest request of Aline and her father consented to remain awhile longer. She did much to encourage Mr. Andrews in his quest for his missing niece.

CHAPTER VII.

RALPH YATES.

In a London suburb a doctor was standing by the bedside of a man who was talking deliriously. He was at that moment crying excitedly: "Stop him, stop him!" The nurse approached the bedside and laid a wet cloth on the sufferer's head and soothed him until he rested as quietly as a child. The doctor asked her if he were ever violent and had she been able to learn how he received his injury? The man was evidently a mulatto of the superior type. The nurse informed him that he had never been violent, but always looked at her so pitifully and pleadingly, as if imploring her to help him remember something. She had made inquiries about him from the neighbors, hoping to learn something of him. They could not tell her much.

She learned there were two men who occupied the cottage together, both were of dark complexion, possibly Spaniards, or some other nationality. They employed an old woman to clean up for them. She had been questioned. It was found that she did not know anything that would throw any light on the matter. It was noticed, however, that the man's companion had disappeared on the day he was found unconscious. The doctor left, after instructing the nurse to keep a strict watch on the patient and not to leave him one moment more than was absolutely necessary, as he was likely to awaken in full possession of his senses. After the doctor was gone, she lowered the lights and took a seat by the bedside of her patient. She must have dropped asleep. She was awakened by no sound, but became wide-awake to find the sick man sitting up in bed staring at her.

In a low voice, he said: "Do not be afraid, but tell me who you are and why I am in bed." She told him that little Johnnie Moss had come to get him to make a kite and had found him lying unconscious in a pool of blood on the floor, that he ran out screaming and the neighbors came. Someone sent for the doctor, who would not allow him to be moved and had employed her to nurse him, with a chore woman to assist her. She gave him some cordial that the doctor had told her to give him in case he awakened in his full senses. Soon after he fell into a calm, restful sleep that lasted until the doctor came. He was glad that the patient had regained his scattered senses and was sleeping soundly and breathing regularly. He sent the nurse to take a much needed rest and he took her place to wait until the sick man should awaken, but he slept on for another hour before he opened his eyes and looked at the doctor smilingly. The doctor gave him some drops that seemed to have a restful effect upon him. The doctor told him that with care he would soon be well again, but admitted that he had a close call. He told him to obey the nurse and get well, that he wanted to talk with him.

Dr. Campbell had become singularly interested in his patient, had studied him well and observed him closely and had concluded the man was honest and upright and felt that, in early life, his environments and associations must have prevented him from succeeding in life's hard battle. He had also noticed the books lying on the table, indicating that his patient possessed great intellectual ability. He became interested in him when he considered the lonely life that he was leading.

One week later Dr. Campbell listened to one of the strangest stories he had ever heard. The man said that his name was Ralph Yates, that he was born of slave parents, but at an early age had run away from his master, leaving a mother and sister behind.

He told him he had been captured by another slave trader and how he finally escaped and made his way to England. He told how he had taken pleasure in relating the events of his early life to his companion, often sitting way into the night relating some incident of his life on the plantation. He also told him of the receipt of the letters and passage money to come back and an identification card which he joyfully showed Marlo, his roommate.

That was only a few days before he was stricken down. He was to leave the next day. Continuing, he said: "As I lay here in the bed the other day the thought came to me that Marlo had struck me and left me, thinking me dead and robbed me of my money and fled. I asked the nurse to go to my little trunk and give me a little tin box where I kept my money, for I was convinced that the Spaniard had proven false to me and had not been my friend, but doctor, I did not know until then of the treacherous one that I had shared so generously with. I was not prepared for the terrible discovery I then made. The money was gone,—that did not surprise me so much; but when all of my letters and my picture was taken, and when I considered that we were near the same age and not unlike each other, my heart grew sick within me for I feared the worst, for with such evidence to prove that he was myself, as no one had seen me since I was a mere boy, it would be a very easy matter to impersonate me."

The doctor listened intently to the incident of lowly life. When he arose to go he had resolved to befriend this man who had been so unjustly dealt with. The doctor, who was also alone, but quite wealthy, had often felt the need of someone to look after him and care for his office. He was on the point of taking a vacation and now he felt that he might take a trip to the United States of America and might combine pleasure with Samaritan work. He had many talks with Ralph, whose recovery was not very rapid, owing to the dangerous wound.

It was now six weeks since he was struck down and before he was able to enter into the doctor's services, and it was another week before they found themselves on a vessel bound for New York.

Omitting many things incident to traveling, they arrived safe at their destination. They immediately proceeded South, taking rooms in the best hotel the place could afford, a few miles from the Andrews' homestead. Dr. Campbell lost no time in locating Mr. Andrews, as he was a man of great prominence. Ascending the steps, he rang the bell, and on being assured the master was at home, sent in his card and was immediately ushered into his presence. Although Mr. Andrews could not remember anyone by that name, he was very much surprised to see a very distinguished gentleman, seemingly having not reached his fortieth year. He had a strong, handsome face, although his features were irregular, but he had the most winning smile and the firm grasp of the hand impressed you more than his personal appearance. He was indeed a splendid type of man. Mr. Andrews greeted him most cordially. There was not much formality in the meeting of the two who possessed so much geniality. After the host had seated him comfortably, he gave his attention to the motive that brought him to the home of this noted Southern planter. After introducing himself he offered his letters of introduction from some of the most distinguished European families. Mr. Andrews scarcely glanced at them, so agreeably had he been impressed by the stranger. Dr. Campbell did not keep his host in suspense long, but told him that his business was concerning someone else.

He told him of Ralph Yates just as that person had told him, relating the circumstances that brought them together, not forgetting to relate the treachery of Ralph's companion. In fact, there was nothing left unsaid. Paul Andrews was shocked and surprised, for the advent of Marlo had been carefully kept concealed from him. He was mystified when reference was made to certain letters that Ralph had received and passage money to come to the plantation, and also the identification card. He could not think who could be so interested that the interest would induce them to go to the trouble to send for him. For one moment a thought came to him that made him turn pale, but he quickly put it away from him, saying: "Oh, no, she could not do that wicked thing!" Yet the thought unnerved him and a look of misery settled on his face and remained there.

Mr. Andrews was greatly agitated when he learned that Zoleeta's uncle was in the neighborhood. Continuing, Dr. Campbell said: "Mr. Andrews, it is my belief that the Spaniard has posed as your niece's uncle and has lured her away." He was very much surprised to learn that the police had not been called in to investigate the matter. As Dr. Campbell was in possession of so much of the family history, Mr. Andrews thought it was well to confide in him, giving as a reason that he had not done so was to avoid publicity. He got up and unlocked the drawer in the desk and gave Dr. Campbell the letter to read that he had taken from Zoleeta's desk addressed to himself. After reading the letter, Dr. Campbell grasped his hand, assuring him of his heartfelt sympathy. His first impression was the same that his host's had been when he first read that fatal letter, but when Mr. Andrews told him that his first impression was wrong, and as soon as he was convinced of this fact he had been working night and day and that evening he was to meet two detectives in company with Zoleeta's betrothed. Dr. Campbell thought that Ralph would be invaluable as he knew the Spaniard. It was agreed that the doctor and his protege should be added to the number.

Some hours later Paul Andrews, Lord Blankleigh, Dr. Campbell, the two detectives and Ralph met at the Wayside Inn, and when they left all felt hopeful that Zoleeta would soon be restored to her loved ones, a prediction which soon came true. It was learned that a man with swarthy complexion was occupying a vine-covered cottage in the lane, but had not been seen lately.

It was also discovered that the tenant was all packed up as if preparing to vacate soon; therefore, it was with grave faces that they prepared to disperse that night. Just then Ralph came hurriedly in, very much excited, saying that he had seen Marlo enter the cottage and as he was about to take a peep in, there came a lady with a long coat on. She was tall and somewhat stout. When he first mentioned a lady all became excited, but knew from the description that it was not Zoleeta. He said that he had run all the way and was sure that she was still there. The detectives hurriedly left and were soon at the cottage. They had just time to dodge behind some bushes as the lady came out. She stood on the steps a moment, but her face was hidden behind a veil. They heard her say: "You must get her away at once." The man replied: "She is still too ill to move," but said, "if you will come here to-morrow evening, I'll tell you just when I will take her away." The woman promised to be there at eight o'clock. She drew her cloak around her and left. The detectives would have followed her, but she entered a waiting cab and was driven swiftly away. They hurried to the inn and reported all they had seen and heard. The next night a few moments before eight o'clock the door of the cottage opened to admit the tenant. A pair of keen eyes noted every movement.

On the outside were another pair of eyes just as keen and watchful. When the Spaniard entered he had lowered the blinds and lighted the lamp. Just then there was a light tap on the door. He cautiously opened it, admitting the woman. She told him to speak quickly, as she did not want to be missed from home. His only answer was to see if the door was tightly closed and being assured of this fact, he folded his arms, and said: "I have everything in readiness to leave and expect to leave the day after tomorrow and I do not expect to meet you again.''

She replied: ''If you will marry the girl, I will give you the money I promised you as soon as I have the proof.''

She had just turned as if about to depart when a voice said: ''Don't move.''

The woman saw Marlo in the grasp of a man. She frantically tore open the door, sped down the walk, followed by the man on the outside. Marlo was soon handcuffed and helpless. In the meantime the man on the outside had a badly scratched face and a button of the woman's coat as evidence of the encounter he had had. The woman had successfully made her escape. Word was sent at once to Mr. Andrews, and in company with the other gentlemen he hurried to the cottage accompanied by Ralph, who recognized Marlo, the Spaniard, as his late companion, and would have attacked him had he not been restrained.

CHAPTER VIII.

ZOLEETA'S ESCAPE.

Zoleeta's recovery was rapid after she began to improve. She at once began to devise some plan to escape, assisted by her faithful Lucy. She had tried to enlist the doctor in her cause, but that man had humored her in a way that showed her irresponsibility, and smiling pityingly, left her.

Lucy told her if it were not for the dogs, they could get away. One day she dropped a water glass and it broke. Then an idea came into her head, showing that she was not so stupid as was supposed. Taking an old shoe she began to crush the glass with the heel of the shoe, but before she had finished she heard the key grate in the lock. She hastily covered the pieces of glass and when old Mrs. Crane entered the room looking around to see what made the noise she had heard, the colored girl was sitting demurely by the bedside fanning Zoleeta.

When the old woman had gone, Zoleeta asked Lucy why she was pounding the glass. The girl only laughed and said that it was only for amusement, but she did not resort to any more amusement that day. The old woman told Lucy to eat her breakfast before going upstairs, but was informed that the invalid had asked her to bring her food up there to eat as she was very lonesome. The old woman did not see any harm in her doing so and raised no objections. Zoleeta was surprised at the large amount of food that Lucy had brought up, but did not eat, saying she had no appetite.

Finally she gathered up the dishes and carried them downstairs and threw the food out at the open window for the dogs to eat.

Late in the afternoon, Silas put his red head in the door, saying he had a flower for the pretty lady. Zoleeta thanked him, but Lucy asked why he did not bring his pony and cart and take the lady out to ride so she could get well, but he said, ''I dare not, for my aunt and uncle would beat me.''

The next day old Mrs. Crane came upstairs, saying that the two dogs were dead, and she knew that Mr. Marlo would be very angry as he had paid a big sum for them. It was evident that she had been drinking and confessed that her husband was drunk and she was afraid that he would beat her as soon as he found it out.

Zoleeta was much better than she would admit as as she wished to gain sufficient strength to escape. When she was alone or with no one except Lucy, she would walk around and felt that she was growing stronger each day. It was finally decided that they would make an effort to get away that day.

Lucy came hurriedly upstairs, telling Zoleeta to come at once as Silas had left the horse and wagon standing in the lane not far from the gate and that the old man and woman were hopelessly intoxicated and that Silas was drinking freely. Lucy had also taken a bottle of wine, knowing well that Zoleeta was not strong and might need it. Zoleeta thought of the dogs and drew back until she was reminded they were dead. They cautiously made their way downstairs and out of the house without being seen or heard, although they thought they heard someone moving about as they passed through the hall.

They had been driving some time before they discovered that they had missed the way and night was drawing on. At last they found themselves on the right road. They then drove rapidly, yet it was near morning when they drove up to a little hotel on the outskirts of the town and paid to have the horse and wagon taken back to the old couple in the forest.

They had yet two miles to walk and it was doubtful if Zoleeta could have walked the distance had it not been for Lucy who supported her with her strong arms, often carrying her over rough places, for it must be remembered that Zoleeta had lost many pounds during her illness. As she drew near her home, she was visibly agitated, yet strange to say, she had no other thought, only the joy of meeting her loved ones. She had lost sight of what the effect might be from the forged letters. She seemed to gain strength as she got a glimpse of the dear old place and it was almost a laborious task for Lucy to keep up with her. Naturally robust and strong, it must be remembered that her strength was greatly used up in waiting upon and assisting our heroine both in the prison home and on the present journey.

It was now early morning. It seemed as if no one was astir. She went to the rear door hoping to find some of the servants who would admit her. Her conjecture was right, for Sam, an old servant who had been in the services of her uncle long before she had been brought there a lonely orphan, who had worshiped her as a child and had sincerely grieved over her disappearance, was there to admit her.

He was speechles with joy and surprised on beholding her and would have shouted the news had not Zoleeta stopped him. He said that all were well, for he did not know of her aunt's harrowing experience the night before and that a physician had to be sent for before daybreak. He told her that her uncle had left home the night before with two gentlemen and had not returned, as he had waited up for him until a message was received stating that he was detained and would remain until morning.

Zoleeta was disappointed to learn that her uncle was away, but was glad that he was well. She went at once to her room accompanied by Lucy. Finding the door locked, she descended to the library to wait until Aline should come down, but on being informed that Mrs. Marshelda was still there, she concluded to let her know of her arrival. She wrote a hasty note to the widow apprising her of her return.

Needless to say that Ruth Marshelda lost no time in coming down and they were soon clasped in each other's arms.

There was too much to explain then and it was not many minutes before they heard a step on the walk and on looking out of the window Zoleeta beheld her uncle. It only took one look at him to convince her that he had suffered by her absence, but there were signs of deep agitation on his face which he was trying to suppress before entering the house. Zoleeta was on the point of running out to meet him, but Mrs. Marshelda held her back, fearing the sudden shock would prove too much for him, so she went out on the porch and laughingly told him that he would not be allowed to enter until he had given a good account of his absence.

He cheerfully agreed to do so, telling her that at last he had a clue to his missing niece, saying, "It was just as you have often told me, that Zoleeta was forcibly detained and the letters forgeries."

Mrs. Marshelda replied: "I would not be surprised to see Zoleeta at any time. If your niece should come home unannounced, would it unnerve you?"

He hastily replied: "Joy seldom kills, and if Zoleeta should come at any moment, I would clasp her in my arms and to my heart without any explanation whatever, for I am convinced that a purer or a better girl never lived."

They had entered the great hall as they were speaking, and at that moment were standing by the library door which was slightly ajar. Mrs. Marshelda said, "Mr. Andrews, God has been good to us and has heard our earnest prayer, Zoleeta has returned and is waiting in there for you," pointing to the library.

For one moment he did not seem to understand until a voice close to him said: "I am here, uncle, and have you no welcome for me?"

Then when Ruth Marshelda saw uncle and niece clasped in each other's arms, she went to awaken Aline and tell her the glorious news. Mrs. Marceaux was also informed of Zoleeta's return. Those around her heard the one word that she uttered—"Lost." They knew not what she meant for she rapidly grew worse and the doctor was again sent for. Her brother had gone to her room with a look of misery on his face and a very heavy heart, when the doctor said that she was suffering from a nervous collapse, presumably from a great shock, and advised him as soon as she grew stronger to take her to the seashore.

Zoleeta sent up to know if she could not go to the sick room, forgetting all that she had suffered from her aunut's cruel persecution. But the mere mention of her name had such a depressing effect on the invalid that it was deemed best that she should not enter the sick room for the present.

It was some time before Mrs. Marceaux was able to travel. Although her brother's heart was almost rent asunder by conflicting emotions, yet she was his sister. Accompanied by Catherine, he took her to the seashore and employed the best nurse he could find, also a good, competent housekeeper. He remained some time and when she had sufficiently improved so as to leave her bed, he returned home.

Catherine did not like the idea of being tied down by an invalid mother and did not feel very gracious towards Zoleeta for returning home and Lord Blankleigh still in the neighborhood and Aline's approaching marriage, yet she in no way connected her mother's illness with her cousin's return. She thought that she might catch Lord Blankleigh's heart on the rebound, as it has been said that one wedding begets another.

Leaving Mrs. Marceaux to the care of her unloving daughter and attendant, we will return to our heroine, and the events transpiring in the immediate vicinity.

Everyone was overjoyed to have Zoleeta home again. Aline's happiness was now complete. There was nothing to mar her approaching marriage, which was solemnized at the appointed time. Everyone remarked that it was providential that Zoleeta had returned before her cousin's marriage, which would have left Mr. Andrews alone, since Catherine was away with her mother.

When Zoleeta first returned, Lord Blankleigh was

immediately sent for. Needless to say, he was over-joyed, for he had been convinced that he had been hasty in judging his betrothed and had been untiring in his zeal to find the missing girl, yet he felt humbled and abashed, when he thought of how quickly he had accepted the statements in the letters, and did not fail to ask her pardon. Placing her hands in his, she had told him there was nothing to forgive, that it semed so plausible, that knowing the facts of her birth as he did it was easy to be misled.

CHAPTER IX.

SAFE AT HOME.

On the evening that Zoleeta made her escape, Marlo was left handcuffed in the custody of a detective, and Ralph, Paul Andrews, Lorn Blankleigh and Dr. Campbell remained at the inn until they had been notified of the capture of the Spaniard. It was suggested that these gentlemen return and in the morning they were to take a carriage and with their prisoner proceed to the place where Zoleeta was held in .captivity, for they had given Marlo the alternative to produce the girl unharmed or be held for abduction, with a long penitentiary sentence.

Paul Andrews arose early and went home as did Lord Blankleigh. After being assured that they would be communicated with at once as soon as they had found the girl.

As our readers know, on Mr. Andrews' arrival at

home, he was overjoyed to find his niece there before him. He at once sent a message back to the inn, but they had departed and when the party arrived at the house in the forest, everything seemed unusually quiet. Not even the barking of a dog to warn the inmates of the approach of strangers.

Marlo was sullen and non-communicative. On entering the house, the silence almost unnerved him. The front door stood open, they entered one room after another only to find everything in confusion. The fire in the kitchen range had died out, although the range was still warm. They searched the whole house only to find that the prisoner had escaped and it seemed the old people with their nephew had flown in evident fear of the consequences of allowing their prisoner to get away.

Marlo wondered where the dogs were. They were soon located, as their dead bodies had not been removed. They had evidently been poisoned. Ralph would have done his former companion bodily injury if he had not been restrained by the others, who had noticed the look of surprise and fear on the face of Marlo, convincing them as much as his protestations that he was as much mystified as they were and seemed on the verge of collapse. Some empty whiskey bottles helped to clear up the mysterious disappearance of that household. They had evidently drunk liberally of the contents and when they had sobered up and realized that the prisoners had gone, lost no time in leaving. There was nothing to do but to notify Mr. Andrews of their failure, which they hated to do.

Dr. Campbell telegraphed to Mr. Andrews the sad news of their inability to find his niece and was overjoyed as a schoolboy as he hurriedly gave the others the news that she was safe at home.

Mr. Andrews agreed not to prosecute Marlo for many reasons, and Zoleeta was reluctant to have the man punished, as he had never been really cruel, only he persisted in his desire to marry her, after the mask had been torn from his face, and he stood revealed as a lover instead of an uncle.

It was decided to give the Spaniard a sum of money and passage to some foreign shore providing that he was never more seen here and that if he ever came back, no mercy would be shown him. He gladly agreed to the proposition, knowing full well that had he been prosecuted, it would mean a long term of years in prison.

But it was destined that he should never leave this country. The morning he was to take his departure found him desperately ill with a low fever. Although having the best medical aid it was fated that he was never to leave this country, for he died before the end of the week. He was given a decent burial and the remainder of the money found on him was given to Ralph as the Spaniard had robbed him of all that he possessed after he had struck him down and fled from England.

Lord Blankleigh had tried in vain to see Zoleeta again after his first greeting on her return home, but was told that she was recuperating after her terrible experience as a captive.

Mrs. Marshelda had departed for her home in the

North and Paul Andrews and his niece were alone.
One morning they were seated in the library in
earnest conversation. Zoleeta was saying, "But,
uncle, I am sure that Lord Blankleigh will release
me from my engagement when he takes into consideration that I can never slight or disown my mother's brother. Of course, I have never met this new
uncle of mine, and I feel there are sacrifices to make
regardless of the effect on my future."

"But, Zoleeta," he replied, "has he not suffered
and waited long enough, and if he is willing to take
you for his wife, knowing all the circumstances of
your birth and parentage, surely you will not send
him away."

She sat in silence for a few moments, then said:
"I can better decide after I have seen my mother's
brother."

Just then Ralph Yates was ushered in according to
appointment. Our heroine was visibly agitated and
had grown very pale. At last she was face to face
with her mother's brother. Did she feel a responsive chord or did she feel as on the other occasion
when she reluctantly accepted the proofs of the false
one posing as her relative?

She was called to herself by her Uncle Paul, who
said, "Zoleeta, this is your mother's brother, your
Uncle Ralph."

She raised her eyes that had been cast down. A
sigh of relief escaped her when she beheld that
manly man standing there. She felt a responsive
chord and was touched as she had not been before.
Holding out her hand, she greeted him warmly while

he stood mute with wonder and surprise at the sight of this beautiful girl, his dead sister's daughter.

For a brief moment they stood looking at each other. There was forged a link which bound them together that already joined them by ties of blood and never until the day of their death was there a shadow of regret in their trust in each other.

Paul Andrews had quietly left the room and not by word or look did he try to influence her decision for or against her ex-slave uncle. She had not told him what her decision would be, yet he had already divined it, for out of the depths of her immeasurable sense of duty, there would be no question of what the outcome would be.

Soon after Ralph had taken his departure, Paul Andrews returned to the room. Zoleeta was still standing by the window where she had been watching her mother's brother take his departure. She turned and greeted her Uncle Paul with a sweet smile. He did not question her as to the result of her interview, nor did he say one word to force her confidence. She told him, however, that her Uncle Ralph had treated her with the utmost consideration, telling her that he was induced to come by the letters that he had received, but as they had been stolen by Marlo, he could not remember the exact contents. Zoleeta told her uncle that Lucy had told her on one or two occasions of her aunt going to see her grandfather and getting the address of someone by the name of Ralph, but she would not listen to her as she did not wish to encourage gossip. They both thought best to send for Lucy and get at the truth of the matter and find out much that they did not understand.

Needless to say, Lucy told of the visits of Mr. Andrews' sister to the cottage and all that our reader is aware of that happened at old Nathan's cabin. In fact, she cleared up the whole mystery and from that day Paul Andrews rarely smiled.

Afterwards, in the presence of her Uncle Paul, Zoleeta held many interviews with her mother's brother. The days went by and the favorable impression made by Ralph increased and he was respected by all.

It was Dr. Campbell's intention to take Ralph back with him, but it seemed as if fate had so decreed it that he had to remain behind. He had contracted a fever, no doubt, from Marlo, and it was many weeks before he was able to be up and around. Not until Dr. Campbell was assured that he was on the road to coplete recovery did he leave him, which he did with genuine regret, for he had become deeply attached to this handsome mulatto whose life had been so void and full of trouble.

When Zoleeta learned of her mother's brother being ill, she at once signified her intention to nurse him. Her Uncle Paul tried to dissuade her, saying, "I will send a competent nurse."

To this she agreed, but added, "I will do my part, and besides, uncle, I am not afraid of the fever."

Her uncle was far from feeling satisfied, and at once sought Dr. Campbell, who had charge of his protege. He protested against Zoleeta going near the sick man, but neither Dr. Campbell's nor her

Uncle Paul's advice and protestations could change her resolve.

Ralph had been removed from the inn and was now installed in the cottage about two miles from the Andrews' home. Zoleeta had taken her faithful Lucy with her and a big strong man to help. They got along nicely and Dr. Campbell had to admit that Ralph's ultimate recovery was as much due to Zoleeta's nursing as to his own administration.

Although Paul Andrews knew that his niece was a good, true, conscientious girl, yet he could not fathom the depths of such immeasurable love and unselfishness as she exhibited by her self-forgetfulness. Dr. Campbell regarded her a little less than a mad woman, yet he could not help admiring her and had he not been a man of principle, he would have disregarded Lord Blankleigh's claim on this lovely girl and tried to win her for himself.

As was expected, many of Zoleeta's friends passed her with the slightest bow of recognition when they would happen to meet her when she would be going for a stroll with her patient, always, however, accompanied by Lucy, who had also developed into quite a nurse and understood many things that were surprising in one so young with such limited opportunities for knowledge. Joe, the big stalwart servant, who had been installed as Zoleeta's assistant, was faithful and true, and like Lucy could be depended upon. It was at this time that Mr. Andrews received the sad news of his sister's fatal illness and hastened to her side.

Mrs. Marceaux's name was seldom ever mentioned

in the Andrews home, but if by chance her name was uttered, you would see a tightening of the lips and a hard look come into the eyes of her brother Paul. He had not forgiven his sister. Even when she was pronounced able to travel, he had not asked her to return to him home. Therefore it was with surprise that among the mail he received was a letter from a stranger living in New York City, informing him that his sister was living in a quiet street and while she had every comfort, she needed companionship. The writer goes on to say that at first Mrs. Marceaux refused to give any information concerning her relatives, finally realizing the seriousness of her condition, "gave me your address." She added, "Your sister has lived alone with one servant. I have learned that her daughter ran away with and married an artist. Her mother has not heard of her since." Continuing, the writer said, "I believe that she is dying of grief and do not think that she will last long."

Paul Andrews did not hesitate. It was his sister and he was hurrying to her. The thought of her being alone, perhaps dying, was almost more than he could bear. Zoleeta wished to accompany him, but he would not consent, but when she received a letter telling her that her aunt had lost her sight, she hastened to her side without waiting for her uncle's permission.

Her Uncle Ralph was now convalescing rapidly at the cottage, and placing everything in the hands of their competent housekeeper in their home she was soon on her way to New York City, knowing that her aunt could not see her. She went immediately to her aunt's address, and was fortunate to meet her uncle as he was coming out. Although he protested, yet he was truly glad to see her, and have her close by. He bitterly opposed her nursing her aunt, without avail. Mrs. Marceaux never got tired of telling her brother how kind and thoughtful her nurse was, but she was continually asking for Catherine.

It was while at the seashore that her daughter had run away with the young artist Her mother had never seen him, but his name was Randolph. She did not know his first name. As soon as she was able to travel, she came on to New York, hoping to find them, as she had heard Catherine speak of this gifted young artist from New York, but whether it was from the city or from some town in the state, she did not know.

Her brother visited many studios in his effort to find Randolph, without success. He also inserted ads without avail. He took trips to other towns in the state, with no better success. He became anxious as it was evident that his sister was failing fast.

It was truly pitiful to see her turn her sightless eyes toward the door each time it opened, hoping that her daughter would come back to her, then her mind would wander. Sometimes she imagined that she was helping her daughter to make an elaborate toilet, saying, "Put this flower in your hair. Put on this lace dress, you must win him. Don't let Zoleeta have him. She is the daughter of a slave. Her ancestors are Ethiopians. Let me tell you softly,"—then she would whisper—"I wrote and told him that she was a negro."

At these times Paul Andrews was compelled to leave the room and begged Zoleeta to return home. Her only reply was, "She can do me no harm now, and I may do her much good. See how quiet she becomes when I touch her and sing to her."

Often when the invalid was asleep, uncle and niece discussed what course was best to take to find Catherine.

Zolesta seldom ever left her aunt's side. She was all devotion and Paul often wondered what he would have done without her. One day her uncle insisted upon her taking a walk and getting some fresh air, telling her that with the help of the maid, he would do nicely until her return.

She had walked for some time when she noticed that she was almost in front of a studio and without one moment's hesitation she entered to make some inquiries. There was no one about the place but a very stupid looking boy who seemed to be cleaning up a very untidy studio. She learned that the artist's name was Guy Randolph and that they had not lived there long, saying that they had rooms upstairs, but did not think that they were home. He did not seem inclined to find out, possibly thinking tht he had answered enough questions, but when Zoleeta had placed a silver dollar in his hand, he went upstairs with alacrity, returning with the information that Mr. Randolph would be down at once. Presently, she heard footsteps. On turning around was surprised to find herself face to face with Catherine.

For one moment, neither could speak a word, then Catherine looked defiantly at Zoleeta as if questioning her right to be there, and Zoleeta realizing there was no time to lose, went to her cousin, and placing her arms around her, told her of her mother's condition, urging the necessity of haste. Catherine told her that she would be ready in a moment, but she did not invite her cousin upstairs.

She soon appeared, accompanied by a dark, handsome gentleman, whom she introduced as her husband. Mr. Randolph seemed very much in love with his wife, but it only required a glance to tell that his wife was indifferent to him. He had a sad, wistful look that went straight to Zoleeta's heart.

After briefly explaining her errand to Mr. Randolph, she and her cousin Catherine started at once. Catherine's husband saw them out, not forgetting to beg of his new cousin to plead with his wife's mother to forgive him for depriving her of her only child, assuring her that he would soon follow them and plead his own cause.

CHAPTER X.

DEATH OF MRS. MARCEAUX.

It was not many days before it became evident the once beautiful Claretta Andrews, now Mrs. Marceaux, was nearing the end of her life's journey. She was overjoyed at the restoration of her daughter, yet there seemed to be an unrest that could not be accounted for.

Finally, she told the nurse that she must speak

alone with her brother. He came at once to her bed-side. Placing her thin hands in his, she told him that she was going to leave him soon, but could not die in peace until she had confessed a great wrong she had done. He would have stopped her, but she begged him to let her proceed.

She told him of her treachery to Harold's orphan child, which our reader is already acquainted with, then adding, ''Brother Paul, I have also done you a great wrong. Before our father died, he gave me a letter to give you. It was the day that you had to go away on business to Rosslyn Court House. Shortly after he gave me the letter, he became unconscious; soon after he died. I was curious to know the contents of that letter. I betrayed my dead father's trust and broke the seal and read what he had written. Look under my pillow and take out that sealed packet you will find there and you will learn what I have known all these years.''

He took the packet and extracted the letter that she indicated was the right one and would have placed it in his pocket without reading it, but she wanted him to read it, and tell her if he would forgive her. He told her that was unnecessary, that she was forgiven already, and to prove that she was forgiven, before he knew the contents, he gathered her thin, wasted form in his arms and kissed her pallid cheeks again and again.

When he was alone, this is what he read:

''My Dear Son:

I am writing this because I think you ought to know. You remember your uncle, Aaron Andrews?

He was my only brother. He died when you were quite a youth. On his death bed he bequeathed to me a slave woman and her two little children. They were pretty children; one was a boy and the other a girl. The mother's chief charm lay in her magnificent black hair, and large flashing eyes. He asked me to treat them well. I asked him who were the children's father. My son, listen to what he told me. He said, 'Brother, when I pass away, those children will be fatherless.' My son, the name of this slave woman who found favor in your Uncle Aaron's eyes was named Barbara Yates, the mother of Ralph and Mildred Yates! Paul, my son, do you not see that your brother Harold married his cousin Mildred, my brother's daugher? True, there was no wedding ring, but ties of blood are more binding. I possibly would not have divulged this secret, but Harold's marriage to his cousin has brought about unlooked for complications.''

There was added a postscript telling him that it was not necessary that his sister be made acquainted with that part of the family history.

When she had finished speaking she seemed so weak that Paul at once summoned Zoleeta to the sick room. She entered so quietly that the invalid was not aware of her presence.

Then in a weak voice, she said, "Paul, dear brother, will you please tell Zoleeta all that I have told you, tell her that for every act of treachery and every pang that I made her suffer that I have suffered ten thousand. Do you think that she will forgive me? Oh, if I could hear her say, with her own lips, 'Auntie, I forgive you,' I could die in peace.''

Paul motioned for Zoleeta to speak. She bent over her aunt, kissing her pallid lips, saying, ''Auntie, I do forgive you, fully and freely from the depths of my heart. We all make mistakes and yours is not unpardonable.''

A beautiful smile illumined the invalid's face as she exclaimed, ''I am so happy, but I want to thank the dear nurse that has been so kind to me. Oh, Zoleeta, I have the kindest nurse, oh, so kind.''

When informed who nurse was, she put out her arms while her niece bowed over her and received the first caress from her dead father's sister. It was evident that the sick woman was fast passing away. Catherine was at once summoned to the room with her husband, who had just arrived, in time to receive pardon and a blessing from the dying woman. With her hand clasped in her brother's and her head pillowed on the breast of her niece, Zoleeta Andrews, the daughter of Mildred Yates, the ex-slave and descendant of the Ethiopians of Africa, Claretta Marceaux breathed her last.

It was a sad return to Paul Andrews' home. He had his sister buried beside her parents. As he stood by the grave of his only sister, he was glad that her last hours had been so full of peace and comfort. As Catherine stood by the side of her husband in her girlhood home, she felt sad and humble, but a wiser girl than she was when she had left home. She had learned to appreciate her handsome husband, and her uncle was very kind to the once wayward girl, whom he felt was more to be pitied than blamed. He offered her and her husband a home as long as they cared to remain and Zoleeta, true to her promise, presented Catherine with a check for a handsome sum as her marriage dower.

In the meantime Guy Randolph sought an interview with his wife's uncle and told him of startling events in the nearby vicinity many years ago before and just after Guy's birth, of which Mr. Andrews was ignorant. It was almost unbelievable, yet he could not doubt the story, as he knew the South could not boast of its moral record, and besides, he felt drawn to this young artist, who through no fault of his, had found so many obstacles in his path to success.

He explained to Mr. Andrews that shortly after his marriage to Catherine, he had been summoned to the bedside of his old nurse, who lived in a distant city. Leaving his wife in New York, he hastened to the dying nurse's side. Startling things were revealed to him. He learned of events that he had never dreamed about.

She had been a most beautiful woman and an ex-slave. "As a boy, I had often admired her great beauty." He told Paul he remembered fighting a boy who once had made a slurring remark about his nurse's color. He had told the boy that he did not care if she were darker than his mother, that she was the most beautiful. Continuing, he told Mr. Andrews that arriving, he found his nurse very sick.

It was evident that she would never leave her sick bed alive. "She told me that she was not my nurse, but my mother, and Colonel Randolph Slayton

was my father. She gave me letters and newspaper
clippings, showing that she had kept herself informed of everything concerning my father and his
affairs. She gave me those and told me to go to old
Mr. Slayton's lawyer. When I learned of my birth
and parentage, I did not care for myself, but how I
wished that I had delayed my marriage for a few
weeks and my wife would have been spared the so-
called disgrace of being united to a man of African
descent.''

Paul Andrews listened with dismay at this revelation and felt thankful that his sister had been
spared the knowledge that her daughter's husband
had descended from that race of people for whom she
felt such bitter hatred. He told Mr. Andrews that
he had not been to see Mr. Slayton's lawyer, as he
had just arrived in the neighborhood and the lawyer
resided in a distant town. Mr. Andrews suggested
going to see the lawyer and consult with him, which
was accordingly done.

Arriving there, he was informed that for years they
had been trying to trace him and if he could prove
his identity, there was a great fortune waiting him.
Guy gave the lawyer some letters to read that he
had received from his mother, thinking her only his
nurse as she had led him to believe. She had also
written the lawyer admitting that he had been
brought up in that belief. After fully establishing
his identity, he was given a letter that had been
intrusted to them by Mr. Slayton a short while before his death, many years before. All that was now
necessary was to sign some papers and he would be-

come a wealthy man, but this Guy refused to do until he had read his father's letter.

"My Dear Son:

When you read this I will be sleeping my last sleep. My days are numbered as the doctors have given up all hopes and I am now trying to make some reparation for the great wrong I have done you and your mother, who was one of the dearest women that ever lived. I feel that I could not rest in my grave if I failed to right this wrong as far as possible. I was left at the age of twenty-three without father or mother, but had inherited vast wealth and scores of slaves. Strange to say that even at that early age, I had developed a mania for saving money until I was the wealthiest man in the country. I had contracted no bad habits and can say without egotism or exaggeration that I could have married any of the great Southern beauties, who gave me every encouragement.

But not until I had reached my thirtieth year was my heart awakened to the charms of a woman, and that woman was your mother. She was no college bred girl, no girl of fashion, but one of my slaves. I had no family ties, no one to please but myself, and this girl was mine by inheritance and doubly mine by common law that was prevalent in the South. She was beautiful, but her chief charms were in her fine, large black eyes. She showed unmistakable signs of refinement and good sense that was remarkable for one brought up surrounded by the debasing environments of slavery.

This slave girl feeling the galling yoke of bondage falling away from her by my preference and the many costly presents I gave her, had no thoughts for future consequences, but lived for me only.

When I realized this poor slave girl was bordering on motherhood, I felt that I was doing my whole duty when I exempted her from all work and all care, establishing her in a cabin by herself with an older woman to wait upon her. She never asked me to marry her. I had no thought of doing so. She felt that she was mine through inheritance and had no voice in the matter, yet at times she looked at me so wistfully and pleadingly that it made me feel very uncomfortable indeed. I did not feel that I was doing a great wrong as the same conditions between master and slave existed all around me, however, at those times, I'd give her an extra piece of gold; but that did not always bring a smile to her face; but when she did smile, it was so full of pathos that I preferred tears.

One day there nestled on her bosom the sweetest baby boy that any father might be proud of. I was wild with joy. She waited until I had exhausted my caresses on the boy and his mother, then said, with all the bitter sarcasm that any cultured woman could say, 'You have allowed your son to be born in bondage, do you intend that he shall be reared as a slave? Do you intend that the fetters that bind the mother shall also shackle the son? And do you intend to give your son a name or shall he remain nameless?'

My son, I was taken by surpirse at her thought of our boy and his rights. I told her to name you after

myself—Guy Randolph Slayton. I gave her a sum
of money that I thought would startle her by the
amount, more money than she had ever possessed in
her life and was prepared to respond to her caresses
that I felt was my due after my magnificent generosity, but I had yet to learn that entering the realms
of motherhood had put a new dignity upon this poor
friendless slave girl. With flashing eyes and flam-
ing cheeks, she threw the money into my face, telling me that it cost more than that to keep my saddle
horse.

It was then, my son, that for an instant as I gazed
upon the face of that beautiful outraged slave girl
I felt that I could renounce the whole world for her
sake. I went back into the house, sat far into the
night thinking, and when I went to bed and to sleep
it was with a clear conscience, for I had resolved to
marry Hebe. That was your mother's name. I felt
that unconquerable love for her that I intended on
arising to go at once to her cabin and make her
happy by telling her so, but on arising the next morning I was called away on business and was gone several days. On my return I accepted an invitation to
a dinner party, met a charming young lady visitor.
She had several admirers, but she seemed to treat
them all alike; finally she showed a decided preference for me. I felt flattered and almost before I
knew it, I had proposed and was accepted. When I
realized that all my plans for making your mother
my wife had gone wrong I had this perplexing problem before me,—what to do about her and my son.

I married the lady I was engaged to, but I didn't
lose sight of the fact that I must provide handsomely

for my boy and his mother. On going to the cabin to make her acquainted with all that I was going to do for her, I was surprised to find the place deserted and learned that she had disappeared on the night that I brought home my bride. No one had seen her go, no one knew where she went.

My wife was a lovely woman, bright and intellectual, yet there was a void in my heart that she could not fill and two years later, when she gave me a little son, she could not understand my lack of exuberant joy such as she felt. I was pleased, but not happy. How could I be when my first born and his mother were homeless wanderers, I knew not where? I then began seriously to realize the awful wrong that I had done to make this poor inexperienced girl an outcast, without home or friends. It would have been a relief to know that you were both dead. I have spent a fortune trying to locate you, but without avail. I have placed this letter in my lawyer's hands and have told him all the circumstances of your birth and year and dates. I have placed fifty thousand dollars to your credit and ten thousand to your mother. My son, I feel that I have done all that I can and can only add that you have already found out from what I have written that I have not been a happy man since I lost your mother and my last thoughts are of her and not of the woman that bears my name. Forgive me, my son, and may God bless you, is the prayer of your dying father. It is not necessary to divulge those facts to my widow or your half-brother, Will Slayton.

(Signed) Your Father,
Guy Randolph Slayton.''

When Guy had read his father's letter he felt very bitter. He took the first opportunity to give the letter to Mr. Andrews to read. Placing the letter in his hand, he watched him as he read it. There was absolute silence afterwards, both seemed to be in a deep study.

The young man was the first to speak, saying, "Mr. Andrews, can you forgive me for marrying your niece?"

Mr. Andrews answered: "While you have married hastily, it was not unpardonable, and when I take into consideration all the facts of the case, I feel satisfied that you were the victim of circumstances and are not wholly to blame."

Grasping his hand, he assured Guy that he fully and freely forgave him, yet that assurance did not seem to make Guy any happier, as he still looked worried. The older man laid his hands on his arm, and said, "Cheer up," but he was reminded of the fact that his wife was not aware of the origin of his birth and was not sure how she would feel about it.

Mr. Andrews also felt that the young man had grave cause to fear the outcome of the revelation to his wife, for well did he know that Catherine had much of her dead mother's makeup and knew that the young husband would have hard work to make her understand that he was not responsible for her position as his wife.

Mr. Andrews at first said there was no necessity of telling her. The secret could remain between the two, and was surprised, yet well pleased, when this young artist husband drew himself up, and said:

"Mr. Andrews, I have always been poor and have never knowingly deceived anyone and I love my wife too dearly to deceive her. I love my honor. There is none in deception, and regardless of what may be the outcome, my duty is clear, I must not shirk it, although a painful one."

Guy also told Mr. Andrews that he did not intend to touch one penny of his inheritance, but his attention was called to the fact that his father had exhausted every resource to find and provide for himself and mother's future comfort. He also reminded him that his father had been left an orphan at an early age and had not seen things at that time as he did later and it was evident that he also was a victim of circumstances, for when he would have righted the wrong done Guy's mother, he was called away and before he could carry out his intentions, he met the woman who afterwards became his wife, and his acknowledgment that his vanity was flattered, but his heart was true, "and he not only asked you with his dying breath to forgive him, but you told me your mother, when she saw the angels hovering over her bed, begged you to forgive your father. It was a beautiful love tragedy." Mr. Andrews further said: "I am sure that some day the world will know and appreciate you, yet you should not lose sight of the fact that although you are now wealthy, you are still young and struggling for fame, and besides your wife has been reared in luxury and is expecting a little stranger before many months, and you ought to give them the first consideration regardless of the past."

CHAPTER XI.

RALPH'S RESOLUTION.

Needless to say that the artist's love for his pretty wife and the imaginary disgrace brought upon her overcame all his scruples and when Catherine left for her home in the North with her talented husband, she was well pleased. She was also delighted with the fortune that came to her husband through the death of a relative, yet at that time it was not made plain to her who that relative was. They did not remain long in New York, but sailed for Italy, where he longed to go for many years to perfect himself in art.

Neither Mrs. Slayton nor her son ever learned of the artist's connection with them, nor when his fame was sung from continent to continent and when she had purchased one of his famous pictures, did she know that the artist descended from a negro slave, not only from the South, but from their own plantation, and was a half-brother of her son, William Slayton.

On her return home, Zoleeta was pleased that her Uncle Ralph had so far recovered as to dispense with Lucy's services and she was only waiting Zoleeta's return before taking her departure. An old woman was secured to take her place at the cottage. Joe still remained there.

Mr. Andrews was glad to be at home again with his niece, yet he was very much concerned about her future, as she had such conscientious scruples about her mother's brother and the lonely, cheerless life he led. She often went to the cottage to see how everything was progressing. Her uncle often remonstrated with her, but her only answer was that she had spent the largest part of her life with her father's people. "And now," said she, "dear uncle, do not oppose me in doing what I am sure my parents would approve of, if they were living."

One day when she went to the cottage as usual, she found her Uncle Ralph in a serious but not unhappy mood. She started at once to dispel the gloom from his brow. She told him that she had long intended to see him comfortably settled in a nice little home of his own, but as she wanted him to express his wishes, she had come to consult him.

She said: "I will place a comfortable sum to your credit in the bank. Uncle Paul approves of the plan and you will make us both happy by accepting it."

Ralph was so overcome with emotion that he could not speak of her kindness for some time, but finally he said, "I deeply appreciate it. When I think of all you have done, and are still doing, and all that you have sacrificed for my sake, I stand abashed to think I have no way to compensate you; therefore, I have made up my mind that I will no longer call myself a man and be selfish enough to allow you to jeopardize your interests for me with your unsurpassed kindness and watchful care. I am again a well man, although no longer young, and I feel that I can make my own way."

"The money taken from Marlo and given to me

as my just right will place me above immediate
want and help me in the days to come. Of course, it
would be a pleasure to be close by where I could see
you sometimes, but it would be unfair to you for me
to remain in the vicinity of your home. Do I not
see that many of your friends are slighting you? I
hope that you may not come to see me again. The
world is harsh and judges cruelly. It would grieve
me very much were you to suffer through your kindness to me. I appreciate your kind offer to place
me in a home of my own and can not find words to
thank you, but I have just received a letter from Dr.
Campbell asking me to return to him and have decided to do so, and was on the point of answering it
when you came.''

Zoleeta could not but admire him for the resolution that he made. She replied: ''I think that Dr.
Campbell would be very fair and treat you well, but
I do not see the necessity of you entering into the
doctor's services.''

Finally she left after telling him to take time and
think the matter over. Her Uncle Paul was not surprised to learn that she had been unsuccessful in her
mission for he had watched Ralph closely ever since
his advent into the neighborhood and was amazed
at his intellectual ability and well pleased at his un-
obtrusiveness and after the closest scrutiny, was convinced that he was a man to be trusted, yet there
were times when a shadow would flit across Paul
Andrews' face when he thought of his lovely niece's
kinship to the ex-slave. At those times he wished
that his brother had chosen one from his own race

to be the mother of his child and it was with pain and sorrow that he recalled the fact that through the treachery of his dead sister that it had been made possible for the relationship to be brought to their knowledge. He sighed heavily as he thought of this.

Little did he think that Zoleeta's ex-slave uncle suffered as keenly as he did and felt that it would have been more merciful if he had been left to die when stricken down by the treacherous Spaniard, and wished that his sister had chosen one of her race for a life's companion. He sighed to think that things would remain as they were until the end. How often he sighed or how bitterly he grieved over the situation none ever knew, and it was not until after his death that Paul and Zoleeta realized the great sacrifice that Ralph had made for her sake.

When they knew all, they stood humbled and silent. Each feeling that they had entertained a prince in disguise. A man who by his true manliness had drawn the curtain of obscurity from their eyes and made those two see that true manhood is not rated by the color of the skin.

Paul Andrews and his niece talked together many times of Ralph and his admirable qualities, his self-reliance and independence.

Zoleeta took this opportunity to broach a subject to her uncle that had long puzzled her. "Uncle," she asked, "why are the Colored people ostracised and scorned by the whites? History teaches us that the American Negroes are descended from the Etheopians of Africa. Now there are various colors. Is not the Caucasian race responsible for their mixed blood? Is it not inhuman and cruelly unjust to mistreat anyone on account of his color? If a person is known to have Negro blood in their veins they are placed beyond the pale of respectability. It is true that I am well received for it is not known that my ancestors were once slaves and sold on the auction block. I feel that I am living a terrible, deceitful life, there are times when I am receiving so much homage my eyes flash with scorn when I think of how my friends and admirers would fall away from me if they knew me to be the offspring of the despised race of blacks, and it is only my love for my father's people that prevents me from proclaiming to the world this secret, that at times weighs so heavily on my heart.''

''A short while ago, I was at Mrs. Moore's. While seated on her porch there came to her house a Colored girl to deliver a note to Mrs. Moore. She did not even ask the girl on the porch although the sun was scorching hot. The girl waited until she had received an answer. All the time she was trying to protect her face from the sun's fierce rays by holding up her hands. After she left, I remarked that the girl looked as if she suffered from the heat? Mrs. Moore simply said that it did not hurt the girl and, ''if you show those Negroes too much consideration, they would become presumptious.''

''The very next day as I was passing the same lady's house, I heard her in angry tones threaten to discharge her coachman for allowing her horses to stand in the sun, although they had been standing there only a few moments, as I saw him when he drove up to the door. I have seen some of our most aristocratic ladies place their arms around the neck of a jet black horse and think nothing of it. I have seen a black horse and a white horse harnessed together, each doing his part without friction, and the negro that we are trying to impress from the pulpit and platform that God, the creator, made us all equal and tell him it is a sin to oppress the weak, when it is an evident fact that Caucasian race is not only the oppressors but they never stop until the weaker races are crucified on the altar of their greed and ambition. I ask, Uncle, who is responsible for this deplorable state of affairs, that, to me, seems a litttle less than barbarism?''

While our heroine was speaking her uncle never once interrupted her, but when she had repeated the question, she paused for a reply. His face had been a study, sometimes flushing red from his temples to his neck, for well did he know the Southerner and his attitude toward the Colored people far better than this pure young girl where the light was trying to struggle through her puzzled brain, for she had often heard remarks that were not intended for her, that had set her to thinking. Her uncle remembered in his boyhood days, on this same plantation where she was now the owner, how he had seen black mothers with their white offspring in their arms and again, how he had seen those same mothers nurse some white babe, whose own mother was physically unfit to nourish it or socially indifferent. He felt uncomfortable when he remembered that he had known slave girls to be sold to other masters because they had learned that they had honor and were fighting to defend it.   Yet he could not tell this pure girl these things, nor was he willing to admit to her that the race of people that he was indentified with and whose blood alone flowed in his veins did not justify their claim of superiority over all the other races.

It shamed his manhood when he thought of his Uncle Aaron and his part in the tragedy of the South. To think that his family had not passed through the ordeal with clean hands? That the Andrews' record had not been a clean one. He told Zoleeta that although it was a great loss when the slaves were liberated, he was glad as he would have given them their freedom as soon as they passed into his hands.

She was glad to hear this. ''Why, Uncle,'' she said, ''Our animals are treated with more consideration than those ex-slaves for when they are worn out and unfit for service, we provide for them as long as they live, yet I have been told that the poor Colored people were liberated and sent out into this world without a dollar and no visible means of support, and what is most surprising, I have also learned that Congress refused to make any appropriation for their benefit, although they fought for freedom and liberty and when they were liberated they were in that destitute condition. Had I been a man, I should not have rested day or night until I had awakened the Nation to the injustice done those ex-slaves, who should have had a certain sum set aside for their use for ten years at least. Oh, Uncle, it is horrible when you think of it! What chance had those poor Colored people to make good citizens? They are what the white people have made them." Continuing she said, her face illumined by a beautiful smile, "I am proud that I am descended from that race of people who have suffered such wrongs, for I would rather be wronged than do wrong."

Paul Andrews was amazed at the clear insight of his niece as to the existing conditions. Uncle and niece talked for some time longer and both realized as she had often told him that it was like a tangled skein of threads, the more they talked the more hopeless it seemed.

Just then Lord Blankleigh was announced. Zoleeta would have escaped had it been possible, but was forced to remain and it was her uncle, who after cordially greeting the visitor, excused himself on the plea of business.

CHAPTER XII.

THE BROKEN TROTH.

Lord Blankleigh was overjoyed at seeing his fiancee and declared that he would not let her out of his sight again, and begged her to name an early date for their wedding, which had been delayed by her abduction by the Spaniad. She told him that while she had been held a prisoner that the effect had not been altogether harmful, that she had considered things then that she had not taken into con-

sideration before and felt that good would come out
of those trying days and had concluded their engagement was a mistake, and it would be doing him
a great injustice to let the marriage take place.

She reminded him of her Uncle Ralph and the ties
of blood that united him and her saying, she would
never let Lord Blankleigh sacrifice himself and his
social standing for her and her kin. He pleaded in
vain. He was forced to depart with a promise that
he might write some time and she would answer his
letters. Although sadly disappointed, he was not
altogether hopeless.

There came one day a package addressed to Mr.
Andrews from across the waters and on unpacking
it, he was both pleased and surprised. A beautiful
picture of Zoleeta as true as life done by Guy Randolph, the artist, who was fast becoming famous.
The picture was called ''My Inspiration,'' a copy of
one that he had on exhibition in Paris. Mr. Andrews
had the picture hung in the library. It was admired
by all. Special mention was made of it in the leading papers, journals and magazines.

One day as Mr. Andrews stood, as he thought,
alone, lost in admiration at the lovely face on the
canvas, he sighed deeply, but whether happily or un-
happily was a matter of conjecture as he ardently
explaimed, ''My brother's child!'' and another sigh
heaved his breast.

He was startled to hear a voice close by, saying,
''My sister's child.'' On turning around was surprised to see Zoleeta's ex-slave uncle standing by
his side. At first, Paul Andrews drew back resent-

fully, feeling that Ralph's presence in that room gazing on his dead brother's child's picture was an intrusion, although he had always shown exemplified courtesy to the ex-slave, but felt that he could not make an equal of him. Never before did he so forcibly realize the marriage law that made him and the ex-slave kin. In silence they stood with their eyes resting on the face displayed on that canvas.

Paul Andrews seemed to be struggling with deep emotion and uncertainty and as Ralph turned to leave the room, it was evident that Mr. Andrews, while standing there, had been fighting a battle and had won, for when the ex-slave turned to go, Harold's brother silently linked his arm in that of the brother of Mildred and they passed from the room together, and the marriage ties that united them were cemented by bonds of friendship, that only ended at the grave.

One day as Mr. Andrews was returning home, he was riding a magnificent high spirited horse recently purchased. He had just dismounted as Ralph came up. Not waiting for the stable boy, he took the bridle to lead the horse away. Just then the horse became frightened at a piece of paper, made a sudden plunge forward with Ralph clinging to the bridle. It was in vain, they called to him to let go, finally he lay unconscious and the maddened animal ran on to the stable. They carried Ralph into the house and sent at once for the doctor.

It was some days before there was any hope given that he would live and some weeks before it was learned that he would never walk again. The doctor

advised him to be put in some institution, but neither
Mr. Andrews nor his niece would hear of it. They
had a bright sunny room fixed up for the invalid,
a good strong and competent nurse installed there
to care for the sick man. Time went on, but he
did not improve. The doctors said that it might be
weeks or perhaps months before there would be
much change.

Some months after leaving America word was received from Catherine that she was the mother of a
darling baby boy. Since then, there had been no
word received from the artist's home.

One day a carriage drove up to Mr. Andrews'
home. A stylishly dressed lady who lost no time
in ascending the steps, stepped out. The door
opened to admit Catherine and her maid. Mr. Andrews and niece were in the invalid's room when he
was sent for. Not knowing who wanted to see him,
he was completely surprised to see his niece.

He at once sent up for Zoleeta, who welcomed
the traveler, yet she felt a foreboding that she could
not account for; however, she hastened to see that
Catherine was resting in her old room with her maid.
After seeing them comfortably settled, she hastened
back to her uncle. He turned a puzzled look towards
her, but she had no inkling why her cousin had returned, but thought after she had rested that she
would explain everything satisfactorily. She had
been at her uncle's home several days, and had offered no explanation why she was there without her
husband and baby. Finally her uncle sent for her.
She entered the library, where he was waiting, with a

defiant look on her face, for she had been expecting the summons.

Her uncle, ever courteous, drew up a chair for her and remained standing until she was seated. He took a chair opposite and did not keep her in suspense long, but asked her why she was there without her husband and child. She replied, "My husband has deceived me, and I have left him. I never expect to see him again."

On hearing this her uncle's face became very grave as he asked her in what way she had been deceived. She said, "Uncle, my husband is a Negro and I do not intend to live with him again. He has deliberately deceived me."

Her uncle listened to her with a pained face without uttering a word until she paused, then he said, "Catherine, where is your baby?"

"Why, uncle," she replied, "I did not want a Negro child and told him so. I also told him that I never wanted to see either of them again. To think my child descended from the black people whose ancestors are Etheopians. Why, I feel as if I shall never hold up my head again."

Her uncle was very stern as he said, "Girl, you have committed a terrible sin. Where is your mother love? Why, the animals in the forests cling to their young. You have deliberately forsaken your husband and child. Your husband is one of God's noblemen. It was to keep from deceiving you that he told you of his origin. Miserable girl, you should kneel at your husband's feet and beg his pardon."

"Why, Uncle, would you have me lower my Southern pride to that low born ex-slave?"

Her uncle replied, ''Granting he was born in those trying days of slavery, he is one of the grandest men I have ever met. I shall send him word immediately that you are here and will return with him, if he comes for you.''

''But, Uncle, I tell you that before I will live with a Negro, I will kill myself.''

''Catherine,'' her uncle said, ''did he offer no explanation how it was he married you withholding the secret of his birth?''

''Uncle, he wanted me to read some letter he claimed that his father had left for him but I do not believe one word of it and refused to be deceived again.''

''Catherine, had you read that letter, you never would have left your husband. He did not know the secret of his birth until after his marriage to you. You remember he was summoned South to the death-bed of his nurse? She proved to be his mother. You have cruelly misjudged your husband.''

''Uncle, that does not alter the fact that my husband descended from the despised race of slaves of the South.''

Her face grew scarlet when she remembered that it was at her suggestion that she had eloped and married this ex-slave, yet he was too magnanimous to remind her of this fact when she had accused him of luring her away from her invalid mother. Still with burning cheeks she remembered it was she who opposed returning to her mother after her marriage and relieving her of all worry and suspense.

Her uncle replied, "Catherine, you must return to your husband."

This she absoluetly refused to do; even the mention of her baby had no effect on her. With a defiant look on her face she left the room.

Her uncle went in search of Zoleeta and told her all the facts of the case. She was very much surprised, as she had not been made aware of the secret of Guy Randolph's birth. "Oh, Uncle!" she said, "surely Catherine cannot mean to desert her little innocent babe and her husband, who, like myself, are but the victims of circumstances? I will go to her at once and convince her of her terrible error."

She immediately sought her wayward cousin, but met with no better success than her uncle.

That night Mr. Andrews wrote to Catherine's husbnad, telling him that she was there with them and would he come for her, adding, however, that he had his heartfelt sympathy. Zoleeta added a few words to console him in his far away home. However, before sending the letter, he sought Catherine and allowed her to read the contents. She told him he could send the letter if he wanted to, but she was firm in her decision that she would never live with him again.

The days went by and weeks had rolled around until it was now three months since the letter was sent to the deserted husband across the water, yet they had not received a single line in reply.

When Guy Randolph had signified his intention to Catherine's uncle to tell his wife the origin of his birth, Mr. Andrews had not approved of the idea, yet he could not help but admire this young man of obscure birth for his courageous determination to have no secrets from his wife.

One evening as he sat in his studio commenting on a picture that he had just finished, Catherine entered and remarked it was a wonderful beauty, her only objection to it was the skin was tinted too dark.

Placing his arms around his wife, he said, ''I am glad that you like it. It is a true reproduction of my mother.''

''But Guy,'' she replied, ''no one would ever think that she was white. She reminds me of some of the ex-slaves of the Southern part of the United States. Some of them were quite beautiful.''

With his arms still around his wife, he replied, ''My mother was a beautiful woman despite the fact she had mixed blood.''

When her husband spoke those words, a look of horror overspread her face. She exclaimed, ''Surely you do not mean that? Oh Guy! Do not jest with me for I would abhor you if that were the case.''

Bending over his wife he replied, ''Catherine, I am not jesting. It was not my mother's fault that she was born a slave, it was not her fault that she was born in bondage, although as soon as possible she severed the fetters that bound her and took me far away where we could breathe the sweet breath of liberty until she died.''

But in spite of his explanation, Catherine repulsed him and when he offered the letter left by his father to substantiate his statement, she took the letter, tore it in fragments and threw it in his face, telling him that she would never live with him again, that he could have his negro child and that she would never willingly look upon their faces again. It was in vain that her husband pleaded with her not to leave him and her child, but she scornfully replied that her mind was made up and she would never change.

For several days he did not see his wayward wife. He was in hopes that she would reconsider her decision and remain. Vain hope! Without one word of farewell she left husband and child.

Day after day, he gazed at his little babe deserted by its mother. Not once did he complain, but night after night he sat in dumb anguish trying to fathom this new sorrow that had fallen upon him and how to meet it. He remembered how his mother in dying had clung to him, how she had endured poverty and privations rather than be separated from her child, yet his wife, who had boasted of the best blood of the South, had not the mother love nor the mother instinct of the poor slave girl who entered motherhood at the will and bidding of her master and had defied the father of her child and taken her babe away, living in obscurity that she might have him always with her. The animals do not forsake their young. The feathered tribe watch over and shelter their brood from the tempest, yet the mother of his child had proven herself devoid of the most beautiful love, a mother's love.

Catherine remained in her uncle's home for many months. Everyone was kind to her, yet she seemed very unhappy. One day Zoleeta found her in tears. Placing her arms around her, she offered consolation, never once referring to the separation of her and her husband or its cause.

One morning Catherine surprised everyone at the breakfast table by announcing her intended departure to her husband and child. She bitterly bewailed the fact that she did not heed the advice of her uncle and cousin and now since she saw how unjust she had been, her face blanched with terror for fear that he would not forgive her. She told her uncle that she had seen her baby in her dreams, and "Oh, Uncle," she said, "if necessary, I will kneel at my husband's feet and beg his pardon." She burst into tears and cried most bitterly.

Her uncle wanted to accompany her to her home, but she would not consent. With her maid, she sailed with the best wishes of all for a happy reunion with her husband. The voyage was uneventful. Catherine was anxious yet dreaded to meet her husband. When the carriage drove up before the door she quickly alighted. A terrible fear possessed her. She could not tell why. She noticed the blinds were closed, the house had a deserted look. For a moment she felt as if she would faint. Her fears were well founded, she learned from the occupant of the house next door that at one time a famous artist had resided there, finally had gone away, no one knew where.

Catherine took rooms in a quiet hotel near by, hoping her husband might return or she might get some information of his whereabouts, thus we leave her for years keeping her lonely vigil, refusing her uncle's cordial invitation to return and remain with them.

The weeks had passed into months, months had passed into years until two and a half years had rolled around since Ralph had been carried into the house unconscious. The end came peacefully with his niece and Paul, his brother-in-law, by his bed-side.

They shed genuine tears of regret, but none of re-morse, as they had done everything possible to re-lieve the sufferer. After the burial, Zoleeta went to the cottage and would have taken Lucy with her, but she could not be found. On entering the cottage, however, she was surprised to see Lucy already there. Her eyes were red from weeping. Zoleeta took charge of whatever letters and papers there were.

On returning home, she sat down to examine them. She wept bitter tears when she read what might be termed a diary, for there was jotted down thoughts and ideas. She felt that it was well that they had fallen into her hands. Taking the papers to her uncle, this is what they read: "Lucy is a good woman, so faithful and true. I have watched her and felt that she would be a good woman for a wife. I am sure that she thinks well of me, for when I was so ill and she thought me asleep, she wept bitter tears over me, saying that she did not care to live if I should die. Oh, I felt so happy and began to improve, thinking that we could marry, then all at once I thought of a dear girl, who had sacrificed so much for me that my marriage might prove a humiliation and a disgrace to her, possibly raising a family dishonor. I thought of all that it would mean to this girl, who is as good as she is beautiful, and if I should die without forming new ties, she would have nothing to remind her of her ancestors, but a memory; so I have crushed this love, my only love, out of my heart. There are times, however, when I long for the end, for my heart has bade farewell to Lucy. May God bless and take care of you, farewell.''

It was then that Paul and Zoleeta learned her exslave uncle had been a man among men and had sacrificed his love to save Harold's and Mildred's child from shame and humiliation.

Some weeks later, Zoleeta sent for Lucy and told her that she was going out on some business and wanted her to accompany her. They came across a neat little cottage which they entered. It contained five rooms and a nice yard, a front and rear porch. The house was beautifully finished and was almost new.

Zoleeta suggested going through it. Lucy was loud in her praise. Zoleeta said, ''Lucy, I am glad that you like it, for it is yours. I had intended to buy it for Ralph, but now I give it to you as a memorial to him, and I shall place a thousand dollars to your credit in the bank. I know that Ralph would like you to have it. I also know that you were very dear to him.''

Lucy burst into tears and cried freely at the mention of his name and Zoleeta's kindness and could not realize that the house belonged to her.

Lord Blankleigh had heard of Ralph's death from Mr. Andrews, had sent beautiful words of consolation to Zoleeta. She did not answer his letter, simply sending an acknowledgment through her uncle.

Aline is a widow now and with her children is at home with her father. The home that has known so much sorrow is now one where peace abides. They had been in her father's home some months when one day Zoleeta was summoned to the parlor, where she was very much surprised to meet Lord Blankleigh. She greeted him with unrestrained delight while he greeted her most rapturously. Whatever she told him must have pleased him very much, for he departed seemingly very happy indeed. She also seemed pleased as she read a letter he had placed in her hand from his mother, telling her that she was waiting to welcome her new daughter, stating she was alone as both of her daughters had married some months before, and so we see all obstacles cleared away for a happy marriage. It has now been five years since she first met her lover.

She felt with Aline and the children back home that her uncle would get along nicely without her. There was nothing to delay her marriage, which was solemnized very quietly owing to the recent death of her uncle Ralph. The last thing that Lady Blankleigh did before leaving for her husband's home in England was to go to Ralph's grave, her distinguished husband walking by her side. He lifted his hat as his wife laid a wreath on that grave.

Paul Andrews, as he watched Zoleeta, with her

husband take their departure, lifted his eyes heavenward and exclaimed, "Harold, dear brother, I have
been loyal to the trust!"

Lord Blankleigh was well satisfied with the reception of his wife by his mother and sisters. Zoleeta's
wonderful beauty was the topic everywhere. Her
jewels were the most rare and costly, her gowns
were wonderful creations of art.

One day Lord Blankleigh laughingly asked his
mother how she liked her Yankee daughter. Her
face flushed red, but she answered unhesitatingly,
"My son, oh, my son, I am pleased! You have made
me so happy!" adding, "I never saw such wonderful beauty and grace combined. You are indeed
blessed."

Two years later when she held her little grand-
son she was very proud and was doing her best to
spoil him. The child grew very much like his father.
His grandmother was very much pleased and relieved of much anxiety for she was fearful that he
might show traits of his mother's colored ancestors,
for it must be remembered that both Zoleeta and
her uncle refused to listen to Lord Blankleigh's plea
that she become his wife unless his mother was made
acquainted with all the facts concerning her parentage.

There had, of course, been a stormy scene between
mother and son. She had threatened to disown him,
his sisters told him disdainfully what they thought
of his intended wife and her people. Finally he had
left his royal home after telling his mother that
he would never return until she would welcome his

wife as a daughter. She received many letters from him, always answering promptly, begging him to come home, but he was firm in his decision and remained away. Many times that proud gray head was bowed with grief at the continued absence of her only son. Finally, when she could endure it no longer she sent for him, telling him that for his sake she would welcome his wife.

Needless to say, Lord Blankleigh hastened to his mother.

One day when little Allen was about three years old a very dear friend of Zoleeta's called in her carriage to take her to a great missionary lecture. Lady Blankleigh went and was surprised when the speaker spoke of the semi-civilized, ignorant negroes who lived in the southern part of the United States of America. There were times her face flushed and then paled as she listened to the exaggerated picture drawn of that race of people from which she descended. She knew, of course, there were many ignorant negroes in the South and there were many others that were a credit to the race and the community in which they resided.

Lady Blankleigh returned home in a very serious mood. That night at dinner a friend of Lord Blankleigh dined with them. As he had been to the lecture he spoke of the degradation that existed among the negroes of the United States of America and expressed his intention of giving a liberal donation to help the cause, and further expressed his surprise that such conditions still existed among such broad-minded citizens that comprised the States.

Our heroine entered into the discussion without the least embarrassment. Her husband made several ineffectual attempts to change the subject but his wife, he noticed, seemed not only anxious to continue the subject, but there was a smile on her face and a beautiful light shone in her eyes.

CHAPTER XIII.

LADY BLANKLEIGH'S MISSIONS.

Several days had passed and Lady Blankleigh seemed as happy as ever, yet there were times that there was a shadow on that beautiful face. One day she entered the room where her husband sat smoking. He immediately arose, removing the cigar from his mouth. She insisted that he finish it. He hesitated to do so, however, until she assured him she came to have a talk with him on a very important subject and refused to begin the conversation until he had resumed his smoking.

They sat in silence for a short while. She seemed to be thinking very seriously, finally she said, "My husband, what I have to say to you may surprise you. I hope you will grant the request that I shall make."

He looked into her serious face with a smile on his handsome countenance, saying, "My dear wife, why so serious? I promise to grant whatever you ask. Have I ever refused you anything at your first request?"

Zoleeta replied, "That is true, as you have anticipated my every wish and have left nothing to be
desired," but smiling, said, "let me warn you not
to make rash promises. You remember the day I
went to the missionary lecture and the discussion
that followed here in our home? It has impressed me more than I can tell. Those missionaries are wrong and while I do not pose as a missionary or a reformer, I feel that there is much good that
I could do for those negroes who have been so unjustly dealt with."

Lord Blankleigh only laughed and said, "My dear
wife, you almost frightened me with your serious
face. My dear, do not hesitate to subscribe any
amount that you wish. I am proud that you possess
such a warm, true heart. Shall I write you out a
check? Do not hesitate. If you wish to build schoolhouses or churches, do so, and spare no expense."

At those words Lady Blandleigh arose, went to
her husband, placing one hand upon his arm and
said, "It is not money I need. It is not only churches
and schoolhouses that I was thinking of. It is to
return to the States from which I came and which
my ancestors were held in bondage."

"But my dear wife, we cannot go now. My mother's health is failing, she has never been the same
since my father and brother perished in the ship-
wreck. We can, as I say, send whatever help is
needed."

She replied, "My husband, you do not understand.
I do not wish to leave your mother in her loneliness.
I thought that I would go and take little Allen with

me and you could often visit us and when our boy
is old enough, we will place him in some university,
until then, I shall keep him under my care with the
best tutors.''

When the full meaning of her words fell on her
husband's ears he was speechless with surprise and
fear. He felt that she had suddenly become bereft
of her senses. Clasping her to his bosom, he said,
''Darling, you do not know what you are saying.
I cannot part with my wife and child, even for a
short while. I glean from your remarks that it may
be for months or perhaps years. No! No! My dear
wife, it is not to be thought of!''

She replied, ''My husband, my heart is set upon
this mission. Do you not see those missionaries are
all wrong? To be helpful to one you must know
the cause of the trouble before you can help them.
Just as a physician must know the cause and nature
of a disease before he can successfully cure his patient and to know how to be helpful to any race
of people and lead them to the goal of their earthly
ambition, to earthly success, you must first find the
cause that retards his footsteps that will in the end
lead him to the eternal heights.''

''How blind our most learned men and women are.
I will admit there is much to be done for the uplift
of the colored people, but we must first educate the
hearts of the Southern whites before we can ever
hope to successfully educate the negro's brain. To
uplift that race of people, despised and mistreated
because their skin is black, we must first change
the attitude of the Southern whites and the calm

indifference of the prejudiced Northerner. In fact, both the North and the South must be made to see that it is their duty to protect the colored man and his rights as citizens of the great United States of America. As it is the colored man feels that he has scant protection under the flag he fought and died for. He feels that every man's hand is against him and his slowly awakening intellect causes him to instinctively feel that there is no place in this beautiful world where he is welcome."

"But, Zoleeta, do you not see that this separation from you and my son would break my heart, and think of the surroundings even under a tutor. He is apt to pick up habits and associates that would be detrimental to his future as my son and heir."

"But, my husband, I promise that just as soon as he arrives at the age for university training you shall superintend it and we will often see each other."

Lord Blankleigh saw that she was determined to carry her point. It was a new side of her character. He did not think with her lovely disposition that she would be so firm, and he grew somewhat stern when he told her that he would never consent.

Zoleeta replied, "I am sorry you withhold your consent, but I feel that it is my duty to go and I must not shirk it, I shall arrange to leave in a fortnight."

Lord Blankleigh said, "My wife, let us have no more of this talk. I positively forbid you to go."

Zoleeta replied, "My Lord, I shall carry out my arrangements to leave in a fortnight."

With those words she left the room, leaving Lord Blankleigh alone with giref and despair. Thus we see the first cloud between our heroine and her husband.

The two weeks had rolled swiftly by. All during the days of preparation Zoleeta, although outwardly calm, was deeply affected by the coming separation from her husband whom she loved most dearly. There was a reserve between husband and wife that remained unbroken. A gloom settled over the once happy home. In the privacy of her room, Lady Blankleigh shed many tears, yet never once did she think of relinquishing her journey and the work she had planned. She felt that it was the hearts of the Southern whites that she wanted to reach and her efforts should be directed along that line. Before the light of intelligence can shed its rays in the black man's brain, the white man must be made to see that his inhumanity to a weak race of people can never lift him above the degrading habits formed by the heel of oppression, crushing out all rights as a human being, much less a citizen. The white man must be made to feel that his attitude towards the negro has been his undoing. Oh, if her husband could only see how the poor colored people had been subjected to all kinds of humiliation, he surely would not oppose her.

She arose to go to him in one last plea. Just then there was a rap on the door and she was pleased to see her husband enter, but one look at that cold, determined face showed her how useless any further appeal was. However, she gave him a loving welcome, but received no response from her caress as he received her kiss. She assured him that she would always teach her boy to love and honor his father and she would write him letters of his progress.

Zoleeta had not noticed her husband's face as he entered and was surprised at the shock she received when he told her that she was not to take her son; that he was to remain with him and his grandmother and with the nurses. That he would have all the care and consideration that she could have bestowed on him. Zoleeta for a moment was unable to utter a word, then with a very white face, said, "Surely, my husband, you will not deprive me of my son? I am leaving your mother her son? Oh, my dear husband, do not deprive me of my child? Let me have him a little while to comfort me when I am far away from you."

For answer he only said, "If you go, you go alone. We part forever."

Zoleeta replied, "Oh, no, take back those cruel words!"

Her husband only repeated, "You have voluntarily given up husband and child, I bow to your decision. The carriage will be at the door at five o'clock, the hour that you told me you would leave."

With tears streaming from her eyes, she cried: "Oh, where is my child—let me kiss him good-bye."

But her husband replied: "You kissed him the last time as he lay in his little bed last night. Accompanied by his nurses, he was taken away for a few days as I wanted to spare you the parting grief."

At those words, Lady Blankleigh seemed suddenly turned to stone, as she looked for one instant on the face of the man she loved so well; then without another word, almost in a condition of collapse, she turned and left the room—a few hours later, the house.

Standing on the deck of the steamer with eyes dimmed with tears Lady Blankleigh did not see her husband in the crowd who had come to take a last look on the face of his beautiful wife, who seemed to have grown angelic in her beauty, subdued with sorrow. He stretched forth his arms in one last silent appeal as the vessel was slowly steaming out into the ocean.

Zoleeta's voyage was without incident. She arrived safely at her destination and was soon comfortably settled. She won many friends. She went about making herself acquainted with the situation, and soon had many of the influential women co-operating with her. It was not long before there was a notable change in conditions. Of course, it required time, but the change was perceptible. She was dearly beloved by all and there were many surmises why this beautiful, intellectual and gifted woman should spend her money and time among them. She did not shun the lowly, neither the white or colored, yet it seemed that she sought companionship among the wealthy and influential whites and the middle class as well.

She often spoke at open air meetings when it was impossible to get a church or hall that would hold the people, so great was their desire to hear her

logical talk on the cause of degradation among the
colored people and the injustice done them. She did
not explain that she thought all acts of injustice were
planned or premeditated for she was sure that some
of the wrong done the Southern negro was uninten-
tional. First, they claimed that the negro was shift-
less and dishonest. Granting the last has a sem-
blance of truth, there was a possible cause. Sometimes they had scarcely enough to feed themselves
and families and were not paid living wages. The
natural result was that they got a habit of helping
themselves, which we all know is wrong. Again, she
said, "I have seen white ruffians walk up and deliberately kick a colored man off the sidewalk if he did
not step aside quickly, when their wives or daughters
came along, and I have been told that wives, sisters
and sweethears of the black men were meanly insulted in the presence of their male relatives or
friends who, if they dared to raise their hand or
voice to protect them, were beaten, clubbed or shot
by those ruffians, who boastfully claimed that they
had shot and killed a vicious negro desperado.

The Southern press lauds them as heroes. The
ministers in the pulpit ask their congregations to
pray for the degraded race of negroes. It is this
class of people that I appeal to, it is the injustice
from the press and platform that makes the negro
feel that every man's hand is against him.

We have neither desire nor inclination to encourage lawlessness to either white or black, but every
broad-minded person will admit that the colored man
has a serious cause for grievance. Needless to say

that after those meetings adjourned there were many men and women who went home and seriously thought over the problem. The result was that there was more benefit from those lectures to the whites. She reminded them that they were the ones who gave the negro his first lesson in dishonesty, for did not they steal from him his country, home and fireside, bring him to a strange country among strange people, unable to speak intelligible dialect to voice his protestations, and could they expect to uplift him morally when by virtue of ownership and force, if necessary, the negro sees his wife, daughter, sweetheart, and ofttimes mother, compelled to submit to shame and dishonor?

When she spoke of the wrongs done the Southern negro, she felt that some very plain talk was necessary to make her meaning clear. At those meetings she requested that no colored persons be admitted for fear they might take advantage of her defense of them to commit unlawful acts. She also called special meetings where the whites were excluded.

Year after year she sacrificed home, husband and child. She crucified herself on the altar of duty for the betterment of her mother's people. When she first took up her self-imposed task, she wrote many letters to her husband, but received no reply. It seems that he had made his word good and cast her off forever. Tonight she sat longer than usual looking at the picture she loved so well. She no longer pictured her boy as a prattling, romping child, for it has now been eighteen years since she left her husband's home. Her boy is now a young man of twenty-one years. She wondered if he looked like his father. She kept herself posted all about her husband and son and knew that her boy had graduated with honors and was at home with his father and the idol of his gray-haired grandmother. In justice let us say that Lord Blankleigh's mother often prevailed upon him to go and bring his wife home, for she had taken a wonderful liking to her beautiful and imperial daughter-in-law.

Zoleeta had grown more beautiful in her mature years and no one ever passed her without turning to look at that queenly woman. There was one thing that she never did, that was neglect her personal appearance. She was always faultlessly dressed. No one ever took her for anything but what she really was,—a perfect lady.

It was shortly after Lady Blankleigh had taken up her abode in the South, after her return from England, that she realized that she would become a mother again. At first she was filled with pleasure to think that she would have someone to lavish her affections upon in her self-imposed exile. Her first impulse was to send her husband the glad news, then her face grew pale for fear that she might be forced to give up her little one, but she thought it was her duty to do so. She did not mention it in her first letter, and as she received no reply from the others, she let the matter drift as it would for the present. She had surrounded herself with every comfort and luxury, with a competent maid and nurse. Strange to say, she had no thought of returning to her English home. If she thought of doing so, she realized that it might be months, perhaps years, before she could answer the call of her mother's people and return and lift up her voice for their interest. However, she decided there should be no cause for future regrets. She at once had her little daughter's birth recorded, giving its father's name and rank and present abode, signed by proper witnesses.

The child at an early age gave evidence of great beauty, but more like her father, with her auburn hair with a tinge of gold that made her beauty beyond description. Her face was wonderfully fair and she had violet eyes that at times seemed almost black. Artists tried in vain to sketch her, but only once did her mother consent. He seemed to catch each line and curve, even the smiling eyes, so much like her father's, seemed to be laughing.

"Mamma," she said one day, "do you like my picture? You are always looking at it," going to her mother and placing her arms around her neck. Her mother fondly kissed her, and said, "Yes, darling, I was only thinking that it is all I will have to console me when you are away at school, for you know, pet, it will only be one short week before I place you in the best school in Boston."

"Oh, mamma," she replied, "I wish I might remain with you." For a moment both were silent, when Zoleeta said, "Daughter, some day your position will be far different from this, and I want you to be able to fill it with dignity and culture." For a moment both remained silent, then her daughter asked, "Mamma, shall I like my father and brother?"

Her mother replied: "Oh, daughter! my daughter,

have I not always told you that your father was
a king among men? That he is the soul of honor,
and that you must love him dearly? You must remember he has been deprived of you all your sweet
young life, so you must make it up to him in the
future by your loving devotion." Continuing, she
said: "Dear, you know on your return from school,
I shall take you to England to your father. As to
your liking your brother, that fact alone should make
him very dear to you."

Her daughter replied: "Mamma, why not take me
there now? I have had the best private teachers, I
have learned the languages and besides I do not want
to go and leave you alone."

Zoleeta laughingly said: "All you say is true, but
there is always something else worth learning. It
will only be for one year and it will seem doubly long
for me as it will be for you with your laughing, care-
free schoolmates." Clasping her daughter in her
arms, she said, "Oh, Agnes, my daughter. I hope you
may always be happy."

After Zoleeta returned from the North where she
had placed her daughter in school, she did not rest
in her labor as there was much to do before leaving
for her husband's home in England. She felt it
was her duty to see that her husband and children
be united. She grew sad at times when she thought
it not improbable that her husband might refuse to
receive her, but she would no longer deprive him of
his daughter. She had given Agnes only the most
meager information about her absence from her husband, home and her son. Somehow, she seemed fear-

ful that her daughter might not approve of the course
her mother had taken. There were times when she
felt that Agnes was not at all concerned about the
existing conditions in the South. Zoleeta did not
wonder much that, as she had been careful that
her daughter should see the most beautiful things of
life. She always tried to make her evenings bright
and happy and forget much of the sadness she saw
around her from time to time, so when she went to
bed and to sleep her last thought would be happy
ones, and a smile would linger on her face.

Agnes had startled her mother when discussing the
beauty of a Southern girl who was at least two-thirds
white, by saying, ''Mamma, the girl is quite pretty,
but I believe I would rather be dead than to know
I had one drop of negro blood in my veins.'' Drawing herself up to her full height, she exclaimed,
''Mamma, dear mamma, are you not glad, too?''

Zoleeta's face paled for a moment and wondered
how her daughter had become possessed of such a
thought. The only conclusion that she could arrive
at was traceable through the Southern blood inherited from her Southern ancestors. Her mother replied, ''Agnes, it pains me to hear you talk so. The
colored people are not responsible for the fact that
they are unfortunately collored. It seems terrible to
criticize them.''

Agnes replied: ''Of course, mamma, I feel sorry
and do all I can to help them, but I am not one of
them and connot express a sentiment I do not feel.''

Agnes had been back from school some time. She
was nearly eighteen years old. A more beautiful

girl was hard to find. One day she came laughingly into the room where her mother sat gazing at the picture of her husband and placing her hands over her mother's eyes, gently taking the picture from her hand, and said: "Mamma, when will you take me to see my father?" Her mother replied: "We will start very soon, my dear. Agnes, your brother is now twenty-one years old. I was just wondering if he were anxious to see his mother. Yes, we will prepare to go in a fortnight, at least." A spasm of pain gripped Zoleeta's heart as she asked herself the question: "Have I lingered too long?" Agnes danced around the room, exclaiming, "Oh, I am so happy!"

Her mother replied: "I hope you may always be happy. You have a bright future before you."

Although Zoleeta had located in the State of Georgia, she was often away for days presiding at meetings. Many times principal speaker at those gatherings. She had on one occasion been sent for in Texas. She found the most deplorable conditions existing, the colored people seemed dull and stupid and were often brutally treated by their white employers until there was noticed a subdued hatred, a smoldering fire that was likely to break out at any time. Zoleeta found much to do. The white population did not take very kindly to her advent in their midst and scoffed at her teachings, yet she persevered and felt very much encouraged. She noticed night after night a very distinguished looking gentleman, possibly between forty-five and fifty years of age, always accompanied by a young man, although

somewhat taller than the elder man, looked as if they
might be father and son. She could not tell why, but
she always felt a sense of security in the presence of
those two. She often found herself looking at the
younger man as if trying to remember who he looked
like, but she could not settle the puzzling question.
The elder man did not resemble anyone that she
could remember that she had ever seen; he wore a
luxuriant growth of beard, had a fine shaped head.
When he walked around or moved about the puzzled
look would deepen on her face; yet she was satisfied
that she had not seen him before. They were both
evidently men of high education; she learned they
were doing excellent work among the colored people.
She also found out for years the elder gentleman had
been laboring to uplift the race of people so unjustly
discrimnated against there and in the surrounding
country as well. She learned that the elder gentleman had been joined by the younger man about two
years previous. They were inseparable.

Zoleeta stayed there many weeks, but whether she
was purposely avoided or circumstances had prevented her from conversing with father and son,
she did not know. She attributed her failure to do
so to be simply circumstantial, for there was no reason to think otherwise, as she had been treated with
the utmost deference by them when they chanced to
meet.

When she left that part of the country, she found
her interest in the couple was not decreasing and
made up her mind that if she ever returned there,
she would try to learn something of them.

One night as Lord Blankleigh sat is his home looking at the picture of his beautiful wife hanging on
the wall, there were lines on his face that were not
there when his wife was by his side. He loved her
as dearly as ever, but he could not forget how she
had defied him and left him and her boy of her own
accord. He had told her it was forever, but his heart
continually cied out to her. Finally he held out his
hands to that silent picture, and said: "My wife, oh,
my dear wife! If I could only see you once more."
His head dropped on his breast and a troubled sigh
escaped his lips. There was a slight touch on his
shoulder, and on looking up, he beheld his son.

"Father," he said, "tell me of my mother. Why she
is not here? I remember when I was quite young
I asked for my mother. You told me when I was
older you would tell me all about her. Again, when
I asked you, you replied when I reached manhood
you would tell me all. Father, look at me," he said.
"I am twenty-one years old today."

Lord Blankleigh started up, and exclaimed: "Is it
possible?" He looked long and earnestly at his son.
He was a fine looking young man, with his father's
pleasing smile and his mother's fine eyes. "Father,"
he said, "grandmother has not forgotten and has
prepared a little feast. Come, she is waiting." The
father took the arm of his son, found dinner ready to
be served. After dinner Lord Blankleigh's mother
retired very soon to her room. She was now getting
very feeble. Father and son were silent for some
moments and Allen again reminded his father, and
said: "On this day you promised to tell me why

my mother is living apart from us. Was she un-
faithful?"

At those words Lord Blankleigh was on his feet in
a second and exclaimed: "My son, if any other man
had asked me that question, I would have knocked
him down. My boy, your mother was the purest
woman that ever lived and had I not been a brute, I
would have gone to her years ago. My son, listen
while I tell you of my cruelty to her."

"Oh, father, do not say that! You, the kindest of
fathers, could not be cruel. You do yourself an injustice."

His father interrupted him, and said: "I will tell
you all and you can be my judge."

He then told his son of his mother's wish to go to
the States to use her influence to better the condition
of the American negro and how he forbade her to go,
Seeing that his opposition failed, "I had sent you,
her baby boy, away so she could not take you, although she pleaded hard, telling me that she would
give you to me a few years later. I told her that if she
went, it should be forever. I have never seen her
since, nor have I ever written to her, although she
wrote to me on several occasions."

"Fathter, oh, father, surely you did not treat my
mother in such a manner? Father, you tell me that
she was denied one last look at me, her baby, that
you have never answered her letters? Oh, father,
that was cruel."

"I know, I know, my dear boy, but do not reproach me, for I am filled with remorse; but there
are reasons that you know not of."

"Father, I think it was a noble sacrifice to go among those people and teach them. Will you let me read those letters? You promised me I should, but if you would rather not, I shall not feel offended; such correspondence may be sacred to your eyes alone."

"No, my son, there is also one for you. Read them all. Here are also some newspaper clippings concerning her work. I shall take a walk in the garden for awhile; in the meantime, you can read them carefully, but my boy, do not judge me too harshly."

Lord Blankleigh had finished his stroll, was standing on the balcony when his son came out. Slipping his arm through that of his father's, he calmly said: "Father, I shall leave at once for the United States. I am going to my mother."

"Oh, my boy, my boy! Do not leave me."

Allen replied: "Father, you have your mother, have had her all those years. My mother has been deprived of her son."

The father replied: "My son, there is something that I did not tell you, that was one of my main reasons for keeping you with me. Do not ask me; it is a secret that rests between your mother and me, and must be buried with us."

His son replied: "Father, it is also now my secret. In one of those letters my mother said: 'It is is not necessary for our boy to know that his mother descended from the race of slaves and that her mother and our boy's grandmother were sold on the auction block. Do not tell him this, he need not know. I am doing much to better the condition of the poor ex-slave which I am so closely identified with.' "

The father exclaimed: "Oh,   y son, have I blundered? Did I give you that letter? I had not intended to do so. I cannot forgive myself. My son, I have guarded the secret so carefully that you might never know."

"Father, there is nothing to forgive. I am proud of my mother and I am going to her."

In the morning when his grandmother learned that he was going to his mother, she clung to his neck and cried. He had not seen his father since early morning. Now as the hour of departure drew ner, he started out to find him, when his father walked into the room, dressed in a neat traveling suit. His son grasped his father's hand, saying: "Father, it is so good of you to see me off. Will you not send a kind word to my mother? Just think what it will mean to her. I am sure that she still loves you."

"No, my son, do not ask me."

Looking into his father's face again, he could not help remarking, "Father, you look ten years younger. I wish I had a late picture of you to take to my mother, and I am sorry that after all those years, you have no message to send her."

Placing his hand on his son's arm, he said: "My son, I shall take the message myself; I am going to my wife. Boy, do you think she will forgive me?"

"Oh, yes, father, and I am so happy."

CHAPTER XIV.

REUNITED.

One evening as Zoleeta was in her room she had been reading, but now she was sitting with her book lying closed on her lap and her eyes had a faraway look in them, when a visitor was announced. She came at once to the parlor, which was richly furnished. She saw a tall, handsome young man standing in the room. Thinking it was one of the young men who had been interested in her work, she went forward with a bright smile of welcome. She was startled at the resemblance to somsone, but before she could utter a word, the young man came swiftly forward, extending his hands, exclaiming. "My mother, oh, my mother!"

Then she knew the resemblance. For a moment she could not speak; then her first words were: "My son, oh, my son! I have prayed for this, but, oh, Allen, tell me quick, where is your father? Can he forgive me?"

"Mother, there is nothing to forgive. Father loves you and awaits your pardon."

"Oh, my son, I now see that I should never have given up home, husband and son; but, my boy, I have done good."

"I know it is so, mother, for we have read of you in the paper. Mother, would you welcome father if he should come to you?"

"Oh, my son, I know joy seldom ever kills, but, oh,

I do not think my heart could contain so much happiness. No, it would not kil me, but after eighteen years, I know that he is now reconciled to our separation.''

Hearing a footfall, she slightly turned her head to see the outstretched arms of her husband as he approached her. She turned very white and seemed about to fall, when her son gently placed his arms around her waist as he heard her exclaim, ''My dear husband,'' and when he saw his father kneel at his mother's feet he quietly left the room.

Finally Lord Blankleigh raised his head, and said: ''My darling wife, can you ever forgive me? I feel that I can never forgive myself.''

Rising to his feet, clasping his wife in his arms, he exclaimed: ''Henceforth your people shall be my people, and your God my God; whither thou goest, I will go.''

Just then Agnes came in carrying a bunch of roses, saying: ''See, mamma, what I have brought you.''

Just then she saw that her mother had a visitor and seemed deeply agitated. It had been Zoleeta's intention to quietly break the news to her husband that he had a daughter as well as a son, but at this unlooked for incident she had grown deathly pale. Her daughter noticing this, sprang to her mother's side as if to protect her, at the same time looking resentfully at the man as being the cause of her mother's deep agitation, but something in that face called up a memory of someone she thought she had seen. For a moment she stood uncertain, then all at once, she remembered the picture of her father that he reminded her of. Like a flash she realized that she was in his presence.

Up to this time neither of her parents had spoken a word. Her father had recoiled a step or two as his daughter was about to greet him. Seeing the action she stepped back and placed her arms around her mother. Although overcome with sorrow and uncertainty, her father could not help but realize that those two who stood before him were the most beautiful women he had ever seen.

Zoleeta with her jet black hair, and Agnes with her auburn locks which hung upon her shoulders, but the beauty which they represented did not lift the doubt of uncertainty from his face. Finally Zoleeta took her daughter by the hand and led her to her father, saying: "My husband, this is your daughter."

Agnes, stretching out her hands to her father, exclaimed, "Oh, papa, have you no love in your heart for me?" and for a moment seemed deeply grieved. One glance, however, was sufficient for the father, and he was convinced that he was the proud father of this surpassingly beautiful girl.

He took a step forward and Agnes was soon clasped in her father's arms. Presently they were conscious of someone else entering the room. There stood Allen, Agnes' brother. He was introduced to his sister. At first he was incredulous and asked why he had never been told he had a sister. Finally Lord Blankleigh told his son to take his sister for a walk. After they had gone he placed his arms around his wife and said: "Again, dear wife, I must beg your pardon for my seeming doubt and I fear my incredulity is beyond pardon.''

Zoleeta replied: "My dear husband, my only excuse for not informing you of having a daughter was, I had received no reply from my letters and I never doubted that your attitude towards me was the same, and oh, my dear husband, Agnes has been such a comfort to me and I was preparing to take her to you and had commenced to pack already.''

Kissing his beautiful wife again and again, he exclaimed: "Oh, my heart cannot contain all of my happiness! Oh, my dear wife, I do not deserve to be so happy. I cannot tell you how proud I was of your success and when I read in the papers and magazines of your glorious work, I was indeed proud of you.''

Husband and wife talked long and Zoleeta told her husband of their daughter's aversion to the negro race, and thought for the present not to tell her, for she never had a sorrow only being away from you and her brother. Both agreed to the proposition and felt that they must warn their son.

A couple of evenings later, word was brought to Zoleeta that a couple of gentlemen wished to see her. Thinking it possible that it was someone interested in her work, and who had heard of her expected departure and wanted to see her before she left, she immediately had them shown in. She was much surprised to see the gentleman and his son who had been of so much interest to her while in Texas some months before. She greeted them most cordially and was not left in suspense long. The elder gentleman said: "Lady Blankleigh, I see you do not remember me." Not pausing for a reply, he said, "I am Guy Randolph, and this is my son, Kenneth."

For one moment Zoleeta felt as if the room was spinning around. She was incapable of speech but warmly extended her hands to both father and son. She hastily summoned her reunited family to welcome the newcomers and cousin as well. The young folks greeted each other most cordially. After a few moments' conversation, at a suggestion from Lady Blankleigh, Allen and his sister accompanied by Kenneth went out on the balcony to get better acquainted.

After they had left the room Guy Randolph briefly explained his presence in the South, the land of his birth. He said that after the departure of his wife, he secured a good competent nurse and housekeeper. He had remained some time longer in his home, hoping that his wife would return. Seeing that she did not, he left the place that reminded him of her. When the boy was old enough he placed him in college. "I came South and all the time that he was in college, I was laboring with my mother's people. I had heard so much of your wonderful success that I often wanted to see you, but remembered I did not know that it was you, as everyone knew you as Mrs. Blank."

Zoleeta replied: "I did not use either my title or full name for fear of embarrassing my husband."

Guy replied: "Imagine my surprise when I saw you and felt for reasons of your own that you preferred not to be known as Lady Blankleigh. And now that you have told me your reason, I really admire you for the consideration that you have shown to your loved ones. I learned through the Society Journal while you were in England that you had a son and heir, but was very much surprised tonight to find that you are the mother of a daughter as well. Oh, Zoleeta, you must be proud of your children. Your daughter is most beautiful, indeed.''

A happy smile came on Lady Blankleigh's face to hear her children spoken of so nicely.

Continuing, Guy said: ''I saw you many times, as I attended all your meetings you held while in our town in the State of Texas. I did not make myself known for fear of embarrassing you, but when I read in the paper that you would soon leave for your home in England, I felt that I could no longer endure the suspense for I longed to hear some news of my wife.''

Zoleeta realized that Guy still loved his wayward wife. She said: ''Catherine left her uncle's home to join you and her baby boy long before I became the bride of Lord Blankleigh, hoping that you were still there. She was very penitent and hoped for your forgiveness. Oh, Guy, why not cable at once? Catherine wrote and told uncle that she had taken rooms close to her old home and would wait for her husband for years, if need be.''

Guy had turned pale, as he exclaimed: ''Can it be true?'' He remembered all the dreary dismal years that he had been parted from his wife. He sighed deeply many times. They talked long and earnestly, and when they parted it was agreed they should all sail on the same vessel.

Guy Randolph and son soon left, promising to see them the next day.

That night before they retired, Kenneth said to his father: "Father, you promised me that some day you would fully explain why my mother is not with us. I have hesitated to ask you before for fear the subject was a painful one to you and should not speak of it now, only you have arranged to return with Lady Blankleigh. I have neither the right or the inclination to interfere with any individual plans that you might make for yourself, but as I am included without my consent to those plans, I feel that I must speak. You remember when you told me once that my mother in her highly nervous state could not endure the presence of her child. There must have been a cause, if she objected to me then, she may do so again. Under those circumstances, I cannot go to my mother, as much as I would like to see her. I often gaze at her picture that you gave me. She must have been very beautiful." He ceased speaking for a moment.

His father sat with bowed head. He felt that the time he dreaded had come. He felt that he could no longer put off telling his son the truth, but would tell it in such a manner that the son would still respect, if not love the mother who had abandoned him when an infant in her arms. Kenneth Randolph was a magnificent speciman of young manhood. He was an athlete in the truest sense of the word. As the father's gaze lingered on his son, his bosom swelled with pride, for well did he know that any mother would feel blessed with such a son, and felt that when he and his wife were reunited, he would wish for no greater earthly happiness; but at his son's words a spasm of pain gripped his heart. He asked himself what, after all, if Kenneth should refuse to accompany him home after hearing the history of his father and mother's disagreement. Seeing that his son was waiting for him to speak, he told him that his mother had accused him of deceiving her. "The basis of the deception was that after our marriage I learned of my mother's humble birth, while my wife boasted of the superior blood of her parents, and fearing that you might inherit inferior blood through my ancestors, therefore, she left you to comfort me so I would not be alone, and returned to her people."

The son replied: "But, father, is one to be despised because he is of humble origin? Do not be afraid to tell me all, I see that you are withholding something from me."

Guy Randolph was very pale when he arose to his feet. Placing his hands on the younger man's arm, he said: "My son, oh, my son! what more can I tell you?" and his head hung on his bosom.

Kenneth said: "Father, forgive me if I seemed persistent. It seems to me there must be other and graver reasons for a mother to desert her babe than the reason that you have given me, and I am sorry that I have caused you so much anguish." Grasping his father by the hand, he said: "Father, I shall persist no longer. We shall not speak of this again. You have been the best of fathers to me and I shall devote the rest of my life to make you happy, and if your wife is waiting for you as Lady Blankleigh told you tonight, then by all means, go to her, and I shall remain here."

At those words, his father exclaimed: "My son, oh, my son, I could not go to your mother without you after all those years of weary waiting."

Father and son remained silent although each one deeply agitated, seemed to be in serious thought. Each seemed to have been fighting a battle and simultaneously won.

Finally Kenneth said: "Father, I will go to my mother," and Guy Randolph exclaimed, "God bless you, my son Kenneth, I will not let you go until I tell you all, and oh, my boy, do not condemn me for you remember I told you that not until I was married to my wife did I learn the facts concerning my ancestors."

And feeling that he was throwing off a burden, he proudly threw back his head, while a beautiful smile lit up his features, saying, "My son, I do not know why it was that I have hesitated to tell what you have asked me. I will hesitate no longer. My boy, my ancestors descended from the Ethiopian race. My mother was a slave. I have nothing to be ashamed of, but that is why my wife left me. I gave up my art to work among my mother's people. Now, my boy, I lay no commands on you. You are of age to choose for yourself your life's work and whatever it may be, you have my blessings."

Up to this time his son had not the remotest idea that he was contaminated with the blood of the despised race of negroes of the South. For one moment he stood appalled. His father went to him, gently touched him on the arm, saying: "Son, it is late, make no rash decision tonight; tomorrow will do."

He turned to leave the room, but was stopped by his son, saying: "Father, for your sake I will go to my mother, but will not promise to remain. I shall return and continue the work among our people. You know I have been admitted to the bar and I feel that the negroes of the South are often in need of legal defense which they are unable to secure for the want of money." Gazing fondly at his father, he resumed, "Your unbounded liberality to me has not made the financial part an issue for me to consider."

Guy Randolph looked as if there was something else he wanted to say, but hesitated to do so. Finally Kennth said: "Father, I am listening."

Whereupon his father said: "My son, will you try to love your mother? I have forgiven her; will you not do so, too?"

"Father," he said, "I will respect my mother; more than that I cannot promise. Remember, she deserted me when a baby in her arms and right here in the South I have seen negro mothers clinging to their infants, seemingly defying death to even separate them; yet my mother willfully and willingly deserted me." Laughingly he remarked to his father, "I suppose I must have my share of conceit, for I do not think that I was displeasing to the eye. Now, father, good-night, or morning, rather, for it is now morning, and we must have a few hours to rest as we have a busy day before us."

We will now follow Mr. Randolph across to his

former home in Italy. They had a pleasant voyage, but to Guy it seemed as if the vessel would never reach port. Finally they arrived and as he reached the vicinity in which he had resided, he was visibly agitated. His son also appeared agitated, but with a tinge of curiosity that, owing to his youth, made his agitation less serious, yet he was anxious to see the mother, who had deserted him because some of his ancestors were colored. He undoubtedly possessed more spirit than his father, presumably inherited from his mother, and was determined to let his mother see that he was not going to fall into the arms that had spurned him when an infant.

Guy Randolph felt how ashamed Catherine would feel when she remembered she had said that she would never willingly look either upon his face again or his negro child. He pictured her bitter regret of all these years that she had been deprived of her husband and her manly son, but he magnanimously made up his mind that he would not reproach his wife or allow her to reproach herself. He resolved to bury the past, and that when Kenneth returned to the United States, to take up his life's work, that there would be nothing to mar his departure. They stopped at a nearby hotel and learned that a Mrs. Randolph had resided there a number of years, but for the last two years had been living in a beautiful cottage just around the corner.

Husband and son hastened there. On making inquiries they were overjoyed to find that she was still there, for Guy had felt a peculiar dread that he could not understand. He was afraid that she might have gone and he would not be able to trace her. A sweet little gray haired woman seemed very glad when she found out who the travelers were, and said: ''Oh, sir, she talked of you to the last and wanted to see her baby boy, but it was not to be. She passed away within the hour.''

When the full meaning of the words fell on Guy Randolph's ears, he would have fallen to the floor had it not been for the strong arm of his son.

''We learned that his wife had always said that he would come. She kept her faith till the very last. No one knew that she was bad off, she just seemed to pine away. She found great comfort in looking on the picture of her husband and regretted that she had none of her baby.''

Guy asked to see his wife alone and when he stood over all that was left of his pretty wife, the hot tears fell fast, as he exclaimed: ''Oh, Catherine, my wife, my wife, you have kept your vow never to look upon my face or that of your son. Little did you think how that vow would be fulfilled.''

He remained some time in the room. Finally Kenneth came in and when he looked upon the pale, sweet face of his mother, he shed genuine tears of regret to think how he had planned to make his mother feel his resentment for her treatment of him and for his father's life wrecked of happiness by her injustice. He knelt beside the casket and for the first time in his life, he called that silent form ''Mother,'' while the tears rolled down his cheeks.

Some weeks later, Guy Randolph and his son paid Lord and Lady Blankleigh a visit, then sailed for the United States, where they took up their abode.

There were many servants in the Blankleigh home that she had left there eighteen years ago. They were overjoyed to learn that Lord Blankleigh was returning home with his wife. They strewed flowers everywhere, and standing there with outstretched arms and silvery white hair, and a smile of welcome on her aristocratic face, stood Lord Blankleigh's mother, and on each side his two sisters, all eager to welcome home Lady Blankleigh, the daughter of an ex-slave, "Mildred Yates."

They were surprised to see that she had brought company. They beheld the most beautiful girl that they had ever seen. Seeing the admiring glances of his mother and sisters and as soon as they were through greeting his wife, Lord Blankleigh took Agnes by the hand and proudly introduced her to his mother and sisters, saying: "This is my daughter, Agnes."

For once in their lives his aristocratic mother and well-bred sisters could find no words to express their surprise and admiration. But every look and feature proclaimed her to be of royal birth. A daughter of the Blankleigh house. They soon, however, recovered their composure, and no one could doubt the genuine warmth of the welcome which Agnes received from her royal kin. Allen laughingly remarked that no one noticed him since his sister had come. But the fond glance that he bestowed on that lovely personage was far from convincing those present that he objected to the attention that was paid his sister. Lord Blankleigh never regretted that he married Zoleeta Andrews, the daughter of an ex-slave.

"FINIS."

SEQUEL TO
BLACK AND WHITE TANGLED THREADS.

Memory's revealing powers turning backward
Over the long vista of receding years,
Sometimes brings smiles, oft-times tears;
Nothing in this world can last,
Only memory, ever revealing the unforgetable past.

KENNETH

CHAPTER I.

It was the dawning of a beautiful September morning. All Nature seemed to be rejoicing, yet on the awakening of this bright autumn day, many hearts were saddened.

Not far from a small, but well populated village in the state of Kentucky, and not many miles from Frankfort, there had been a terrible railroad disaster. It was 7 o'clock in the morning when the physicians hastily drew on their garments in response to their respective calls to care for the wounded.

The residents in the nearby vicinity opened their doors and worked with the doctors to alleviate the pain of the sufferers. In many instances the only thing that could be done for the sufferer was to receive the last message to some dear ones waiting in vain for their return.

Not far from the wreck was the well-appointed office of Dr. Phillip Grayson, who had many of the victims carried to his office, and who, with the help of his assistant, cared for them. Some were able to leave for their homes unassisted, but there was one case that was most serious. It was that of a young girl about nineteen years of age.

Her hair was of a golden brown and hung in beautiful disorder over her shoulders, framing a face that could not be strictly termed beautiful, but it was one that showed at a glance that the owner was a person of culture, refinement and wealth. Her clothing, although plain, was of the finest quality. Her skin, which was very fair, now appeared unnaturally white. Her forehead was high, almost too high for a girl, yet it did not detract from the otherwise lovely face. If you could have seen her eyes you would have pronounced them the most beautiful feature of the face. They were of that shade of gray that seemed to darken into the shade of a pansy. On her fingers were two costly rings, but there was no inscription on them. In fact, there was nothing to establish her identity by which her friends might be communicated with.

Dr. Grayson worked faithfully over her, but his renowned skill seemed of no avail. It looked as if the fair sufferer would pass into the Great Beyond without even regaining consciousness. The doctor felt very much disturbed as he watched over the stricken girl, so he sent his assistant to the scene of the disaster, hoping to find some clew to her identity.

He was alone, the last of the wounded having departed or having been carried away by friends or relatives. He continued to work over his patient without result. Once he thought he noticed a quivering of an eyelash, but if so, it was so slight that he was not sure and it had not been repeated. As he stood watching and waiting for some change, the 'phone rang. It proved to be a message from his assistant informing him that the lady had been identified, and that her father was on his way to the doctor's office.

As Dr. Grayson was expecting the visitor, he was at once admitted.

"I would like to see the doctor," said the gentleman.

"I am the doctor," replied Dr. Grayson.

For a moment the visitor almost forgot his daughter, so great was his surprise at this unexpected information. And then growing indignant at what he considered an untimely jest, he haughtily drew himself up to his full height and sternly said:

"I wish to see Dr. Grayson, who has been attending my daughter."

"I am Dr. Grayson," calmly replied the doctor, "will you please step this way?"

Upon his reply the doctor was subjected to the most insulting scrutiny. Dr. Grayson was six feet tall, broad shouldered, broad intellectual forehead, dark complexion, so dark that no one could doubt his origin as being that of a direct descendan of the negro race. He had not that mixed blood that is characteristic of the American negro, yet he was a handsome man with piercing black eyes, straight nose, a fine mouth with even white teeth that not even his silky beard could conceal. He had none of the heavy features peculiar to the race with which he was identified. His hair was crisp and wavy and he wore it in a slight pompadour. He was a man of culture and refinement, and, though noted for his geniality, he was not exempt from that quick way of speaking so habitual to professional men. He was a young man, not more than thirty years of age.

Dr. Grayson led the way to his patient, who

showed signs of returning consciousness. Through the doctor's skillful ministrations, he was rewarded by seeing her eyes open. Touching the father on the arm, he motioned him to speak to his daughter as soon as she sufficiently gained consciousness. Seeing her father bending over her, she asked where she was.

"With father, darling," replied the father.

She smiled sweetly but lapsed into unconsciousness once more. Turning to Dr. Grayson the gentleman asked why his daughter had been brought there. His tone was both arrogant and insulting. The doctor, with a twinkle in his eye, unobserved by the visitor, replied with dignity:

"For treatment, sir, and it is only by prompt treatment that she is still alive. She is still in a serious condition."

Mr. Blair, the banker (for so the girls' father proved to be), haughtily replied:

"I shall have my daughter removed at once and placed under the care of my family physician, hence, I shall no longer require your advice."

Dr. Grayson, seeing the banker's attitude toward himself and his determination to remove his daughter, thought that any protest he might make would be in vain, so he refrained from making any.

Mr. Blair, taking a well filled purse from his pocket, asked for his bill.

"I haven't made out a bill, as cases of emergency like this are usually free and I have done no more for your daughter than I would have done for any other human being," responded Dr. Grayson.

Only the anxiety for his daughter prevented the banker from further showing how very distasteful it was to him to have one of the doctor's race administer to his daughter, and as soon as he could get the proper conveyance and attendance, he had his daughter removed to his palatial home, where she was soon under the care of the family physician. Her recovery was very slow. Sometimes her recovery seemed very doubtful but youth is a great factor as a healing power and Alice, in time, was able to sit up and converse.

One day she was talking to her mother when quite unexpectedly she fainted away. It was long before she was revived and her mother becoming alarmed hastily sent for the doctor, but he was out of town. Two other physicians were sent for but they were away on urgent cases and it could not be told just when they would return. The parents knew not what was best to do. Finally Mrs. Blair said: "Let us send for Dr. Grayson."

At first the father refused to have him, but Alice looked so wan and pale that he reluctantly gave his consent. Then, too, he remembered that old Dr. Cowan, the family physician, had said that the doctor who had first handled the case had shown remarkable skill, otherwise Alice would have succumbed to her injuries.

Accordingly Dr. Grayson was sent for. He found the patient in a high fever and it became necessary for him to make repeated calls. Often his face was very serious as his patient continued in a delirious state.

CHAPTER II.

DOCTOR AND PATIENT.

One day, when Dr. Grayson called, he found his patient much improved and felt relieved to think that his services should shortly be dispensed with, as he knew that the banker so desired.

On his next visit the nurse was out and Mrs. Blair was taking a much needed rest, having been assured that all danger had passed. As the doctor stood looking down at the sick girl, lying so quiet, he thought she must be asleep; but on bending over her, he was surprised to see her open her eyes and putting up her arms, ask to be raised. The nurse was no-where to be seen and the doctor felt compelled to assist her. This he did and was again surprised, somewhat uncomfortably so, when she rested her head upon his bosom and clasping her arms around him, assured him that she would always remember him and begged him to think of her sometimes.

Dr. Grayson hastily disengaged her arms from around him, gently lay her back on the pillows, while her face was suffused with blushes. Soon the nurse returned and was informed that Miss Blair was progressing nicely. Dr. Grayson said that he would not call again as he had learned that Dr. Cowan had returned and was sure that he would advise them. He spoke cheerily to his patient, bidding her goodbye. He gave the nurse a cordial parting word and was just departing when Mr. Blair arrived. He scarcely spoke to or noticed the doctor.

Dr. Grayson told Mr. Blair just what he had told the nurse, adding: "Your daughter is doing nicely and if your physician has not returned, I would advise you to take her to the seashore, but under existing circumstances, the matter must rest with you and the superior experience of Dr. Cowan, who has had many years of practice."

Extending his hand to the banker, which was ignored, he expressed a wish for Miss Blair's speedy recovery.

Mr. Blair replied: "I am glad that you realize that there is no further necessity for your coming again and I hope that you will remember this."

Without any further delay Dr. Grayson lifted his hat, entered his car, and was soon whirled out of sight.

CHAPTER III.

DR. GRAYSON AND KENNETH RANDOLPH.

Dr. Grayson had been born and reared in the North. His parents had been thrifty and industrious. Having only one child, they spared no pains in educating him for his chosen profession. He had spent some years abroad, chiefly in Berlin, and had made great progress there, winning notable mention in the medical world. From there he went to London and did himself credit and was often consulted on most important cases.

After five years of study and practice, he returned to his home in the United States with well earned honors, announcing that he would establish himself in the South, as he believed there he would find a much broader field in which to work. He was soon a recognized power in the medical world and was called in consultation by the most eminent physicians and skilled surgeons. In fact, his knowledge was so great that no note was taken of his color, and by his noble bearing and courtesy, he proved that true manhood was not rated by color.

Yet there were times when he met some of his professional brothers in public places that it seemed quite difficult for them to remember him. But there was one who never forgot him. This was Kenneth Randolph, an attorney, and it was through him that Dr. Grayson was called to the home of very poor people to treat a little colored boy who had been almost, if not quite, blinded by a little white lad.

Be it said in justice to the white boy, that the injury to the colored child was not committed maliciously, for he dearly loved the colored boy, who had been his playmate ever since they were babies. The nurse would take Herbert Drake, the wealthy man's son, to see James Taylor, the little colored boy, whose mother was a poor washwoman. At the time of the accident to little James' eyes, the children were about five or six years old. Often when the Drake household was alarmed because of the disappearance of little Herbert, and some one would think to go to poor Mrs. Taylor's, they would find the rich man's son there, perhaps enjoying the plain, but wholesome food cooked in James' humble home. Often the nurse found the little truant unmanageable if he could not take James back to his home with him.

One day the washwoman had been prevailed upon by the nurse to permit James to return home with her. She gave a reluctant consent, saying that she was afraid that he would be in the way. After he had been washed and cleaned, they started for Herbert's home. Little did the mother or anyone imagine how disastrous that visit would end, a visit that ended in a never-to-be-forgotten tragedy.

There was to be a select family reunion the next day. A few of the most exclusive families had been invited. They were to go picnicing in the woods with all sorts of good things to eat, and little Herbert's heart nearly broke when he learned that James could not go. He asked mamma and papa, uncle and aunty, even the nurse, to take James, but they all answered, "No."

His father became impatient and said, "My little loyal man, wait until James gets white, then you may take him along. There will be no black people there."

Poor Herbert felt very bad to have to tell James that he could not go, after he had, in his childish way, boasted that he should. He and James sat disconsolately in the back yard with tear-dimmed eyes, trying to plan some way, in their baby minds, how to accomplish making James white.

All at once, little Herbert jumped up and exclaimed, "You stay here until I come back and I'll tell you what we will do."

Finally he returned from the stable, with a brush

and a mysterious looking can and a towel. He then said, "James, do you remember the day when Jack, the stable boy, made the kitchen floor so black with his dirty shoes and cooky got so angry with him? He went to the stable and got this very thing, for I went with him. He rubbed this stuff in the can upon the floor, then taking the brush scrubbed it off, and it was ever so black, blacker than your face, and that is pretty black. When he got through it was so white, as white as I am. I'll put some of this on your face and make you white and then you put on one of my suits. Won't that be fun?"

At first James was afraid it would hurt, but when Herbert told him of the pretty clothes, he said, "Alright, I won't cry, I'll be brave like the Indians in the book."

Herbert said, "That will be jolly, and now while I make you white, I will tell you pretty stories that nurse told me and then you won't feel the pain."

James tried hard to be brave, but the mixture burnt him so bad, his eyes began to smart and burn, his face felt afire; finally he could stand it no longer. First a stifled moan, then some tears, then screams that brought out the entire household to see what was wrong. All stood horified, when Herbert told them what he was doing to James and why it was necessary. No one knew what was to be done; none thought of sending for the doctor.

The poor boy meanwhile suffered untold pain as the fluid was known to contain poison of the most dangerous kind. Some of it had gotten into his eyes. There was danger of losing his sight, perhaps other

complications might follow, as it was suspected he
had swallowed some of the fluid. It was suggested
that he be taken to his mother, which was accordingly done. With nothing more substantial than
some weak apologies and a liberal amount of advice
accompanied by some well known home remedies,
possibly ineffectual even in minor cases.

The poor woman told Mr. Drake that she was too
poor to get a doctor and she was then given some
liniment that only increased the pain to the already
inflamed and swollen face and its application had
to be discontinued. Added to the remedy spoken of,
the sufferer was given a suit of Herbert's cast-off
clothes. It was then that both the white and colored
residents in the neighborhood protested and urged
the poor widow to take her boy to the city doctor,
then go to a lawyer, state the case and sue for dam-
ages.

The poor woman exclaimed, "How can I go to a
lawyer? I have no money and now I will not have
time to earn much from washing, as my poor child
will have to be attended to."

One woman spoke up and suggested that there
was a fine lawyer in the City Hall Square who took
all deserving cases free of charge and directed just
where to go.

She had been directed to the office of Kenneth Randolph, noted attorney. Kenneth listened to all details and was so very gentle, and noting the poor
woman's evident distress and inability to explain her
meaning intelligently, put her at her ease and was
very indignant at the heartless manner in which she

had been treated. He sent her home after assuring her that her boy should have medical treatment at once. He also promised to handle the case for her by instituting proceedings against Mr. Drake, the wealthy lumberman, unless it was satisfactorily settled out of court.

As soon as the widow had gone, Kenneth called up Dr. Grayson and explained as much as possible concerning the case and urged him to go at once to the widow's home. Then come to see him, as he would be responsible for the bill. Kenneth had often met Dr. Grayson at public places and was much impressed by his dignity and bearing and had learned much of this dark skinned physician who was an honor to the profession. An intimacy sprung up between them that was to last through life in a way they least expected.

Needless to say, the two men took an active interest in little James. His mother was very grateful and although Dr. Grayson worked faithfully, he found it necessary to call in an eye specialist. It was as he first thought, very doubtful if the lad would ever see again. But out of the unbounded generosity of Kenneth there was no expense spared to restore the sight of the injured child.

CHAPTER IV.

DR. GRAYSON AND THE MILLIONAIRE'S DAUGHTER.

When Dr. Grayson returned from the banker's residence, he was much perturbed concerning the emotion displayed by Alice Blair. He felt that her mistaken sense of gratitude had led her into indiscretions and embarrassments to them both. He felt that it was a fortunate circumstance that brought old Dr. Cowan home at this time, relieving him of the embarrassing, if not dangerous, position in which he found himself. Although not a conceited man, he could not forget the partial caress that had been bestowed upon him and the vivid blush that followed. Several times he had passed Miss Blair in her car and had lifted his hat in response to her smiling recognition.

Some weeks later he returned to his office very much exhausted from two strenuous days and nights at hard work. He laid off his coat, loosened his collar, thinking to rest for a few moments. He was soon sleeping soundly, only to be partly awakened by a soft, caressing touch on the forehead. Quickly he was fully aroused and found Alice Blair standing by a table, seemingly lost in admiration of some beautiful flowers in a vase, with her face covered with blushes. The doctor hastily donned his coat, mildly apologizing for having it off.

Dr. Grayson, as we have stated, was a man of culture and refinement, and his professional dignity prevented him from expressing undue surprise at her visit to his office. He regretted the necessity, if there was one, however. He smilingly held out his hand and said, "This is indeed a pleasant surprise, but I hope there is no recurrence of the old trouble."

Still with her face suffused with blushes, she took the chair that he placed for her and replied, "I do not feel as well as usual and felt that I would like to consult you about my true condition."

For a moment the doctor's gaze rested upon the face of the beautiful girl seated before him and he concluded that if the case was to be diagnosed by looks and appearances he would have said that her health was perfect. Although reluctant to make the examination, he did so. At the conclusion of which he felt that her appearance was not deceptive and could find no cause for her belief that she needed medical aid.

He told her that she was getting along nicely, perhaps she was a little nervous, and continuing, he said, "On my last visit to you, I told Mr. Blair that I felt the sea breeze would be beneficial to you. I suppose that your physician did not recommend it, and as I was no longer being consulted about what would be best for you, it would be construed as presumption on my part were I to further advise you."

"But, Doctor," she replied, "I do not want Dr. Cowan's advice. He is getting old and doty and I told father and mother so."

The doctor answered, "I presume, then, that it is with your parents' consent that you are consulting me now?"

She truthfully replied that it was not. "Father

said that there was nothing the matter with me, just as if he knew how I felt." And with the tears dangerously near falling from her eyes, she exclaimed, "No one cares for me." And with this she arose to leave.

The doctor had risen and stood ready to open the door for his fair visitor as he answered and assured her that every one was deeply interested in her and that if at any time Mr. Blair felt that his services were required he would only be too glad to serve to the best of his ability. "But," he continued, "it would be quite unprofessional to infringe upon the rights of another."

She answered, "I will not have that old fogy doctor's advice or services either."

Dr. Grayson was silent for a moment, then he replied, "Men of my profession may appear gruff and indifferent, that is because we cannot allow sentiment to enter into our profession, as it would unfit us for our chosen work. Yet we hearily wish for the welfare of our patients. I am proud that it was in my power to give you timely aid in your distressing condition, and thereby helping to restore your health."

"Forgive me if I seem ungrateful, but Doctor, please do not bar your door against me, for I feel that I must come again," she said as she laid her hand on his sleeve.

"Miss Blair," he replied, "my office is a public one, and I have neither desire nor inclination to act so discourteously to anyone, especially a former patient."

She was visibly agitated and soon afterwards left. She found it necessary to lower her veil before entering her car to be driven home, where she gained her room unobserved by any member of the family. Locking the door, she took a flower out of her dainty hand bag that she had surreptitiously extracted from the vase of flowers on the doctor's table, and upon that silent blossom she bestowed caresses as if it could understand and would keep her secret.

After Alice Blair's departure, Doctor Grayson felt very much disturbed, for well did he know to allow the banker's daughter to come and go at will would not be treating her fair, besides he was a man of irreproachable character that had never been assailed. Such a procedure would be misconstrued, having the appearance of a clandestine arrangement, rather than for medical treatment, and he resolved that if she came to his office again to make it quite plain to her that if the visits were to continue, it would be well for her to be accompanied by some member of the family or by the expressed wish and approval of her parents.

Two weeks later she again visited the doctor's office. He was out and his assistant had been called away to another city by the illness of his mother and had not returned. She wrote a note, carefully sealing it, expressing a desire to see the doctor, saying that she would call again after office hours.

When Doctor Grayson returned and had read her note, he felt very much depressed. He had tried hard to think that she had no special interest in him, but matters were beginning to look very grave, and he felt that possibly after all he had made a mistake in thinking so lightly of the matter.

He scarcely knew what to do, but was more determined than ever to reason with the young lady. She could hardly be cognizant of the facts existing between the races. He felt that the daughter of a banker had not been permitted to be present or discuss those events, the environment in which she had been reared being so exclusive and perfect.

The doctor noticed that she was inclined to be somewhat self-willed, but out of the generosity of this big hearted, broad-minded man, he had at that time attributed this trait to nervousness, the result of a fevered brain. Even after taking all these things into consideration he was not really assured of what the outcome of the coming interview would be; however he would tell her of existing prejudice. That he would be judged harshly, likely be condemned unheard, possibly driven out of the town, or worse, perhaps his life would be the forfeit.

But aside from that, he felt that he must protect his former patient, that cruel calumny should not touch her with the finger of scorn. Strange to say, while eager to protect the banker's daughter, there had been no awakening in his heart for the many charms of this lovely girl. He was not self-important, in fact, so far his profession had filled his heart and mind and he had no other desire than to become famous in his chosen work.

Yet there were times that he sighed, as he often thought of a lovely black eyed girl in his far away home town. Her complexion was of that dark color that left no doubt in your mind of the race of people that she was identified with. She was younger than he, yet he felt that when he would take a wife, he would seek Odene Lester. He knew that she was unwed and felt ere long he would lay his heart at her feet.

While the doctor sat thus thinking of the past and present and future possibilities, Alice came in. He arose at once, extended his hand in greeting, then he placed a chair for her, and remained standing until she was seated. She noticed the absence of warmth in his greeting and her face flushed painfully; however, she asked him if he got her note. Without waiting for a reply and seeing the open note lying on the table, she said, "O, I see that you have."

He replied, "I hope that as soon as you are rested you will acquaint me of the important matter that you have referred to."

Had Alice been an older and a wiser woman, she would have been warned by that habitual quick and professional way of speaking that there was a lack of sentiment in his heart for her. She felt that he spoke somewhat harshly, too much so, yet she could not fathom the cause. She, therefore, forgot all the pretty little things that she intended to do and say to charm this dignified, austere doctor.

She burst into tears and cried unrestrainedly for some moments, causing him to refrain from saying many things that should be said, to such an extent as to weaken his resolve, thinking that he would put it off until some future time, when her nerves would be stronger and less likely to such extreme agitation. When she grew more composed, he decided to follow his original plan and began to tell her at that time of race prejudice and its direful influence that was sweeping this country from city to city, from coast to coast and that her frequent visits would be misconstrued, not forgetting to remind her how she would be ostracized by her people and misjudged by his. But she would not be convinced.

How grateful he was for an urgent call that made it impossible to continue the conversation, but at her earnest appeal promised to see her soon.

As she left his office, she was not quite happy, yet more hopeful. She did not lower her veil over her beautiful pansy colored eyes.

CHAPTER V.

AN ENIGMATICAL SITUATION.

That night Dr. Grayson and Kenneth Randolph were seated in the former's office. The young lawyer remarked, ''I do not look like a despairing lover, do I, who has just returned from the presence of one who has declined the honor to become his wife, but such is the case. You remember, Doc (that was the familiar term with which Kenneth addressed the young doctor, and in the same familiar terms was addressed in return as Kenneth), that I once told you that I was very much interested in a young lady belonging to one of the most exclusive families.

"I hesitated for family reasons to ask this lady to marry me, for there is said to be a skeleton in every closet, and there is one in mine, left there by my ancestors, and I hesitated to drag it forth."

As he paused for a moment, Dr. Grayson answered and said, "What need to drag it forth? What have you to do with the lives of your ancestors? They lived their lives in their way, you must live yours, and as long as you have lived a clean life and re-morse has no place in your conscience then why not let the past bury its past. I think that I know you too well to feel that you have ever done aught to shame your manhood."

Kenneth replied, "I am not downcast nor would I have you believe me fickle, but, Doc, let me tell you, I know now that my heart was never touched by cupid's arrow as deeply as it should have been con-sidering my anticipations for a future to be spent with her. I must confess that I lost my heart as I was hastening to hear my fate.

As I was being ushered into the parlor, the most beautiful girl that I had ever seen, who could not have been over seventeen or eighteen years of age, came down the stairs. She was tall and slender, her hair was that auburn shade that painters rave about, and as her eyes looked into mine, for a moment, they seemed almost black. She was very fair, in fact her beauty was dazzling. Doc, you may smile, but I am determined to win this girl for my wife. I cannot tell why I feel thus, but I know that I shall be suc-cessful. Failing to do so, I shall go to my grave unwed. I learned that she was the sister to the girl that I went to see. She had just returned from boarding school in the North, where she had spent three years.''

The doctor listened to Kenneth with varied thoughts, resembling in a way, his own case, only the circumstances were reversed. While there had been no question of marriage in his case, yet he had tried to convince the lady that any sentiment between them would be frowned upon, in fact it would not be tolerated. As Kenneth stopped speaking, the dictor remarked, that it was fortunate that the young lady had discovered before too late that his heart had been given to another and wished him success in winning the affection of the charming lady that he had just spoken about.

The two men sat in silence for some time, each busy with his own thoughts. Finally Kenneth looked at the doctor somewhat curiously for a moment and was convinced that there was something on the doctor's mind that was troubling him, and said, ''What is it, Doc? Out with it. You know that I am your friend and whatever it is that is troubling you, I am sure will come out all right.'' But the doctor was not so sanguine and told Kenneth so. However, he related all that our reader already knows concerning himself and the banker's daughter, careful not to mention her name or repeat any incident that would enlighten the young attorney as to her identity. And strange as it may seem, whether purposely or unintentionally, Kenneth had not revealed the name of the lady who had rejected him or her charming young sister.

After listening to the doctor, Kenneth could not help but admit that there was great cause for worry for the outcome of the future of the couple and felt that the gravity of the situation needed no exaggeration and frankly told the doctor so, but assured him that if he could be of any assistance to him in any way that he would help him to the extent of his ability.

The doctor said, "I am no coward, but I am afraid that it will mean for me to leave these parts where I have, by hard work, established myself. I am ranking in science and skill with my white associates. In many instances, surpassing them."

Kenneth thought long over the situation and wondered who the lady could be. He knew that the doctor was the soul of honor and felt that under no circumstances would he approach or take advantage of any lady whom he came in contact with, professionally or otherwise. Yet he also knew that he would receive no justice there if he remained.

Kenneth sat long thinking over his friend's predicament. He felt that if the doctor remained there would be many obstacles to his continued success. Kenneth knew that the doctor and he had descended from the same race of people and wondered if he could have hope for his suit if these facts were known. He had intended to reveal all to the lady whom he had asked to marry him, but there had been no necessity to do so as she had refused the honor.

For the first time in his life he felt himself a coward; for the thought of not winning Dian, filled him with unspeakable despair. Should he take his friend's advice and live his life and let the past sink into oblivion! It seemed best, but would his conscience be at rest? Would it stand for it? He was weighted down with the burden of the secret and it was the pricking of his conscience that caused him to seek the advice of his friend, the doctor, without revealing it even to him.

He often met Dr. Grayson but there had either been no time, desire or inclination to discuss the subject that meant so much to those two men. He also frequently met Alice Blair who had rejected his suit, but as there had been no deep affection between them, there was an absence of embarrassment and, they usually extended and received courtesies in the most friendly manner.

CHAPTER VI.

ALICE AND DIAN.

One morning as the banker and his family were seated at the breakfast table, he glanced at his eldest daughter and said, "Alice, I notice that Kenneth has not been here for some time. He is a brilliant young barrister, a clean and capable man. I thought by this time, he would be wanting to deprive me of my eldest daughter. Not that I want to lose you, but he is a man that any woman might feel proud of. Dian is young yet and we hope to keep her with us for some years to come. Is not that so, mother?" appealing to his handsome wife. Mrs. Blair who laugh-

ingly said, "Why father, have you turned match-
maker? but it is as you say, Kenneth is a brillant
young man and some day will become famous."

Mr. Blair replied, "Oh, no, but I miss the young
man." Up to this time Alice had not spoken, but
seeing all eyes turned on her, replied with as much
composure as she could command, although her face
flushed, that she had declined the honor of becoming
the wife of Kenneth Randolph.

Had a bombshell exploded, it would not have filled
them with greater consternation beyond that she
would not enlighten them why she had rejected the
young attorney.

Dian thought her sister must be very difficult to
please, for as young as she was, she had noticed the
maneuvers of mothers to capture this rising young
lawyer for their daughters. On one or two occasions, she tried in vain to win her sister's confidence,
thinking that although young, she might be able to
help her sister to a better understanding with the
rejected suitor, but was curtly informed that she
need not bother about her affairs that she never
would marry Kenneth. To her mother she gave the
same unsatisfactory answer.

Dian was greatly surprised when a few evenings
later Kenneth monopolized her company at a very
grand reception. He begged permission to call. She
shyly granted his request. She was not vain nor
conceited and did not realize that the young attorney
was deeply smitten with the charms of the sister of
the girl who had rejected him. Possibly it was the
though of this rejection that caused Dian to be very
kind to her visitor.

That was only the beginning and it was not long before Kenneth was a recognized suitor for Dian Blair, youngest daughter of Jarvis Blair, the banker. There had been no bethrothal and Dian's beauty had brought her many lovers who sued in vain for her hand.

Mr. and Mrs. Blair felt very much disturbed on account of Alice, she seemed restless and ill at ease, she lost her rosy color, but to all questions concerning her health, she replied that she was quite well.

One day Dian surprised her in tears and was startled when Alice threw her armes around her neck asking if she could keep a secret. Dian replied that she would respect any confidence that she might give. In fact it seemed to her that life was made up of surprises. Alice informed her that she was in love with a man that she was afraid that she would never gain the consent of her parents to marry. Although she said, he is a high class, cultured gentleman.

Dian was speechless at this announcement. She could not think of any gentleman of their acquaintance that her sister favored as a suitor. She felt, however, that it was this unknown lover that had won her heart, hence the rejection of Kenneth.

Alice continued, I love this man dearly, and as Dian had thought, her sister said, it is for the love of this man that I refused Kenneth. "You need not blush for me, for we did not care for each other, and it is a notable fact that he did not break his heart over the rejection, but found one to bestow his heart's affection upon, much fairer and prettier than I." Kissing Dian affectionately she asked her if she was not worthy of her confidence. "If so tell me dear, if it has been settled."

Dian replied, "Oh, sister, I am indeed most happy or will be if mother and father give their consent. Kenneth is coming tonight to ask them." And blushing prettily, it was her turn to embrace her sister. She said, "Wish me success, just as I wish that you may win their consent to the marriage of the man of your choice whom you so dearly love."

Alice replied, "Sister, my parents would rather see me sleeping in my grave than to marry this man."

Dian replied, "Sister, as you have not told me your lover's name, I cannot voice my opinion. I fear that I am too young and inexperienced to give you an intelligent opinion. In fact I feel that my judgment will be gauged by expressions of love and I fear that may not always prove satisfactory, but you have my sincere sympathy and I pledge myself to do all that I can for you to insure your future happiness, if you will only tell me how I can best serve you."

The sisters talked long, but on separating Dian was still perplexed over her sister's mysterious love and the unknown lover. She truly sympathized with her and what seemed to be her unfortunate love.

Alice did not feel comfortable after confiding in her sister and somehow felt vexed at herself for that outburst of confidence. And when Kenneth came that evening to ask for her sister's hand, she locked herself in her room, a prey to conflicting emotions, not from regret, for she had not loved the young barrister, yet she felt irritable that he was so easily con-

soled over the termination of their love affair. She
did love Dr. Grayson and the emotion she felt was
from fear and suspense and a sense of shame at the
clandestine way she used to see him. She blushed
painfully as she asked herself this question, "Is he
really my lover? He does not seem overjoyed that
I have lost my heart to him. Does he love me?"
Tears filled her eyes as she could not answer the
question with satisfaction.

Some hours later as Dian was going to her room,
she rapped at her sister's door. Receiving no reply,
she proceeded to her own room where for a long
while she sat turning the beautiful solitaire diamond ring on her finger put there by Kenneth with
the consent of her parents.

CHAPTER VII.

KENNETH'S PLEA FOR THE COLORED LAD.

Time went on and in three more days the trial of
Taylor versus Drake would take place in the court-
house. Dr. Grayson was to be an important witness
as he had been first called to treat little James Taylor, the colored washwoman's son, the victim of his
little innocent playmate.

The coming trial was eagerly looked forward to
and when the morning dawned, bright and clear, the
courtroom was crowded. Many were unable to gain
admission. Among those who were admitted were
Mr. and Mrs. Blair, accompanied by their daughter,

Dian, who had prevailed on them to take her, in fact she knew that her lover was to plead for the colored lad and she was most anxious to hear him.

Alice refused to attend, saying that she was not interested and had no desire to mix in such a heterogeneous crowd of people.

The case was presented in due form. The first witness called was a maid in the Drakes' employ. She testified that on that day she had heard children crying and as she had seen Herbert and James go to the rear of the house, she hastened there to learn what might be the trouble. She found Herbert trying to wipe James' face. Both of the children were crying. In answer Herbert said, that his papa had told him that James would have to be made white before he could go to the picnic with them, so he was trying to get the black off of his face.

The wealthy lumberman was next called, but denied that he had told his son to use any method or remedy and had spoken thoughtlessly. He was then asked if he had given James' mother any financial aid in the three months of suffering of the lad and her inability to provide as formerly on account of the condition of her little son's care. Mr. Drake was undoubtedly confused, but managed to say that he had not.

Next his little son Herbert was put on the stand. Although badly frightened at first, he made a fine witness for his little chum, but unknowingly a bad one for his father. Tears rolled down the little fellow's cheeks when he said "I tried so hard, but the black would not come off." Finally bursting into tears, he said, "I didn't mean to hurt James and I wanted so bad to take him to the picnic. He can have my little pony and cart," and running up to the judge, he cried, "oh, Mr. Judge, please don't send me to jail and do not put little James in jail, I will be good to him. He did not do anything." And before he could be restrained he jumped down, ran to the chair where Jimmy sat beside his mother, with his eyes carefully bandaged, threw his arms around James' neck and bravely said, "I won't let them take you to jail, I told them not to, but I will go, I am not fraid. And when I get to be a big man, I will take care of you."

The scene between the two playmates was most pathetic and many shed tears at the loyalty of Herbert to his chum.

Dr. Grayson testified concerning the lad's condition when he was called in a few hours later. When the doctor took the stand, many necks were craned to get a look at this eminent physician whose fame had preceded him.

Dr. Evans, the eye specialist, testified that he had been called in and at the time. He said it was a matter of doubt if the lad ever again would have his sight. Yet he concluded that youth ofttimes performed wonders, but there was not much hope for recovery of sight in this case.

Other witnesses were called, the last to testify was James' mother. She told of Mr. Drake's absolute refusal to give her financial aid, not even to pay the doctor's bill. This concluded the evidence.

When Kenneth Randolph, the noted attorney,

arose to plead for the washwoman's son, you might have heard a pin fall, so profound was the silence. He dwelt on the large heartedness of the rich man's little son and his faith in his father's word and guidance by his advice. When the father told him that little James was to be made white before he could participate in their pleasures that was only to be enjoyed by the white people, little Herbert felt that James would be all right if his skin was white. Straightway from the depths of his little loyal heart, he did what he thought his father had expected him to do to make his playmate white. He in his childish judgment, took the same means and process to remove the colored skin that he had seen used on the floor with such satisfactory results.

Kenneth's plea to the jury was eloquent and convincing. He dwelt on the terrible calamity that was worse than death. Doubtless the child was blind for life and besides, he was handicapped by prejudice and discrimination. His race of people are ostracized and find it most difficult to exist when in full possession of all of God's given faculties. What a future for this child that may live to be ninety or a hundred years of age. It is enough to make the angels weep.

I ask the jury if $50,000 is not a small compensation, yet that is all I ask. It should be twice that sum. Think of the hardships of the poor mother who will also suffer. Will there be one dissenting voice to keep from this child what is his just due.

In the years to come when little Herbert with his large heart has arrived at the age of manhood, he will thank you for being the means of providing for his little playmate blinded by his error, the error of his loyalty to little James, his boyhood chum.

And again, gentlemen, does it not seem a strange freak of nature that little Herbert should be so broad minded when his father has shown his littleness when he sent the widow some liniment and a cast-off suit of clothes of his son as a compensation for his blighted future life.

And what of the mother? Oh, terrible is the day when we fail to reverence woman, especially a mother. Again I ask what kind of a woman, herself a mother, that had not that human spark of feeling for another. One would have thought that for the sake of the love her little son bore the colored lad, would have appealed to her most tenderly. Let me tell you what Herbert's mother did. She sent some cookies to James and a tract to the mother advising her to trust in God.

Gentlemen, look at this child and thank God that you are spared the affliction and suffering and out of gratitude, if nothing else, give this lad $50,000, not a cent less.

The defense was weak, and the verdict in favor of the plaintiff was rendered without the jury leaving their seats. A shout went up that the court could not quell and Kenneth had covered himself with glory.

Dian and her mother were in tears. The jury was thanked and lauded for their fairness.

Little Herbert did not know what it was all about, but heard some one say that James is going to have a lot of money. He clapped his hands gleefully and running to James, exclaimed, "Oh, James, you can have a pony and cart prettier than mine."

Kenneth made his escape as soon as possible, but not before his bethrothed had spoken a word in praise. He would have accompanied them to their car, but the surging crowd, all eager to shake hands with him, made it impossible to do so.

When Dian reached home she flew to her sister's room and threw her arms around her neck and said, "Oh, sister, you should have been there, my Kenneth is a king. The way he defended the colored boy was just grand. He won the case. We will read all about it in the paper, I am sure there will be extras out, and oh, sister there was a colored doctor that testified. I tried to remember his name. I think it was something like Gray or Grayson, I do not remember which. If I was a colored girl, I would almost give my life for such a man. Although dark, he was quite handsome. His physique was magnificent, in fact he was the finest specimen of Afro-American manhood that I have ever seen. He had the most winning smile. I did not know that a colored person could have such an admirable personality." So great was her enthusiasm that she had failed to notice her sister who had first grown white, then red. She felt that she had got Dian's opinion of her lover unsolicited.

Dian was very happy and talked incessantly until the dinner bell rang. Then accompanied by her sister, she descended to the dining-room where the trial was the theme of conversation.

Alice remained quiet, but changed color when her mother said to her father that Dr. Grayson was really a fine looking man and quite intelligent. Receiving no reply, the conversation drifted into other channels.

Soon after dinner Kenneth arrived. Alice congratulated Kenneth on winning the case and on the plea of a headache soon retired to her room.

CHAPTER VIII.

THE REFLECTIONS OF ALICE.

Returning to her room Alice gave way to her pent-up feeling. She soliloquized thus, "Have I given up the substance for the shadow?" And as on a previous occasion asked herself this question, "Had either of her lovers loved her?" Of course, she felt that Kenneth would have married her had she accepted him, yet she now knew that he had never really loved her, not because he had been solaced by her sister's charms, but he had never wooed her in a manner that convinced her that his happiness was in her hands.

He had never looked at her as he did at her sister. His face was never transfigured when she entered a room as it did when in the presence of Dian. She had never been jealous of her young sister, although she knew that she was marvelously beautiful and had felt relieved that her rejected lover found such unalloyed happiness in his love for Dian, such as he had never, or ever would, have felt for herself.

And now as she sat alone, thinking over these things and taking into consideration Kenneth's prominence and his rapid approach to fame, his charming personality, she could not help but realize that her sister had chosen well. ˙Her only solace was, that she and Kenneth had never loved each other. Still, soliloquizing, she asked herself this question, "What modern woman would not have left the question of love out to be the wife of this brilliant young attorney?" He was the substance and it was with a feeling of deep regret that she had given up the substance and was grasping for the shadow.

Her face flushed scarlet as she realized that this doctor, the descendant of the despised race of black slaves, had not sought her out to be his life companion. He had not asked her to be his wife, yet she felt that she had lowered herself in his estimation, by her silent and unsolicited avowal of love for him. She intuitively felt that he did not spare her feelings, he had not lost his heart to her, he had made no advances and showed simply tolerance of her. She felt that he did not love her. She had not touched his heart. And this was brought forcibly to her realization one day when she unexpectedly entered his office and found him gazing on the picture of a girl. On questioning him, he admitted that at one time she had been a school mate of his and was some years his junior.

Another time while waiting for the doctor to return, she opened a drawer in his desk and found that same picture with these lines written across the back, "Odene, my love." Now as she thought of all these things, she could not help but feel that she was really pursuing a shadow.

She got up and walked to the long mirror and gazed long at the image reflected there and was satisfied with the reflection. She wondered if the doctor would always remain insensible to her charms. She felt that his former school mate held a cherished possession of his heart that she so much craved. She seated herself again with her head bowed upon her hands, revolving in her mind what would be the outcome of her fatal love.

As she sat in silence she heard the merry laugh of her sister in the spring-time of her early love, and for the first time felt a feeling of envy and jealousy.

Alice knew that even if Dr. Grayson had really loved her their happiness would be clouded by the fact that any engagement that should exist between them would not be tolerated. It would be frowned upon. As he said, she would be ostracized and he to save his life, would be driven into exile.

She had learned of her father's prejudice to the colored race, and that he would not rest until he had crucified her lover on the altar of hate. No, she could not see perfect happiness, even if she possessed the doctor's love which she knew that she did not have. As she viewed all points, she could not but admit that they were not very flattering to her. She thought of Kenneth. Did she regret the rejection of his suit? She began to think that she did, yet she did not love him, but she felt revengeful because he had gained such apparent happiness by her refusal to become his wife and felt offended because he was so unexpressibly happy. Try as he would, he could not conceal his great joy at having won her sister and was a constant visitor.

She could only see Dr. Grayson in the most clandestine manner, and then those stolen moments were always at her suggestion and management. She asked herself if she enjoyed those moments. The doctor was never rapturous, received her tender affection in almost complete silence that was most embarrassing as it was humiliating to this high bred, beautiful southern girl. He simply tolerated her, his undisguised indifference wounded her pride as well as saddened her heart. She could not complain of his treatment to her as a lady. He was ever kind and thoughtful, yet he would not profess a false sentiment that he did not feel.

From the depths of his heart he pitied the girl for her indiscreet love and her inability to crush out this feeling that was likely to prove disastrous to both; yet she seemed to live on the meagre crumbs of his tolerance, torn by the knowledge of his preference for the colored girl and the happiness of her discarded lover, Kenneth, and her sister, Dian.

As their wedding day approached, she wondered how she could endure it. There was steadily growing in her heart a bitter hatred for those two lovers who had nothing but the kindest feelings in their hearts for her. And before she went to bed that night she drove the first shaft into the pure young heart of Kenneth's betrothed.

CHAPTER IX.

A SISTER'S HATRED.

After bidding her lover a fond good night, Dian went happily upstairs, seeing a light in her sister's room, knocked softly and was admitted, and on Alice's invitation, sat down upon a low stool by her side. She was so happy and her youth had not made her observant. Therefore, she did not notice the cloud on Alice's brow, but her face covered with blushes, told her sister that Kenneth had pleaded for an early marriage, although her parents favored a longer delay, but Kenneth had proven that he could plead as successfully out of court as well as in one, and win. Consequently, they were to be married in three months.

Alice didn't know why, but she was surprised and visibly agitated at this announcement. She knew that it would come, but felt that a long engagement might mean a broken troth, and if she failed to win the doctor, she thought she might have possibly won the young attorney to his first infatuation. Therefore, when Dian received no reply, after making this announcement, although she paused for congratulations, she looked up into her sister's face and saw that it was deathly pale. She at once apologized for not inquiring about her sister's headache.

Continuing she said, "I fear that you are still suffering. Is there anything I can do for you? Let me bathe your head."

Alice replied, "I do not need your aid nor your

sympathy, but I am sure that you will need sympathy when you realize how people speak so pityingly of you saying that it is too bad that you could not get a lover of your own without taking your sister's.''

Dian was both hurt and surprised at her sister's words and the scornful tone of her voice warned the young girl that her sister was not only displeased at this approaching marriage, but was very unfriendly to the coming event that she looked forward to with so much pleasure.

She arose to her feet and said, ''Alice, I fear that you are not well or you would not speak thus. You did not love Kenneth,'' and Dian, unthinkingly, made a mistake when she continued speaking saying, ''as Kenneth did not love you, and does love me, I cannot see that we have done any wrong as to call down such ill-natured remarks, and dear sister you should rejoice that I am happy just as you will be when you have won over our parents' consent to your marriage to the man of your choice which I hope will be soon.''

Alice replied, ''You need not think of my future now, for it seems that you have only thought of your own and it is very inconsistent that you should pretend to care whether I am happy or not, since it pleases you to glory in winning my lover whom I rejected to save you from the sneers and jeers of the people who knew that you were in love with the man who had asked me to marry him.'' Dian, who had grown as pale as Alice had grown red with passion, at this cruel attack on her and her absent lover, replied, "Sister Alice, it is false; I never won your lover and never did aught that could be so construed. You made the announcement to the surprise of mother, father and myself that you had rejected Kenneth, and sister, while I do not boast of conquest. I had many admirers and suitors; I had no need to come between you and your lover. I would have scorned to do anything so contemptible."

"That is it," Alice replied, "the question is why you did not accept some one else!"

Dian replied, "I am sorry that you feel thus, but I must repeat that I did not steal your lover. I do not think that you are well and I deem it very unsisterly to continue this discussion that is painful to both of us. I will bid you good-night, hoping that in the morning you may view matters more clearly."

She opened the door to pass out, but before the door had closed, Alice said, "I do not want you to think that I envy you your fickle lover, and I do not think that Kenneth would feel flattered if he had heard his betrothed's unrestrained raptures over the negro doctor. He might feel that he had a rival."

At this unlooked for insult, Dian was speechless, but disdainfully refused to answer and went to her room. She had been so happy when she had entered her sister's room. Now her heart was filled with fear. She knew not what to expect. Her sister's demeanor was a revelation to her. She resolved, however, to say nothing of the conversation to any one, hoping that Alice would feel sorry by morning and would lose no time and hastily admit that she did not mean all that her words implied.

CHAPTER X.

KENNETH AND HIS FATHER.

Mr. Randolph sat in his luxurious apartment, his gaze resting upon the recently finished picture of his deceased wife. The opening and closing of the door made him aware of the return of his son who had been away attending to some legal business. He immediately arose and stretched forth his hand in response to the hearty greeting of his son who had advanced into the room exclaiming as he did so, "Hello Dad," a greeting that always reminded him of his son in his early youth, and in truth he liked that frank boyishness expressed in those words far better than the later dignified and perhaps a more correct term of "Father" that his son invariably addressed to him since he had grown older. Continuing, he asked, "Have you finished the picture of my beautiful mother?"

Mr. Randolph replied, "I have and want your opinion."

Kenneth said, "I fear that my opinion will not count for much considering the picture is done by the famous artist, Guy Randolph of Paris, France, now residing in the United States, the home of his birth." Both father and son laughed at Kenneth's witticism.

Mr. Randolph laughingly said, "I think your profession will make a humorist out of you."

Father and son lived luxuriously, but with the entire absence of gaudiness. Everything was artistic, from the beautiful decorated walls to the laying of a rug or the placing of a vase. The hangings were draped in the most artistic fashion, in fact everything was artistic in design and harmonious in selection.

Having partaken of their well cooked and well served dinner prepared by an experienced house-keeper who looked after the needs of the two gen-tlemen, who were inseparable. They repaired to the den or smoking room, then after seating themselves, Mr. Randolph passed the cigars to his son, remark-ing that they were of a new brand and were very fine. He looked for a moment at his son as if wait-ing for him to speak, seeing that he did not he said to Kenneth, ''Have you told Dian's parents as I have advised you to do, that you have mixed blood. That your ancestors descended from the black race of slaves?''

Kenneth replied, ''Father, I am a coward when I think that possibly to divulge this secret might be the cause of losing her.''

'''Then, my son, if she spurns you, she is unworthy of your love and devotion.''

''But father, if you could see Dian you would know that she is as good as she is beautiful.''

''Then, my son, why hesitate? I cannot consent to meet your betrothed until I can meet her with a clear conscience that there will be no embarrassment by concealing a fact of such vital importance. Until you have done so, I must refuse to meet my son's future wife. You know, Kenneth, the unhappy and fatal results of the discovery of my origin after my marriage, but in that case you know that I was entirely innocent, not knowing that my mother was tainted with the blood of that despised race of slaves. Remember boy, your motherless youth, note your father's wrecked life by those events, do not have a repetition of the life of your father.''

Kenneth said, ''Father, I will do as you say, only I shall first tell Dian as I feel that she is the only one to be considered first, as it is with her that I expect to live and to enjoy complete happiness.''

''But, my son, do you not see that it is unfair to her parents to be the last to be made acquainted with those facts.''

''Father, it may be as you say, but I must confide in my betrothed.''

''Well, my son, let it be as you say, but lose no time and as the hour is yet early, I would call this evening. Although you say that she does not expect you, not knowing of your return, I am sure it will be an agreeable surprise.''

''Oh, Father, how kind of you to suggest me going tonight. I was most eager to do so, but I thought it would be selfish to leave you alone the first night after an absence of nearly a week.''

Mr. Randolph looked long and lovingly at his handsome, distinguished son and felt no uneasiness as to the result of the revelation he was to make to his beautiful fiance whom he was most anxious to meet. Having heard so much of her beauty, not only from Kenneth, for people in love are not always the best judges of the beauty of the one they desire to possess for their own, but the journals and magazines always find some new beauty in the charming

Miss Dian Blair, the youngest daughter of Jarvis Blair, the banker.

After Kenneth had changed his traveling suit, he returned to his father and told him that although he would not remain late, yet he thought it best not to sit up for him, for well did he know his father's habit of not retiring before his return, it mattered not how late the hour.

After his departure, the artist's gaze rested upon the face of the wife whom he had loved and lost many years before death had claimed her. He had felt sure from many facts that he became acquainted with shortly after he lost his wife that caused his heart to go out to her in great pity, for he realized that her mind had been warped by the cruel teachings of her mother whose prejudice and hatred for the colored people had made her unjust and she had conveyed that hatred to her youthful daughter whose mind had not matured and was susceptible to those teachings and bore fruit that was the wrecking of his home and happiness.

Yes, Guy Randolph freely forgave his lost wife and cherished in memory only the lovely things that stood out in her life although they may have been hard to detect, those lovely things by one not in love with Catherine Randolph, but her husband not only remembered them, but magnified them in his mind to such an exaggerated degree that one not acquainted with the true facts of her character would imagine that Mr. Randolph still mourned a sainted wife who had left noble deeds as a monument. And we have evidence that Catherine had repented of her injustice to her husband and infant son, therefore, we should commend Guy Randolph rather than condemn him for his loyalty to the memory of his beautiful wife, who had by years of waiting for the husband she had so cruelly deserted and the baby she abandoned, made atonement.

CHAPTER XI.

KENNETH AND DIAN.

Kenneth lost no time in getting to the home of Mr. Blair and was cordially received by the family. Dian greeted her lover rapturously for it was indeed an agreeable surprise.

The lovers soon found themselves deserted by the other members of the family and the evening being fine, they went out on the balcony. Kenneth seemed unusually quiet. Dian said, "I don't think you are pleased to see me after your long absence."

Whereupon Kenneth, laughingly replied, "My long absence was only five days, but each day seemed longer than the preceding one. I cannot express how happy I am to be in your presence once more. If I appear to be less talkative than usual, it is because I was wondering whether your love would change."

"Oh, Kenneth, how can you imagine such a thing!" And to prove her sincerity, she nestled closely to him and allowed him to kiss her repeatedly."

Kenneth said, "Dian, I have something on my

mind that I feel I ought to tell you before our wedding day. It is the ghost of the past."

"Then why disturb it? Let it rest, Everyone has a skeleton in the closet and they keep it there whenever it is possible."

"But, Dian, suppose some day it should walk out from under lock and key, it might startle you."

"Oh, Kenneth, how you frighten me by your serious talk. I am sure that there is nothing that will make me love you less. Is it something that you have done in the past?"

"No, my darling, I have not knowingly done a mean act in my life."

"Then Kenneth, why will you persist in dragging forth this skeleton?"

"Dian, what I referred to happened before my father was even born."

"Before your father was born, then why not let the secret rest if there is one!"

"Yes, darling, there is a secret, and in spite of your charitable feeling, I must tell you this, and if you feel that you cannot link your name with mine, then I bow submissively to your will. Dian, my grandmother was a mulatto slave, she was a beautiful octaroon girl, descended from the slaves of the south. My father was the only child. He married a beautiful white girl who deserted him as soon as she became aware of the fact. She left me, an infant, to console my father for her desertion of him, but my father was not aware that he had descended from the race of colored people until after his marriage. My mother died without ever seeing my father or myself

again. I learned afterwards that she repented and
went back to the deserted home. My father had tak-
en me and gone elsewhere. She remained near the
deserted home until her death where we found her a
few hours after she had passed away."

Dian did not interrupt Kenneth while he was laying bare the secret of the past that had been so fatal
to them and by the shadows of that past still hovering over their heads. "Oh, Kenneth, my poor Kenneth, what a sad life your father must have spent
with only a little babe to cheer him, and, oh, what a
sad childhood without a mother's love and tender
care."

"But my darling, my father was so good and so
devoted to me that perhaps I did not miss my mother
as I had not been accustomed to seeing her. Only
now as I see mothers hovering over their little ones,
then I sigh for just such a remembrance."

"Oh, Kenneth, I am so glad that you have told me
this and I promise to make up to you for all the pet-
ting that you missed when a little child."

"But Dian, my father petted and indulged me in
such an extravagant fashion that many of the people who knew that I was motherless predicted that
I would not amount to much."

"But Kenneth, dear, let us think no more of the
sad past and let me make you happy."

"Oh, Dian, my dear girl, have you forgotten the
race of people that I am descended from? Do you
know that such a marriage would not be tolerated
by your family or friends? That such a union would
be frowned down on?"

"Oh, Kenneth, what care I for the world and besides you are as white as I am and who knows how many of the white race have some colored blood in them. Of this I am sure, that they are not proclaiming it from the housetops and why should you? And unless you refuse to marry me, we will marry on the day set for the ceremony." And throwing off the sadness that had momentarily settled on them, she laughed merrily and exclaimed, "Oh, how romantic it seems and knowing the secret is shared with no one else makes it doubly sacred."

Kenneth replied, "Let us not make any further plans until I have told your parents." Dian exclaimed, "Oh, no that is not necessary to tell them, they are living their lives, we must live ours. It might make them unhappy, although they love you as a son as they never had one. Yet it is a risk, best not assumed. Let the past bury the past."

"But, oh, Dian, if later on you should regret being united to one identified with the American Negro, it would kill me."

"Oh, Kenneth, Kenneth, how can you cherish such unkind thoughts of me? Can you doubt my love for you and if you refused to wed me, I shall remain unwed."

Kenneth exclaimed, "Oh, Dian, my darling, I am so happy it shall be as you say. Father was right, he said that your love for me would out-weigh birth or past traditions, attributable to the colored race of people, he was only waiting for this to welcome you as his daughter."

CHAPTER XII.

DR. GRAYSON'S RESOLVE.

Dr. Grayson sat in his office reflecting on the past and present of which Alice Blair was the center of those reflections. He could not lavish on her an affection he did not feel. He resolved to tell her that his heart was already bestowed on Odene Lester. He also resolved to write at once to Odene and if she accepted him, all would be well, but in event she refused him, he would not take his bruised heart to Alice to heal, he could not let her sacrifice her happiness and in return receive the dead ashes of his love that some other woman had kindled and was burnt out for her portion. No, he could not do that. It would be unfair to her and shame his manhood.

To strengthen this resolve, he at once took up his pen and wrote to Odene Lester. In part he wrote explaining his long silence telling her of his early struggles and privations and how step by step he was rising to fame. How he had never forgotten her and felt that it would have been unfair to bind her by any promise while he was undergoing so many privations and enduring much which was hard to bear, but now he was proud to say that he, not only laid his heart at her feet and was now able to supply the necessities of life, but she could enjoy the luxuries of life as well. Stating that he had looked forward to the time that he could offer her a heart that was true and in his anxiety hoped for an early and favorable reply. This done he felt that he had taken a decisive step to place a lasting barrier between himself and the banker's daughter. Not that he felt that he could not trust his heart, but it was hard to resist the sad wistfulness, silent plea and tear dimmed eyes of Alice Blair. Proving that his mind was irrevocably made up, he arose at once, went out and mailed his letter, not wanting to trust it to the hands of another. This done he felt his senses relieved, yet he dreaded the interview that he knew must come.

CHAPTER XIII.

ALICE.

Dr. Grayson was kept very busy, had just returned from making a special call when the door opened and Alice came in, looking incomparably beautiful, she never looked more lovely. The doctor stood the test. His heart did not thrill in her presence. He was safe. He greeted her most cordially and seated her in the most comfortable chair he could find. She noticed that he was formally polite, and did not show any loverlike pleasure at her visit. After inquiring after her health and feeling assured that she was well, he said, "Miss Blair, I was just thinking of you."

At those words, she smiled happily, saying, "I am very glad that you think of me sometimes."

He replied, "I think of you quite often. My

thoughts at this time were that I wish to have a talk with you.''

She blushed prettily, but without waiting for a reply, he continued. ''Miss Blair, I am sorry if I have misled or encouraged you to think favorably of me, I shall never forgive myself, if you will experience any embarrassment from our confidence which I shall keep a profound secret, it matters not what sacrifice I have to make to do so.'' (Little did he think at that time the great and cruel sacrifice that he would have to make would come.) When he started to speak, the blush died out of her face, leaving her extremely pale, then she buried her face in her dainty lace handkerchief while she was convulsed with sobs.

Dr. Grayson pitied her from the bottom of his heart and regretted that he had caused her pain. Never once did he in his mind allow himself to remember how she gave her love unsolicited. Never would he admit that she had not that maiden modesty that should have been her safeguard. No he could only pity and not blame her.

Finally she raised her head, and said, ''Doctor, your words and attitude convey to me that you are planning a life apart from me. When you speak of the past as if done with forever as far as we two are concerned.''

He replied, ''Miss Blair, anyone ought to feel honored and blessed by the true love of a good woman and I feel that there is some one more worthy of you than I am, that some day will lift you to the realms of bliss and you will then thank me that I did not take advantage of your kindness to blight your future, possibly a life filled with remorse and regret.''

She arose to her feet, her face dyed scarlet, saying, ''You showed me every kindness, encouraged me and led me on to think that you loved me as you have taught me to love you. Now you calmly tell me that you have no love for me and scorn the love that I have bestowed on you. I cast aside my maiden modesty for what? Do you know what you are? I will tell you if you do not know. You are a Negro descended from the despicable race of black slaves. Do you know what would be your fate if it was known that you had insulted one of my race? Do you know that a word from me, a banker's daughter, telling of the discourtesy you have heaped upon me, would be punishable by death, possibly in a most horrible form?'' She paused for want of breath.

Dr. Grayson never once interrupted her and now as she ceased speaking, he still remained silent from sorrow and surprise. He knew that she told the truth that if she just spoke the word, that his life would pay the penalty. Yet he knew that what she had said about his advances and encouragements was absolutely false, but he realized that his word would not stand against hers, even if he should speak those words. Yet if he knew that they were given credence, he would not speak them.

He reverenced woman too much to pull her off that sacred pedestal where man by his reverence had placed her. No, he could not expose her to the shame and ridicule to the few who might believe. No, he could not do this. He felt no sacrifice too great to shield the woman who loved him so fondly. He took a step toward Miss Blair and said, "You surely do not realize what you are saying or what you are accusing me of. I am sorry that you think so well of me. Now, if this be so, then why would you have me suffer? Does one usually prove one's love by injustice to the object of one's affection? Oh, Miss Blair, I have always regarded you as one of the highest types of womanhood. Let me keep that opinion of you. I am sure that you are worthy of it."

Then Alice asked him, "Is it because you love Odene Lester?"

At first Dr. Grayson thought not to answer her question, but thinking it best to leave nothing unexplained, as they were not likely to have another confidential talk, he admitted that he had hoped some day to lead Miss Odene Lester to the altar, as she was very dear to him.

Miss Blair exclaimed, "Would you pass me by for a colored girl?"

He calmly replied, "She is one of my people."

She further said, "I am young, far too young to pass my future in sorrow, but if I must I will not suffer alone. A woman scorned thinks only of revenge."

Dr. Grayson replied, "You mistake me, I do not scorn you, I have nothing in my heart only the best wishes for your future happiness and comfort and may God bless you in every walk of life."

Alice cried, "You break my heart, then ask God to bless. I want none of your good wishes. I hate you.'' Then, before he could reply, she quitted the room. He stood where she had left him until he heard her car whirling away.

CHAPTER XIV.

THE WEDDING.

Up in her room, shut out from the noise and bustle of happy excitement incidental to wedding preparations, sat Alice Blair. It was on the eve of the wedding. Mrs. Blair was filled with anxiety for Alice, who at the last moment refused to serve as maid of honor at her sister's wedding. She had pleaded illness and in truth it seemed as if her statement was correct, but it was of the mind and not the body. She had never shown the least bit of kindness to Dian since their stormy interview three months before when she had accused her sister of stealing her lover, although Dian had done her utmost to bring about a better feeling between them. She was so happy and hated to see her sister otherwise. Mrs. Blair had questioned both of her daughters, but could elicit no explanation from either, but a mother's love and a mother's instinct almost told her the facts of the situation. She pitied her eldest daughter from the depths of her heart, but held Dian, her youngest daughter, blameless.

When all hopes of Alice being maid of honor was passed, Alice walked into the room, filled with chattering, excited and happy young girls, and announced that she would serve her sister in that capacity. Later on, when Dian was alone with her, she thanked her sister lovingly for so deciding, but Alice told her very coldly that she did not want her thanks for she knew it was deceit, that she had only decided to do so for her own reasons.

The wedding was a brilliant affair. Dian was a dream, an indescribable vision of loveliness, dressed in pure white, her veil caught up by fragrant orange blossoms. No one ever pays much attention to the bridegroom, but on this occasion, it was impossible to overlook that handsome specimen of American manhood. Kenneth was naturally handsome, but today, with Dian by his side, he looked indeed transformed. He was, as she had expressed on former occasions, her king. Alice made a beautiful maid of honor and her serenity disclaimed any thought that she regretted that her sister had won Kenneth. But alone in her room, you would have thought different had you seen the beautiful dress crumpled and trode upon by the bride's sister. Yes Alice regretted it.

Among the presents received was a beautiful loving cup from Dr. Grayson, and from England a beautiful diamond necklace, from Lord and Lady Blankleigh. Agnes also remembered her handsome cousin and if a tear fell on the token she sent to the bride of Kenneth, no one ever knew nor did any one hear the sigh from her heart as she felt the force of those words, "Of all sad words of tongue or pen, the saddest are these, it might have been." And strange to say that Kenneth's wife was not unlike Agnes, the hair, eyes and all near the same color. Perhaps there was something that he was not aware of in Dian that was suggestive of his far away cousin that immediately gave Dian a place in his heart.

Guy Randolph was pleased with his son's choice and presented her with a beautiful diamond bracelet. To Kenneth, a handsome check. The happy couple went away to be gone three months. Lady Blankleigh had thought to extend an invitation to spend the time with them in their English home, but at her suggestion Agnes briefly said that she thought it would be very tiresome to have them there. Lady Blankleigh looked at her daughter somewhat curiously, not so much at the words, but the tone in which they were spoken. Then all at once there was a revelation unlooked for. She said no more, however, but she knew that when suitor after suitor was rejected and years were rolling by, that Agnes' heart had been deeply smitten by Catherine's handsome talented son.

CHAPTER XV.

HARVEY GRAHAM.

One evening as the Blairs sat at dinner, Mrs. Blair said, "Father, I received a letter from Dian and Kenneth. They are having an enjoyable time."

He replied, "I am very glad, I am sure."

Continuing, she said, "Alice received one by the same mail, did you not dear?" Thus appealed to, she replied that she had, but it was unimportant.

"Dian seems to think that I am a jockey or a servant. She said that Brown Bess would miss her can-
ter over the hill and as my horse had gone lame,
that I was to use Bess and she would get exercise,
besides I would have the pleasure of the ride."

Her mother replied, "Oh, no, she did not mean
that you were a servant, the stable boy can exercise
the horse, so we will say no more about it."

Mr. Blair said, "By the way, daughter, I have
seen Harvey Graham here quite often lately. If I
were you I would not encourage his attention as he
does not enjoy the best reputation. Remember, I
place no commands on you, but I give you timely
warning."

Alice replied that Mr. Graham seemed quite nice.
Mr. Blair did not reply. Soon after he arose from
the table. Alice went to the piano and was playing
a lively tune when Mr. Graham was announced.
After a general conversation with Mr. and Mrs.
Blair and a neighbor, who had preceded him by a
few moments, he went with Alice for a stroll in the
grounds. When they had got a safe distance from
the house, Alice said, "I will marry you only on
one condition, that I spoke of on your last visit."

"But, Miss Blair, I do not see how I can do anything to Dr. Grayson to turn the public against him.
I have found that he is very popular as well as skillful and is held in the highest esteem by the profession. And what is most singular, he attracts one
against his will. It is a pity that he is colored, for
a more magnificent man I have never seen, regardless of the fact that his skin is dark."

Alice replied, "I did not ask you for your opinion of this doctor, and if I am not worth a little favor, you will please take me back to the house."

At this Mr. Graham replied, "Miss Blair, I will do anything to win you for my wife." So she unfolded a plan so contemptible that he even hesitated to do, as it would bring untold misery to innocent ones. They talked long and earnestly and when he left he had the assurance that Alice would become his wife as soon as everything was carried out as planned.

Harvey Graham was the son of a grocer, but some years ago he had fallen heir to a considerable fortune, which he hastened to get rid of by gambling and riotous living and was looking around for means to replenish his fast diminishing fortune. When he sought and obtained the introduction to the banker's daughter, her father had warned her, but she paid no heed. Her mother talked with her of the man's dissipated habits but without avail. Alice seemed to have turned from a pure, innocent, lovely girl to a peevish, irritable woman.

When she returned to the house, she did not enter but remained on the porch. When her father went out, he found her alone. Mr. Graham, she told him, had been gone some time. She soon entered the house and proceeded to her room.

In the morning, as Alice did not come down to breakfast, her mother sent word telling her that they were waiting and was very much startled when she learned that Alice was too ill to rise. Dr. Cowan was at once sent for and looked very serious as he pronounced it a case of brain fever. Two trained nurses were installed, but the patient did not improve. Other eminent physicians were called in consultation, all pronounced it a serious case. Her life seemed to hang by a thread. Some one suggested sending for Dr. Grayson. He was accordingly sent for, but after looking at the sick girl could give them no hope and went away a prey to conflicting emotions. His heart was filled with profound pity for the stricken girl. Dian and Kenneth were sent for. The young bride hovered tenderly over her sister, forgetting her false accusations and injustice.

One day she regained consciousness and asked for her mother. The nurse left the room, but remained in close call. When alone with her mother, she said, "Mother, I am going to die, but I must ask one request of you."

Her mother exclaimed, "Oh, my darling, do not say that, I am sure you will get well."

But Alice replied, "No, mother, I feel that I have not much longer to live. Will you grant my request?"

Her mother, with tears rolling down her cheeks, promised to do anything that she could to make her happy.

Then she said, "Mama, send for Dr. Grayson."

Her mother replied that he had been there.

She smiled and said, "Is that so?"

Her mother replied that she was unconscious at the time and did not know of his visit.

"But, mother, you do not understand, I must see him alone. Oh, mother, do not delay."

Her breath came in short gasps. Her mother started at the change and hastily called the nurse, while she went to find Mr. Blair. He was near by waiting the outcome of his daughter's illness. When told of Alice's request, Mr. Blair was perplexed, he could not tell why, but he only knew that there was something in that request that he could not understand. And old Dr. Cowan, who had been there earlier, told them that there was something on their daughter's mind and she would never recover unless the trouble was removed and if they knew of anything that she desired, to lose no time in satisfying that desire. So, without further delay, Dr. Grayson was sent for. He remained for some time with her. When he left, it was noticeable that he was nervous and distraught for one of his profession. It was not long after before nurses and doctors were flying to and fro as the patient was worse, alarmingly so. Finally she rallied and expressed a wish to be alone with her mother and father. What was said no one knew, but when Mr. Blair went from the bedside of his daughter, he was fatally stricken and ere the week went by he was laid in the vault beside his ancestors.

CHAPTER XVI.

ALICE'S REQUEST.

When Dr. Grayson returned to his office, he telephoned to Kenneth, who was detained at his office. Kenneth arrived at once. Dr. Grayson said, "Kenneth, no man ever needed advice more than I do. You remember I told you of a wealthy man's daughter's fancy for me. You remember I told you that I did all that I could to discourage her."

Kenneth replied, "I remember it all and I know that you were talking truly for I could see that you did not love this lady and her presence was distasteful to you. I heartily sympathize with you, but tell me what has occurred to make you look as you do. Why, you look ten years older."

He replied, "She came to my office two or three times since I saw you. I felt that I could not let her compromise herself thus and you also remember I told you of Odene Lester. I decided to marry her. When this girl came to my office the last time, I had a decisive talk with her and told her that I expected to marry Odene. I wrote to Odene just previous to this girl's last visit to my office. She became hysterical and threatened to publicly accuse me of trying to dishonor her. Oh, Kenneth, you know, I have too much reverence for a woman that one should suffer at my hands."

Kenneth replied, "Oh, Doc, surely you have been mistaken in your judgment of her. She surely is not a lady to begin with," said Kenneth. "I do not want you to tell me anything that you care to withhold, but I feel that I could help you so much better if I knew the name and the position of this young lady. I promise you, Doc, I shall be as secret as the grave."

Dr. Grayson replied, "I have not finished. At this moment the lady is at death's door and I was sent for a short while ago. She had made known to her parents her desire to become my wife before she died and I have just received a letter from Odene making me supremely happy by accepting my humble self."

When Dr. Grayson spoke of this lady being at death's door, Kenneth went white and exclaimed, "My God, the name, the name, Doc!"

The doctor felt that he could not expose Kenneth's wife's sister, even when the question was repeated. The doctor answered, and said, "I have too much respect for her to betray her confidence in me."

Continuing he said, "I would sooner have my tongue plucked out by the roots."

Kenneth had received his shock and could not help thinking that Alice Blair was the lady who had given her love unsolicited. When he had become more calm, he stretched forth his hand, grasping that of the doctor's, exclaiming, "Doc, you are one of God's noblemen to shield a woman who has threatened to tear down all that you have built up, possibly your life would have been jeopardized. Oh, Doc, such nobility of character!"

It was some time before they grew composed

enough to take up the thread of conversation again. Dr. Grayson continued, that he was so surprised and saddened at the request that he soon left her presence without any promise to accede to her request.

Kenneth said, "Oh, Doc, what will you do?"

The doctor replied, "How could I comply with Odene's letter of acceptance in my pocket. This young lady's father was frantic and it would not surprise me if he is not very ill before another day. The mother is in hysterics, everyone else is mystified, for no one else knows what was said in that room and it must remain a secret, but oh, Kenneth, you are so wise, tell we what to do. If I were to marry her, she says that possibly she will not linger long, then I could marry Odene, but oh, Kenneth, it is a dangerous thing to do. I have heard of such cases before that the consummation of such a marriage acted like a tonic and the patient fully recovered."

"No, it would be unjust to both."

Just then Kenneth was called to the 'phone, telling him of the serious illness of Mr. Blair, making it necessary for him to hasten there at once. It was not long before Dr. Grayson was sent for. He hesitated to go.

CHAPTER XVII.

DR. GRAYSON AND MRS. BLAIR.

Although it was a long distance from Dr. Grayson's office to the millionaire's home, yet he did not take his car, but went on foot, for he wanted to think. His mind was torn by conflicting emotions. He found himself involved in a network of complications by no fault of his own unless his love for Odene Lester should be so construed. But he resolved in spite of the almost intricate position he found himself in that he would be loyal to his betrothed, the only woman that he ever loved.

When he arrived at the mansion, he was met by his true friend, Kenneth. Upon inquiring after Alice, he was informed that she had rallied and was asking for him. Dr. Grayson said, "As much as I sympathize with your sister-in-law, I cannot be untrue to the one I have promised to marry and will not prove myself less than a man by not only perjuring myself at the altar, but to make false vows to the dying. No, Kenneth, I cannot do so."

Kenneth replied, "I respect your views. Your decision is a noble one, but it seems hard to refuse to comply with her request and she is so young to die. Mother is on the verge of a collapse while father lies cold in death in the room there, pointing to the library where the body of the millionaire lay ready for burial.

Just then the door of the room softly opened and

Mrs. Blair, the grief stricken widow, entered, and with outstretched arms advanced to her son-in-law and exclaimed, "My son, oh, my son, Alice is dying and her cry is for Dr. Grayson." And before Kenneth could tell her that the doctor was there and she had not discovered his presence, she continued by saying, "I do not feel that I can give up my daughter. Yes, sometimes I think that I would rather see her taken out with her father than to accept this man as my son-in-law."

It was then that Kenneth said, "Mother, the doctor is here, let him speak for himself."

Mrs. Blair was very much startled and was in a hysterical condition and cried out, "What have you done to my daughter to bring her to the state she is now in? It was not manly in you to take advantage of your professional visit to win her heart and by so doing become a member of my family."

Dr. Grayson had not uttered a word while she heaped abuse on his head. He felt if the mother only knew how he had tried to combat her daughter's growing sentiment for himself, she would realize how unjust her accusations were, but he would rather have had his tongue cut out than to tell this proud mother, this prejudiced Southern woman, these facts.

Kenneth had tried to stop the avalanche of words, but to no avail. Still Dr. Grayson stood there silent, silence that condemned him in the eyes of the haughty widow, who continued by saying, "My children have never been denied anything in their lives and feeling that Alice will not be with us much longer, I will not refuse to consent to her request, but I want you to thoroughly understand that any presumption on your part to take advantage of your connection with my family will not be tolerated.''

This last insult was more than her magnanimous son-in-law could stand for and taking her gently by the arm he started to lead her out of the room, when Dr. Grayson stopped her. His face had grown stern and showing what an effort it had cost him to remain silent under the insults that he had been subjected to. He said, ''Mrs. Blair, spare yourself all uneasiness in regard to my advent into your family. My face is not white, but black people have pride. I have no intention whatever of becoming a member of your family. The idea of so doing is as repugnant to me as to you and regardless of the outcome of your daughter's illness, I absolutely refuse to lower my standard of manhood by becoming by law your son. Hoping for your daughter's complete recovery, I have the honor of bidding you a good afternoon.''

At this unlooked for decision, that Mrs. Blair was not prepared for, she burst into tears and cried hysterically while she exclaimed, ''Do you mean to tell me that you refuse to marry my daughter? You ought to be glad of the honor. You, whose ancestors were slaves. Do you mean to insult me thus, me an unprotected widow? Oh, Kenneth, my son, how can you stand by while I am grossly insulted?''

Kenneth replied, ''Mother, oh, mother, you do not realize what you are saying. Dr. Grayson is one of God's noblemen. Some day you will find out.''

Just then Dian came swiftly and silently in the

room, her eyes swimming in tears, and seeing Dr. Grayson, grasped him by the arm, hysterically crying, "Come, do come, and save sister, she is dying, but is continually calling for you."

He tried to tell her that he had an urgent call, but she appealed to her mother and husband to have the doctor see her sister, and much against his will he was ushered into the sick room.

There lay Alice, seemingly near death. She was so still, then starting up wildly, saying, "Sister, has the doctor come yet?"

Her mother said, "Alice, daughter, Dr. Cowan has just left and said that you were to be a good girl and try to sleep."

She put out her thin arms and cried, "Oh, mother, I do not want Dr. Cowan, I want Dr. Grayson. Mama, tell him that I cannot die in peace if he does not come to me."

The doctor had been standing in the shadow unobserved by the sick girl, a prey to the most distressing thoughts and was very much startled when the sick girl addressed her sister, saying, "Sister, I am sorry that I cannot live in a husband's love as you do, but see that it is engraved on my headstone, 'Alice, the beloved wife of Dr. Phillip Grayson.' Tell father to be good to the doctor when I am gone."

She did not know that her father had died of the shock of learning of her mad love for this colored doctor.

Continuing, she said, "Sister, fix my hair pretty so that the doctor will not be ashamed of his bride. He is late coming, but I know he had to go for the minister."

At those words, the doctor, unable to restrain himself, quietly left the room unobserved by all except Kenneth, who followed him out. Taking up his hat he accompanied him on his return.

They walked silently for some time. Then Kenneth slipped his arm in that of his friend and said, "Doc, can you not do this? It will only be for a little while and then a final release? Do not think of those wild words of a mother, frenzied with grief and despair and her brief widowhood and her eldest daughter slipping into the great beyond. Oh, Doc, I know it is hard. I do not think I ever heard of a case so sad in all of my life."

Dr. Grayson replied, "It was hard to stand there and take the abuse that I did awhile ago. The accusation was unjust, but I would have suffered ten thousand tortures rather than have said one word that would have reflected detrimentally on the woman who cherished such a warm regard for me and was brave enough to confess it. Think not that I hesitate or harbor any feeling of resentment at this time of sorrow on that account. The hour of sorrow is not the hour to cherish ill-natured feelings, it matters not how great the provocation. Possibly if I had no one to think of but myself, I might have made the sacrifice, but I cannot and will not sacrifice Odene. I would give years of my life to restore that girl to health and happiness. Just think how proud I was that it fell to my lot to save Miss Blair in that terrible wreck less than three years ago. Now I begin to think that it would have been far better if it had been other hands that had ministered to her instead of mine. My heart goes out in great pity for Miss Blair, but I must be true to my betrothed, true to myself and trust in God to make all things right.''

They were near Kenneth's office. He took the hand of Dr. Grayson in his, pressing it warmly, telling him that he must see his father and let him know how things were transpiring at the Blair homestead.

CHAPTER XVIII.

DR. GRAYSON PROCURES MARRIAGE LICENSES.

The next morning as Dr. Grayson was drawing on his gloves preparatory to going out, his office door was hurriedly pushed open and Dian, followed by Kenneth, her husband, entered. She was very pale, but resolute. She immediately approached the doctor and said, ''Oh, doctor, will you not save sister's life, there is nothing that we can do that will avail and it rests entirely with you.''

Continuing, she said, ''Complying with her request possibly may not save her, but even if we must lose her we do not want her cries ringing in our ears and it may be only for a little while, then release.''

The doctor was silent, but he realized that there was a relentless fate pursuing him from which there seemed to be no escape. He wanted to save Dian's sister, but not at the cost of his and Odene's future happiness. But if it could be accomplished in a professional way, he would not only be willing, but would work day and night to make her well.

Kenneth saw a look on Dr. Grayson's face that he had never seen there before. He spoke to his wife and said, "Come, I will place you in your car, I will be home presently."

After sending his wife home, he returned to the doctor's office and said, "Doc, do not do it. I am sure it will come out right."

The doctor did not answer, but picking up his hat, which he had laid down when the visitors had entered, he said, "Come with me, Kenneth."

Kenneth did not question him. He dared not do so, but after they had walked some distance, it was not until the doctor turned to go into the license clerk's office that he became aware of the doctor's intention. Grasping the doctor by the arm, he said, "Doc, don't make the sacrifice."

The doctor replied, "I feel that I will only be lending myself for a little while and I can no longer refuse and the death angels hovering nigh." He signed deeply as he repeated, "Odene, poor Odene," then turned and walked away with the documents in his pocket that would bind him to Alice Blair.

Did ever an expectant bridegroom feel so utterly wretched and sad. He did not want Alice to die, but he would not take the step that he was about to take if he thought that she might possibly recover. No, he felt that in a few days or possibly hours that he would be free to claim Odene and for the first time in his life Dr. Grayson was contemplating doing a dishonorable thing, and that was to

deceive the girl who had promised to be his wife,
for he felt that he could not tell her of Alice and he
was sure the Blairs would not be anxious to have it
known, so there was no need to make Odene unhappy
and some day in the future when his happiness was
assured he would tell her all.

CHAPTER XIX.

DR. GRAYSON AND ODENE.

After reaching the sidewalk, Dr. Grayson turned
to Kenneth, "I have a very important call to make,
then I will proceed to Mrs. Blair's."

After parting from Kenneth, the doctor realized
that he had left an important paper that he wanted
and was hastening to get it when some one exclaimed, "Oh, Doctor, how glad I am to see you."
And there before him stood Odene, his betrothed.
For a moment he was incapable of speech. There
was a startled look on his handsome face. Odene
noticed it and became alarmed, but he rallied and
asked her when she had come, meanwhile he said,
"I am on the way to the office, come with me."

She walked beside him, explaining that her mother's sister in a nearby village was quite ill and they
had been telegraphed for and she had motored from
there and was stopping at the hotel, intending to
give him a surprise, which, she laughingly said, she
was sure she had for he did not seem fully recovered. By this time they had arrived at the office,

and, unseen by anyone, he clasped her to his heart
in unrestrained joy that the force of the embrace
almost made her cry out, when like a flash the knowledge came to him: Like a serpent reclining on his
bosom were the papers that would unite him and
Alice Blair in the holy bonds of matrimony, and
pushing Odene almost roughly aside, he strode across
the room and before she could ask him to explain
his strange conduct, he sat down and bowed his head
upon the table. Just then Odene saw a paper lying
on the floor and feeling privileged drew from the
long envelope the fatal license and read with horror,
while her face showed great anguish, the name of
Dr. Phillip Grayson and Alice Blair, the date was
that very day. Then it flashed on her the cause of
his strange conduct when she had met him and now.

She calmly drew off her engagement ring, laid it
on the marriage certificate, quietly opened the door
and departed, feeling that death would have been
preferable.

The closing of the door aroused the doctor. He
looked around to find the room empty and with eyes
distended gazed upon the silent evidence of his perfidy. He hastened to the door, but he could not see
her, and try as he would he could not remember
the hotel that she was stopping at and really he
could not recall whether she had told him. However,
he called up two of the most prominent ones, but
without success. He then called up a very exclusive
boarding house and received the information that
the lady had been there but had left and they could
not tell where she had gone. He felt that he must

find Odene and explain all. He could not help but wonder why fate had been so remorseless and did not rejoice to hear, when he did not arrive at the Blairs, a message from Kenneth, saying the crisis was passed and Alice would live, adding, "Accept my congratulations, you are saved."

It seems as if Kenneth must have followed his message for in a very short time he entered the office, smiling his satisfaction, but upon seeing the troubled look on the doctor's face, said, "Why, I do believe that you regret not having to marry my fair sister-in-law. Why, man, you look as if you have been through a spell of sickness. Can you not realize the good news that you and the lovely Odene, whom I am most anxious to see, can be wedded, and if I were you, I would hasten to do so for I am not sure that as soon as Alice recovers and realizes how she has compromised herself, she may endeavor to make you feel that you are responsible for the position in which she finds herself placed. To say the least, it is unenviable and may cause you more trouble."

Dr. Grayson had not uttered a word yet. Now he pointed to the marriage license and a solitaire ring lying on it, and then while Kenneth stared unable to understand what it meant, Dr. Grayson told him all there was to tell. It was not much, but, oh, it meant years of untold misery for him. Needless to say that Kenneth's heart bled for his friend, who for no fault of his own was made to suffer so bitterly. There was nothing to say that could help his friend, but he left, telling him to call upon him if there was anything he could do. He also told him that Mr. Blair would be buried on the morrow.

CHAPTER XX.

ODENE.

To describe Odene's feelings when she read that fatal letter that meant that all was over between herself and Dr. Grayson. She went at once to where she was stopping and was soon on her way back to the village. On arriving at her aunt's, she was informed by her mother that her aunt was much better. The physician had told her the danger was past. She also told her daughter that the wealthy Mr. Maxwell from New York had been there to see her. He had recognized her that morning when he had seen her enter the car and was driven away, and on making inquiries, learned that we were stopping with relatives. Continuing she said, "Odene, it seems strange that he does not seek to marry some one of his race. It is true you are not fair, and cannot be mistaken for white. He has not been deceived."

Whereupon Odene replied and said that he did not care, that he was willing and would renounce the whole world for her sake.

Mrs. Lester replied, "Daughter, he must really love you. It is not often that a girl has been honored by two such offers as you have, but I think after all you have chosen well when you decided to marry Dr. Grayson. They say that his knowledge and skill is phenomenal. He has published medical books that have surprised the most eminent physicians and the most skillful surgeons. You have returned sooner than I expected. I am glad that you decided to wait for my chaperonage, for I did not like the idea of you going to town alone. I am sure that I shall be able to go with you tomorrow as the nurse is very competent.''

Odene replied, ''Mother, I have changed my mind. I think after all I shall marry Mr. Maxwell.''

Mrs. Lester was speechless with surprise and answered, ''Surely, Odene, you do not love this man, for how often you have denied yourself to him when he called. At first I felt pleased that he showed so much determination to see you. After learning from the photographer who was the original of the picture on exhibition and when you refused to see him, he continued sending flowers and books just as if you were one of his race. It is true that my father, who was your grandfather, was white. He loved my mother and when he died he left her so well provided for that I was enabled through the death of my mother and my inheritance from that source to educate you in the best college in the north. As far as education and culture goes, you can rank with any lady in the land.'' And looking proudly on her lovely daughter, she added, ''No one need be ashamed of your looks.''

Then, going back to the subject that had so much interest to those two. Mrs. Lester looked on the beautiful face of her daughter and realized that there was something wrong. When she asked Odene what was the matter, her daughter answered, ''There is nothing wrong, mother.'' And for the first time in her life deceived the mother who had always been her companion and confident.

Her mother replied that Mr. Maxwell had expressed a desire to call and she had given him permission to do so. "But, Odene, dear, think well what you are doing. I am sure that the doctor loves you and will make you a good husband and I have always felt that you returned his love."

While they were speaking there was a ring at the door that proved to be a messenger from Mr. Maxwell with a lovely bouquet of flowers for the sick room and a note for Odene begging her to see him for a few moments. Odene sat down and answered it at once assuring him that she would be pleased to see him that evening. Needless to say that when he arrived, he was most cordially received. He felt encouraged by the smiling greetings and again pressed his suit and was made happy by her answer.

He told her that he was afraid that her heart was in the keeping of the young physician. He said, "Darling, you have been so kind to make me happy by promising to become my wife. I thought that I was so near losing you that I now plead for an early marriage. Oh, Odene, if you only knew how I have followed you from place to place and how despairing I have been, you will again make me happy by naming an early day."

For the second time that evening, he was made supremely happy when she replied, "It shall be whenever you wish."

He said, "Odene, it is not as if I was a young man and could wait a long time. You must remember that I am twice your age and I am impatient for the day that I shall call you my own.'' Kissing her tenderly, he laughingly said, ''If it is left to me, I would say before the end of the week and I would take you abroad, then you could purchase lavishly of everything that you wish, knowing that you were deprived of a girl's delight—a trousseau.''

Odene, placing her hands in his, replied, ''Let it be the day after tomorrow.''

At those words, Reginald Maxwell kissed her again and again and told her that he would spend the rest of his life in making her happy.

After his departure, Odene at once sought her mother and told her that she had promised to marry her aged suitor. Her mother was prepared for this announcement, but not wholly pleased for there was something that had come over her daughter that she could not understand.

CHAPTER XXI.

CONVALESCING.

Alice Blair's recovery was rapid. She was sitting so quietly one evening when her mother was alone with her that Mrs. Blair said, ''Daughter, what are you thinking about?''

Alice replied, ''Will you please tell me if Dr. Grayson was here when I was so very sick?''

Her mother was filled with consternation at those words. She would like to have said no, but Alice was

watching her so intently that she replied, "Yes,"
adding, "You know that he is very skillful and it
was thought best to consult him, but do not worry,
he will not come again."

Alice replied, "No, there will be no need. Now,
mother, will you tell me who knows of my desire to
wed Dr. Grayson?"

Mrs. Blair hastily replied that no one takes any
account of what is said by one who is delirious.

Alice replied, "That is true, mother, but I was
not delirious and I felt that I was dying but I knew
all that was transpiring around me. Mama, did
anyone tell the doctor that my life was in danger
and any refusal to comply with my request might
prove fatal? But, of course, there was no necessity
to tell him, he being a physician, he must have
known. But, mother, I ask you again, who knows
of this desire of mine? Does Kenneth know?"

When she asked this last question, her face flushed
scarlet when she remembered that she rejected him,
and for him, above all others, to know how she had
been humiliated for this colored doctor, who had
not only showed how distasteful such a marriage
would be to him, but showed that he had not one
spark of affection for her and had demonstrated that
not even to save her life would he marry her.

Continuing, she said, "Mother, tell me all and from
today it shall be a closed book in my life's history."

Thus importuned, with many sobs and tears, her
mother related all the circumstances. And in justice
to her mother, who spoke of Dr. Grayson in the highest terms, giving it as her belief that the doctor had

hesitated for fear of embarrassment of the family by uniting himself to her daughter. She said it only went to prove that Dr. Grayson knew more than all the rest of the doctors together. The result was proven by your recovery. Next she asked for her father and was told that he had met with an accident. Then she said, "Mama, I remember when I requested to marry the doctor, father was taken ill. Is he not better?"

Her mother replied that he was much better and it was some days before she was told the truth. She cried bitterly and felt that she was the cause, and from that day she asked no more questions concerning what transpired while she was sick.

One day when she was in the parlor, Harvey Graham was announced. Alice received him coldly. When he told her that he was ready to carry out the scheme that she had planned when she was suddenly taken ill, she informed him that she felt that she could not marry him, therefore, would not expect him to render his service, with the hopes of winning her hand as she had promised him. However, she told him that she would see him soon as she was now able to walk about in the grounds. Sometimes her better nature prevailed and she felt that she would not seek revenge on Dr. Grayson, but she could not but remember with the bitterest humiliation that not even to save her life would Dr. Grayson marry her. No, she could neither forget nor forgive and resolved that she would show him no mercy.

CHAPTER XXII.

A CHILD SHALL LEAD THEM.

One day as Alice was taking a walk, she became very tired and stopped for a few moments to rest. There was a thick growth of bushes and on the other side some little children were playing. One little girl said: "Let's play stealing somebody's little child, and you be the child's mamma and you must cry, and I will say, that little black Susan stole it, and then you will be Susan's mother and whip her."

The other little girl spoke up, and said: "Oh, no, let's pretend that a man stole her and we will pretend to hang him."

One little girl spoke up, and said: "Oh, girls, those are wicked thoughts. Let us play taking good things to poor people and read the Bible, tell pretty stories and make them laugh. That would be better than to make them cry. And my mother said that sometimes we just imagine somebody hurts us when they don't." And she said: "Even if they do hurt us, it would be petter to be good to them and then God would love us. And do you know, they say that heaven is so much prettier than this world that I want to go there. Mamma said that she was going there and that is why she would never tell a story or make anyone sad."

One little girl exclaimed: "There comes little Jane. Let's ask her to pray. She prays so pretty it just seems that she sees God and is talking to him just as we talk to each other."

When little Jane, who was only ten years old, reached them, her little friends told her what they had been talking about. So the girls all knelt down while she prayed. In her prayer she said: "Dear Jesus, not only forgive those that do wicked things, but please stop those that are thinking of doing wicked things."

The children were so busy that they did not hear a convulsive sob on the other side of the hedge, but soon left as happy as good children could be.

Dr. Grayson was saved from a terrible revenge. Alice Blair saw herself revealed as she had never been before, and with tears streaming from her eyes, resolved to be a better woman. She was being led to the heights by those little innocent children. After drying her eyes, she returned home, went to her room, remained during the rest of the day. The next day she surprised her mother by asking her to take her abroad. As they had nothing to keep them here and felt that a few months of travel and change would do her good, her mother was overjoyed, as she had asked Alice on several occasions to take a trip, but she had always refused. In less than a month, Alice Blair and her mother had left the South. Alice felt that she could no longer face Kenneth or Dr. Grayson.

Several days later, Mr. Randolph, with a badly sprained ankle, had sent for Dr. Grayson. While seated in Mr. Randolph's apartment, who was still living alone—Dian or Kenneth could not prevail upon him to live with them—Kenneth came in and after being assured that his father was doing nicely,

warmly greeted Dr. Grayson, asking him if there
was much sickness. He replied that he was pleased
to say there was no increase of sickness. Mr. Randolph laughingly turned to Dr. Grayson, and said:
"Kenneth accused me of undue hilarity at my
friend's wedding that caused me to make a misstep,
injuring my ankle."

Kenneth replied: "Oh, by the way, dad, you promised to tell me of your friend's wedding."

Mr. Randolph said: "I had to go to Louisville the
day before yesterday. I met a friend whom I have
not seen since Kenneth was in college. This man
is somewhat younger than I, possibly about 40 years
of age, while I am some years older. He recognized
me as I did him, only he looked much younger than he
really was, and seemed to be as happy as a school boy.
He placed his arm within mine and confided in me
that he was on his way to get a license to marry a
lovely girl many years younger than himself. They
were to marry in the parlors of a hotel with only
her mother and one or two of the hotel guests as witnesses. This gentleman, Reginald Maxwell, belonged
to the most exclusive set; therefore, I was much surprised when he married this charming girl, named
Odene Lester. No one could blame him, however,
for his wife is a beautiful colored girl, highly cultured. They say that he has been in love with her
for a long while, but was led to believe that her heart
had been given to another."

Reginald Maxwell and his bride were still abroad.
They appeared to be quite happy. Odene was always
considerate and kind to her husband, while he fairly

worshiped his lovely wife. He lavished costly jewels
and rich gowns on her until she told him that she
could not use them all. If she was ever sad or unhappy, she kept it concealed from her husband and
he began to think that after all, she had not cared
for the talented doctor. However, Odene had much
spirit and could not forget how Dr. Grayson had
rapturously embraced her and at the same time had
in his pocket a license to marry another. She could
not understand his perfidy. She had set him up as
an idol and he had proven himself mere clay and the
image she had exalted on the sacred altar of her
heart lay shattered at her feet. When she thought of
those things, she felt no regret for having united herself to one who showed how deep and true was his
love. She not only encouraged his caresses, but
caressed him warmly in return. She was not only
learning to appreciate him, but her heart was so
deeply touched that she felt almost content at her
lot. Yet there were times when she was restless and
her eyes grew dim with unshed tears.

They returned home after an absence of one year
abroad and were located in New York, her husband's
home. Mrs. Blair and Alice are still abroad and
doubtful if they shall return for some months to
come.

When Mr. Randolph mentioned Odene Lester as
the name of the girl his friend had married, Kenneth
was filled with consternation. Although he had felt
very much concerned when the doctor had told him
of Odene's unfortunate discovery of the license and
the broken troth, the engagement ring reposing on

the fatal document, neither he nor the doctor were
prepared for the decisive steps Odene had taken.
The only conclusion that they could arrive at was
that some persistent admirer was near and that she,
in a fit of pique, had accepted him and consented to
an immediate marriage. Kenneth had not told his
father of Dr. Grayson's predicament, but the doctor
gave him permission to do so and soon left. Mr.
Randolph expressed genuine regret that it was his
misfortune to make the announcement so harshly and
hastened to communicate his regrets to the man
whose life was so full of bitterness and turmoil.

Dr. Grayson arrived home in a troubled state of
mind. It was hard to believe that Odene was lost
to him forever. Forgetting for the moment that he
was about to commit an act that would have separated them just as effectually, he bowed his head upon
his hand and wondered why he had been pursued so
relentlessly by fate. He arose, taking the ring and
license, put them away together, declaring that he
would never look upon either again. He worked
harder than ever, gave himself no time to rest, finally
it was noticeable that he was losing flesh and looked
very bad. He was advised to take a needed rest,
but he declined to do so until one day he was found
unconscious in his office. This was followed by a
slow fever and it seemed he would never arise, but
when he did, he was only a mere shadow of his
former self. He decided to travel. He went abroad,
worked in the hospitals of Berlin. It was while in
Berlin that Dian received a telegram that her mother
had passed away and her sistser was bringing the

body home. Mrs. Blair was laid beside her husband.
Dian and Kenneth prevailed on Alice to remain with
them, but this she resolutely refused to do. Some
months later, they received a letter from Alice telling them that she had joined the Red Cross nurses
and would remain abroad.

CHAPTER XXIII

DR. GRAYSON'S ILLNESS.

Dr. Grayson had been away now two years when
he accepted an invitation to visit one of his old patients who resided in Scotland. He needed rest and
felt that he would get a complete rest in the little
hamlet, but there was an epidemic of fever and we
find the doctor working harder than ever until, overcome himself, and as he had not been strong since
four years previous when he was so dangerously ill,
a nurse was installed there. When she was ushered
into the sick room she turned very white and seemed
on the point of fainting, but soon rallied when she
saw that the patient was dangerously ill and it was
necessary to have another nurse.

It was now the third week of his illness. The danger was passed, but he was very weak. Finally he
began to recognize objects. It was then the nurse
spoke of leaving. She seemed afraid that he would
recognize her and such was the case. Before she
could leave he asked: "Where am I? And, Miss
Blair, how came you here?" Alice answered his

questions, but told him not to talk. He lay quietly
for a while watching her as she moved around the
room, putting things in order, fixing the flowers in
the vase. He lay there thinking of the past and
sighed when he realized that Odene was lost to him
forever and wondered if Alice still cherished any
affection for him. He knew that he would never
more be happy, but he might make her happy. So
one day, as the nurse sat reading to him, he placed
his hand over the page, and said: "I would rather
talk." He said: "Miss Blair, I feel just like a culprit to let you administer to me after my seeming
lack of appreciation for your past kindness to me
and your present interest. I can only offer you the
ashes of a dead love, but I wish it was in my power
to make your life happier than the past."

She replied: "I neither ask nor expect your love.
That is not yours to give as you have already bestowed it on another."

Dr. Grayson answered and said: "Surely you have
heard that Odene has been the wife of another for
more than four years."

Alice exclaimed: "No, I did not know." And her
face grew pale. Somehow she felt that she could
marry this doctor, but she asked herself this question: "Would she be satisfied with the second place
in his heart?" Alice was only a woman and knowing that he held the first and only place in her heart,
that she would be happy. She placed her hand in
Dr. Grayson's and promised to be his wife.

Just then there was a rap at the door. She opened
it and admitted Mark Rogers, the assistant nurse,

who had been invaluable in the sick room. Mark bowed in silence as he handed in the mail that consisted of a letter for the doctor that seemed to have followed him from place to place, so numerous were the postmarks, and some papers. The letter was from Kenneth. While the doctor read his letter, nurse Alice took up the papers and almost the first thing that met her eyes was the great legal battle won by the noted lawyer, Kenneth Randolph, in New York in the United States of America. The case spoken of was that of a beautiful widow who was about to be defrauded out of her valuable property left by her deceased husband.

The article went on to state how a few years previous society had been startled by the announcement that Reginald Maxwell, the wealthy retired merchant, had married a beautiful colored girl by the name of Odene Lester. His death occurred about a year previous to the suit. When Alice read those lines she became faint, her face was colorless, as she realized that Odene was free and that the doctor was forever lost to her. At last she lifted her eyes to the man she had promised to wed. His face was set, but showed resolution. She realized that his letter must have contained bad news. She had no idea what it was; she did not connect it with the article that she had just read in the paper, for she thought that piece of information would have made him supremely happy and to have considered it a most fortunate circumstance that he was made aware of Odene's widowhood before he led another to the altar. Yet she could not understand the shocked expression that rested upon his face. He seemed near collapse.

Forgetting her own misery, she advised him to take a rest as he was not strong. She hastily summoned Mark Rogers, the assistant nurse, but he was soon himself again, declaring that there was no cause for anxiety and was soon chatting as pleasantly as ever, seemingly in the best of spirits. Yet he mentally exclaimed: "It is fate, cruel fate, that is pursuing me," and silently prayed for strength to carry out the resolution that he had made. He had resolved to marry her who had sacrificed so much for him. Who had renounced kin and country, had jeopardized her social standing in the country that had given her birth. She had severed home ties, and all for his unworthy self. And she knowing all that he had suffered through the loss of one that he held most dear, was willing to take the pieces of his shattered heart still bleeding from the wounds inflicted by the colored girl, and would devote the remainder of her life in curing those wounds and if the scars should remain, she would still feel that she had something to do. She would heal that scar by such love and devotion that he would in time give her his entire love. As he thought of Alice's love so rare and beautiful, there came to him a revelation. A light illumined that handsome face that had been so gloomy and from the very depths of his heart, he felt that God had been very good to him. He at last realized that his love for Alice had been increasing each day and did not regret his betrothal to her and felt that he had been blind. He said: "I will

spend the balance of my life in making her happy,"
and asked his Father in heaven to make him worthy
of this noble girl.

Although the doctor had declared that there was
no cause for anxiety as he was feeling all right, yet
Alice and Mark left him to himself. Soon after he
went in quest of Alice. He found her seated in the
little vine covered porch. Her eyes were red as if
from weeping. He gently took her hand, pressing
her fondly to his bosom. She drew herself from him,
yet he retained her hand, which she appeared reluctant to let him hold. He asked her to name an early
day for their marriage that they might leave the
almost deserted hamlet. He had seated himself by
her side. She seemed to be deeply agitated. He
again drew her to him, begging her to answer and
make him happy. For answer, she placed the paper
in his hands with the fatal article uppermost. Her
only words were: "Odene is free. She is a widow."

Dr. Grayson was not aware until then that the
article was in the paper. He was genuinely dis-
tressed, for he had refrained from mentioning the
matter to her. He gently replied: "I know it, but
she is nothing to me and we will carry out the plans
as we have arranged. We will take a long sea voyage for you need a rest as well as I do."

CHAPTER XXIV.

NURSE ALICE.

Before the doctor's proposal of marriage, Alice was making preparations to leave, accompanied by the old housekeeper who had been pressed into service as she had no relatives and nowhere to go. Alice knew that the doctor was getting along nicely and that Mark was a good conscientious nurse and that her services could be dispensed with, consequently, she continued those preparations. The doctor, still seated by her side, begged her to name an early day for their marriage. She answered, and said: "I will tell you in the morning." He had to be satisfied with that. The next morning he arose bright and early, drew aside the curtains from the window of his small but well kept room, feeling very happy over the prospects of leading to the altar the woman of his choice, his queen.

As he stood there looking out of the window, he thought he saw what appeared to be a woman disappearing over the ridge. She stopped, glanced backward, reeled as if about to fall. He watched her until she had disappeared from view. He stood for some time afterwards thinking of the event. He could not tell why, but somehow the woman had interested him. Finally dismissing her from his thoughts, he went in search of his betrothed. He did not find her in the little room where they ate their meals, although the table was daintily spread, so he sat down and waited. Presently the old Scotch housekeeper and Mark entered. The doctor greeted them both pleasantly, again taking up some papers that he had been examining. Presently old Mrs. Briggs, the housekeeper, asked him if he would not eat his breakfast before it got cold. He looked somewhat startled and surprised, then said: "Please tell Miss Blair that I am waiting." He had not noticed that Mark held a sealed note in his hand, he immediately opened it, although he was agitated and his hands shook nervously. This is what he read:

"Dr. Grayson:

My Esteemed Friend.—In spite of the fact that we are forever parted by fate, I shall always feel that you are indeed my friend.

It would be most cruel, indeed, were I to keep you bound by a proposal that you made me and I accepted. I know that you feel that it is your duty and would persist in carrying out the arranged plans, but dear friend, I cannot and will not allow you to sacrifice your principles of honor for my sake. Duty and love do not always go hand in hand through life. Sometimes it becomes a sin to do what we claim is duty and it is with a sense of shame that I remember the time in the days past when I cast aside my maidenly modesty to influence you to pretend a sentiment for me that you did not feel. Yet out of your big magnanimous heart, you would make me your wife. I feel that it is pity, not love, that has prompted your desire to marry me. I wish that I could feel otherwise. Scorn me if you will, but do not pity me.

If you should think of me in the future, think of

me only as Nurse Alice and may God bless you in
every walk in life. Please do not seek me. Let this
be good-bye forever.

ALICE."

As soon as the doctor recovered from his surprise,
he asked what she had said. Mark replied: "She
said that her services were no longer needed and
hoped that I would remain with you. But as I have
planned to go away immediately, that will be impossible."

The doctor felt that it would have been better had
he died. He felt like giving up. Then like a flash,
it came to him that it was Alice he saw disappearing
over the ridge. He reproached himself for not making an investigation. He realized his stupidity and
what it might cost him. He doubted if ever he would
be able to trace her, but was determined to make the
effort.

He immediately began to pack for a journey and
was quite sorry that Mark could not go with him,
but their destinations lay in opposite directions. The
doctor was sorry to lose Mark as he had learned to
like the youth who had been bereft of all of his people by the cruel ravages of the fever epidemic. He
had just reached the age of two and twenty. He
wanted to study for the ministry, but his progress
had been retarded by adversities. Dr. Grayson would
have given him a well filled purse to help him in his
chosen profession, but the young man courteously
declined, remarking that he could make his own way.
He did not tell the doctor that he did not wish to
obligate himself to him, to the man who had won

Nurse Alice's heart, nor of the many sleepless, agonizing nights that he endured. He resolved that henceforth, to endeavor to concentrate his future life to the service of his maker and forever put all thoughts of Miss Blair from him. Often, oh, how often, he had noticed how tenderly she cared for the stricken man. Her very touch seemed to be a caress. Sometimes Mark thought that he would die from the terrible pain that was eating out his heart and it was with a feeling of satisfaction, if not happiness, that he watched her departure. Feeling that he had probably been mistaken in regard to the feeling that existed between her and the doctor, he resolved to find her and plead his own cause and ask her to be his wife. He knew that he was a poor man, but would work for her as no man ever worked for a woman. He did not know of her wealth, but was satisfied that she had been reared amid the best surroundings, culture and refinement.

CHAPTER XXV.

MARK AND ALICE.

He was fortunate to find her in less than two weeks and so changed that he scarcely recognized her. Mark had stopped in a little church to rest on a hot, sultry day. He saw her there and spoke to her. At first she hesitated to speak, but she always liked the youth who seemed so lonely and friendless. She allowed him to walk home with her and gave him per-

mission to call when he wished. She told him that
as she needed rest that it was her intention to remain
there for a fortnight or more, provided that he did
not disclose her retreat. He readily agreed to keep
her abode secret. He went to see her, telling her of
his great love. At first she gave him no hope, but he
seemed so alone and she had cast herself adrift from
her people. Then she began to look more favorably
upon his suit. She knew that she did not love him,
and not until she had told him all was she satisfied.
Sometimes during the narrative, her face was scarlet
and eyes dim with tears, but she did not spare herself. She exonerated the doctor from all blame.

Mark listened in silence. When she had finished,
he drew her to his arms, and said: "Poor girl, if you
only bestow one-half of the love and devotion on me
that you have on Dr. Grayson, I will be content."
And when he imprinted a kiss on her lips, sealing
this betrothal, she did not object and made him happy
by telling him at the expiration of her stay there,
that she would become his wife.

He felt it would be a pleasure of love to work and
provide for her and was very disappointed when she
told him that she had enough for both. She wanted
to see her future husband's ambition crowned with
success. And without his knowledge, the next day
she went to see a prominent lawyer in the village.
When she left there, she felt much happier, knowing
that, come what would, Mark was well provided for.

A few days later he went to the now deserted hamlet and disposed of a little cottage, all that was left
to him. He realized the small amount of money,

enough for present needs, saving him the embarrassing necessity of allowing Alice to provide in their early stage of matrimony.

She missed him the few days that he was absent, and on his return did not withdraw from his embrace. Was Alice Blair fickle? No, she was not. But having lost the man that she truly loved, she resolved to marry one that she felt she could make happy. What it cost her to renounce her old love, none can tell.

One day, about three days before their marriage was to be solemnized, Mark was surprised on his arrival at the little vine covered villa to find her seriously ill. The village physician found out that she was evidently a lady of birth and refinement, and lost no time in having some of the best people in the town interest themselves in the beautiful young stranger so near death. She had been constantly calling for Dr. Phillip Grayson since morning, and when Mark arrived they naturally thought it was he. He was immediately ushered into the sick girl's chamber and none will ever know what the promised husband of Alice Blair suffered to hear his betrothed babbling about the doctor, begging him not to let Odene take him away.

Before the end came, she expressed a wish to be buried under the Italian skies. With her last breath, she whispered the name of Phillip Grayson with her head resting on the breast of Mark Rogers, her intended husband. Her funeral was attended by the most notable people in the town and floral tributes showed the great esteem in which she was held by the villagers.

Dr. Grayson went to London to an address that he had given to Mark Rogers in case that he should find Alice while he worked on each clew without success. He frequented the hospitals, thinking that she would likely follow the vocation of nurse, but it was of no avail, she had disappeared as completely as if the earth had swallowed her up. And as he had not heard from Mark, he felt that he, too, had been unsuccessful in his search. Strange, he had almost completely lost sight of Odene.

He felt that she had marred his life. He failed to take into consideration that he had planned to deceive her. He lost sight of the fact, had he married the banker's daughter when she lay at death's door, and had she passed away, not until then would Odene Lester have been aware of his marriage. Yet he felt that Odene had treated him badly by her hasty marriage to the retired merchant. He thought of all the sacrifices that Alice had made for him and how willingly she renounced all, and even after his refusal to marry her when she was so badly stricken that death was threatening to take her young life, yet how in the fever stricken Scottish hills, she had risked her life and nursed him. He thought of her gentle and soothing touch and had often wondered when she rested, so faithful was she to his wants and comforts. He had told of his early love, his hopes and how they had ben blighted by the girl that was to have been his wife.

Alice forgave him all and promised to become his wife when he received that fatal letter and the announcement in the paper of Odene's widowhood that

drove Alice from his side. He felt that Alice thought
that she would be doing him injustice were she to
marry him now when his first love was free. He had
felt that death would have been a release. He had
not realized how dear Alice had become to him until
he had lost her. As he sat there in the room in the
hotel, thinking of all these things, he realized that
Odene had only wounded his pride, but Alice his
heart.

He was not a fickle man. He was fully satisfied
that if he could find Alice and make her his wife, the
world would hold nothing else to be desired. He felt
much depressed, but was determined not to leave
England until he had found her. As he sat thus
gloomily reviewing the past, Mark Rogers was ushered in. Dr. Grayson grasped his hand. He had not
expected him, but a letter.

His first words were: "Have you found her?"
Mark did not reply at once. He seemed incapable of
speech. He gravely bowed his head. Dr. Grayson
exclaimed: "Thank God! Tell me quick where to
find her." Continuing, he asked: "Why did you
lose time in coming, when you might have wired
me?" And in his excitement and rapidity of speech,
he had failed to notice his visitor's face. Finally
the doctor said: "For God's sake, speak and tell
me where to find her."

Mark answered: "I found her, only to lose her
again."

Dr. Grayson was speechless with amazement by
such a blunder. Finally he asked: "Tell me how
after you found her, you managed to lose her?"

Mark replied: "Alice is forever at rest."

The doctor sprang forward and grasped the other's arm and in a broken whisper, commanded Mark to tell him all. He sank into a chair and listened while he was told all that the reader is acquainted with. Also revealing his own love for Nurse Alice. How he had worshiped her and knew how hopeless that love was and how bitterly he had fought his mad love that seemed to be consuming him. And when he had accompanied her to her beautiful vine covered villa, he could no longer conceal his love for her and when she had said that she never intended to wed, finally she promised to become his wife. "However, before she plighted her troth to me, she told me of her promise to you and the article in the paper that made her promise void, that the circumstance was beyond your control, that her life was forever severed from you that she would never willingly be in your presence again,—that is when she promised to consider my proposal. Consequently, when I went to see her the next day, she told me if I was willing to pick up the burden of the tangled threads of her life that she would become my wife. But we were fated not to wed. She was stricken with the fever, and in her weakened condition, could not rally."

The doctor knew that Mark was an exceptionally fine young man, far above the average, had always been regarded thus, but in his misery and disappointment, was inclined to be unjust.

Therefore, he replied with much hatred: "I sent you to find my betrothed and you have acted the part of a traitor to steal my intended bride. Fool that I was to trust you. There was never a more dishonorable act.'' And, loosening Mark's arm, said: "I would not soil my hands with such a miserable coward. Else I would throw you bodily out!"

Although the blood rose to Mark's face during this bitter denunciation, yet he stood still, without uttering a word. The doctor continued: "You tried to cheat me and lost." He stopped for want of breath.

Then Mark replied: "I, too, loved this fair nurse, but not until she had assured me that she found it impossible to become your wife did I plead my own cause. I suppose that we both loved Miss Blair,— our love must have been different. Had she asked me to have you brought to her or to have been conducted to you, I should have done so, knowing that I was promoting her happiness, knowing full well that my own heart would break. You think you suffer, but, oh, God, think how I must have felt when the woman that I expected to lead to the altar died with your name upon her lips, her head pillowed on my breast!''

And boy though he was, he strode up to this distinguished physician, many years his senior, and of a much larger physique, and exclaimed: "Do you understand? No, you do not. You who have gone onward and forward to fame, have yet to learn the inward machinations of human hearts. You have lost sight of that vein of sentiment in the hearts of the young. While you pursued fame, you in your narrow pursuits in the medical world, will never know what it cost me to see her beautiful pansy colored eyes rest on me without recognition, calling me Phillip, her Phillip. I tried to make her understand, but could not, and it made her happy to think that it was you that her fever parched lips pressed instead of mine. I had planned a home where we two could be so happy together."

For a moment he remained silent, the thick sobs choking him. Finally he said: "I am going far away and spend the rest of my life as a missionary in a foreign land." And holding out his hand to the man that had spoken so scathingly to him, said: "I cannot part in anger from one she loved so dearly, nor can I forget that we both loved her—God only knows which loved her best."

The doctor stood abashed at the rebuke from this boy preacher. Taking the hand extended to him, he said: "I am sorry. None can fathom the depths of such sorrow as yours." Continuing, he said: "Once I offered to assist you in your chosen work. You rejected my offer, but in the name of our sainted Alice, take this check, I pray, for the heathen."

At another time Mark would have refused, yet he knew that the doctor would be happier, and, laying aside his feelings, he accepted it. Then after directing the doctor to where Alice was buried, he hastened away. Dr. Grayson went to Naples, Italy, and had a costly shaft erected to her memory, with the simple words inscribed, "At Rest."

CHAPTER XXVI.

HERBERT AND JAMES.

Dr. Grayson then prepared to return to the United States, but ere he set sail the great world war broke out. He entered the service for he felt that he must work, work. But before enlisting, he sent word to Kenneth and Dian of their sister's death. Both wept bitterly for the sister who had died in a foreign land among strangers and requesting that her body rest under Italian skies. He also sent Alice's jewelry and other possessions thereby establishing without a doubt all the sad facts of their lost loved one and one day they stood beside the grave of their sister whom they had loved so well and had entreated in vain for her return.

Dr. Grayson worked unceasingly. He administered to many as they lay on the field, but everywhere he went he could hear words of praise of the blind evangelist who not only gave spiritual comfort, but was proficient at nursing as well. Dr. Grayson had not seen this evangelist, but one day he heard someone say, "There comes the blind preacher." And glancing down the aisle of the hospital ward, he was surprised to see one of his race. He was a man of medium height. He had on a neat fitting suit. He carried a bible in his hand, but he was not seen to open it. He had also partially regained his sight, yet he still wore dark glasses. A holy light shone on his countenance that reflected from above.

Miss Jones, a nurse, said, "I hope that he will be able to comfort that poor soldier brought in this morning. At times he is delirous, then he appeals to someone to take a message home, but before he can dictate a message, he relapses into unconsciousness."

The evangelist stopped at the cot of the soldier and taking hold of one of his hot restless hands, he placed his other hand on the brow to calm the sufferer. As the minister counseled him to look to Jesus, he spoke of how the Saviour suffered and died. He realized that the soldier's hours were growing short. He noticed that he had become sightless. But he continued saying, "Look to Jesus, do you hear!"

Whereupon the dying soldier answered, "Yes, yes I do. Take a message to my mother and tell her that all is well."

The evangelist bent his head to catch the whispered voice, "I am Herbert Drake, my parents live in a village not far from Louisville, Kentucky, in the United States of America." It was then that the preacher, who was none other than James Taylor, the little playmate of Herbert Drake and was blinded by him by an accident, was so visibly affected that he could scarcely speak, but he realized that Herbert's life was fast ebbing away. He aroused himself and once more repeated, "Do you hear!"

Herbert replied, "I can hear, but I cannot see you."

Then James Taylor said, "Do you remember the little colored boy in your home town by the name of James Taylor, or did any one ever tell you about him?''

He replied, ''Oh, yes, yes. As I grew older, I was told how I made blind the little chap and it has been the wish of my life to meet him and ask his forgiveness, but it cannot be. But if you should come across him, say that with my last breath that I wished for his pardon.''

Then the evangelist again asked him, if he could hear. And being assured as before, the evangelist bowed low over the cot of the dying soldier and said, ''Herbert, I am James Taylor, your childhood playmate.''

Then Herbert seemed to shrink from him, saying, ''Oh, I know that you hate me, but I did not know.''

The tears were now falling fast from the evangelist's eyes as he clasped more tightly the hand of the dying soldier assuring him there was nothing to forgive that he had not been intentionally harmed and that his mother, who had passed into the realms of the great beyond, had often told him the story of his affliction and impressed upon him that he was a loyal friend and that if he ever met him that he was always to remember that. She told him that he was a good boy and would make a good man.

''Oh, James, did she say that? then I can die happy.'' He soon passed away. Some months afterward when peace was declared, James Taylor, the blind evangelist, walked into the steamship's office. He met Dr. Grayson there, who had not the opportunity before to speak to James Taylor. He did so at once. He told James how he had been called

in to attend him when his eyes were injured. They
sailed on the same vessel and parted in New York.

Dr. Grayson lost no time in calling upon Kenneth
and Dian with the sad mission. Kenneth warmly
thanked the doctor for his kind services and was
much pleased at the costly stone of Italian marble
erected there and would have paid for the shaft, but
the mere mention of so doing, filled the doctor with
such unspeakable sorrow, that Kenneth ceased to
refer to it. He knew the doctor felt that it was his
right. When Kenneth was alone in his office with
the doctor, the doctor told him all that had occurred
between them. He dwelt on how tenderly he was
cared for by Alice when he was stricken with the
fever. He spoke of the fatal article in the paper
and its consequence and direful ending. He spoke
in glowing terms of the young theologian and his
hope to make her his wife. Yet he could not tell
his friend how she had died with his name upon her
lips. It flavored too much of egotism. Strange as it
may seem, Dian grew very cold and unfriendly toward Dr. Grayson whose life had been so closely
woven in and associated with her family. She treated
him with scant courtesy and ill-concealed contempt.
The doctor could not help but notice and feel the injustice of it. Yet he felt that it was but natural
for Alice's sister to associate him with all the misery and unhappiness that befell her beautiful sister.
Kenneth remained the ever true friend of the doctor and tried to apologize for the change in Dian,
his beautiful wife. The doctor only pressed his
hand and said, "I understand." They often ex-

change office visits, but the doctor declined all invitations to the young attorney's home, neither mentioned Odene's name.

One afternoon as Kenneth sat alone in his office, a lady was ushered into his presence by the office boy. Kenneth arose at once and courteously invited her to be seated, but she hesitated to do so. Although her veil was lowered, yet he thought that he saw a bright smile on the face. The lady did not keep him in suspense long. Lifting her veil at the same time extending her hand, she exclaimed, "Cousin Kenneth, have you forgotten me!" All at once he recognized Agnes Blankleigh. He greeted her most cordially. After she was comfortably seated, he took a seat opposite and asked her when she had arrived and if Lord and Lady Blankleigh were with her. She informed him that she came over with Dr. and Mrs. Campbell, a dear friend of her mother. She also explained that she had not been feeling so well lately and a sea voyage was recommended and as Dr. Campbell was coming to America, he insisted that she should accompany his wife.

Kenneth told her that her looks did not indicate that her health was not good and declared that she was beautiful beyond description. She stopped him asking him if he was not afraid of making her vain. She was not unlike his wife. While Agnes' hair was more of a red gold, Dian's hair was decidedly auburn with a gold tint, so rare and much sought for by artists for their masterpieces. He asked her where they were stopping. She told him, at the St. Clare Hotel, but did not know how long that they would remain in Louisville.

Kenneth and Dian were now residing just outside of the city, having located there soon after Dian's mother had passed away. Kenneth had a luxurious law office on a popular street in the city. Agnes had no trouble in locating him and succeeded in giving him a complete surprise. After a pleasant hour, she arose to depart, declining an invitation to let him drive her out to his home in his car. He promised, however, to bring Dian to see her the next day. Although Dian had come home from college, the proud possessor of a well-earned diploma, had also received private instructions in the most exclusive society etiquette, yet it was with some misgiving that she prepared to call on her husband's royal cousin. She wore a neat calling costume that was indeed most becoming as well as appropriate. Kenneth introduced his wife to his cousin Agnes who mentally exclaimed, ''What a beautiful woman.''

Kenneth, who loved his wife and was proud of his cousin, was delighted to see them meet so cordially, conversing as easily as if they had known each other for years. Dr. and Mrs. Campbell returned from a drive as Kenneth and Dian were taking their leave. Dian invited Dr. and Mrs. Campbell to accompany Agnes the next day to dinner. They also exacted a promise from their fair English cousin to spend some time with them as their guest. When the callers had departed, Mrs. Campbell remarked on the beauty of Dian and her beautiful hair. Soon Agnes went to her room to dress for dinner, but it was sometime before she began to make her toilet. She could not tell why, but she felt disturbed, not

only by the beauty of Dian, but her future possibilities as a great belle. She knew that Dian had never
realized how wonderfully beautiful she was and felt
if ever she awakened to that fact and took advantage of it, that she would have the world at her feet.
As for her part, she would never encourage her to
be any other than what she was, the wife of a promising attorney.

But for Kenneth, how much she admired her distinguished cousin. None ever knew. She could not
help but feel that Dian was unworthy to be his wife,
feeling that she was unappreciative of that honor.
She felt a gloom settling over her that was hard to
dispel. The next day, Dr. and Mrs. Campbell and
Agnes were the guests of Kenneth and Dian. When
Agnes had divested herself of her long cloak that
completely enveloped her, she stood revealed in all
her aristocratic beauty, arrayed in a most becoming
toilet of dull blue with bodice of silver brocade,
edged with tiny black ostrich feathers with turquoise
ornaments, with the exception of a diamond spray
in her golden brown hair. When Dian had dressed
to receive her guest, she asked Kenneth if she would
pass inspection of her English guest. He assured
her that she was always beautiful no matter what
she wore. Although she was never envious of anyone's attire, yet she did not want to appear dowdy
on this occasion that would stand out conspicuously
as the first time that she had entertained her royal
cousin and her distinguished friends. But when she
viewed her cousin's toilet, she felt that her own
dress was very commonplace indeed, yet she had put

on a white silk dress, simply made. Her only ornaments, a spray of Ivy Leaves at her belt.

It was not that she could not afford elegant clothes,
but she preferred to dress more simply in accord
with the society that was considered very smart in
that city. But we all know there could be no comparison with Blankleigh Castle of England and its
regal society with this little southern town. Dian
was a perfect hostess. She had efficient servants
that on this occasion did not fail her. And as Kenneth viewed the well appointed table, he smiled his
approval at his wife. Mr. Randolph was now an
inmate of his son's home, having been persuaded to
come when Kenneth had moved to his present abode.
He greeted the guest most cordially, being an artist,
he was not slow to arrive at the conclusion that
Agnes was faultlessly gowned, besides being very
beautiful. Dr. and Mrs. Campbell were delighted
with Dian and made Kenneth promise to bring her
to visit them in their English home. Kenneth was
very courteous to Agnes and greatly admired her.
After dinner, he took her out on the balcony while
Dian and Mrs. Campbell were discussing household
affairs.

Agnes said to Kenneth, "Cousin, when are you
coming to visit us? I read so much about your career
that I am really proud of my talented cousin and
want my friends to meet you."

He replied, "Nothing would give me more pleasure and I hope some day to avail myself of your
kind invitation."

Mrs. Campbell was calling Agnes. She and Kenneth entered the long window leading from the balcony. It was not long before they had taken their departure. The next day as Kenneth sat in his office, busily looking over some important papers, Agnes was ushered in. She said, "I could not resist the temptation to stop for a moment as I was passing." Glancing at the papers scattered over his desk, she remarked, "If you are too busy, I shall proceed at once as I had the car wait for me." But he would not hear of her going, declaring that the business could wait. As he arose to place the papers in the safe, Agnes could not help but admire her cousin, whose perfect physique had made him a target for all who saw him. His rich brown hair was combed back from his intellectual forehead revealing a face full of manly beauty.

CHAPTER XXVII.

KENNETH AND AGNES.

Agnes left the office in a reflective mood. She was too high bred and aristocratic to admit to herself that she was disappointed because his wife still held her husband's love so securely. For Kenneth's face would light up when Dian's name was mentioned, yet Agnes had shown him as plainly as she dared, that she was cherishing a very warm place in her heart for her distinguished cousin. She made many visits to his office. He couldn't tell why, but he did not mention them to Dian.

It was not long before he was not only expecting those visits, but anticipated them with great pleasure. One day as she yas preparing to leave after an unusually pleasant visit and as Kenneth was holding her hand, bending over it as if about to kiss it, the door opened. He turned to see his father walk in. His face turned red as he dropped her hand and stammered a greeting, not the usual kind of genuine pleasure that he always extended for he knew that his father had seen. Agnes extended her hand to Mr. Randolph who acknowledged the greeting somewhat coldly. She soon took her leave.

Mr. Randolph walked over to his son, laying his hand firmly on Kenneth's arm as he remarked, "My son, I was surprised at your attitude when I entered this room. Why does Agnes come here?"

Kenneth replied, "Father, I did not invite her and could not be guilty of such discourtesy as to ask her to leave."

His father then asked, "Is this the first visit here since the one on the day of her arrival?"

Kenneth, ever truthful, answered it was not, but could not remember just how many times.

His father replied, "If you did not welcome her, she would not come. It is not treating Dian fair. My boy, you have the dearest wife in the world. You have her heart. Treasure it well. One of her little white hands is worth more than a thousand lords or dukes' daughters who for vanity's sake will make a conquest of any man who is willing to be her slave. She has no heart and will make trouble. So beware and be true to Dian."

Kenneth chafed under his father's lecture, but after his nervousness wore away he became more bold and declared that no one intended to harm Dian and he felt that Agnes was entitled to some consideration. Mr. Randolph left his son's office in a very disturbed state of mind and was determined to check all intimacy between Kenneth and his cousin. The matter was not referred to again. Dian never heard of those visits and ere many days Agnes came as her guest as had been planned. Although Mr. Randolph endeavored to frustrate any clandestine meeting between the two, yet they often met unobserved. Finally he was convinced that Dian had something on her mind as she lost color and was very listless. He asked her to consult a doctor, but she declared there was nothing the matter.

Kenneth's attention was called to the fact that Dian was ailing, but he could see no cause for anxiety. Dian saw little of her husband after his cousin was domiciled in their house. He must turn the music for Agnes or she wanted him to drive the car for her, then she wanted him to tell some of the great cases he had won. He was only too willing. He seemed to forget that Dian existed. She never complained, yet he was courteous and pleasant to her always. One day when they were looking at some photographs as Dian crossed the room, she dropped one on the floor and before she could recover it her husband had quickly stooped and picked it up, restored it to her, placing them in their right positions, thus saving her the trouble of doing so. She smiled her thanks. As she turned to go, he held the

door open for her, then a spasm of pain contracted
her heart as she realized that he had not even asked
her to remain. She could hear them laughing and
talking together.

That evening there was quite a number of invited
guests for dinner. Agnes was resplendent in a dress
of pink velvet trimmed in rare old lace that was very
becoming. Many admiring eyes followed her. Every
one was in a joyful mood. The dinner was indeed
a success. They had the three servants besides
Jane, Dian's special maid pressed into service to
help wait on the guests. When she had left the room,
one distinguished guest, a judge, remarked, "That
was a very neat looking maid. She reminded me
of a young girl I saw once. She was on trial for
dishonesty, but the real culprit confessed before she
died. I felt very sorry for her for she seemed of
the better class. She is only part colored."

Dian said, "Oh, Kenneth, I said my instinct was
seldom at fault. When Jane came to me, she had no
reference. She admitted that she had trouble, but
was innocent, but she would not explain the nature
of her trouble and my husband did not want me to
hire her, but I was so impressed in her favor that
I gained my point."

The conversation then drifted to the poor. One
lady remarked, that she felt sorry for the colored
people in a general way and was always ready to
do all she could to help them. Some of them remarked, there are many of them quite beautiful. One
old gentleman said, that he gave to all the poor
regardless of color.

The next day, when the family was alone, Agnes referred to the conversation declaring that if she had a drop of Negro blood in her, she would cut herself and let it flow out. And if she married a man that had Negro blood and she had not been aware of it before that she would leave him. Turning to Dian, she asked, "Would you not do so?"

Dian remarked, "If my husband had Negro blood and only two drops, I would puncture his breast and drink one drop so I would feel that we were equal and feel proud of it."

Whereupon Agnes replied, "Oh, Dian what plebeian thoughts. I could never hold up my head again."

Neither Kenneth nor his father made any remarks, nor joined in the discussion until appealed to, then they said that love that could not stand the test, was not love, only a poor substitute. However, Mr. Randolph said, "This is unfair that all should be arrayed against Agnes and that he felt that mixing the races did not always bring happiness nor always end in misery.

Agnes spoke again and said that no one can impose on me, for I do not care how fair one is I could tell if they were contaminated with Negro blood.

When they had separated for the night, Kenneth thought much about Agnes' views and was convinced that the secret of Lady Blankleigh's parentage had been religiously kept and that her daughter was spared the humiliation that such knowledge would bring her. He thought of Dian, his noble hearted wife, who would gladly share that blood that most people thought was a stigma. He felt that she was far superior to her English cousin and made up his mind to be unusually devoted to his lovely wife who was brave enough to give her view and meant it.

But the next morning when they met at the breakfast table, he was once more under the spell of his fascinating cousin and was at her beck and call. His father had found it necessary to speak to him again about his evident neglect of Dian.

Some days later, Mrs. Campbell came to let Agnes know that Dr. Campbell was called home immediately and he had engaged passage by the next steamer which would leave on Thursday and to catch it they must leave at once. She concluded by saying, that she had left the maid packing.

Agnes had been gone a fortnight when one evening Kenneth went to his desk in the library and opening a drawer, brought forth a package of papers, yellow with age and said, "Dian, do you not think that you ought to examine those papers that you found in the drawer of your mother's desk? They may be important." She replied, "I have often thought of doing so, but thought I would wait until you could assist me. However, we will do so now." Upon unfolding one paper, it proved to be a marriage license issued in May, 1848, in Sussex, England, to Gregory Blankleigh, eldest son and heir of Lord Gregory Blankleigh to Alma Jane Lawrence. Kenneth realized the similarity of the names as that was Lady Blankleigh's name, but her husband's name was Allen, so he felt it had no connection.

Dian said, "Kenneth, mama's name was Alma; what
can it mean?"

He replied, "We cannot find out anything more
from the certificate. The solution must be in the
letters, but I hesitate to read what must have been
a sacred correspondence of some kind. So Dian,
read them. I feel sure that we are about to make
an important discovery of some kind."

"Oh, Kenneth," she replied, her face aglow with
excitement. "Suppose I have descended from royalty."

He laughingly replied, "These facts may relate
to someone else, but read the letters and see if they
will throw any more light on the subject."

Taking them as they were dated, the first one read
as follows:

"London, England.

Alma, my dear wife: How I wish that the day
was here that I could openly claim you before the
whole world. I must admit that I am a coward,
every time I think that I will tell father, then I put
it off. Consequently it remains untold. But I will
put it off no longer. Keep the marriage certificate
safe and I will write to you soon. Hoping to convey
the joyful news that we are forgiven and though
only a curate's daughter you will find a sincere welcome in the family of a lord. With many kisses,
I am

Ever your true husband,

GREGORY BLANKLEIGH.

"London, England.

My dear wife Alma: The house is full of invited

guests and I do not want to speak of our marriage
until the family is alone. But they will leave in a
few days, then I am sure that I can fly on the wings
of love and bring home my beautiful bride.

As ever your devoted husband,

GREGORY.''

"London, England.

My dear wife: Your letter is before me and I know
how disconsolate you must feel. I hope you will
be my acknowledged wife before the little one arrives. The death of your mother must be hard for
you, and me, your husband and protector, so far
away. Father has just informed me that he wants
to take me on a sea voyage with him. As my little
brother, Allen, is too young, it seems that it will be
best for me as I shall have him alone. I will tell
him all. Who knows but what we will make a point
to see you for I shall tell him the first night or day
that we go abroad. Hoping best results, I remain,

Yours anxiously and devotedly,

YOUR HUSBAND GREGORY.''

CHAPTER XXVIII.

DIAN MAKES A DISCOVERY.

After reading those letters, even Kenneth, with all
his dignity, was visibly excited. Dian exclaimed,
"Oh, Kenneth, my mother descended from Lady
Blankleigh's family. My mother told me that her

father was an Englishman and died at sea shortly
before she was born. My mother was only a young
girl when her mother died and that she was named
Alma after her mother. My mother said that when
my grandmother died there was scarcely anything
left for her support. Before dying, she tried to tell
her about some papers, but was too weak to be understood. So we thought no more about it. My
mother was only 16 when she met my father who was
over twice her age. At that time, he was only a
bank clerk but had quite a snug fortune inherited
from his father. My mother being an orphan, agreed
to an early marriage."

Kenneth replied, "Oh Dian, do you know that you
are an heiress to the Blankleigh estate and millions
and that your grandfather was heir and you are a
direct descendant, cutting off the younger son with
a small portion? But I think that he inherits the
titles, and you the lands. I must look it up."

As they were discussing this strange discovery,
Kenneth's father came in and he was told the news.
He too, showed some excitement and said, "Children, do you not remember that I said there was a
strong resemblance between Dian and Agnes? Dian
is Lord Allen Blankleigh's greatniece, while her
mother was his niece. Dian, you and Agnes are second cousins. Is it not wonderful. Where have those
papers been all this time?"

When all was explained, their father said, that
immediate steps should be taken and that Dian
should come into her own. Dian said, that she could
not think of depriving Lord and Lady Blankleigh

of what they had enjoyed all those years and Kenneth felt the same, yet he felt that Dian had been kept out of it long enough. Yet he concluded to make no arrangements whereby Lord Blankleigh should be dispossessed without due consideration. Dian and Kenneth had plenty of money and felt that the inheritance would not add to their pleasure and had almost decided to let things go on as they were and would consider all angles before making any disclosures that would affect their royal relatives. However, Dian was but a woman and after all felt that it lay in her power to humiliate Agnes, who had taken such pains to snub and ignore her on every possible occasion, depriving her of much of her husband's society. So taking those things into consideration, Dian felt that she must claim her own. She had heard so much of Lady Blankleigh's nobility that she felt that she would hate to see her lose the millions that the estate represented. However, as everything was so new and so uncertain that she could scarcely think of the great possibilities that her inheritance would afford her. Kenneth would make rigid investigation regarding the English laws before presenting her claim to the Blankleigh estate.

For several days the subject was discussed from every point of view. Finally at the end of a fortnight, Kenneth was enabled to congratulate his wife as the heiress of the Blankleigh estate and its immense revenue. And yet he could not say that this knowledge made him happy. He thought of Agnes and her imperial beauty. How she would no longer be the heiress, only the daughter of an impoverished lord. He did not want Agnes to suffer through Dian's claim, and resolved more than 'ever to have a serious talk with his wife and if possible see that she put forward no claim.

Kenneth did not realize that he had any special interest in his cousin beyond relationship. He did not realize that Dian was more beautiful than Agnes, and that with the same advantages, would some day make society wake up and gasp at her wonderful beauty. His thoughts seemed to be with Agnes, yet he was not fickle. But if we would go back over the period of a few years, we would see him a rejected suitor of the sister of his wife and he felt that when he had won Dian that the world held no greater boon to his happiness. Whether it was Agnes' decided preference for her distinguished cousin, was something that he had not considered and her effort to keep him near her side flattered his vanity and besides he was proud of his cousin's preference for him.

He had no desire to neglect his wife and did not see the shadow stealing over her beautiful face and her eyes grow dim. He did not notice her great effort to be correctly dressed as she had noted his admiration for the exquisite gowns worn by Agnes. She spent money freely, yet she felt there was something wanting to make her efforts a success and felt relieved when her cousin had returned to her English home. And now she felt radiant as she felt that she would stand on equal footing with Lord Blankleigh's daughter and mentally resolved that they should not look down upon her and that her husband should feel neither fear nor shame. She had received a good education and knew that she only had to review her accomplishments and all would be well. And when she and Kenneth would go to England that she would be very considerate in making her claim. But Dian was grieved and disappointed when Kenneth announced at dinner one evening that when he returned from abroad that he hoped to bring Dian good news to the effect that every one felt very cordial toward her and would not contest her claim. Mr. Randolph looked up from his plate and asked, "Is not Dian going with you? Now would be a good time to make them the visit that they have been urging upon you and take your wife."

Mr. Randolph had noticed the look of disappointment on Dian's face and also remembered that he had found it necessary to remind his son of his seeming disloyalty to his wife when Agnes was visiting there, and he was determined, if possible, to give them no opportunity of being together.

Kenneth answered his father and said, "I do not think it best to take Dian this time as it might embarrass Lord and Lady Blankleigh." The truth was, his determination to evade making the claim in his wife's name, feeling that he could make Dian forego her claim. She did not need the money and had never been associated with royalty, therefore, could not miss any of its social environments.

Dian noticed that her husband did not want her to accompany him and answered, "Very well, I shall remain at home." Mr. Randolph said no more at that time, but when Kenneth went to his office, he rapped upon Dian's door, after a moment's delay, she opened it to see Kenneth's father standing there. He noticed there were traces of tears in her eyes.

He said, "Dian, come into the parlor, I want to speak to you." She led the way into the room. Mr. Randolph did not keep her waiting long, but said, "Daughter you agree to remain at home and let Kenneth sail alone. Now I am going to speak confidentially to you. Kenneth will not leave here for a month or six weeks on account of the celebrated case he has on hand. I want you to improve your time by making some purchases for the trip because you are going with him and you are going to claim your own. I have made art a life time study and I know just what you will need for to start with, I will give you a list, get the best and you will see that Kenneth takes you to Paris before going to London. I want you to put yourself unreservedly in the hands of Worth, the greatest costumer the world has ever known and spare no expense. In the meantime while he is clothing you, I want you to employ a woman, whom I shall recommend, to instruct you the ways of royal society. Do this if possible without your husband's knowledge and let the surprise be complete. I shall run to New York in a few days and if Kenneth does not object, you might take Katy and go along. I may be of service to you."

When Mr. Randolph commenced to speak, Dian was speechless, surprised. She did not think that it would be right to go if Kenneth did not approve. Yet she also felt that his father would not have advised her to go if there would be any harm

done by her going. She was young and when she
realized what it would mean to her, she gladly consented. Her face beamed with smiles while from
her lips issued forth happy laughter. Yes, Dian
was very happy and as there had been no more said
concerning her accompanying Kenneth abroad, he
gladly gave his consent for her to take Katy and go
to New York on a little trip. At the expiration of
a week, when she had returned home, if Kenneth had
not been so much occupied with other matters besides
his impending trip, he would have noticed how beautiful Dian was and how happy she looked. Her joyful anticipation of her trip abroad had worked a
wondrous change in her.

Two days before he was to take his departure,
Kenneth was never more surprised when at supper
table, Dian calmly announced that she had changed
her mind and would accompany him on his trip. His
face flushed and he replied, somewhat irritably, "It
is too late to prepare for the journey."

She laughed happily and said, "I am all ready."
Yet he did not seem altogether pleased. Mr. Randolph was very much engrossed with his supper and
did not appear to notice what was being said. Kenneth remained silent until the meal was finished, then
pleasantly remarked that the trip would be made
more pleasant than he had anticipated, and kissing
his wife fondly he went out to attend to some matters that required his attention.

After Kenneth left, Mr. Randolph said, "Dian,
when you and my son were wedded, I presented you
with a diamond bracelet. I could not then give you

another jewel that held such painful association for me and all those years I have had it locked away from all eyes. My wife for whom I had purchased it, was taken by death.'' Opening a jewel case, he displayed the most beautiful diamond brooch and earrings that dazzled the eyes, ''I have sent to Paris for a diamond tiara.''

Dian exclaimed, ''Oh, father, you are too kind.''

He replied, ''It makes me very happy to see you so happy. Lady Blankleigh has some of the rarest gems in London and I noticed Agnes was resplendent with jewels when she was here and you must remember that you are now a member of the royal family and must dignify your new honors. I will advise Kenneth to buy you a set of emeralds when you arrive in Paris.''

CHAPTER XXIX.

THE ARRIVAL IN ENGLAND.

Kenneth and Dian had a pleasant voyage. They were the cynosure of all eyes. Kenneth was a splendid type of American manhood who showed that American independence with every move. Dian, with her unusual beauty, was much admired. Their devotion to each other was the theme of many conversations.

Arriving in Paris, Kenneth took Dian to many places of interest. She went to the art galleries, the grand operas, in fact, she was wondering how she would ever get time to make her purchases without his knowledge as he was ever by her side. It was fortunate that he met a young attorney whom he had met in Boston and on Dian's assuring her husband she would not be lonely, he went around many places with the Hon. Frank Parkerson. Dian spent some days at the costumers and with Mme. Von Blake who taught her English etiquette while Worth clothed her in rich garments. He raved over her form, her hair and her great beauty was made more pronounced by each costume. At last all was complete.

Kenneth was somewhat amazed by the number of boxes delivered at their hotel each day. She gave fabulous sums to Worth. Kenneth bought her jewels.

At last they took their departure for the home of Lady Blankleigh. Kenneth had made several attempts to dissuade Dian from pressing her claim. Although he spoke with much feeling of Lady Blankleigh's mature age, yet his thoughts were with Agnes. He did not want to see her suffer and determined to make one more appeal to Dian and get her to promise to let matters rest as they were, but she invariably replied, "We will be governed by circumstances." With that he had to be content. She did not tell her husband that his father had talked the matter over with her advising her what to do.

The travelers were cordially received. Lord and Lady Blankleigh had been notified of their coming. They were charmed with Dian and marveled at her wonderful beauty. Agnes had resented it mentally ever since she knew that Kenneth was bringing his wife. She alone of that happy family felt that her presence would be a bar to their pleasure. She felt as his cousin, that she had a claim on him and unjustly felt that if it had not been for Dian—well—

They had arrived early in the day and Lady Blankleigh expressed her satisfaction as that night there was to be a dinner party and the travelers could get some rest. Agnes had noted with some uneasiness the exclusive style of Dian's traveling dress and wondered how she had acquired such taste, but felt that there would be a difference in their dresses at dinner as she had such exquisite dinner dresses and felt no worry over what a girl from the States would wear, although she was good looking. Agnes chose for her dinner gown one of blue with pearl ornaments. Her shoulders and arms looked like chiseled marble. Her dress was enveloped in rare lace that hung in graceful folds to the floor. Her golden brown hair was dressed in the most becoming style. Yes, Agnes was a beautiful girl and as Kenneth got a glimpse of her on her way to the drawing room, he mentally exclaimed, "There is none so beautiful," and was somewhat anxious to follow her.

Hastening to Dian's room, he rapped and asked her if she was nearly ready.

She answered, "In a moment, dear."

He was somewhat impatient when the maid opened the door and in an irritable tone began to complain, but the words refused to come. Was that Dian, that royally beautiful woman! Impossible! She had on a dress of the rare color that matched her red gold hair, in fact, it looked as if the material had been

woven from those tresses. Rare lace of exquisite
design and texture added to the richness of the costume. She wore emeralds and diamonds. None can
describe her hair. It was a decided auburn with a
tint of gold dressed in a girlish fashion that made
her ravishingly beautiful. Finally he exclaimed,
"Oh, Dian, how beautiful. My darling wife. I am
so proud of you."

She laughed and said, "Oh, Kenneth, do not make
me vain, but tell me will I do?"

For answer, he proudly escorted her downstairs
and for a time forgot his cousin Agnes who had
noted at a glance every line of Dian's exquisite dress.
Although too well bred to show any surprise, she
felt a pang of jealousy that she had never felt before. She felt that Dian had won.

There was quite a large number present and Kenneth was the lion of the evening. The dinner passed
off pleasantly, everyone seemed happy. If Agnes
seemed a trifle unstrung no one noticed it.

A few evenings later, Sir John Benton, a noted
lawyer, noted for his legal decisions in many cases
settling intricate tangles of the law, was discussing
at the dinner table the outcome of an unknown heir
springing up having never been heard of before and
contesting for the estate which another relative had
held in possession for many years. He had proved
his claim and came into his own. It was a remarkable decision, yet it was just and justice won.

Kenneth said, "That reminds me of a case somewhat similar that has come to my notice and I have
been called upon for advice. The party in question

that I refer to is a lady. Her mother was the only
child of a lord, yet her mother died without this
knowledge for she had failed to examine some papers
as they were both young and thoughtless. She then
married a man who soon made a name for himself
in the financial world. She never gave a thought to
her mother's affairs or who her father was. She
knew that her father was dead. She was very happy
in her husband's love. They had two daughters.
Now, father and mother and one of the girls are
dead. The living girl, on looking over the papers,
finds that her mother's mother, her own grandmother, was married secretly to a lord, but had died
without the marriage being revealed. Now this lady
is the only direct descendant of this lord, her grandfather. This lord had a younger brother who would
be a granduncle to this girl. The question is, is this
girl entitled to any part of the estate descending
from her grandfataher.''

Sir John had been listening keenly to the narrative and when Kenneth had finished he said, ''If she
holds unquestionable proof that her grandmother
was legally married to this lord and that her mother
was the only issue to that marriage and the lady in
question is the only surviving member of her
mother's family, then she succeeds to all the estates
and the revenues therefrom. The younger brother
succeeds to the title, but little else unless there has
been special provisions made through a will. But
as the matter stands, the lady in question can claim
all of the estate.''

While he was talking, Dian had grown very white.

Kenneth said, "I am very glad that you have explained so fully your English laws."

Lord Blankleigh said, "I believe in justice, but I feel if some one would disposses me after so many years, I would feel it a rank injustice. After a man has reared his family in a royal manner and then is compelled to step down, I fear that I should not do so very graciously."

Lady Blankleigh said, "If it was proven beyond doubt I would yield the scepter to the rightful owner and wish him or her success and happiness."

Agnes smilingly said, "That is just like mama, but I think I would agree with papa and contest the claim."

Her brother Allen spoke and said, "As we are not called upon to relinquish our rights, let us be magnanimous and extend a cordial greeting to our would-be successor."

All joined in the laugh that followed. But if you had noticed there was no mirth in Kenneth or Dian's laugh.

That night Kenneth and Dian spoke again on the subject. Kenneth felt more than ever his adversion to present his wife's claim and Dian, after hearing the discussion and learning how each felt on the matter, felt less inclinded to do so.

"But Kenneth dear," she said, "I feel like we are just sneaks and sailing under false colors and I am really getting nervous. I do wish that we knew just what to do. It is not a matter of money with us, but I would like the rank that is mine legally and absolutely."

They were both silent for some time, then a light broke over Dian's face and she exclaimed, "Oh, Kenneth, let us trust Lord Blankleigh, the one that is most involved. But with the promise not to divulge it to another member of the family." Kenneth replied, "Oh, Dian, not a bad idea."

They talked for some time longer both agreeing to talk the matter over with Dian's uncle. The next morning Kenneth asked for an interview with Lord Blankleigh. They had been in the library but a few moments when Dian asked and received permission to enter.

Kenneth said, "My Lord, I have a matter of great importance to lay before you."

Before he could proceed any further, Dian said, "Lord Blankleigh, we will only take you into our confidence by promising that you will not tell the secret to anyone until I give you permission to do so."

Lord Blankleigh was surprised but said, "You do not mean that I shall not tell my wife! I have never kept a secret from her in my life and should not like to begin now."

Then Kenneth said, "This is one that you will feel that it will be best on your part to withhold from her."

Lord Blankleigh asked, "How long must I maintain this silence?"

Dian said, "Till I give you permission to speak."

He replied, "Mrs. Randolph, it is hard to refuse a woman a request, but with honor I will give you the required promise and it matters not under what

stress or condition, I will never reveal it to anyone
without your permission."

As our readers know the import of this secret we
will not repeat the legality or linger over the house
of the Blankleighs. He was handed a marriage certificate of Gregory Blankleigh and Alma Jane Lawrence. He was surprised beyond words for none
ever knew that his brother had married. Then he
was given the letters that she had received from her
husband just before he sailed on that fatal trip. He
wrote of his hopes to acknowledge his marriage before the birth of their child. He read all of these
letters and then the truth flashed upon him that if
that child was living, if a boy, he would be the lord
of all the estate and title. If a girl, she would inherit all except an empty title.

When he had read them all, he asked, "Did the
child live?"

Kenneth answered and said, "It did and it was a
girl."

Lord Blankleigh replied, "She must be nearly as
old as I am."

Kenneth replied, "She died a few years ago leaving two daughters, only one now survives that family. Father, mother and sister all dead."

Lord Blankleigh asked, "Where is this girl? She
would be my brother's granddaughter. Do you know
where she is?" Then it flashed on him that that
must have been the case that Kenneth was discussing with Sir John Benton. He also remembered
how he had said that if a claimant should come forward that he would contest his rights. Now he felt

that all was slipping away and that he was power-
less to do anything. He thought of his wife and
children and laid his head upon the table and
groaned aloud.

He again repeated, "Kenneth, where is she to be
found? This woman that will come to strip me of
all except an empty title?"

Kenneth motioned to Dian to speak, at the same
time he said, "I have an appointment to make and
will speak to you again."

He left the room as Dian placed her hands on
Lord Blankleigh's bowed head and said, "I am here,
uncle."

He lifted his head, he seemed dazed, and said,
"Where is she?"

She repeated and said, "I am here, uncle; I am
the girl who will not strip you of your possessions."

He said, "Dian, Oh, Dian, is it you, really you?
How did it happen?"

She told him how year after year the papers,
yellow with age, had laid in a little black trunk in an
attic room and after her mother's death, that she
and Kenneth had gone through the papers and made
the discovery. And to make it complete there was a
true likeness of his brother at the age of 21 years.

"Dian," he said, "your resemblance to my family
are conclusive proofs. I must go and find my wife."

Dian restrained him, saying, "Remember your
promise, for I will hold you to it." She said, "Lord
Blankleigh, may I call you uncle when we are alone?
I am wealthy in my own right, my father was a
multimillionaire banker. At the death of my parents
and sister, I was left with unlimited wealth. My

husband is wealthy. I do not need money. I have never been associated with royalty and I do not miss anything that I have never been accustomed to or possessed.''

Lord Blankleigh said, ''It matters not what our feelings are on that point, I feel that you have been deprived of your rights long enough and I shall take immediate steps to restore to you your own.''

Dian said, ''But, Uncle, I will not take it. Think of how Agnes will be humiliated. Oh, Uncle, listen to me. I absolutely refuse to take possession. Kenneth and I thought that you ought to know that your brother had been married, but did not want to deprive you of what you had considered your own for so many years.''

Dian had gathered up the papers, tying them together. Lord Blankleigh reached for them and she said, ''Uncle, see, I will make it impossible for you to thrust this property on me,'' and before he became aware of her intention, she threw them into the grate where a slow fire was burning to dispel the chill of this early spring day.

When he realized what she had done, he sprang forward and recovered them with only a small portion of them partly burned. Then, going to her, he placed his arms around her and pillowed her head upon his breast as he said, ''My dear noble girl.''

By this time Dian was in tears. He continued to caress her, saying, ''Oh, Gregory, dear brother, you have left an angel.'' ''And Kenneth,'' he cried, ''your wife is a jewel.'' So absorbed they were with each other that they did not see that others had witnessed their embrace.

CHAPTER XXX.

LADY BLANKLEIGH'S SORROW.

Lady Blankleigh, on passing the library and seeing the door ajar and correctly thinking that she
heard her husband's voice was about to enter the
half open door, but she was not prepared for the
scene that met her gaze. There stood Lord Blankleigh with Dian in his arms, kissing and caressing
the lovely girl, who returned his caresses. Lady
Blankleigh turned from the scene with a very white
face. In all her married life, her husband had never
given her cause to doubt his fidelity and it had often
been remarked upon that they had set an example
of enjoying a life time of honeymoon, so great was
their devotion to each other, and if any one had told
her that her husband was false, she would have been
most indignant and it would not be repeated. But
she was compelled to believe what she herself saw.
She scarcely knew how she gained her room, and
sometime later Lord Blankleigh entered and was
surprised at her lack of warmth to his greetings the
first time since their marriage. He felt deeply
concerned and inquired if she was ill. She replied
that she had a headache and surprised him when she
petulantly refused to let him rub her head as he often
did on former occasions when she had suffered the
same complaint.

However, she went down to dinner as if nothing
had happened and to all inquiries as to her head re-

plied that she was better and the noble girl who was willing to discard her inheritance to save her and family from humiliation, she scarcely noticed at all, a breech of etiquette that she had never before been guilty of and she had always been considered the most charming hostess, always being most amiable to all that were thrown under her roof. After dinner when all had returned to the drawing room, Dian was pressed to sing. She sang as she never did before and Kenneth was very proud of his wife. The party circle broke up, each going to their rooms.

It had been decided to give a great ball for the guest the following week. Although possessed of great wealth, neither Dian nor Kenneth had ever witnessed such preparations for so grand a ball. Kenneth remarked to Dian, saying, "Darling, I hope that you have selected a gown worthy of the occasion."

She answered quite calmly, "I think so."

That morning Lord Blankleigh on seeing Dian going to the music room, had followed her and said, "Oh, Dian, my dear niece, give me permission to tell my wife all. Remember I have never had a secret from her before." But Dian had noticed how languid and listless Lady Blankleigh was and told him that she did not think that his wife was well and would under no circumstance tell her of it.

As they stood conversing in low tones, it was again their misfortune to be observed and their actions misconstrued. Agnes had seen them enter the music room and it was not the first time that she had

noticed the seemingly clandestine meeting. She
scornfully repeated to her mother those meetings,
but as she turned away from the door she encountered her mother and from the shadow on that pale
face, realized that her mother needed no information
in regard to those secret meetings and lovingly placing her arms around her mother's waist, they
both ascended the stairs together almost in silence.
Agnes asked permission to enter her mother's luxurious boudoir and when mother and daughter were
seated, Agnes, with the impassioned blood of youth,
declared that she would tell Kenneth to take his wife
away. But Lady Blankleigh would not hear of such
a thing, but did discuss plans to go to the seashore
to recuperate.

Kenneth and Dian had both noticed a coldness
from their hostess and daughter, but had not the
slightest idea what had occasioned it. Kenneth remembered with shame how Dian had been ignored
in their own home by his cousin Agnes, and now
she openly scorned her, while Lady Blankleigh simply ignored her. Dian was tearful as she and Kenneth tried to find a solution for the change of treatment they were receiving in their kin's palatial
home. Kenneth said, ''We will leave for our home
the day after the ball.'' For he was justly indignant.

The guests were arriving, and the band was dis-
coursing rare music in the grand ball room of Blankleigh castle. Kenneth had rapped for admission to
his wife's dressing room. Dian did not keep him
waiting. She told the maid to open the door and if

Kenneth had been surprised at his wife's rich dinner gown, he was almost incredulous at her appearance in her lovely ball dress of rich lustrous white velvet, a tiara of diamonds rested upon her red gold hair, from her neck suspended a diamond necklace, a large brooch of the same gems and a stomacher of brilliants that dazzled the eyes. He could not understand how she became possessed of so many costly diamonds. She laughingly told him how she and his father had conspired to surprise him. She told him that she, at her father's advice, had gotten the tiara in Paris. His father had written to the famous jeweler there and he had it ready for her. She also told him how she had placed herself in the hands of an impoverished lady belonging to one of the royal families, also how Worth had done the rest. As Kenneth beheld his lovely wife, there came to him the first time a regret that Dian could not or would not take her rightful place in the royal family to which she belonged.

Pen cannot portray the sensation that Dian created and Lord Blankleigh again sought the lovely girl and tried to induce her to let him claim her before all the world. But to all of his entreaties, now seconded by her husband, she steadfastly refused. Again finding her alone near a curtained alcove, Lord Blankleigh pleaded with her to tell his wife. As they emerged from the shadowy retreat they encountered Agnes, who disdainfully passed Dian without any pretense of having seen her. Dian felt the snub and Kenneth had from a short distance away seen the whole thing and deter-

mined that nothing could induce him to remain in
a house where they were the recipients of so much
discourtesy. He would take Dian to a hotel and
they would finish their sight seeing without further
inconvenience to their royal kin. Dian had been
presented at the Court of St, James by Lady Blankleigh at the same time that several other Americans
had also been honored. So they felt that they could
get along as they had made many friends who were
making it very pleasant for them. But there were
times that Dian longed for their less pretentious
home in the United States.

Two years have gone by since Dian and Kenneth
returned from their visit abroad. There had been
but little communication between the families. One
day a letter arrived for Kenneth. On reading it
his face became serious. Lord Blankleigh was seriously ill and was continually asking for Kenneth
and Dian. Could they come? It was from Lady
Blankleigh. Kenneth passed the letter to Dian and
when she had finished reading it he asked her if
they should go. Dian, ever kindhearted and unmindful of the slights received, felt that if they
could be of any service to the stricken man, that it
was their duty to go. But ere they could sail they
were shocked and grieved beyond expression, on entering the studio one morning, to find Mr. Randolph's spirit had fled. In his hands he held the
picture of his departed wife, Catherine. Some years
previous he had his wife's body removed from Paris
and his body was laid beside her. All colors and
creeds forgotten. And Kenneth not only mourned

over the recent grave, but tears fell freely on the grave with the inscription of "Mother," and before he and Dian departed for England they strewed flowers on the graves of their loved ones.

The death of Kenneth's father delayed their departure, yet in their grief they did not forget Lord Blankleigh and sent them a cablegram apprising them of their bereavement. They also wrote to Lady Blankleigh, telling her that if her husband was no worse to tell him that he was absolved from all promises that he had made them and that they would be with them at the earliest possible moment. Lady Blankleigh was mystified by the words of the letter and on entering the sick room where her husband sat in a large easy chair, she was about to ask him what it meant, but on beholding a letter in her hand and noting the foreign postmark, asked, "Will they come?" at the same time exclaiming, "My dear wife, I want everything righted before the summons."

Lady Blankleigh placed the letter in his hand and on receiving it he read those precious words that he had longed for.

Lifting his eyes to heaven, he exclaimed, "Oh, Father, I thank Thee, I thank Thee. Call the children. Tell Agnes and Allen to come. Oh, that I am spared to see everything righted."

But neither son nor daughter had come in. Both were cantering in the parks. The secret had been kept so long that Lord Blankleigh decided not to wait for the children, knowing that they could be told later. Lady Blankleigh noticed his excitement,

begged him to wait awhile until he grew more calm.
This he refused to do. He told her of his brother's
secret marriage and his ignorance of the fact until
Kenneth and Dian came and told everything connected with the transaction and the nobility of Dian,
her attempt to burn the will, the promise he gave
to keep the secret, out of her great love for you and
consideration for Agnes and Allen, who had always
been known as joint ehirs to the estate. Then Lord
Blankleigh almost collapsed when his wife, in a half
fainting condition, fell on her knees at his feet, her
beautiful long black hair only sprinkled with a few
silver threads, fell around her almost covering her
face that had at first been pale but was now scarlet,
when she remembered how she had by her cruel,
unjust suspicion, driven from her door the noblest
woman on earth. Lord Blankleigh was greatly agitated when she pled for forgiveness, the tears running down her cheeks, and not until she grew more
calm did he understand her great agitation. She did
not spare herself.

Lord Blankleigh, ever ready to shoulder the blame,
took it all upon himself especially when he remembered how often he waylaid his beautiful neice, begging her to release him from a promise he had so
rashly made before he was made aware of the seriousness of the facts. Agnes and Allen were told
all the facts. It was then remembered how strong
was the likeness between Agnes and Dian. Agnes
felt very remorseful of the treatment that Dian had
received at her hands and to make atonement for the
past she immediately made every one happy by an-

nouncing that she had accepted Prince Elderstrom for her future companion and ere Dian and Kenneth arrived had almost completed her arrangements for the ceremony and regretted very much that the death of Kenneth's father would make it impossible for Dian to serve as matron of honor at the early date the prince had pleaded for.

CHAPTER XXXI.

KENNETH AND DIAN'S ARRIVAL.

When Kenneth and Dian arrived, Lady Blankleigh folded Dian in her arms while the tears rolled down her cheeks, exclaiming, "My dear, dear niece, my noble girl. Your uncle has told me all. Oh, Dian, can you forgive me for all the slights that you have received here in your own house? My generous girl, you had it in your power to turn us all out, yet you refrained from doing so. Lord Blankleigh has sent for his lawyer and will take immediate steps to restore your own to you."

Dian replied, "Oh, Auntie, Kenneth and I do not want it. Let all remain as it was."

"But Dian, you must take it, the doctor has ordered your uncle to a warmer climate to remain possibly two or three years, and who else should occupy the house but yourself? Agnes will soon be married."

They agreed to let the matter rest and besides Lord Blankleigh desired the change.

When Dian entered the room her uncle clasped her
in his arms, saying, "Oh, Dian, I feel so much better
since the burden of the secret is lifted from me.
You are indeed a noble girl."

It was decided that Dian and Kenneth should take
up their abode in the palace at the earliest possible
moment. They returned to America and settled up
all business. Kenneth's law partner, a conscientious
man, was fast making a name for himself and ere
many weeks went by, Kenneth and Dian were holding their rightful positions without the world knowing that the royal family of Blankleighs had been
subjected to any change.

Three years have rolled around and the travelers
are not thinking of returning, although reports are
that Lord Blankleigh had fully recovered. Princess
Agnes lives scarcely fifteen miles from her old home.
She and her lovely cousin, Kenneth's wife, are much
sought after. Their beauty is the theme of every
one. Agnes has buried the romance of her youth
and there are times that she thinks tenderly of Kenneth. She puts such feelings aside, for she has a
husband who adores her and such love will win over
youthful romances and if Agnes is not supremely
happy, she is at least contented with no lingering desire for what might have been.

Kenneth and Dian are supremely happy, for there
are childish voices in the mansion now, yet their
eyes often grow misty with tears as they wish that
Kenneth's father had been spared to them. Their
two children have learned to speak with gentle reverence of their grandparents that they have never

seen, Guy Randolph and his wife Catherine, and often stand and look up at the "bootiful" pictures of grandma and grandpa.

Since Kenneth has gone to England to live, Dr. Grayson missed him very much. He had moved from the south and is now located in New York, and although Odene lived there also, he made no effort to see her. When he met Mrs. Maxwell at a public reception, he asked for and received permission to call. He took the opportunity to explain the presence of the marriage license he had in his possession on that fatal day that he had last seen her in his southern town. She was not only surprised, but out of the depths of her heart she pitied him, knowing for the first time that he was a victim of circumstances over which he had no control. She regretted her part in the unhappy past, yet she had nothing but words of praise for her deceased husband, stating that their married life had been one of contentment. She was still very beautiful and was much sought after, but she sent them all away. While Dr. Grayson admired her very much, he could not forget the lone grave in sunny Italy. His hair was well sprinkled with gray, yet there were many who would have given much to win this famous doctor. Alice had been dead now five years and Odene was still a widow.

One day the doctor was announced. She happily received him and insisted on him taking the seat she offered. He took her hand in his and said, "Dear Odene, the spring time of our love was blighted, the summer time of affection has passed, the autumn

time of our lives is approaching. Let us pass
through the glorious autumn of love to the sunset of
life together, to the crossroads. Our lives have been
one of tangled threads. My heart is hungry for your
love. My home is barren and lonely. I need your
presence. Do not send me away. I know I am not
worthy, but God helping me, I shall devote the remainder of my life to make you happy.'' She placed
her hand in his and named an early day.

He is a devoted husband. If there are times when
she sees a far away look in his eyes, she knows that
his thoughts are of the lone grave under Italian
skies, but she says nothing, but is ever tender and
gentle and does not reproach her husband for any
lingering sentiment that he might cherish for the
memory of Nurse Alice.

They had no children, but they adopted a pretty
little baby girl whose mother had passed away in
the charity ward in one of the great hospitals there,
and upon investigation learned that there was no
one to claim it. And as his wife caressed the little
one, her husband put his arms around her, saying,
''Shall we name it after you, Odene?'' But she
lifted her eyes to his face and gently said, ''We will
call her 'Alice.' ''

''FINIS.''

ABOUT THE EDITORS

Henry Louis Gates, Jr., is the W. E. B. Du Bois Professor of the Humanities, Chair of the Afro-American Studies Department, and Director of the W. E. B. Du Bois Institute for Afro-American Research at Harvard University. One of the leading scholars of African-American literature and culture, he is the author of *Figures in Black: Words, Signs, and the Racial Self* (1987), *The Signifying Monkey: A Theory of Afro-American Literary Criticism* (1988), *Loose Canons: Notes on the Culture Wars* (1992), and the memoir *Colored People* (1994).

Jennifer Burton is in the Ph.D. program in English Language and Literature at Harvard University. She is the volume editor of *The Prize Plays and Other One-Acts* in this series. She was a contributor to *Great Lives from History: American Women*, and, with her mother and sister, coauthored two one-act plays, *Rita's Haircut* and *Litany of the Clothes*. Her creative non-fiction has appeared in *There and Back* and *Buffalo*, the Sunday magazine of the *Buffalo News*.

Maggie Sale is Director of the Undergraduate Women's Studies Program and Assistant Professor of Women's Studies at Columbia University, where she is also Assistant Professor of English and Comparative Literature. Her writings on U.S. American and African-American literature and culture have appeared in *American Literature* and *African American Review*.